The-Complete-Leadership-Collection-Vol-1

The Art of War, The Prince & Meditations —
Timeless Lessons on Strategy, Power and Self-
Mastery

A Modern Translation

Adapted for the Contemporary Reader

Sun Tzu | Niccolò Machiavelli
Marcus Aurelius

Translated by Tim Zengerink

Table of Contents

Preface - Message to the Reader

What If You Could Help Rebuild the Greatest Library in Human History?

Thousands of years ago, the Library of Alexandria stood as the crown jewel of human achievement — a sanctuary where the collected wisdom of every known civilization was gathered, preserved, and shared freely.

And then, it was lost.

Through fire, conquest, and the slow erosion of time, humanity lost not just books — but ideas, dreams, discoveries, and stories that could have changed the world forever.

Today, the Library of Alexandria lives again — and you are invited to be a part of its restoration.

Our mission is simple yet profound:

To rebuild the greatest library the world has ever known, and to translate all timeless works into every language and dialect, so that no seeker of knowledge is ever left behind again.

By joining our movement to rebuild the modern Library of Alexandria, you become part of an unprecedented mission:

- **Unlimited Access to the Greatest Audiobooks & eBooks Ever Written:**

  Instantly explore thousands of legendary works—Plato, Shakespeare, Jane Austen, Leo Tolstoy, and countless more. All instantly available to read or listen, placing a complete literary universe at your fingertips.

- **Beautiful Paperback & Deluxe Editions at Printing Cost**

  Own any title as an elegant paperback, deluxe hardcover, or stunning collectible boxset—offered to you at true printing cost, delivered straight to your door. Build your personal Library of Alexandria, crafted for beauty, built for durability, and worthy of proud display.

- **Fresh Translations for Modern Readers—in Every Language & Dialect**

  Enjoy timeless masterpieces reimagined in clear, contemporary language—no more outdated phrases or obscure references. Alongside the original versions, we're tirelessly translating these classics into every language and dialect imaginable, ensuring accessibility and understanding across cultures and generations.

- **Join a Global Renaissance of Literature & Knowledge**

  You directly support expanding our library, publishing deluxe editions at true cost, translating works into all global languages, and bringing humanity's greatest stories to people everywhere. By joining today, you're not just preserving a legacy of masterpieces; you set in motion a powerful wave of literary accessibility.

Become a Torchbearer of Knowledge.

Join us for free now at **LibraryofAlexandria.com**

Together, we will ensure that the light of human wisdom never fades again.

With gratitude and a shared love of knowledge,
The Modern Library of Alexandria Team

Visit:

www.libraryofalexandria.com

Or scan the code below:

Introduction

Masters of War, Rule, and Self —
Strategy, Power, and the Inner Command

The Complete Leadership Collection (Vol. 1) brings together three of history's most enduring texts on the art of command—Sun Tzu's The Art of War, Niccolò Machiavelli's The Prince, and Marcus Aurelius' Meditations. Written in vastly different times, places, and contexts, these works share one unifying goal: to teach how power is gained, maintained, and most importantly, governed. Each offers a distinct but complementary philosophy of leadership: strategic awareness, political realism, and moral self-mastery.

This volume presents more than tactical instruction. It offers a layered meditation on human nature, decision-making under pressure, and the moral complexities of authority. These texts are neither outdated relics nor abstract musings. They are blueprints—ruthlessly pragmatic, psychologically nuanced, and ethically demanding. They continue to shape political theory, business strategy, military command, and personal leadership across the globe.

This introduction explores the foundational ideas of each text, their historical roots, and the enduring relevance they carry for leaders today. To lead well is to know not just how to direct others—but how to govern oneself.

The Art of War:
Strategic Clarity and the Power of Perception

Attributed to the Chinese general and strategist Sun Tzu, The Art of War is a 5th-century BCE military treatise that has transcended its origins to become a global manual for leadership in conflict, negotiation, and competition. Its philosophy is grounded in paradox and principle. Victory, according to Sun Tzu, is not about brute strength, but about subtlety, foresight, and adaptability.

The key lessons of The Art of War include:

- Know yourself and know your enemy. Without this dual awareness, failure is assured. With it, victory is effortless.
- All warfare is based on deception. Misleading opponents, creating illusions, and exploiting uncertainty are central to success.
- The greatest victory is won without battle. The ideal commander triumphs before conflict begins by shaping conditions and controlling perceptions.
- Flexibility is strength. Rigidity invites collapse; fluid strategy allows survival in shifting landscapes.
- Leadership requires harmony. A general must understand morale, timing, geography, and the temperaments of both troops and terrain.

Though grounded in military tradition, The Art of War is not a handbook for violence. It is a treatise on how to navigate opposition wisely and efficiently. The real battlefield, Sun Tzu suggests, lies in the mind: success belongs to the calm, alert strategist who sees the invisible threads between force, timing, and perception.

For the modern leader, The Art of War teaches strategic clarity, restraint, and perspective. It urges commanders to act decisively but think deeply—to recognize that victory is not domination, but influence skillfully applied.

The Prince:
Power, Pragmatism, and the Mechanics of Rule

Written in 1513 by Niccolò Machiavelli, The Prince is perhaps the most controversial political treatise in Western history. Often mischaracterized as cynical or immoral, the book is better understood as a brutally honest guide to navigating the unstable world of political power. It does not describe what rulers ought to be, but what they must be in order to survive.

Machiavelli, a Florentine diplomat and political thinker, lived during a time of intense political volatility. Italy was divided into warring states, manipulated by foreign powers, and plagued by betrayal. The Prince was his response: a mirror held up to power, unadorned by idealism.

Its core lessons include:

- It is better to be feared than loved, if one cannot be both. Fear preserves authority more reliably than affection.
- The appearance of virtue is more important than virtue itself. Reputation shapes perception; perception shapes power.
- A ruler must learn to act against morality when necessary. Ethics must yield to necessity when the state is at risk.
- Fortune is like a woman—it favors the bold and can be shaped by daring. Leaders must seize opportunity with vigor and courage.

Machiavelli does not celebrate tyranny—he studies effectiveness. His prince is not a monster, but a realist who understands that human beings are fickle, self-interested, and often irrational. The wise ruler knows when to be merciful, and when to act decisively without guilt.

For the modern leader, The Prince is not an instruction manual for cruelty. It is a warning against naïveté. It reminds us that leadership requires more than ideals—it requires intelligence, timing, and the ability to read both allies and enemies with precision. In a world where appearances and alliances shift constantly, the Machiavellian lesson is not amorality—it is strategic lucidity.

Meditations:
Stoic Discipline and the Moral Authority of the Self

Written by Roman Emperor Marcus Aurelius during his campaigns in the 2nd century CE, Meditations is not a philosophical treatise—it is a private journal. Yet its pages contain some of the most profound reflections on leadership, duty, and self-discipline ever written. In stark contrast to the cold calculation of Machiavelli, Marcus offers a deeply personal and moral philosophy rooted in Stoic principles.

Stoicism teaches that while we cannot control what happens to us, we can control how we respond. Marcus applies this lesson to imperial rule, grappling with power, mortality, ambition, and justice. His aim is not to dominate the world, but to govern himself.

His key teachings include:

- You have power over your mind—not outside events. Real strength lies in mastery of one's thoughts and emotions.
- Live according to nature and reason. Virtue is not an external standard, but the alignment of one's actions with what is just and wise.
- Do your duty without complaint. Leadership is a burden to be borne with humility and endurance.
- Death is natural and unavoidable. Obsession with fame or pleasure is distraction; tranquility comes from accepting the transient.
- People will act unjustly. Your role is to respond justly and remain true to your character.

Meditations is the counterweight to The Prince. Where Machiavelli teaches adaptation to the world, Marcus Aurelius teaches resistance to its corruption. Where The Prince advises appearing virtuous, Meditations insists on being virtuous. Where Machiavelli dissects power, Marcus questions its true value.

For the modern leader, Marcus Aurelius offers a mirror not of the crowd, but of the conscience. He teaches that greatness begins not in conquest or rhetoric, but in silent integrity. His message: to rule others well, one must first rule oneself.

A Triad of Leadership: Strategy, Survival, and Self

Read together, these three texts form a triptych of leadership:

- The Art of War shows how to think strategically.
- The Prince shows how to wield power pragmatically.
- Meditations shows how to live and lead with inner strength.

None of these works is complete alone. Each responds to a different dimension of leadership. Sun Tzu's clarity without Marcus' integrity risks detachment. Machiavelli's realism without Stoic principle can lead to cruelty. Marcus' virtue without strategy may invite failure.

A wise leader must balance them all. They must plan like Sun Tzu, act with the clarity of Machiavelli, and reflect with the conscience of Marcus. These are not ideals—they are imperatives in a world that rewards speed over substance, noise over wisdom, and ambition over character.

Welcome to The Complete Leadership Collection (Vol. 1). May these three masters teach you how to lead—not by domination or pretense, but through clarity, realism, and the enduring strength of moral authority.

The Art of War

Sun Tzu

Introduction

I. Brief Biography of Sun Tzu

Origins and Early Life

Sun Tzu, originally named Sun Wu, was born around 544 BCE in the state of Qi, which is now part of Shandong, China. The name Sun Tzu, by which he is better known, is a title meaning "Master Sun." Though much of his early life is still unknown, historical evidence suggests he came from a family with strong roots in military strategy and learning. This background likely helped shape his extraordinary skills in warfare and tactics, setting him up for the distinguished career he would later have.

As a young man, Sun Tzu began gaining a reputation for his sharp mind in strategy, though historical records about him are somewhat scarce. The lack of solid information has only made his life more fascinating, with parts of his story seeming like a mix of history and legend. His eventual rise to fame as a general and thinker was based not just on his practical knowledge of warfare, but also his ability to apply general ideas to real-life situations. His famous work, *The Art of War*, would form the foundation of his lasting influence, even though much of his life story has been blended with myths.

Military Career and Rise to Prominence

Sun Tzu's skills in military strategy didn't go unnoticed. He served under King Helü of the state of Wu, a role that gave him the chance to show his expertise on a larger stage. His ability to turn hopeless situations into victories earned him respect across the region. One of the biggest examples of his brilliance was when he defeated the state of Chu, which was much bigger and had more resources. This win highlighted his talent for outsmarting opponents with greater numbers and supplies.

The defeat of Chu was more than just a military win; it strengthened Wu's power and stability during a time when warfare between Chinese states was constant. Sun Tzu's strategies often used psychological tricks and deception, with clever tactics to weaken his enemies' morale before any fighting began. His deep understanding of terrain, human nature, and the use of deception made him stand out among other military minds of his time. These achievements earned him lasting fame and confirmed his place as one of the greatest military strategists in Chinese history.

Creation of The Art of War

It was during this period of political upheaval and near-constant warfare that Sun Tzu is believed to have authored The Art of War. The Warring States period (475–221 BCE) was a time of great instability, with various factions vying for control of China. In this context, Sun Tzu's strategies and insights were not only revolutionary but essential for survival.

Rather than a theoretical treatise, The Art of War is a distilled collection of Sun Tzu's accumulated experiences and the military wisdom passed down from generations before him. The text, composed of concise aphorisms and principles, is a practical guide intended for military leaders facing the challenges of warfare. Sun Tzu's approach to warfare emphasized the importance of strategy over brute force, and many of his insights remain highly applicable even in the modern world. His genius lay in his ability to condense complex concepts into simple, memorable phrases that have stood the test of time.

Even today, The Art of War continues to influence a wide array of fields beyond the battlefield, from business to sports, and remains a touchstone for anyone seeking to understand the nature of conflict and strategy. The timelessness of Sun Tzu's work speaks to his mastery of the art of warfare and his ability to provide wisdom that transcends the ages.

II. Historical Context

Sun Tzu lived during one of the most chaotic times in Chinese history, a period historians call the Spring and Autumn period, which later became the Warring States period (around 771–221 BCE). This era saw the weakening of the Zhou Dynasty's power, leading to constant wars between rival states. Regional leaders fought for control, with alliances constantly shifting and battles happening frequently. The political scene was unstable, and military skill was vital not just for winning but for survival.

As states competed for dominance, warfare was about more than just expanding territories; it was necessary for keeping sovereignty. Even small mistakes could lead to the complete destruction of a state, making military leaders crucial to the survival of nations. It was in this intense environment that Sun Tzu's strategies developed. He created his tactics not only to secure victories but to ensure long-term survival in a world where states were often annexed or destroyed. His strategies responded to a reality where the stakes were incredibly high, offering insights that went beyond war and into the political dynamics of the time.

The fierce competition for power among Chinese states during the Warring States period required new approaches to warfare, focusing on cunning, intelligence, and strategy rather than just raw strength. Sun Tzu's writings came out of this era of near-constant conflict, where he understood that success depended on outsmarting the opponent, not just overpowering them. His methods were designed for a time when a single wrong move could lead to disaster, stressing careful planning and the need for preparation in an unpredictable and dangerous world.

The Role of Warfare in Ancient China

In ancient China, warfare was much more than just battles fought on the field; it was closely connected with politics, philosophy, and governance. Leaders during this time were expected not only to be skilled in battle but also to be strong in diplomacy and statecraft.

Military action was often a tool used to achieve political goals, and leaders had to balance the challenges of internal governance while also preparing for outside threats. Sun Tzu's approach to warfare reflects this larger understanding, as he constantly stressed the importance of planning ahead, being flexible, and understanding both the enemy and one's own forces.

Warfare during this period was all-encompassing. It involved logistics, governance, and diplomacy, areas where military leaders needed to show not only strength but also wisdom. Sun Tzu's strategies, which often focused on winning without fighting, came from this broader view of conflict, where preserving resources and maintaining the stability of the state were as crucial as defeating the enemy. His well-known principle, "The supreme art of war is to subdue the enemy without fighting," demonstrates his understanding of the long-term effects of war. Instead of seeking short-term victories at great costs, he promoted strategies that would protect the state's power while weakening the opponent's will.

During Sun Tzu's era, military leaders were expected to grasp the moral and philosophical sides of warfare. Confucian values influenced Chinese society deeply, shaping how rulers led and how they fought. Leaders were judged not just by their military successes but by their ability to keep order and promote justice. Sun Tzu's work reflects this, as it puts great importance on the qualities of leadership and the ethical aspects of warfare. He supported the idea of a wise and virtuous leader, one who could inspire loyalty among soldiers while staying calm and focused in the chaos of battle.

The political landscape was always changing, with alliances breaking as quickly as they were formed. Espionage, deception, and psychological warfare became key tools for staying ahead. Sun Tzu's contributions to the art of war went beyond just battlefield tactics; they involved understanding the enemy's mind and manipulating both physical and mental conditions to achieve victory. He understood that sometimes the best battle is the one that's won before it even starts.

His insights into psychological manipulation, deception, and moral unity within an army were direct responses to the complex and high-stakes world of ancient Chinese warfare.

In this world of shifting power and constant conflict, Sun Tzu developed his principles not as abstract ideas but as practical tools for survival and dominance. His belief that victory could be achieved in ways other than battle was groundbreaking in a time when brute strength often ruled. His strategies focused on flexibility, intelligence, and the power of unpredictability. By continuously adjusting to changing situations, he believed a general could turn even the most desperate circumstances into opportunities for success. In this way, his work is not only a reflection of his era but a timeless guide for those looking to navigate conflict with wisdom and precision.

III. Philosophical Background

Sun Tzu's ideas didn't develop in isolation; they were influenced by the major philosophical traditions of ancient China, especially Daoism and Confucianism. Daoism, which emphasizes balance, harmony, and non-contention, had a deep impact on his strategic thinking. At its core, Daoism teaches that one should move with the natural flow of the universe, rather than resist it. This belief in flexibility and adaptability is reflected in Sun Tzu's view that a good leader must be flexible in both thought and action, ready to adapt to changing situations instead of sticking rigidly to a set plan. The idea of winning with minimal force—ideally without fighting at all—embodies the Daoist principle of achieving results with the least effort, which is central to The Art of War.

Moreover, Daoism's focus on harmony is seen in Sun Tzu's approach to warfare as an art where the best outcomes are those that avoid conflict altogether. He recognized that forcing a victory often brings about unnecessary destruction and loss, not just in terms of lives but also resources and morale. Instead, he advocated for strategies that involved subtlety, psychological manipulation, and careful planning, all aligned with the natural course of events. Sun

Tzu's famous saying, "The supreme art of war is to subdue the enemy without fighting," reflects Daoist wisdom, where the soft overcomes the hard, and the flexible triumphs over the rigid.

Confucianism also played a key role in shaping Sun Tzu's philosophy. Confucian values like duty, ethical conduct, and governing with moral integrity are present in his view of leadership. In Confucian thought, a leader's role is not just about winning; it includes the well-being of the people and the pursuit of order and justice. Sun Tzu's writings, although focused on military strategy, emphasize that a good general must also be a wise and virtuous leader. This aligns with the Confucian ideal of the "Junzi," or the gentleman, who leads by moral virtue and serves as a role model. Sun Tzu believed that an effective leader earns loyalty and trust, not through fear or force, but through wisdom, fairness, and calm decision-making. The combination of Confucian ethics and Daoist practicality creates a balanced framework for Sun Tzu's strategies, making The Art of War not just a guide to military success but also a blueprint for ethical leadership.

Core Principles of Sun Tzu's Philosophy

The Importance of Strategy Over Force

At the core of Sun Tzu's philosophy is the belief that strategic insight is more valuable than brute strength. He argues that the best victories are those achieved without fighting, highlighting the need for careful planning, foresight, and the use of intelligence rather than relying solely on physical power. For Sun Tzu, a leader's role is to outthink their opponent instead of outfight them. He advocated for a strategic approach that reduces the costs of war, both in terms of human lives and resources. Instead of direct conflict, Sun Tzu advises military leaders to disorient their enemies, target their weaknesses, and use deception to gain an advantage. To him, a well-fought battle is one that ends before it even starts, with the enemy defeated by the unseen forces of superior strategy.

Flexibility and Adaptability in Warfare

One of Sun Tzu's key principles is that rigid plans often lead to failure. Success on the battlefield depends on the ability to adapt and respond to constantly changing conditions. He teaches that no two battles are the same, so no single strategy can work for every situation. Instead, Sun Tzu emphasizes the need for flexibility, urging generals to stay fluid in both thought and action. In his view, the best leaders are those who can read the terrain, understand their troops' morale, anticipate their enemy's moves, and adjust their tactics as needed. By avoiding predictable patterns, a leader can keep their opponents off balance, staying one step ahead.

Flexibility goes beyond just physical movements on the battlefield. It includes mental agility, the ability to think quickly, and the willingness to abandon a failing plan for a better one. Sun Tzu believed that sticking stubbornly to a plan, no matter how well thought out, could lead to disaster if it didn't fit the situation. His philosophy encourages leaders to be like water, adapting to the shape of their environment, changing form as conditions change, and always finding a way to move forward. This principle of adaptability has made The Art of War highly relevant in many areas beyond the military, including business and sports, where the ability to pivot in response to new challenges is often the key to success.

Psychological Warfare

Another core element of Sun Tzu's philosophy is his deep understanding of the human mind, both in terms of the enemy and one's own troops. He places great emphasis on psychological warfare, believing that many battles are won or lost in the mind long before they are fought on the battlefield. A leader who can demoralize the enemy, spread confusion, or instill doubt has already set the stage for victory. Sun Tzu advocates using tactics such as deception, misinformation, and surprise to weaken the enemy's confidence and will to fight. By showing strength when weak or pretending to be disorganized when ready to attack, a leader can manipulate the enemy into making costly errors. To Sun Tzu, deception is not just a tactic—it is the essence of warfare.

Equally important is understanding the psychology of one's own troops. Sun Tzu teaches that a successful leader must know how to keep their forces united and their morale high. Soldiers who trust their commander, believe in their cause, and feel confident in the strategy are far more likely to fight bravely and with determination. Sun Tzu believed that a wise general knows how to inspire and motivate, how to reward loyalty, and how to manage fear and uncertainty within the ranks. In his view, leadership is just as much about fostering the right mindset as it is about military skill.

The Role of Leadership

At the core of Sun Tzu's strategic thought lies Sun Tzu believed that leadership is essential to the success of any endeavor, whether military or otherwise. The qualities of a great leader, in his view, go beyond tactical skill. A leader must possess wisdom, remain calm under pressure, be decisive, and uphold moral integrity. For Sun Tzu, leadership isn't just about giving orders; it's about guiding one's people with a steady hand and clear vision. The ability of a leader to inspire trust and unity among their troops is often the key to determining the outcome of a battle.

In The Art of War, Sun Tzu stresses that a leader must deeply understand human nature and manage both resources and emotions wisely. A good leader knows when to be strict and when to show compassion, when to give rewards and when to administer punishment, always balancing authority with wisdom. The leader's role is to create harmony within the ranks, ensuring that everyone, from the highest officers to the lowest soldiers, works together as a unified team. Sun Tzu believed that leadership was the ultimate factor in determining success, and that no amount of strength or resources could make up for a lack of vision and guidance from the top.

For Sun Tzu, leadership is both an art and a responsibility. It requires not only the skill to create great strategies but also the wisdom to carry them out with compassion and integrity. His insights elevate the role of a leader to that of a moral authority, making it clear that true power comes not from dominance but from understanding and mastering oneself, the situation, and those who follow.

IV. Key Themes and Structure of The Art of War

The Art of Strategy

At the core of The Art of War is the idea that victory is achieved through careful planning and strategic foresight. Instead of depending on brute force or sheer numbers, Sun Tzu highlights the importance of intelligence, preparation, and the thoughtful management of resources. To him, a successful campaign begins long before the actual battle. It requires a leader to evaluate not only their own strengths and weaknesses but also those of their enemy. This involves understanding the terrain, the morale of the troops, and the timing of actions. A well-planned strategy, in Sun Tzu's view, allows one to control the battlefield before the enemy even realizes they are being outmaneuvered.

Sun Tzu explains that strategy is the key to using minimal resources for maximum effect. It's not enough to simply fight well; one must fight smart, knowing when to strike and when to hold back. His focus on strategic thinking teaches that victory often belongs to those who understand when to avoid fighting altogether. For Sun Tzu, the greatest generals are those who can win wars without engaging in combat. His insights encourage readers to look at the bigger picture of their challenges, whether in warfare or life, and to approach them with deliberate, calculated actions rather than reacting on impulse.

The Principle of Deception

One of the most enduring and thought-provoking principles in The Art of War is the role of deception. Sun Tzu's famous statement, "All warfare is based on deception," sums up his belief that a commander's true strength lies in their ability to mislead and outsmart the enemy. Deception isn't just a tactic—it's a fundamental part of strategy, allowing a leader to shape the enemy's perceptions and decisions. By creating a false sense of security or concealing one's true intentions, a skilled leader can manipulate their adversary into making costly errors. Misinformation, fake retreats, and surprise attacks are all tools in the strategist's toolkit.

In Sun Tzu's philosophy, deception is about gaining the upper hand through psychological means. The aim is to make the opponent feel secure where they are weak and vulnerable where they are strong. By hiding one's true strengths and revealing only what is necessary, a general can keep the enemy in a constant state of doubt. This unpredictability, according to Sun Tzu, is essential for achieving success. His teachings on deception go far beyond the battlefield and have proven valuable in many areas of modern life, including business negotiations, competitive sports, and political strategy.

Adaptability and Flexibility

Throughout The Art of War, Sun Tzu consistently emphasizes the importance of adaptability in the face of changing circumstances. A leader who clings to a single plan or strategy, regardless of the evolving situation, is bound to fail. Instead, Sun Tzu advocates for a flexible approach, where a commander can pivot quickly and seize opportunities as they arise. In his view, the ability to adapt is a defining quality of a great general. Sun Tzu compares the ideal leader to water, which conforms to the shape of whatever contains it. Just as water flows around obstacles, a successful commander must move with the ever-changing conditions of warfare.

This principle of adaptability aligns with Sun Tzu's belief that no two battles are alike. The unpredictable nature of conflict requires a mindset open to change, whether in tactics, alliances, or terrain. Leaders must be able to set aside preconceived notions and embrace the fluid nature of their surroundings. Sun Tzu's insight extends beyond military situations to modern leadership challenges, reminding readers that success often depends on staying flexible, innovative, and responsive to new information.

The Role of Morale and Unity

For Sun Tzu, victory is not merely about having the largest army or the most skilled fighters. The morale of the troops and the unity of the command structure are just as vital to success as any weapon or strategy. Soldiers who trust their leader and believe in their cause are much more likely to perform well under pressure than those who are demoralized or divided. Sun Tzu places significant importance on treating soldiers with respect, addressing their needs, and inspiring them with a sense of purpose. A general who can command loyalty and cultivate unity within the ranks is far better prepared to face the challenges of war.

Additionally, Sun Tzu underscores the need for clear and consistent leadership. A general must be decisive and fair, maintaining discipline while also knowing when to show compassion. The bond between a leader and their soldiers is a crucial element in creating a cohesive and effective fighting force. Internal harmony can often be the deciding factor in battle, especially when facing difficult circumstances. Sun Tzu's teachings on morale and unity go beyond the battlefield, offering valuable insights for modern leaders in business, politics, or personal endeavors. They remind us that a team's success often hinges as much on its internal dynamics as it does on external factors.

V. Influence and Legacy of The Art of War

Influence in East Asia

The Art of War has been a foundational text in East Asia for centuries, deeply influencing the philosophies and practices of military leaders, scholars, and political strategists. From China to Japan and Korea, its principles have shaped the ways wars were fought and how empires were governed. In China, where Sun Tzu first developed his strategies, dynasties studied the text to refine their military tactics, using its teachings to defend and expand their territories. Beyond the battlefield, The Art of War guided Chinese governance, diplomacy, and statecraft, serving as a manual for leaders who sought to balance power, strategy, and ethics.

In Japan, The Art of War became prominent during the Samurai era, especially in the development of Bushido, the warrior's code of honor. Japanese military leaders, including figures like Oda Nobunaga and Tokugawa Ieyasu, drew inspiration from Sun Tzu's principles. His teachings on discipline, adaptability, and the importance of psychological warfare resonated deeply with the samurai ethos, further embedding The Art of War into Japan's cultural and military traditions. The text's influence reached beyond warfare, shaping how political leaders approached negotiations and alliances.

Korea also embraced Sun Tzu's strategies, applying them in times of internal conflict and external threats, particularly during struggles with neighboring states. For centuries, Korean scholars and military generals turned to The Art of War when planning defenses and military campaigns, finding in its pages the strategic insight and adaptability needed to navigate complex geopolitical landscapes. Sun Tzu's focus on intelligence, deception, and strategic positioning over brute force made his work a vital resource in East Asia's long history of warfare and statecraft.

Influence in Modern Warfare

As the centuries went by, The Art of War spread beyond East Asia and started to influence military strategies around the world. Its ideas were eventually adopted by Western military leaders and strategists, especially during the 19th and 20th centuries when warfare became more complicated. For example, Napoleon Bonaparte is said to have been greatly influenced by Sun Tzu's teachings. His military campaigns across Europe showed how effective it was to use strategic surprise, careful planning, and taking advantage of the enemy's weaknesses—all key elements of Sun Tzu's approach.

In the 20th century, Sun Tzu's influence could be seen especially in guerrilla warfare tactics. Revolutionary leaders like Mao Zedong in China and Ho Chi Minh in Vietnam used The Art of War's focus on psychological warfare, deception, and asymmetrical tactics to defeat stronger and better-equipped enemies. In Vietnam, during the conflict with the United States, Ho Chi Minh and his generals applied Sun Tzu's strategies very effectively, using the jungle terrain and psychological endurance to weaken their enemy's determination and eventually force their withdrawal.

Today, The Art of War is often studied in military academies alongside other classic works on strategy and tactics. Its ideas have shaped both the theoretical and practical education of military officers around the world. From Sandhurst in the UK to West Point in the United States, Sun Tzu's teachings still provide important lessons about leadership, intelligence gathering, and the moral aspects of warfare. His belief that the best victories are those won without fighting connects well with modern military thinking, where political and economic strategies often work alongside or instead of traditional battles.

Beyond the Battlefield: Business, Sports, and Politics

While The Art of War started as a military guide, its influence has spread far beyond the battlefield. In the business world, leaders and entrepreneurs have used Sun Tzu's principles to navigate competitive markets, secure good deals, and manage teams effectively. The strategic use of resources, understanding the competition, and adapting to changes are all ideas from The Art of War that have been applied to the corporate world. Today, it's common for business executives to look to Sun Tzu for advice on everything from launching new products to negotiating mergers.

Likewise, sports coaches and athletes have found value in Sun Tzu's focus on preparation, adaptability, and mental strength. Competitive sports, like warfare, require knowing your opponent, anticipating their moves, and adjusting strategies as the game goes on. Whether in battle or in sports, the ability to stay calm and outsmart the competition is universally important.

In politics, The Art of War has also left its mark. Leaders use its ideas when approaching diplomacy, forming alliances, and even running election campaigns. Politicians often apply Sun Tzu's tactics to influence public perception, undermine rivals without direct conflict, and take advantage of timing and positioning. The text's focus on intelligence gathering and strategic alliances is especially relevant in modern politics, where behind-the-scenes efforts can determine the outcome of public contests.

A Lasting Legacy

The Art of War remains a timeless resource, providing guidance that transcends time, culture, and discipline. Whether on the battlefield, in the boardroom, or in everyday life, Sun Tzu's strategies have endured because they are rooted in a deep understanding of human nature and the complexities of conflict. His ability to simplify the chaotic and often harsh realities of war into clear, actionable principles continues to inspire leaders across various fields.

As we move further into an age where technology and information play increasingly larger roles in conflict and competition, Sun Tzu's teachings on deception, intelligence, and adaptability feel more relevant than ever. His insights remind us that victory is not always achieved through strength alone, but through careful thought, ethical leadership, and a deep understanding of the human element in every pursuit.

Sun Tzu's influence on both ancient and modern warfare, along with his broader impact on business, politics, and leadership, solidifies The Art of War as one of the most important and lasting texts on strategy. His legacy continues to shape how people approach conflict, competition, and success, offering timeless wisdom that resonates with each generation.

Chapter 1 - Laying Plans

Sun Tzu said: The art of war is critically important to the State. It can be the difference between life and death, leading to either safety or ruin. Therefore, it must always be carefully studied and never ignored.

The art of war is based on five key factors that must be considered in every military decision. These factors are: (1) The Moral Law; (2) Heaven; (3) Earth; (4) The Commander; (5) Method and discipline.

The Moral Law ensures that the people are fully united with their ruler, making them willing to follow him, even risking their lives without fear of danger.

Heaven refers to the natural conditions, like day and night, cold and heat, and the changing of seasons.

Earth involves distances, both large and small, areas of safety and danger, wide open spaces and narrow paths, and the possibilities of survival or death.

The Commander represents the qualities of wisdom, honesty, kindness, courage, and strictness.

Method and discipline cover the organization of the army, the ranks, the roles assigned to each soldier, and the control of supplies and resources.

These five factors must be studied in depth by those who seek to understand the art of war. By mastering them, a ruler can win the loyalty of the people and command a strong, unified army capable of facing any challenge.

The Moral Law creates harmony between the ruler and the people, inspiring them to follow without hesitation, even in the face of great danger.

Heaven includes the cycles of day and night, the changes in temperature, and the timing of seasons. Some interpret this as a reflection of the broader workings of nature, like the balance of forces or natural elements.

Earth includes not just physical distances but also the dangers and safety that different terrains bring, whether they are wide open plains or narrow mountain passes. These elements can determine the chances of survival or death.

The Commander stands for qualities that inspire trust and loyalty—wisdom, honesty, kindness, bravery, and firmness in discipline. These virtues are essential for strong leadership.

Finally, Method and discipline ensure that the army is well-organized, with clear roles and responsibilities, and that resources are well-managed. These elements ensure that the military is prepared for anything and that chaos is avoided during battle.

Method and discipline mean organizing the army into its proper divisions, assigning ranks among the officers, maintaining roads to ensure supplies can reach the army, and controlling military spending.

These five principles should be well-known to every general: the one who knows them will be victorious; the one who does not will fail.

Therefore, in your planning, when trying to understand the military situation, use these principles as the basis of comparison, in this way:

Which of the two rulers follows the Moral Law? (That is, who is in harmony with their people?)

Which of the two generals is more skilled?

Who has the advantage of favorable conditions from Heaven and Earth?

On which side is discipline enforced the most strictly? (There is a story about Ts'ao Ts'ao, a strict disciplinarian who once followed his own rule so closely that he sentenced himself to death for letting his horse damage crops. Instead of execution, he was convinced to cut off his hair as punishment.)

Which army is stronger, both in physical strength and spirit?

Which side has officers and soldiers who are better trained? (Wang Tzŭ once said that without constant practice, officers will hesitate when forming for battle, and without constant practice, the general will be uncertain when a crisis comes.)

Which side has greater consistency in rewarding good actions and punishing bad behavior?

By considering these seven points, I can predict who will win or lose.

The general who listens to my advice and acts on it will win: such a person should be kept in command! The general who ignores my advice and does not act on it will be defeated: such a person should be dismissed!

While you follow my advice for success, also take advantage of any favorable circumstances that go beyond the usual rules.

As circumstances change, you should adjust your plans accordingly. (Sun Tzu, as a practical soldier, rejects rigid reliance on theoretical principles. He warns us not to rely too heavily on abstract rules because, as Chang Yu says, while the basic principles of strategy can be explained clearly, you must adapt to the enemy's actions to secure a favorable position in battle. Before the Battle of Waterloo, Lord Uxbridge, commanding the cavalry, went to the Duke of Wellington to ask about his plans for the next day. He explained that if he suddenly had to take command, he would need to know the plans. The Duke listened quietly and asked, "Who will attack first tomorrow—me or Bonaparte?" Uxbridge answered, "Bonaparte." "Well," replied the Duke, "Bonaparte hasn't told me his plans, and since my strategy depends on his, how can you expect me to tell you mine?")

All warfare is based on deception. (This wise and profound statement is acknowledged by all soldiers. Col. Henderson notes that Wellington, known for many military qualities, was especially skilled in hiding his movements and deceiving both friend and foe.)

When we are able to attack, we must make it seem as though we are not ready; when using our forces, we must appear inactive; when we are near, we must make the enemy believe we are far away; and when we are far away, we must make him believe we are close by.

Lure the enemy with baits. Pretend to be in disarray, and then crush him. (Most commentators, except Chang Yu, interpret this as "when he is disorganized, crush him," but it's more natural to understand this as another example of how deception works in war.)

If the enemy is well-prepared at all points, be ready for him. If he is stronger, avoid him.

If your opponent has a bad temper, provoke him. Pretend to be weak so that he becomes overconfident. (Wang Tzŭ, as quoted by Tu Yu, compares this tactic to how a cat plays with a mouse, pretending to be weak before suddenly striking.)

If the enemy is resting, don't let him have peace. (This likely means to keep up pressure on the enemy, although Mei Yao-ch'en suggests it could mean "while we rest, let the enemy exhaust himself." The Yu Lan interprets it as "lure him on and tire him out.")

If his forces are united, divide them. (Many commentators offer an alternative explanation: "If the ruler and his subjects are in harmony, cause division between them.")

Attack the enemy where he is unprepared; appear in places where you are not expected.

These military strategies that lead to victory must not be revealed in advance.

A general who wins a battle makes many calculations in his temple before the battle begins. (Chang Yu notes that in ancient times, a temple was set aside for a general about to lead an army, where he could carefully plan his campaign.)

On the other hand, a general who loses a battle makes few calculations ahead of time. Thus, many calculations lead to victory, while few calculations lead to defeat. How much worse it is when no calculations are made at all! It is through understanding this that I can predict who is likely to win or lose.

Chapter 2 - Waging War

[Ts'ao Kung comments: "He who wishes to fight must first calculate the cost," which prepares us for the realization that this chapter is not primarily about what we might expect from its title, but is instead focused on the planning of resources and strategies.

Sun Tzu said: In warfare, when there are in the field a thousand swift chariots, an equal number of heavy chariots, and a hundred thousand soldiers clad in armor (the swift chariots were lightly built and, according to Chang Yu, were used for attack; the heavy chariots were stronger and designed for defense. Li Ch'uan suggests that the heavy chariots were also light, but this seems unlikely. It's interesting to note the similarities between early Chinese warfare and that of the Homeric Greeks. In both cases, the war chariot was central to military formation, surrounded by groups of foot soldiers. As for the numbers here, it is said that each swift chariot was accompanied by 75 footmen, and each heavy chariot by 25 footmen, dividing the army into a thousand battalions, each consisting of two chariots and a hundred men), with provisions sufficient to sustain them for a thousand li (2.78 modern li make up a mile, though the length may have varied somewhat since Sun Tzu's time), the total daily expenditure, both at home and at the front—including the entertainment of guests, small items like glue and paint, and the sums spent on chariots and armor—will amount to a thousand ounces of silver per day. This is the cost of maintaining an army of 100,000 men.

When you engage in actual combat, if victory is slow to come, the soldiers' weapons will grow dull, and their enthusiasm will fade. If you lay siege to a town, you will drain your strength.

Additionally, if the campaign is prolonged, the state's resources will not be able to bear the strain.

Now, when your weapons are dulled, your enthusiasm has waned, your strength is drained, and your resources are depleted, other leaders will rise to exploit your vulnerability. At that point, no one, no matter how wise, will be able to prevent the inevitable consequences.

Thus, while we have heard of foolish haste in war, cleverness has never been associated with long delays. (This brief and challenging sentence has puzzled commentators. Ts'ao Kung, Li Ch'uan, Meng Shih, Tu Yu, Tu Mu, and Mei Yao-ch'en all comment that a general, though typically unwise, might still win by sheer speed. Ho Shih adds that while haste may be foolish, it at least saves energy and resources, whereas prolonged campaigns, even if skillful, lead to disaster. Wang Hsi avoids the difficulty by saying that lengthy operations age the army, drain wealth, empty the treasury, and bring suffering to the people; true cleverness avoids these pitfalls. Chang Yu argues that as long as victory is possible, even hasty actions are preferable to overly cautious delays. However, Sun Tzu does not explicitly suggest that ill-considered haste is better than well-thought-out but prolonged strategies. Instead, his point is more cautious: while speed may sometimes be unwise, delays are always foolish, if only because they lead to national impoverishment. When considering Sun Tzu's point, the example of Fabius Cunctator inevitably comes to mind. Fabius deliberately measured the endurance of Rome against Hannibal's isolated army, reasoning that Hannibal would suffer more in a prolonged campaign in foreign territory. However, whether Fabius' strategy would have worked in the long run is debatable. Though the reversal of his approach led to the disaster at Cannae, this only suggests a negative presumption in favor of his tactics.)

Only someone who fully understands the horrors of war can fully comprehend the value of conducting it in a profitable manner. (That is, with speed. Only those who recognize the devastating consequences of a long war can truly grasp the supreme importance of bringing it to a swift conclusion. Although only two commentators favor this interpretation, it fits the logic of the context better than the alternative rendering, "He who does not know the evils of war cannot appreciate its benefits," which is clearly pointless.)

The skillful commander does not call for a second levy, nor are his supply wagons loaded more than twice. (Once war begins, he will not waste valuable time waiting for reinforcements, nor will he retreat to gather fresh supplies, but will instead cross the enemy's border without delay. While this may seem like a bold strategy, history's greatest military leaders, from Julius Caesar to Napoleon Bonaparte, have all emphasized the importance of time—that is, being slightly ahead of the enemy—over numerical superiority or careful logistical calculations.)

Bring war materials from home, but rely on the enemy for provisions. In this way, the army will always have enough food to meet its needs. (The Chinese word translated here as "war material" literally means "things to be used" and is understood in the broadest sense. It includes everything needed by the army, except for food.)

When the state treasury is poor, the army must be supported by contributions from far-off places. Relying on distant sources to sustain the army leads to impoverishment of the people.

The beginning of this sentence does not connect smoothly with the next, though it is clearly meant to do so. The arrangement is so awkward that it suggests some corruption in the text. It rarely occurs to Chinese commentators that an amendment might be needed to clarify the meaning, so they offer no help here. The Chinese words Sun Tzu used to indicate the cause of the people's impoverishment refer to a system where farmers sent their corn directly to the army.

But why would it fall to them to maintain the army in this way, unless the State or Government was too poor to do so?

On the other hand, the presence of an army nearby causes prices to rise, and high prices lead to the people's wealth being drained. (Wang Hsi says that prices increase even before the army leaves its own territory. Ts'ao Kung believes this applies to an army that has already crossed the frontier.)

When the people's wealth is drained, the farmers will suffer from heavy demands placed upon them.

As their wealth is lost and their strength is exhausted, the homes of the people will be left bare, and three-tenths of their income will be consumed. (Tu Mu and Wang Hsi argue that the people are actually deprived of seven-tenths of their income, but this is difficult to extract from the text. Ho Shih adds a characteristic note: "The people are the essential part of the State, and food is their heaven, so is it not right that those in authority should take care to protect both?")

Meanwhile, government expenses for damaged chariots, worn-out horses, breastplates, helmets, bows and arrows, spears and shields, protective coverings, oxen for transportation, and heavy wagons will consume four-tenths of the total revenue.

Thus, a wise general makes it a priority to forage from the enemy. One cartload of the enemy's provisions is worth twenty of one's own, and similarly, a single picul of their supplies is worth twenty from one's own stores. (This is because twenty cartloads of provisions will be consumed during the transportation of one cartload to the front. A picul is a unit of measure equal to 133.3 pounds, or 65.5 kilograms.)

Now, to defeat the enemy, our soldiers must be stirred to anger; and to gain any benefit from defeating the enemy, they must receive rewards. (Tu Mu explains: "Rewards are necessary so the soldiers understand the benefit of beating the enemy. When spoils are captured from the enemy, they should be distributed as rewards, so that all the men will have a strong desire to fight, each for his own gain.")

Therefore, in chariot warfare, when ten or more chariots are captured, the soldiers who take the first one should be rewarded. Our flags should be substituted for the enemy's, and the captured chariots should be integrated and used alongside our own. Captured enemy soldiers should be treated kindly and kept.

This is called using the enemy's resources to strengthen one's own forces.

In war, your main objective should always be victory, not prolonged campaigns. (As Ho Shih remarks: "War is not something to be treated lightly." Sun Tzu reiterates here the central lesson of this chapter.)

Thus, it is clear that the leader of armies holds the fate of the people in his hands, and it is his actions that determine whether the nation will be at peace or in danger.

Chapter 3 - Attack By Stratagem

Sun Tzu said: In the practical art of war, the best course of action is to take the enemy's country whole and intact; to shatter and destroy it is not as good. Likewise, it is better to capture an entire army than to destroy it, better to capture an entire regiment, detachment, or company than to destroy them. (According to Ssu-ma Fa, an army corps consisted of 12,500 men; Ts'ao Kung says a regiment contained 500 men, a detachment could consist of any number between 100 and 500, and a company could range from 5 to 100 men. However, Chang Yu gives the exact figures of 100 for a detachment and 5 for a company.)

Therefore, to fight and win in all your battles is not the highest excellence; the highest excellence consists in breaking the enemy's resistance without having to fight. (Once again, no modern strategist would disagree with these words. Moltke's greatest victory, the surrender of the enormous French army at Sedan, was achieved virtually without bloodshed.)

Thus, the highest form of generalship is to thwart the enemy's plans. (Perhaps the word "thwart" does not fully capture the meaning of the original Chinese, which implies not merely defending by countering each of the enemy's strategies, but actively attacking. Ho Shih explains this clearly in his note: "When the enemy plans to attack us, we must anticipate him by launching our attack first.")

The next best course is to prevent the enemy's forces from combining. (This involves isolating him from his allies. We must remember that Sun Tzu is referring to the many states or principalities into which China was divided in his time.)

After that, the next best option is to attack the enemy's army in the field. (That is, when his forces are already gathered and at full strength.)

The worst course of action is to besiege walled cities.

The rule is not to attack cities with walls unless it is absolutely necessary.

(Another good piece of military advice. If the Boers had followed this in 1899 and not spread their forces thin around places like Kimberley, Mafeking, or even Ladysmith, they likely would have had the upper hand before the British were really ready to fight back.)

Building mantlets, movable shelters, and other war tools will take up three whole months.

(It's not completely clear what the Chinese term translated as "mantlets" really meant. Ts'ao Kung says they were "large shields," but Li Ch'uan gives us a better idea, describing them as protection for soldiers attacking the walls of a city up close. This suggests they might have been like the Roman testudo, a formation where soldiers would use their shields to form a shell. Tu Mu claims they were wheeled vehicles for defense, but Ch'en Hao disagrees. See earlier, II.14. The term also referred to turrets on city walls. The "movable shelters" were more clearly described by various commentators: they were wooden, missile-proof structures with four wheels, covered with raw hides, used in sieges to transport soldiers safely to and from the city walls, often to fill up moats with dirt. Tu Mu adds that nowadays they are called "wooden donkeys.")

Building up ramps against the walls will take another three months.

(These were large mounds or earth ramps built up to the height of the enemy's walls to spot weak points in the defenses and to tear down the fortified turrets mentioned earlier.)

The general, unable to keep his anger in check, will send his men to attack like a swarm of ants.

(This vivid image from Ts'ao Kung comes from the sight of an army of ants climbing up a wall. It means the general, losing patience due to the delay, may order an attack before his war machines are ready.)

As a result, one-third of his men will be killed, and the city will still not be taken. These are the terrible outcomes of a siege.

(We are reminded of the heavy losses suffered by the Japanese in their recent siege of Port Arthur.)

A skilled leader defeats the enemy's troops without ever having to fight; he takes their cities without needing to lay siege; he brings down their kingdom without long, drawn-out battles.

(Chia Lin points out that the leader only removes the government but does not harm individuals. A classic example of this is Wu Wang, who, after ending the Yin dynasty, was celebrated as the "Father and mother of the people.")

With his army fully intact, he will challenge for control of the Empire, and by doing so, without losing a single man, his victory will be complete.

(Because of the double meanings in the Chinese text, the second part of this sentence could also mean: "And thus, since the weapon has not been dulled by overuse, its sharpness remains perfect.")

This is how to conquer through strategy.

In war, if our forces outnumber the enemy ten to one, we surround him; if five to one, we attack him.

(Immediately, without waiting for any further advantages.)

If we are twice as numerous, we split our army into two.

(Tu Mu disagrees with this advice, and at first glance, it seems to go against a basic rule of warfare. However, Ts'ao Kung offers an explanation: "When we are two to one against the enemy, one part of our army can be used in the regular way, and the other can be used for a special maneuver." Chang Yu adds more clarity: "If our army is twice the size of the enemy's, we should split it into two groups—one to face the enemy head-on, and the other to attack from behind. If the enemy responds to the front attack, he can be crushed from behind; if he reacts to the rear attack, he can be defeated from the front." This is what is meant by saying that 'one part may be used in the regular way, and the other for a special maneuver.' Tu Mu doesn't understand that splitting the army is an irregular strategy, just as concentrating the army is the regular strategy, and he is too quick to call this a mistake.)

If we are evenly matched, we can engage in battle.

(Li Ch'uan, supported by Ho Shih, rephrases this as: "If both sides are equal in strength, only a skilled general will choose to fight.")

If we are slightly weaker, we can avoid the enemy.

(The meaning "we can watch the enemy" is an improvement on this, but there isn't much solid backing for this version. Chang Yu reminds us that this advice only holds if other factors are equal. A small difference in numbers can often be balanced out by greater energy and discipline.)

If we are greatly outmatched, we can retreat.

Even though a small force may put up a stubborn fight, in the end, it will be overcome by a larger force.

The general is the foundation of the State: if the foundation is solid in all areas, the State will be strong; if the foundation has weaknesses, the State will be weak.

(As Li Ch'uan puts it briefly: "A gap shows a weakness; if the general's ability is not perfect—if he isn't fully skilled in his role—his army will lack strength.")

There are three ways a ruler can bring disaster to his army:

(1) By ordering the army to advance or retreat without knowing that it cannot follow those orders. This is called crippling the army.

(Li Ch'uan adds: "It's like tying the legs of a racehorse so it can't run." You might think "the ruler" in this case is far away, trying to direct the army from a distance. However, the commentators interpret it the opposite way, quoting T'ai Kung: "A kingdom shouldn't be ruled from the outside, and an army shouldn't be commanded from within." Naturally, during a battle or when close to the enemy, the general shouldn't be right in the middle of his own troops, but should stay a little apart. Otherwise, he might misread the situation and give wrong orders.)

(2) By trying to govern an army in the same way he runs a kingdom, without understanding the conditions within an army, a ruler causes unrest in the soldiers' minds.

(Ts'ao Kung notes: "The military and civil spheres are entirely different; you can't handle an army with soft, delicate treatment." Chang Yu adds: "Humanity and justice are the foundations for governing a state, but not for leading an army. Opportunism and flexibility are military virtues, not civil ones.")

(3) By using officers without making distinctions between them,

(This means the ruler doesn't carefully assign the right person to the right role.)

because he doesn't understand the military principle of adapting to circumstances, he undermines the soldiers' trust.

(I follow Mei Yao-ch'en here. Other commentators refer to the officers employed, not the ruler as in the previous sections. Tu Yu says: "If a general doesn't understand adaptability, he should not be put in charge." Tu Mu quotes: "A skilled leader will employ the wise, the brave, the greedy, and the foolish. The wise man enjoys proving his merit, the brave man seeks to show his courage in action, the greedy man quickly seizes opportunities, and the foolish man fears nothing, even death.")

But when the army is restless and distrustful, conflict will arise from the other feudal princes. This brings chaos into the army and throws away any chance of victory.

From this, we know that there are five key factors for victory: (1) He will win who knows when to fight and when not to fight.

(Chang Yu says: If he can fight, he moves forward and attacks; if he cannot fight, he retreats and defends. Victory is certain for the one who understands when to attack and when to defend.)

(2) He will win who knows how to manage both larger and smaller forces.

(This isn't just about the general's ability to count numbers accurately, as Li Ch'uan and others suggest. Chang Yu explains this better: "By using the art of war, a smaller force can defeat a larger one, and vice versa. The secret is understanding the terrain and seizing the right moment. As Wu Tzŭ says: 'With a larger force, move on easy ground; with a smaller force, seek difficult ground.'")

Chapter 4 - Tactical Dispositions

Ts'ao Kung explains the meaning behind the title of this chapter: "marching and countermarching by the two armies to find out each other's condition." Tu Mu adds: "It is through the positioning of an army that its state can be revealed. Hide your positioning, and your condition remains secret, leading to victory; expose your positioning, and your condition becomes clear, leading to defeat." Wang Hsi comments that a good general "ensures success by adapting his tactics to those of the enemy."

Sun Tzǔ said: The skilled fighters of the past first made sure they could not be defeated, then waited for the right moment to defeat the enemy.

The power to avoid defeat is in our own hands, but the chance to defeat the enemy comes from the enemy himself.

(That is, of course, due to a mistake on the enemy's part.)

Thus, a skilled fighter can always protect himself from defeat,

(Chang Yu explains that this is done by "concealing the positioning of the troops, covering up tracks, and taking constant precautions.")

but he cannot always ensure he will defeat the enemy.

Hence the saying: One may know how to win but still not be able to achieve it.

Protecting oneself from defeat involves defensive tactics, while defeating the enemy involves taking the offensive.

(I keep the meaning found in a similar passage in §§ 1-3, despite the fact that the commentators disagree with me. Their interpretation, "He who cannot conquer takes the defensive," is reasonable, but this version seems clearer.)

Being on the defensive suggests a lack of strength, while attacking shows an abundance of strength.

A general skilled in defense hides in the deepest recesses of the earth;

(Literally, "hides under the ninth earth," a metaphor for complete secrecy and concealment, so the enemy doesn't know his location.)

while a general skilled in attack strikes from the highest heavens.

(Another metaphor, meaning he falls upon his enemy like a sudden thunderbolt, against which there is no time to prepare. Most commentators agree with this interpretation.)

Thus, on one hand, we have the ability to protect ourselves; on the other, the ability to achieve a complete victory.

To see victory only when it is clear to everyone is not the height of excellence.

(As Ts'ao Kung says, "the key is to see the plant before it has sprouted," meaning to foresee the outcome before the action begins. Li Ch'uan mentions the story of Han Hsin, who, before attacking the much larger army of Chao, which was heavily fortified in the city of Ch'eng-an, told his officers, "Gentlemen, we are going to destroy the enemy and will meet again at dinner." His officers didn't take him seriously and gave doubtful replies. But Han Hsin had already devised a clever plan, and as he predicted, he captured the city and crushed his enemy.)

It is also not the height of excellence if you fight and win, and the whole world says, "Well done!"

(True excellence, as Tu Mu says, lies in planning secretly, moving quietly, and outsmarting the enemy's plans so that victory is achieved without a drop of blood being shed. Sun Tzŭ praises achievements that "the world's clumsy thumb and finger cannot grasp.")

Lifting an autumn hair is not a sign of great strength;

("Autumn hair" refers to the fine fur of a hare, which is softest in autumn when it starts growing back. This phrase is commonly used by Chinese writers.)

Seeing the sun and moon is not a sign of sharp vision, and hearing the sound of thunder is not a sign of quick hearing.

(Ho Shih provides examples of true strength, sharp vision, and quick hearing: Wu Huo, who could lift a 250-stone tripod; Li Chu, who could see objects as small as mustard seeds from a hundred paces; and Shih K'uang, a blind musician who could hear a mosquito's footsteps.)

What the ancients called a clever fighter is someone who not only wins, but wins with ease.

(The second part literally means "one who, while conquering, excels in conquering easily." Mei Yao-ch'en explains: "He who only notices the obvious wins his battles with difficulty; but he who sees beneath the surface wins with ease.")

For this reason, his victories bring him neither a reputation for wisdom nor credit for bravery.

(Tu Mu explains this well: "Since his victories are achieved under circumstances that remain hidden, the world at large knows nothing of them, and he gains no reputation for wisdom. Since the enemy surrenders without bloodshed, he gets no credit for bravery.")

He wins his battles by making no mistakes.

(Ch'en Hao says: "He avoids unnecessary marches and pointless attacks." Chang Yu explains the connection: "One who tries to win by brute force, even if skilled in fighting pitched battles, may sometimes be defeated. But one who can foresee the future and understand conditions before they arise will never make a mistake, and thus always win.")

Making no mistakes ensures victory because it means defeating an enemy who is already defeated.

Thus, the skilled fighter places himself in a position where defeat is impossible and never misses the moment to defeat the enemy.

(A "counsel of perfection," as Tu Mu notes. "Position" isn't just about the physical location of troops; it includes all the preparations and arrangements that a wise general makes to ensure the safety of the army.)

In war, the victorious strategist seeks battle only after victory is already assured, while the one destined for defeat fights first and then looks for victory.

(Ho Shih explains this paradox: "In warfare, first make plans that will guarantee victory, then lead your army into battle. If you rely on brute strength alone without first using strategy, victory will no longer be guaranteed.")

The ideal leader follows the moral law and adheres strictly to method and discipline; by doing so, he can control success.

In terms of military methods, there are: first, Measurement; second, Estimation of quantity; third, Calculation; fourth, Balancing of chances; and fifth, Victory.

Measurement depends on the Earth; Estimation of quantity comes from Measurement; Calculation comes from Estimation of quantity; Balancing of chances comes from Calculation; and Victory comes from Balancing of chances.

(It's hard to distinguish the four terms clearly in Chinese. The first seems to refer to surveying and measuring the ground, which allows us to estimate the enemy's strength and make calculations from that information. This leads to a weighing of chances—comparing the enemy's chances with our own. If the scale tips in our favor, victory follows. The difficulty lies in the third term, which some commentators interpret as a calculation of numbers, making it nearly synonymous with the second term. Perhaps the second refers to considering the enemy's general situation, while the third refers to estimating his numerical strength. Tu Mu suggests that once relative strength is known, we can apply cunning strategies. Ho Shih supports this, but with a weaker interpretation, indicating that the third term points to calculating numbers.)

A victorious army facing a defeated one is like a pound's weight against a single grain.

(Literally, "a victorious army is like an i (20 ounces) weighed against a shu (1/24 of an ounce); a defeated army is a shu weighed against an i." This illustrates the huge advantage a disciplined, victorious force has over one demoralized by defeat. Legge, in his note on Mencius, I.2.ix.2, defines the i as 24 Chinese ounces and corrects Chu Hsi's claim that it equals only 20 ounces. However, Li Ch'uan of the T'ang dynasty supports Chu Hsi's figure.)

The rush of a victorious force is like water bursting through a dam into a chasm a thousand fathoms deep. This concludes the section on tactical dispositions.

Chapter 5 - Energy

Sun Tzŭ said: Controlling a large army is based on the same principles as controlling a small group; it is simply a matter of dividing them into smaller units.

(This means splitting the army into regiments, companies, etc., each with its own subordinate officers. Tu Mu reminds us of the famous conversation between Han Hsin and the first Han Emperor. The Emperor asked, "How large an army do you think I could lead?" Han Hsin replied, "No more than 100,000 men, Your Majesty." "And how about you?" asked the Emperor. Han Hsin responded, "Oh, the more, the better.")

Fighting with a large army under your command is no different from fighting with a small one; it's just about using signs and signals to communicate.

To ensure that your entire force can withstand the enemy's attack without breaking, you need to use both direct and indirect maneuvers.

(Now we come to one of the most interesting parts of Sun Tzŭ's teachings: the discussion of cheng (direct) and ch'i (indirect). These two terms are tricky to fully grasp or consistently translate into English, so it's helpful to consider what various commentators have said. Li Ch'uan explains that cheng is a frontal confrontation, while ch'i is a diversion to the side. Chia Lin says: "When facing the enemy, your troops should be arranged in a conventional way, but victory comes from using unconventional maneuvers." Mei Yao-ch'en adds: "Ch'i is active, while cheng is passive; waiting for the right moment is passive, but action itself brings victory." Ho Shih explains: "We must make the enemy think our straightforward attack is secretly planned, and vice versa. Thus, cheng can become ch'i and ch'i can become cheng." He uses the example of Han Hsin, who marched his army toward Lin-chin but suddenly sent a large force across the Yellow River in wooden tubs, catching the enemy off guard. In this case, the march on Lin-chin was cheng, and the surprise maneuver across the river was ch'i."

Chang Yu summarizes these ideas by noting that military writers disagree on the definitions of cheng and ch'i. Wei Liao Tzŭ says, "Direct warfare favors frontal attacks, while indirect warfare favors attacks from behind." Ts'ao Kung says, "Going directly into battle is cheng, while appearing behind the enemy is ch'i." Li Wei-kung adds, "In war, marching straight ahead is cheng; turning movements are ch'i." These writers treat cheng and ch'i as separate and fixed, but they don't realize that the two can blend together and switch, like two sides of a circle. A comment on the T'ang Emperor T'ai Tsung goes deeper: "A ch'i maneuver becomes cheng if we make the enemy believe it is cheng; then our real attack will be ch'i, and vice versa. The secret lies in confusing the enemy so they cannot understand our true intentions."

In simpler terms, any operation is cheng if it draws the enemy's attention, and ch'i if it catches them by surprise. If the enemy recognizes a movement meant to be ch'i, it becomes cheng.)

The impact of your army should be like a grindstone smashing against an egg—this is achieved through understanding weak points and strong ones.

In all battles, the direct method may be used to engage the enemy, but indirect methods are necessary to secure victory.

(Chang Yu explains: "Develop indirect tactics steadily, either by striking at the enemy's flanks or attacking from behind." A brilliant example of indirect tactics deciding a campaign was Lord Roberts' night march around Peiwar Kotal during the second Afghan war.)

Indirect tactics, when applied efficiently, are as limitless as Heaven and Earth, as unceasing as the flow of rivers and streams. Like the sun and moon, they end only to begin again; like the four seasons, they pass and return.

(Tu Yu and Chang Yu see this as referring to the changing use of ch'i and cheng. However, Sun Tzŭ isn't specifically talking about cheng here, unless, as Cheng Yu-hsien suggests, a part of the text about cheng was lost. As mentioned before, ch'i and cheng are so interconnected in military operations that they cannot be considered separately. This passage expresses the almost endless resourcefulness of a great leader.)

There are only five musical notes, yet their combinations create more melodies than can ever be heard.

There are only five primary colors—blue, yellow, red, white, and black—yet their combinations produce more hues than can ever be seen.

There are only five basic tastes—sour, acrid, salty, sweet, and bitter—but their combinations yield more flavors than can ever be tasted.

In battle, there are only two methods of attack—the direct and the indirect—yet their combination creates an infinite number of maneuvers.

The direct and the indirect lead into each other, like a circle that has no end. Who can exhaust the possibilities of their combination?

The advance of troops is like the rush of a torrent, powerful enough to carry stones along its path.

The quality of decision is like the well-timed swoop of a falcon that enables it to strike and destroy its target.

(The Chinese here is tricky, and a certain key word in this context resists the best efforts of translation. Tu Mu defines this word as "the measurement or estimation of distance." But applying this meaning to the falcon, it seems to refer to the instinct of self-restraint, which prevents the bird from swooping down on its prey until the right moment, along with the ability to judge when that moment has come. The analogous quality in soldiers is the important skill of holding back their fire until the exact moment when it will be most effective. When the Victory went into action at Trafalgar, moving at hardly more than a drifting pace, it was under heavy fire for several minutes without returning a single shot. Nelson waited coolly until he was in close range, at which point the broadside he unleashed inflicted devastating damage on the enemy's nearest ships.)

Therefore, the skilled fighter will be fearsome in his attack and prompt in his decision.

(The word "decision" likely refers to the measurement of distance mentioned earlier, holding off until the enemy is close enough to strike. However, I also believe that Sun Tzŭ meant this word figuratively, similar to our own expression "short and sharp." Wang Hsi's note expands on the falcon's method of attack, adding: "This is how the 'psychological moment' should be seized in war.")

Energy may be compared to the bending of a crossbow; decision, to the release of the trigger.

(None of the commentators seem to grasp the true meaning of this simile. The key point is that energy, like the force stored in a bent crossbow, only becomes effective when released by the decision to pull the trigger.)

Amid the turmoil and chaos of battle, there may seem to be disorder, yet there is no real disorder; amid confusion, your formation may appear to lack head or tail, yet it remains unshakable against defeat.

(Mei Yao-ch'en says: "When the subdivisions of the army have been arranged in advance, and the various signals have been agreed upon, the separating, joining, dispersing, and regrouping that occurs during battle may give the appearance of disorder, but true disorder is impossible. Even if your formation seems headless and without direction, your forces will not be routed.")

Simulated disorder requires perfect discipline; simulated fear requires courage; simulated weakness requires strength.

(To make this translation clearer, the sharp paradox of the original needs to be softened. Ts'ao Kung hints at the meaning in his brief note: "These things are all meant to disrupt the enemy's formation and conceal one's true condition." Tu Mu explains it plainly: "If you want to appear confused to lure the enemy, you must first have perfect discipline; if you want to display fear to trap the enemy, you must have great courage; if you want to show weakness to make the enemy overconfident, you must have great strength.")

Hiding order beneath the appearance of disorder is simply a matter of dividing the army into smaller units.

(See earlier, § 1.)

Concealing courage under a display of timidity requires a reservoir of hidden energy.

(The commentators interpret a specific Chinese word here differently than elsewhere in the chapter. Tu Mu says: "When the enemy sees that we are in a favorable position but make no move, they will believe we are truly afraid.")

Masking strength with weakness is accomplished through strategic positioning.

(Chang Yu recounts the story of Kao Tsu, the first Han Emperor. He wanted to attack the Hsiung-nu, so he sent spies to gather intelligence on their condition. However, the Hsiung-nu, anticipating this, hid all their strong soldiers and healthy horses, and only allowed the spies to see old soldiers and weak animals. As a result, all the spies advised the Emperor to attack. Only Lou Ching opposed them, saying: "When two countries prepare for war, they naturally try to show their strength. Since our spies have only seen old and weak forces, this must be a trick, and attacking would be unwise." The Emperor ignored this advice, fell into the trap, and was surrounded at Po-teng.)

Thus, one who is skilled at keeping the enemy on the move uses deceptive appearances, to which the enemy will respond.

(Ts'ao Kung notes: "Create the appearance of weakness and need." Tu Mu adds: "If our forces are stronger than the enemy's, we can pretend to be weak to lure them in; but if we are weaker, we must make the enemy believe we are strong so they stay away. In fact, the enemy's actions should always be based on the signals we choose to give." There is an anecdote about Sun Pin, a descendant of Sun Wu: In 341 B.C., the state of Ch'i was at war with Wei, and Sun Pin was sent to face the general P'ang Chuan, who was his personal enemy. Sun Pin said: "The Ch'i state is known for cowardice, so our enemy will underestimate us. Let's take advantage of this." When their army crossed into Wei territory, Sun Pin ordered 100,000 campfires on the first night, 50,000 on the second night, and only 20,000 on the third night. P'ang Chuan, in pursuit, thought: "I knew these Ch'i soldiers were cowards; their numbers are already less than half." Sun Pin retreated to a narrow pass, knowing that P'ang Chuan would arrive after dark. There, Sun Pin had a tree stripped of its bark and inscribed: "Under this tree, P'ang Chuan will die." As night fell, Sun Pin hid archers nearby, instructing them to shoot when they saw light. When P'ang Chuan arrived, he struck a light to read the inscription on the tree, and was immediately shot down by arrows, throwing his army into confusion. [Tu Mu's version of the story is more dramatic, though the Shih Chi suggests that after the defeat of his army, P'ang Chuan committed suicide in despair.])

He sacrifices something, knowing the enemy will snatch at it.

By offering baits, he keeps the enemy on the move; then, with a group of carefully chosen men, he waits to ambush him.

(With an adjustment suggested by Li Ching, this reads: "He lies in wait with the main body of his troops.")

The clever combatant relies on the effect of combined energy and does not demand too much from individuals.

(Tu Mu explains: "First, he assesses the overall power of his army as a whole; then he takes individual abilities into account and uses each person according to their talents. He does not expect perfection from those who lack it.")

This is why he can select the right men and make use of their combined strength.

When he employs combined energy, his fighters become like rolling logs or stones. A log or stone remains still on level ground but moves when placed on a slope. If it is square, it stops, but if it is round, it rolls down.

(Ts'ao Kung refers to this as "the use of natural or inherent power.")

Thus, the energy generated by skilled fighters is like the momentum of a round stone rolling down a mountain thousands of feet high. This concludes the discussion on energy.

(Tu Mu points out that the main lesson of this chapter is the critical importance of rapid maneuvers and sudden charges in warfare. "With such tactics," he adds, "great results can be achieved with even small forces.")

Chapter 6 - WEAK POINTS AND STRONG

[Chang Yu tries to explain the sequence of the chapters in this way: "Chapter IV, on Tactical Dispositions, dealt with offense and defense; Chapter V, on Energy, covered direct and indirect methods. The skilled general first familiarizes himself with the theory of attack and defense, and then focuses on direct and indirect methods. He learns how to vary and combine these two methods before moving on to the topic of weak and strong points. The use of direct or indirect methods arises from attack and defense, and recognizing weak and strong points depends on understanding these methods. Therefore, this chapter follows directly after the one on Energy."]

Sun Tzŭ said: Whoever is first to arrive on the battlefield and waits for the enemy will be well-prepared for the fight; whoever arrives second and has to rush into battle will be tired and worn out.

Therefore, the clever combatant imposes his will on the enemy and never allows the enemy to impose his will on him.

(A mark of a great soldier is that he fights on his own terms or not at all.)

By offering advantages, he can lure the enemy to approach; or by causing harm, he can prevent the enemy from drawing near.

(In the first case, he entices with bait; in the second, he strikes a key point the enemy will be forced to defend.)

If the enemy is resting, he can harass him;

(This passage can be cited as evidence against Mei Yao-ch'en's interpretation of I. § 23.)

if the enemy has plenty of food, he can starve him out; if the enemy is quietly encamped, he can force him to move.

Appear at points the enemy must rush to defend; march quickly to places where you are not expected.

An army can cover great distances without suffering if it travels through areas where the enemy is absent.

(Ts'ao Kung summarizes this well: "Emerge from the void—like a surprise attack—and strike at vulnerable spots, avoid defended places, and attack where you are least expected.")

You can be certain of success in your attacks if you only strike at places that are undefended.

(Wang Hsi explains "undefended places" as weak points, meaning areas where the general is lacking in ability, the soldiers lack morale, the walls are not strong enough, precautions are too lax, reinforcements arrive too late, supplies are insufficient, or the defenders are in conflict among themselves.)

You can ensure the safety of your defense if you only hold positions that cannot be attacked.

(That is, where none of the weaknesses mentioned above exist. There's an interesting nuance in interpreting this line. Tu Mu, Ch'en Hao, and Mei Yao-ch'en suggest it means: "To make your defense completely secure, you must even defend places that are unlikely to be attacked," and Tu Mu adds, "How much more so for places that are likely to be attacked." However, this interpretation doesn't balance well with the preceding clause, which is important in the highly antithetical style typical of Chinese writing. Chang Yu seems closer to the point by saying: "The skilled attacker strikes from the topmost heights of heaven [see IV. § 7], making it impossible for the enemy to defend. Thus, the places I will attack are exactly those the enemy cannot defend. The skilled defender hides in the deepest recesses of the earth, making it impossible for the enemy to locate him. Thus, the places I will hold are precisely those the enemy cannot attack.")

Therefore, the general who is skilled in attack confuses the enemy, so they do not know what to defend; the general who is skilled in defense confounds the enemy, so they do not know what to attack.

(An aphorism that sums up the essence of the art of war.)

O divine art of subtlety and secrecy! Through you, we learn to be invisible, through you, we learn to be inaudible;

(Literally, "without form or sound," in reference to the enemy.)

and thus, we hold the enemy's fate in our hands.

You can advance and be absolutely unstoppable if you strike at the enemy's weak points; you can retreat safely and avoid pursuit if your movements are quicker than the enemy's.

If we want to engage in battle, we can force the enemy to fight, even if he is hiding behind a high wall and a deep trench. All we need to do is attack another place that he will be forced to defend.

(Tu Mu explains: "If the enemy is the invader, we can cut off his supply lines and seize the roads he must use to retreat; if we are the invaders, we can aim our attack at the ruler himself." It's clear that Sun Tzŭ, unlike certain generals in later conflicts such as the Boer War, did not believe in frontal assaults.)

If we do not wish to fight, we can prevent the enemy from engaging us, even if our encampment is only outlined on the ground. All we need to do is confuse him with something strange and unexpected.

(This concise phrase is paraphrased by Chia Lin as: "even though we have constructed neither walls nor ditches." Li Ch'uan adds: "we bewilder him with strange and unusual tactics," and Tu Mu illustrates with three anecdotes. One example is Chu-ko Liang, who, when stationed at Yang-p'ing and about to be attacked by Ssu-ma I, unexpectedly struck his flags, silenced his drums, and opened the city gates, showing only a few men sweeping the grounds. This strange move made Ssu-ma I suspect a trap, causing him to withdraw his army. What Sun Tzŭ is advocating here, therefore, is nothing less than the skillful use of "bluff.")

By discovering the enemy's plans while keeping our own concealed, we can concentrate our forces, while the enemy is forced to divide his.

(The conclusion may not seem obvious at first, but Chang Yu, following Mei Yao-ch'en, explains: "If the enemy's plans are visible, we can attack him with a united force; meanwhile, if our plans are kept secret, the enemy will have to split his forces to guard against attacks from multiple directions.")

We can form a single, united force, while the enemy must divide into smaller parts. Thus, we will have a whole army against only fragments of the enemy's force, meaning we will be many against their few.

If we are able to attack an inferior force with a superior one in this way, the enemy will find themselves in great difficulty.

The location where we intend to fight must not be revealed, because this will force the enemy to prepare for possible attacks at several different points.

(Sheridan once explained General Grant's victories by saying that "while his opponents were kept fully occupied wondering what he was going to do, he was focused mainly on what he was going to do.")

With the enemy's forces scattered in many directions, the number of troops we face at any given point will be relatively small.

For if the enemy strengthens his front lines, he will weaken his rear; if he strengthens his rear, he will weaken his front. If he strengthens his left, he will weaken his right, and if he strengthens his right, he will weaken his left. If he sends reinforcements everywhere, he will be weak everywhere.

(Frederick the Great, in his Instructions to his Generals, wrote: "A defensive war tends to lead us into making too many detachments. Generals with little experience try to defend every point, while those who understand their profession focus only on the main objective, allowing small losses to avoid greater ones.")

Numerical weakness arises from having to prepare against possible attacks, while numerical strength comes from forcing the enemy to make such preparations.

(Colonel Henderson described the highest form of generalship as "compelling the enemy to disperse his army, then concentrating a superior force against each fraction in turn.")

If we know the place and time of the coming battle, we can gather our forces from even the greatest distances to fight.

(Sun Tzŭ is referring to the careful calculation of distances and the expert use of strategy that allow a general to divide his army for a long and rapid march, then bring them together at precisely the right place and time to confront the enemy with overwhelming strength. A dramatic example of this in military history is the appearance of Blücher at the critical moment during the Battle of Waterloo.)

But if neither the time nor place of battle is known, then the left wing will be powerless to help the right, the right will be equally unable to help the left, the front will not be able to relieve the rear, and the rear won't be able to support the front. This is even more true if the furthest parts of the army are separated by over a hundred li and the nearest by several li.

(The Chinese text here lacks precision, but the idea is likely that of an army advancing toward a rendezvous in separate columns, each with orders to meet on a specific date. If the general lets the detachments march haphazardly without precise instructions on when and where to meet, the enemy could destroy the army piece by piece. Chang Yu's note clarifies: "If we do not know the enemy's concentration point or the day they plan to engage, our unity will be lost as we prepare for defense, and the positions we hold will be insecure. If we suddenly encounter a strong enemy, we will be forced into battle in a disorganized state, with no mutual support between wings, vanguard, or rear, especially if there is a great distance between the leading and rear divisions of the army.")

Even though, by my estimation, the soldiers of Yüeh outnumber us, that will not give them any advantage in achieving victory. I say, then, that victory can be achieved.

(Unfortunately, this confident claim was not borne out. The long-standing feud between Wu and Yüeh ended in 473 B.C. with the complete defeat of Wu by Kou Chien, and Wu was absorbed into Yüeh. This likely occurred long after Sun Tzǔ's death. Chang Yu is the only commentator to note the apparent contradiction here, which he explains: "In the chapter on Tactical Dispositions, it is said, 'One may know how to conquer without being able to do it,' whereas here, it says that victory can be achieved. The difference is that in the former chapter, discussing offense and defense, it is acknowledged that if the enemy is fully prepared, victory is not guaranteed. But this passage refers specifically to the soldiers of Yüeh, who, according to Sun Tzǔ's calculations, would remain unaware of the time and place of the impending battle. That's why he says here that victory is possible.")

Though the enemy may have greater numbers, we can prevent him from engaging in battle. Devise schemes to uncover his plans and assess the likelihood of their success.

(An alternate reading offered by Chia Lin is: "Know beforehand all strategies that will lead to our success and the enemy's failure.")

Provoke him, and observe the principle behind his activity or inactivity.

(Chang Yu explains that by noting the enemy's emotional reactions—whether joy or anger—when disturbed, we can deduce whether his strategy is to remain passive or take action. He gives the example of Cho-ku Liang, who sent a woman's head-dress as an insulting gift to Ssu-ma I, provoking him to abandon his cautious, passive tactics.)

Force the enemy to reveal himself, so you can discover his weak points.

Carefully compare the enemy's army with your own, so you will know where strength is abundant and where it is lacking.

(See also IV. § 6.)

In making tactical plans, the highest achievement is to keep them hidden.

(The paradox loses some sharpness in translation. Concealment here doesn't necessarily mean literal invisibility (see § 9 above), but rather not showing any signs of what you intend to do—keeping your thoughts and plans completely veiled.)

Hide your dispositions, and you will be protected from the prying eyes of even the most clever spies and the schemes of the wisest minds.

(Tu Mu explains: "Even if the enemy has intelligent and capable officers, they will not be able to make any effective plans against us.")

How victory is brought about using the enemy's own tactics is something the masses cannot understand.

Everyone can see the tactics by which I win, but no one can see the strategy behind that victory.

(That is, people can observe the outward methods used in winning a battle, but they cannot see the long process of planning and the combinations of strategies that precede it.)

Do not simply repeat the tactics that won you a previous victory; instead, let your methods be shaped by the infinite variety of circumstances.

(Wang Hsi wisely notes: "There is only one core principle of victory, but the tactics leading to it are countless." Compare this to Colonel Henderson's view: "The rules of strategy are few and simple, and can be learned in a week. However, knowing them will not teach a person to lead an army like Napoleon any more than knowing grammar will teach someone to write like Gibbon.")

Military tactics are like water; for just as water flows away from high ground and moves quickly downhill,

so in war, the way is to avoid the strong and strike at the weak.

(Like water, which follows the path of least resistance.)

Water shapes its course according to the nature of the ground over which it flows; in the same way, a soldier works out his victory in relation to the enemy he is facing.

Therefore, just as water has no constant shape, so there are no constant conditions in warfare.

He who can adjust his tactics to match the situation and succeed in winning may be called a captain born of heaven.

The five elements (water, fire, wood, metal, earth) are not always equally dominant;

(Wang Hsi notes: "They dominate in turn.")

The four seasons give way to each other in succession.

(Literally, "they do not always remain in the same place.")

There are short days and long days; the moon waxes and wanes.

(See also V. § 6. The point here is to illustrate the ever-changing nature of war by comparing it to the constant shifts in nature. The comparison is not entirely perfect, however, since the regularity of natural phenomena differs from the unpredictability of war.)

Chapter 7 - Manoeuvering

Sun Tzŭ said: In war, the general receives his orders from the sovereign.

After gathering an army and concentrating his forces, he must blend and harmonize the various elements within it before setting up camp.

(Chang Yu explains: "This refers to creating harmony and trust between the higher and lower ranks before going to battle." He also quotes Wu Tzŭ: "Without harmony in the State, no military campaign can be undertaken; without harmony in the army, no battle formation can be made." In a historical romance, Sun Tzŭ is portrayed telling Wu Yuan: "In general, those who wage war must resolve all internal issues before attacking an external enemy.")

After that comes tactical maneuvering, which is more difficult than anything else.

(I've slightly adjusted the traditional interpretation of Ts'ao Kung, who says: "From the time we receive the sovereign's instructions until we set up camp opposite the enemy, the tactics are the most challenging." It seems more accurate to say that tactics and maneuvers truly begin after the army has marched out and encamped. Ch'ien Hao's note supports this view: "For recruiting, concentrating, harmonizing, and fortifying an army, there are many established rules. The real challenge comes when we start tactical operations." Tu Yu also remarks that "the greatest difficulty is in seizing favorable positions before the enemy does.")

The difficulty of tactical maneuvering lies in turning the indirect into the direct, and transforming misfortune into advantage.

(This sentence is one of Sun Tzŭ's typically condensed and somewhat cryptic expressions. Ts'ao Kung explains: "Make it seem as though you are far away, then cover the distance quickly and arrive before your opponent." Tu Mu says: "Deceive the enemy so that he becomes relaxed and slow while you advance with utmost speed." Ho Shih offers another perspective: "Even if you have difficult terrain to cross or natural obstacles in your way, this disadvantage can be turned into an advantage through rapid movement." Famous examples include Hannibal's crossing of the Alps, which put Italy at his mercy, and Napoleon's similar feat two thousand years later, resulting in the victory at Marengo.)

Thus, taking a long and circuitous route, while luring the enemy out of position, and although starting later than him, managing to reach the goal before him, demonstrates skill in the art of deviation.

(Tu Mu references the famous march of Chao She in 270 B.C. to relieve the town of O-yu, which was under siege by a Ch'in army. The King of Chao initially sought advice from Lien P'o, who considered the distance too far and the terrain too difficult for a relief mission. However, Chao She, acknowledging the risk, boldly stated: "We will be like two rats fighting in a hole—the braver one will win!" After setting out with his army, Chao She marched only 30 li before stopping to build fortifications for 28 days, ensuring the enemy's spies would report this delay. The Ch'in general, thinking Chao She was unwilling to save a city outside Chao's direct control, relaxed. But as soon as the spies left, Chao She launched a forced march, covering two days and one night, and arrived so swiftly that he seized the advantageous North hill before the enemy knew of his movements. The result was a decisive defeat for the Ch'in, forcing them to abandon the siege and retreat.)

Maneuvering with a disciplined army is advantageous; with an undisciplined multitude, it is most dangerous.

(I adopt the reading of the T'ung Tien, Cheng Yu-hsien, and the T'u Shu for clarity. The commentators using the standard text suggest that maneuvering can be either profitable or dangerous, depending on the general's skill.)

If you march a fully equipped army to seize an advantage, chances are you will be too late. However, sending a flying column for the task often requires sacrificing baggage and supplies.

(Some of the Chinese text is unclear even to the commentators, who paraphrase it. I offer my own translation cautiously, as there seems to be some deeper corruption in the text. Nonetheless, it is apparent that Sun Tzŭ disapproves of undertaking a long march without proper supplies. See § 11 below.)

If you order your soldiers to roll up their coats and make forced marches without stopping day or night, covering twice the usual distance in one go, traveling a hundred li to gain an advantage, the leaders of all your three divisions will end up in the hands of the enemy.

The strongest men will be at the front, while the exhausted ones will fall behind, and following this plan, only one-tenth of your army will reach the destination.

The moral of this, as Ts'ao Kung and others have pointed out, is that you should not march a hundred li to gain a tactical advantage, whether with or without your baggage train. Maneuvers like this should be limited to shorter distances. Stonewall Jackson said: "The hardships of forced marches are often more painful than the dangers of battle." He rarely asked his troops for extraordinary efforts. It was only when he planned a surprise attack or when a rapid retreat was urgently needed that he sacrificed everything for speed.

If you march fifty li to outmaneuver the enemy, the leader of your first division will be lost, and only half of your army will reach the goal.

If you march thirty li for the same purpose, two-thirds of your army will arrive.

From this, we can understand how difficult tactical maneuvers can be.

An army without its baggage train is lost; without provisions, it is lost; without supply bases, it is lost.

I think Sun Tzŭ meant "stores accumulated in depots." But Tu Yu says "fodder and the like," Chang Yu says "goods in general," and Wang Hsi says "fuel, salt, foodstuffs, etc."

We cannot form alliances until we understand the plans of our neighbors.

We are not fit to lead an army on the march unless we are familiar with the terrain—its mountains and forests, its pitfalls and cliffs, its marshes and swamps.

We will not be able to take advantage of natural terrain unless we make use of local guides.

In war, practice deception, and you will succeed. In the tactics of Turenne, deceiving the enemy, especially about the number of his troops, played a very important role.

Only move when there is a real advantage to be gained.

Whether to concentrate or divide your troops must be determined by the circumstances.

Let your speed be as swift as the wind,

(The simile is especially fitting because the wind is not only fast but, as Mei Yao-ch'en notes, "invisible and leaves no trace behind.")

and your formations as dense as a forest.

(Meng Shih's comment comes closer to the meaning: "When marching slowly, order and ranks must be preserved" to guard against surprise attacks. Natural forests don't grow in rows, but they do have the quality of compactness and density.)

When raiding and plundering, be like a raging fire,

(Compare with the Shih Ching: "Fierce as a blazing fire that no one can stop.")

and when holding your position, be as immovable as a mountain.

(This applies when defending a position from which the enemy tries to dislodge you or, as Tu Yu suggests, when the enemy is trying to lure you into a trap.)

Let your plans be as dark and impenetrable as night, and when you strike, hit like a thunderbolt.

(Tu Yu quotes a proverb from T'ai Kung: "You cannot close your ears to thunder or your eyes to lightning—they are too fast." Similarly, an attack should be so swift that it cannot be countered.)

When plundering the countryside, divide the spoils among your men,

(Sun Tzŭ aims to curb the abuses of indiscriminate looting by ensuring that all booty is placed in a common stock and fairly distributed among the troops.)

and when you capture new territory, divide it into allotments for the soldiers.

(Ch'en Hao advises: "Quarter your soldiers on the land and let them sow and cultivate it." By following this principle, harvesting the land they invaded, the Chinese succeeded in carrying out some of their most memorable expeditions, such as Pan Ch'ao's march to the Caspian, and, in more recent times, the campaigns of Fu-k'ang-an and Tso Tsung-t'ang.)

Think carefully and plan before taking any action.

(Chang Yu quotes Wei Liao Tzŭ, saying that we should not leave our camp until we understand the enemy's strength and the intelligence of their general. See the "seven comparisons" mentioned earlier.)

The one who masters the art of deception will win.

(Refer to previous sections for more on this.)

This is the essence of maneuvering.

(These words would naturally end the section, but what follows is an excerpt from an older book on war, which no longer exists but was still known during Sun Tzŭ's time. The style of the passage isn't noticeably different from Sun Tzŭ's own writing, and no commentators question its authenticity.)

The Book of Army Management says:

(It's worth noting that earlier commentators don't provide much information about this book. Mei Yao-ch'en calls it "an ancient military classic," and Wang Hsi refers to it as "an old book on war."

Considering the centuries of warfare between different kingdoms in China before Sun Tzŭ's time, it's likely that military wisdom had already been written down in earlier times.)

On the battlefield,

(This is implied but not directly stated in the text.)

spoken commands don't carry far enough, so gongs and drums were introduced. Similarly, normal objects can't be seen clearly in the chaos, which is why banners and flags are used.

Gongs and drums, banners and flags, are used to focus the ears and eyes of the army on a single point.

(Chang Yu explains: "When sight and hearing are concentrated on the same object, the movements of as many as a million soldiers will be as coordinated as those of a single man.")

When the army forms a united body, it becomes impossible for the brave to advance alone or for the cowardly to retreat alone.

(Chuang Yu quotes: "Equally guilty are those who advance without orders and those who retreat without orders." Tu Mu tells a story of Wu Ch'i, who was fighting the Ch'in State. Before the battle began, one of his soldiers, renowned for his daring, went out on his own, captured two enemy heads, and returned to camp. Wu Ch'i had the man executed immediately. When an officer protested, saying, "This man was a good soldier and shouldn't have been beheaded," Wu Ch'i replied, "I know he was a good soldier, but I had him executed because he acted without orders.")

This is the art of managing large masses of men.

In night fighting, use signal fires and drums, and in daytime battles, use flags and banners to influence the ears and eyes of your soldiers.

(Ch'en Hao mentions Li Kuang-pi's night march to Ho-yang with 500 mounted men. They made such an impressive display with torches that the rebel leader Shih Ssu-ming, despite having a large army, didn't dare oppose their passage.)

An entire army can be robbed of its spirit.

(Chang Yu says: "In war, if a spirit of anger can fill the entire army at once, its attack will be unstoppable. The enemy's soldiers will be most eager when they first arrive, so we should not fight right away. Instead, we should wait until their enthusiasm fades before striking. This is how their spirit can be taken from them." Li Ch'uan and others tell a story from the Tso Chuan about Ts'ao Kuei, an advisor to Duke Chuang of Lu. When Lu was attacked by Ch'i, the duke prepared to fight at Ch'ang-cho after hearing the enemy's first drumbeat. Ts'ao said, "Not yet." Only after the enemy's drums sounded a third time did he give the order to attack. The army of Ch'i was defeated. When asked why he delayed, Ts'ao Kuei explained: "In battle, a courageous spirit is everything. The first drumbeat raises this spirit, but with the second it weakens, and by the third it's gone. I attacked when their spirit was gone and ours was at its peak." Wu Tzŭ lists "spirit" as the first of the "four important influences" in war, adding, "The value of an entire army—a mighty host of a million men—depends on one person: such is the power of spirit!")

A commander-in-chief can also lose his presence of mind.

(Chang Yu notes: "Presence of mind is the most vital quality for a general. It enables him to restore order from chaos and give courage to those who are panicking." The great general Li Ching once said, "Attacking does not simply mean assaulting walled cities or striking an army in battle. It also involves shaking the enemy's mental balance.")

A soldier's spirit is at its highest in the morning,

(As long as he has had breakfast, I suppose. At the Battle of the Trebia, the Romans made the mistake of fighting on an empty stomach, while Hannibal's men ate at their leisure. See Livy, XXI, liv. 8, lv. 1 and 8.)

by noon, it starts to fade; and by evening, his only thought is to return to camp.

A wise general, therefore, avoids fighting an army when its spirit is high, but attacks when it is sluggish and ready to retreat. This is the art of studying moods.

To remain disciplined and calm while waiting for disorder and confusion to arise among the enemy: this is the art of maintaining self-possession.

To be close to the goal while the enemy is still far, to wait in comfort while the enemy struggles, to be well-fed while the enemy is hungry: this is the art of conserving strength.

To refrain from attacking an enemy whose banners are in perfect order, or from engaging an army that is calm and confident: this is the art of understanding circumstances.

It is a basic military principle not to advance uphill against the enemy, nor to confront him when he is descending.

Do not chase an enemy who pretends to flee; do not engage soldiers whose spirits are high.

Do not take a bait offered by the enemy.

(Li Ch'uan and Tu Mu, showing a surprising lack of insight, take this literally as food or drink that might be poisoned by the enemy. Ch'en Hao and Chang Yu point out that the saying applies more broadly.)

Do not obstruct an army that is returning home.

(The commentators explain that a soldier whose heart is set on returning home will fight with extreme determination against anyone who tries to stop him, making him too dangerous to oppose. Chang Yu quotes Han Hsin: "Unbeatable is the soldier who desires nothing but to return home." A remarkable story is told of Ts'ao Ts'ao's resourcefulness in San Kuo Chi, chapter 1. In 198 A.D., Ts'ao was besieging Chang Hsiu in Jang, when Liu Piao sent reinforcements to cut off his retreat. Ts'ao was forced to withdraw but found himself trapped between two enemies guarding each exit of a narrow pass. In this desperate situation, he waited until nightfall, dug a tunnel into the mountainside, and set an ambush. Once the entire enemy army had passed, Ts'ao's hidden troops attacked from behind, while he turned to confront them from the front, throwing them into chaos and defeating them. Ts'ao later remarked, "The bandits tried to stop my retreat and forced me into a desperate fight; that's how I knew how to defeat them.")

When you surround an army, leave an opening for escape.

(This doesn't mean you should let the enemy flee. The purpose, as Tu Mu explains, is to make the enemy believe there is a way to escape, preventing them from fighting with the desperation of those with no hope. As Tu Mu adds, "Once they believe they have a way out, you can then crush them.")

Do not press a desperate enemy too hard.

(Ch'en Hao cites the saying: "When birds and beasts are cornered, they will use their claws and teeth." Chang Yu advises: "If your enemy has burned his boats and destroyed his cooking pots, fully committed to the outcome of the battle, you must not push them to the extreme." Ho Shih illustrates this with a story about the general Fu Yen-ch'ing. In 945 A.D., he and his colleague Tu Chung-wei were surrounded by a much larger Khitan army in a barren, desert-like area. Their small Chinese force was suffering due to a lack of water. The wells they dug ran dry, and the soldiers were reduced to squeezing moisture from lumps of mud. Their numbers dwindled rapidly, and Fu Yen-ch'ing declared, "We are desperate men. It is better to die for our country than to be taken captive with our hands tied." A strong wind was blowing from the northeast, filling the air with dense clouds of sand. Tu Chung-wei wanted to wait for the storm to pass before launching their final attack, but another officer, Li Shou-cheng, saw an opportunity and said, "They are many, and we are few, but in this sandstorm, our numbers won't be clear. Victory will go to those who fight hardest, and the wind will be our ally." Fu Yen-ch'ing then led a sudden and unexpected cavalry charge, routing the barbarians and breaking through to safety.)

Chapter 8 - Variation of Tactics

The heading literally means "The Nine Variations," but since Sun Tzŭ doesn't enumerate them specifically and has already stated (V §§ 6-11) that deviations in strategy are practically limitless, we are inclined to agree with Wang Hsi, who explains that "Nine" represents an indefinitely large number. It simply means that in warfare, tactics should be varied to the greatest extent possible. I am unsure how Ts'ao Kung interprets these Nine Variations, but it's suggested they are related to the Nine Situations discussed in chapter XI. This view is also supported by Chang Yu. Another possibility is that something has been lost, which is suggested by the unusual brevity of the chapter.

Sun Tzŭ said: In war, the general receives his commands from the sovereign, assembles his army, and concentrates his forces.

(This is repeated from VII. § 1, where it fits better. It may have been included here simply to provide a start for the chapter.)

When in difficult terrain, do not set up camp. In areas where main roads intersect, join hands with your allies. Do not remain in dangerously isolated positions.

(This situation is not one of the Nine Situations listed in the beginning of chapter XI, but it does appear later on (§ 43). Chang Yu defines it as being located across the border in enemy territory. Li Ch'uan says it refers to land where there are no springs, wells, flocks, or firewood. Chia Lin describes it as a region of gorges, cliffs, and steep terrain with no clear roads forward.)

In situations where you are trapped, rely on strategy. In a desperate position, you must fight.

There are roads that should not be followed,

(Li Ch'uan says this applies especially to narrow passes where ambushes are likely.)

armies that must not be attacked,

(It might be more accurate to say "there are times when an army should not be attacked." Ch'en Hao explains: "When you have an opportunity for a small advantage but cannot achieve a decisive victory, it is better not to attack, to avoid exhausting your troops.")

towns that should not be besieged,

(Compare III. § 4. Ts'ao Kung shares an example from his own experience. While invading Hsu-chou, he bypassed the city of Hua-pi, which lay in his path, and advanced deeper into the country. This strategy paid off with the capture of fourteen key cities. Chang Yu advises: "Do not attack a town that, even if captured, cannot be held or, if left alone, will not pose a threat." Hsun Ying, when urged to attack Pi-yang, responded: "The city is small and well-fortified; even if I succeed in taking it, it won't be a great achievement, but if I fail, I will be ridiculed." Sieges made up a significant part of warfare in the seventeenth century, but Turenne emphasized the value of marches, countermarches, and maneuvers. He remarked, "It is a great error to waste soldiers on capturing a town when the same effort could win an entire province.")

positions that should not be contested, and commands from the sovereign that should not be obeyed.

(This is difficult for the Chinese, given their strong respect for authority. Wei Liao Tzǔ, as quoted by Tu Mu, states: "Weapons are instruments of evil, conflict opposes virtue, and a military commander stands against civil order." Nonetheless, the reality remains that even the emperor's wishes must yield to military necessity.)

The general who thoroughly understands the advantages that come from varying tactics knows how to manage his troops.

The general who does not grasp these advantages, even if he is well aware of the terrain, will not be able to make effective use of his knowledge.

(Literally, "to get the advantage of the ground," meaning not only securing favorable positions but also making the most of natural advantages in every way possible. Chang Yu explains: "Every kind of terrain has its own natural features and also offers room for variation in plans. How can these natural features be used to their full potential unless topographical knowledge is combined with a flexible mind?")

Thus, a student of war who has not mastered the art of varying his strategies, even if he knows the Five Advantages, will fail to make the best use of his soldiers.

(Chia Lin explains that these Five Advantages refer to obvious and generally beneficial courses of action, such as: "if a road is short, it should be taken; if an army is isolated, it should be attacked; if a town is in a precarious state, it should be besieged; if a position can be stormed, it should be attempted; and if consistent with military operations, the ruler's orders should be obeyed." However, there are circumstances in which these advantages may not be used. For instance, "a certain road may be the shortest route, but if it is filled with natural obstacles or if the enemy has laid an ambush there, it should not be followed. A hostile force may be vulnerable to attack, but if it is desperate and ready to fight to the last, it is better not to strike.")

Therefore, in the wise leader's plans, considerations of both advantage and disadvantage are combined.

("Whether in an advantageous or disadvantageous situation," says Ts'ao Kung, "the opposite state should always be kept in mind.")

If we balance our expectation of advantage with awareness of possible disadvantages, we may successfully accomplish the most important part of our plans.

(Tu Mu comments: "If we want to gain an advantage over the enemy, we must not focus only on that goal. We must also consider the possibility of the enemy inflicting harm on us and include that in our calculations.")

If, on the other hand, we are always ready to seize an advantage even in difficult situations, we can free ourselves from misfortune.

(Tu Mu explains: "If I want to escape from a dangerous position, I must not only consider the enemy's ability to harm me but also my own ability to gain an advantage over them. If my plans balance both considerations, I will succeed in getting out of danger. For example, if I am surrounded by the enemy and only focus on escaping, the weakness of my strategy will encourage the enemy to pursue and crush me. It would be much better to encourage my troops to launch a bold counterattack and use the advantage gained to break free from the enemy's grasp." See the story of Ts'ao Ts'ao in VII. § 35, note.)

Reduce the enemy's leaders by causing harm to them.

(Chia Lin lists several ways to harm the enemy, some of which are quite unique: "Entice away the enemy's best and wisest men, leaving him without good advisors. Plant traitors in his country to disrupt government policies. Stir up intrigue and deceit, sowing discord between the ruler and his ministers. Use cunning tricks to weaken his men and drain his resources. Corrupt his morals with insidious gifts that lead him into indulgence. Unsettle his mind by presenting him with beautiful women." Chang Yu, following Wang Hsi, offers a different interpretation: "Force the enemy into a position where he is bound to suffer harm, and he will eventually submit on his own.")

Create difficulties for them,

(Tu Mu explains that this phrase means to create problems that affect the enemy's "assets"—things like a large army, a rich treasury, harmony among soldiers, and the consistent execution of orders. These are what give us leverage over the enemy.)

and keep them constantly occupied.

(Literally, "make servants of them." Tu Yu says: "Deny them any opportunity to rest.")

Offer deceptive attractions and lure them into rushing to a specific point.

(Meng Shih provides a great example of this idiom: "Make them forget pien (the reasons for acting cautiously) and hasten in our direction.")

The art of war teaches us to depend not on the chance that the enemy will not come, but on our own readiness to meet him; not on the hope that he won't attack, but on the certainty that we have made our position unassailable.

There are five dangerous flaws that may affect a general:

(1) Recklessness, which leads to destruction.

("Bravery without forethought," as Ts'ao Kung puts it, causes a man to fight blindly, like a mad bull. Chang Yu says, "Such an opponent should not be met with brute force but can be lured into an ambush and killed." Wu Tzŭ also points out that too much emphasis is often placed on a general's courage, forgetting that courage is just one of the qualities a general should have. A brave man who fights recklessly, without understanding what is truly advantageous, must be condemned. Ssu-ma Fa adds that "simply rushing to one's death does not guarantee victory.")

(2) Cowardice, which leads to capture.

(Ts'ao Kung explains that the word "cowardice" refers to someone "who is too timid to advance and seize an advantage." Wang Hsi adds that it describes someone who flees at the first sight of danger. Meng Shih gives a more detailed interpretation: "He is focused on surviving at all costs," meaning someone who avoids taking risks. But, as Sun Tzŭ knew, success in war often requires risk. T'ai Kung noted: "He who lets an advantage slip will eventually face real disaster." In 404 A.D., Liu Yu chased the rebel Huan Hsuan up the Yangtsze River. Though Liu Yu's forces were much smaller, Huan

Hsuan, fearing the consequences of defeat, prepared a small boat attached to his warship for a quick escape. This lack of resolve destroyed his soldiers' morale. When the loyalists launched a determined attack using fireships, Huan Hsuan's forces were completely routed. They had to burn all their supplies and fled for two days without stopping. Chang Yu also tells a similar story of Chao Ying-ch'i, a general of the Chin State, who kept a boat ready during a battle with the Ch'u army in 597 B.C., so he could escape first if defeated.)

(3) A quick temper, which can be provoked by insults.

(Tu Mu tells the story of Yao Hsing, who in 357 A.D. was opposed by Huang Mei, Teng Ch'iang, and others. Yao Hsing shut himself inside his walls, refusing to engage. Teng Ch'iang, knowing Yao's fiery temper, suggested launching constant attacks to provoke him. He believed that Yao, once angered, would come out to fight. This strategy worked—Yao Hsiang left his defenses, was drawn into a trap as far as San-yuan by the enemy's fake retreat, and was ultimately defeated and killed.)

A delicate sense of honor that is easily wounded by shame is another potential fault.

This doesn't mean that a sense of honor is a flaw in a general. What Sun Tzǔ criticizes is being overly sensitive to slander or criticism, the kind of person who is too easily hurt by insults, even when they are undeserved. Mei Yao-ch'en wisely notes, though it may sound contradictory: "Those who seek glory should not worry too much about public opinion."

The fifth fault is being too concerned for the well-being of his men, which causes unnecessary worry and trouble.

Again, Sun Tzǔ isn't suggesting that a general should neglect the welfare of his soldiers. He simply means that focusing too much on their comfort can lead to poor decisions and lost opportunities. This short-term thinking can ultimately cause greater suffering for the troops in the long run because defeat, or a longer war, will be the result. A misguided sense of pity can lead a general to make choices that go against his better judgment, such as relieving a city under siege or sending reinforcements to a detachment under heavy pressure. In the South African War, it's now accepted that our repeated attempts to relieve Ladysmith were strategic errors that failed to achieve their goal. In the end, it was the general who decided to stop letting sentiment for a small part of the army override the needs of the whole who finally succeeded. I recall an old soldier trying to defend one of our generals, who had notably failed during this war, by saying that he was "so kind to his men." In saying this, though he didn't realize it, he was actually condemning the general according to Sun Tzŭ's principles.

These are the five dangerous flaws in a general, which can ruin the conduct of war.

When an army is defeated and its leader is killed, the cause can almost always be traced back to one of these five flaws. Keep them in mind.

Chapter 9 - The Army on The March

Sun Tzu said: Now we turn to the important task of setting up camp and keeping a close eye on the enemy. When traveling through mountainous areas, it's important to move quickly across the mountains and stay near the valleys.

(This is because the dry, barren highlands can leave your troops without enough food or water. It's better to stay near places where water and grass are plentiful. Wu Tzu, an ancient military strategist, once said, "Don't camp in natural ovens," which means avoiding the entrances of valleys where the heat can become unbearable and where you could easily be trapped. Chang Yu provides a historical example: During the Later Han dynasty, a bandit named Wu-tu Ch'iang hid his troops in the hills. Instead of attacking directly, General Ma Yuan, who was sent to capture him, took control of the areas with water and other supplies. Ch'iang's troops soon ran out of provisions because they hadn't secured the valleys. With no access to resources, they were eventually forced to surrender.)

When choosing a campsite, always pick slightly higher ground.

(This doesn't mean the highest mountain peaks, but rather low hills that give you an advantage over the surrounding area. High ground lets you see the battlefield more easily and makes your camp less vulnerable to surprise attacks.)

It is also important to set up your camp so that it faces the sun.

(Some commentators, like Tu Mu, believed this meant facing south, while others, like Ch'en Hao, thought it meant facing east. Either way, the idea is that facing the sun gives your camp better visibility and warmth, making it more comfortable and easier to defend.)

In mountain warfare, one of the key rules is to never climb uphill to attack the enemy. It's better to hold the high ground and force the enemy to come to you. After crossing a river, always move away from it quickly.

(Ts'ao Kung explained this as a strategy to lure the enemy into crossing the river after you, where they will be more vulnerable. Chang Yu added that moving away from the river ensures that you have the freedom to maneuver, preventing the enemy from blocking your retreat or cutting off your supply lines.)

If the enemy is crossing a river, don't attack them while they're in the middle of the crossing. Wait until half of their forces have crossed, then strike.

(Li Ch'uan refers to Han Hsin's famous victory over Lung Chu at the Wei River as an example of this tactic. Han Hsin's forces built a dam upstream at night and crossed the river to fake a retreat. Lung Chu, thinking Han Hsin's army was retreating in defeat, followed him across the river. At that moment, Han Hsin's troops broke the dam, sending a flood downstream that cut off Lung Chu's army. In the resulting chaos, Han Hsin's forces attacked decisively, killing Lung Chu and routing his army.)

If you're preparing to fight near a river the enemy hasn't crossed yet, don't position your troops too close to the river.

(Doing so could give the enemy the chance to plan a better crossing or force you into a defensive position when you could have set up an ambush instead.)

If you're stationed near a river, make sure to place your boats upstream from the enemy, and always keep your camp facing the sun.

(As mentioned before, being upstream gives you a tactical advantage, allowing you to control the flow of water. This applies whether your forces are on the riverbank or in boats. Facing the sun provides better visibility and can also give you a psychological advantage.)

Never move upstream to meet the enemy.

(Tu Mu warns that, since water flows downward, camping in a lower position is dangerous because the enemy could flood the river or poison the water and send it downstream to your camp. Chu-ko Wu-hou also advised against moving against the current in river warfare, as this would allow the enemy to use the natural flow of the river to their advantage.)

When it comes to river warfare, that's all you need to keep in mind. However, when crossing salt marshes, your only goal should be to get through them as quickly as possible.

(Salt marshes are inhospitable. They have little fresh water, the grass is scarce and not nutritious for animals, and the flat, open terrain leaves your forces vulnerable to attack.)

If you must fight in a salt marsh, camp near a source of fresh water and grass, and position your back against a group of trees.

(Li Ch'uan mentions that trees can signal safer ground, while Tu Mu points out that trees can protect your rear and reduce the chances of a surprise attack from the enemy.)

This concludes the rules for fighting in salt marshes. When fighting on flat, dry land, choose a position that is easy to access, with slightly rising ground on your right and behind you.

(Tu Mu quotes T'ai Kung, who recommended positioning your army with a stream or marsh on the left and a hill on the right. This setup offers natural defenses and strategic advantages.)

By following this rule, you will have danger in front of you and safety behind. This concludes the guidelines for warfare on flat land.

These principles of terrain management are the four essential branches of military strategy: (1) mountains, (2) rivers, (3) marshes, and (4) plains. Understanding these principles helped the Yellow Emperor defeat four kings.

(Some scholars question whether the Yellow Emperor truly defeated four kings, as historical records like the Shih Chi only mention his victories over Yen Ti and Ch'ih Yu. However, the Liu T'ao suggests he fought and won seventy battles, ultimately uniting the empire. Ts'ao Kung speculates that the Yellow Emperor established a feudal system with four princes holding the title of emperor. Meanwhile, Li Ch'uan believes that the art of war began with the Yellow Emperor, who learned it from his wise minister, Feng Hou.)

All armies prefer to occupy high ground rather than low ground because high ground offers advantages for both health and combat. Low ground, on the other hand, is often damp and unhealthy for troops.

(Ts'ao Kung advises generals to prioritize finding fresh water and good pasture for their animals to maintain the health and well-being of their forces.)

When choosing a campsite, look for hard, dry ground. This will help keep your soldiers healthy and reduce the risk of illness.

(Chang Yu adds that dry conditions help prevent diseases from spreading, which can be as dangerous as any enemy.)

Whenever possible, position yourself on the sunny side of a hill or slope, with the incline behind you and to your right. This will benefit your soldiers and allow you to make the best use of the natural terrain.

After heavy rains in higher regions, if you encounter a swollen river covered with foam, you must wait for the water to recede before attempting to cross.

Avoid areas with steep cliffs, narrow passes, or deep gorges with fast-flowing streams. These are natural traps—easy to enter but difficult to escape from. Places surrounded by steep banks or filled with water at the bottom should be avoided at all costs, as they are like natural prisons where you could easily be trapped.

(Dense forests with thick undergrowth, where spears cannot be used, should also be avoided, as well as quagmires and other soft ground that makes it difficult for chariots or horsemen to pass.)

While you should avoid such places, try to lead the enemy into them. If you face the enemy in such terrain, position them so that the natural obstacles are behind them, limiting their ability to maneuver.

If your camp is near hilly terrain, ponds surrounded by tall grasses, or woods with dense undergrowth, these areas must be thoroughly searched, as they are ideal hiding spots for enemy spies or ambushes.

When the enemy is nearby but remains still, it is a sign they are relying on the natural strength of their position. When they are distant and try to provoke a battle, they are likely trying to lure you out of your defensive position and into a trap.

If the enemy's camp seems easy to approach, be cautious—it may be a trap. Movement among trees in a forest is a sign that the enemy is advancing, likely cutting down trees to clear a path for their troops.

Birds suddenly taking flight may indicate an ambush. Startled animals could signal an impending attack.

If dust rises in a high column, it means chariots are approaching. If the dust is lower and spread out, infantry is on the move. Dust that moves in several directions suggests soldiers are gathering firewood, while small amounts of dust moving back and forth indicate the army is setting up camp.

When the enemy uses humble words but increases their preparations, it's a sign they are planning an attack. They may be pretending to be weak to make you feel secure.

If the enemy's camp looks humble but their preparations are intensifying, they are likely preparing for an assault. In one case, an army tried to demoralize its enemy by mutilating prisoners and desecrating graves, but this only strengthened the defenders' resolve. The defenders launched a clever counterattack by sending oxen with burning torches tied to their tails into the enemy's camp, causing chaos and helping them reclaim lost cities.

Aggressive words and forward movements often mean the enemy is preparing to retreat.

When light chariots are positioned on the flanks, it signals the enemy is getting ready for battle.

Peace offers that come without a sworn agreement usually signal a trap.

If the enemy's soldiers are running about and quickly forming up, the decisive moment is near.

If some soldiers advance while others retreat, it is likely a trick designed to confuse and mislead you.

Soldiers leaning on their spears are likely weak from hunger, and if they drink water immediately after getting it, the army is suffering from thirst.

If the enemy hesitates to act even when given an opportunity, it is a sign their troops are exhausted.

If birds are gathering in a specific area, it means that spot is unoccupied.

Noise at night suggests the enemy is anxious, while disorder in their camp indicates the general has lost control.

If the enemy's banners are being moved around frequently, it could mean there is rebellion in the ranks. Anger among the officers suggests that the soldiers are worn out.

When an army begins feeding its horses with grain, slaughtering cattle for food, and not hanging up its cooking pots, it means they are prepared to fight to the death.

When soldiers whisper in small groups, it indicates unrest in the ranks. Frequent rewards suggest the enemy is running low on resources, while excessive punishments point to severe internal problems.

If a general talks boldly but then hesitates out of fear of the enemy's numbers, it reveals a lack of intelligence. When envoys come with polite words, it usually means the enemy is seeking a truce.

If the enemy's troops stand facing yours for a long time without fighting or retreating, they may be preparing a surprise attack. Stay alert.

If your forces are roughly equal to the enemy's, you should be able to hold your position, but attacking head-on would be risky. Instead, gather your strength, watch the enemy closely, and wait for reinforcements.

A leader who underestimates the enemy and doesn't plan ahead will ultimately be defeated.

Punishing soldiers before they are loyal to you will lead to disobedience. However, if they are not disciplined after they become loyal, they will be ineffective in battle.

That's why it's important to first treat soldiers with kindness, then later enforce strict discipline. This is the path to victory.

If commands are enforced consistently, the army will be disciplined. If not, the soldiers will become disorderly. A general who trusts his men while making sure his orders are followed will strengthen both his leadership and his army.

Chapter 10 - Terrain

Sun Tzŭ said: We can identify six kinds of terrain:

(1) Accessible ground;

(Mei Yao-ch'en explains this as ground that is well-supplied with roads and ways of communication.)

(2) Entangling ground;

(Mei Yao-ch'en describes this as "net-like" terrain, where if you enter, you may become entangled.)

(3) Temporizing ground;

(This is ground where you can delay or hold off.)

(4) Narrow passes; (5) Steep heights; (6) Positions far from the enemy.

(It is hardly necessary to point out the issues with this classification. There is a strange lack of logical reasoning in the unquestioning acceptance of these overlapping categories.)

Ground that both sides can freely move across is called accessible.

On this type of terrain, you should arrive before the enemy, take the higher, sunnier spots, and carefully guard your supply lines.

(The general meaning of this last phrase, as Tu Yu explains, is "not to allow the enemy to cut your communications." In view of Napoleon's statement, "the secret of war lies in the communications," it would have been helpful if Sun Tzŭ had elaborated more on this important subject here and in other sections. Col. Henderson says: "The line of supply is as vital to the life of an army as the heart is to a human being. Just as a duelist who finds his opponent's weapon threatening his life and his own guard out of place must adjust to his opponent's movements, the commander whose communications are suddenly threatened finds himself in a bad position. He may be forced to change all his plans, divide his forces into isolated groups, and fight with fewer troops on unprepared ground. In such a situation, defeat could mean the ruin or surrender of his entire army.")

If you follow these steps, you will be able to fight with an advantage.

Ground which can be abandoned but is hard to re-occupy is called entangling ground.

From a position of this sort, if the enemy is unprepared, you may sally forth and defeat him. But if the enemy is prepared for your coming, and you fail to defeat him, then, return being impossible, disaster will ensue.

When the position is such that neither side will gain by making the first move, it is called temporizing ground.

(Tu Mu says: "Each side finds it inconvenient to move, and the situation remains at a deadlock.")

In a position of this sort, even though the enemy should offer us an attractive bait,

(Tu Yu says, "turning their backs on us and pretending to flee." But this is only one of the lures which might induce us to quit our position.)

it will be advisable not to stir forth, but rather to retreat, thus enticing the enemy in his turn; then, when part of his army has come out, we may deliver our attack with advantage.

With regard to narrow passes, if you can occupy them first, let them be strongly garrisoned and await the advent of the enemy.

(Because then, as Tu Yu observes, "the initiative will lie with us, and by making sudden and unexpected attacks we shall have the enemy at our mercy.")

Should the enemy forestall you in occupying a pass, do not go after him if the pass is fully garrisoned, but only if it is weakly garrisoned.

With regard to precipitous heights, if you are beforehand with your adversary, you should occupy the raised and sunny spots, and there wait for him to come up.

(Ts'ao Kung says: "The particular advantage of securing heights and defiles is that your actions cannot then be dictated by the enemy." [For the enunciation of the grand principle alluded to, see VI. § 2]. Chang Yu tells the following anecdote of P'ei Hsing-chien (A.D. 619-682), who was sent on a punitive expedition against the Turkic tribes. "At night he pitched his camp as usual, and it had already been completely fortified by wall and ditch, when suddenly he gave orders that the army should shift its quarters to a hill nearby. This was highly displeasing to his officers, who protested loudly against the extra fatigue which it would entail on the men. P'ei Hsing-chien, however, paid no heed to their remonstrances and had the camp moved as quickly as possible. The same night, a terrific storm came on, which flooded their former place of encampment to the depth of over twelve feet. The recalcitrant officers were amazed at the sight and owned that they had been in the wrong. 'How did you know what was going to happen?' they asked. P'ei Hsing-chien replied: 'From this time forward be content to obey orders without asking unnecessary questions.' From this it may be seen," Chang Yu continues, "that high and sunny places are advantageous not only for fighting, but also because they are immune from disastrous floods.")

If the enemy has occupied the high ground before you, do not pursue him, but instead retreat and try to lure him away.

(Li Shih-min's turning point in his campaign in 621 A.D. against the rebels Tou Chien-te, King of Hsia, and Wang Shih-ch'ung, Prince of Cheng, was his capture of the heights of Wu-lao. Despite this, Tou Chien-te still tried to help his ally in Lo-yang and was defeated and captured. See Chiu T'ang Shu, ch. 2, fol. 5 verso, and also ch. 54.)

If you are far from the enemy and the strength of both armies is equal, it is not easy to provoke a battle,

(The key is that you shouldn't undertake a long, tiring march, which would leave you exhausted while the enemy remains fresh and alert, as Tu Yu explains.)

and fighting in such conditions will put you at a disadvantage.

These six are the principles related to the terrain.

(Or, "principles relating to the ground." See I. § 8.)

A general in a position of responsibility must carefully study them.

Now, an army can face six different calamities, not due to natural causes, but because of the general's mistakes. These are: (1) Flight; (2) Insubordination; (3) Collapse; (4) Ruin; (5) Disorganization; (6) Rout.

If one force is thrown against another ten times its size, the outcome will be the flight of the smaller force.

When the common soldiers are too strong, and their officers are too weak, the result is insubordination.

(Tu Mu refers to the case of T'ien Pu [Hsin T'ang Shu, ch. 148], who was sent to Wei in 821 A.D. to lead an army against Wang T'ing-ts'ou. While he was in command, his soldiers treated him with disdain, openly disrespecting him by riding donkeys around the camp in large numbers. T'ien Pu couldn't control this behavior, and when he finally tried to engage the enemy, his troops scattered in all directions. Afterward, he tragically committed suicide.)

When the officers are too strong and the common soldiers too weak, the result is collapse.

(Ts'ao Kung says: "The officers are eager to advance, but the soldiers are weak and suddenly collapse.")

When higher-ranking officers act out of anger and fight the enemy on their own initiative, without waiting for the commander-in-chief to assess whether they are ready for battle, the result is ruin.

(Wang Hsi comments: "This refers to a general who becomes angry without reason and fails to recognize the capabilities of his subordinate officers. This leads to intense resentment and ultimately brings disaster upon him.")

When the general is weak and lacks authority, and when his orders are not clear or precise,

(Wei Liao Tzŭ in chapter 4 says: "If the commander gives his orders decisively, the soldiers will not need to hear them twice. If his actions are carried out without hesitation, the soldiers will not have doubts about following them." General Baden-Powell also emphasizes, saying: "The key to getting good results from your trained men lies in clear instructions." Wu Tzŭ, in chapter 3, adds: "The worst flaw in a military leader is indecision; the greatest disasters in an army come from hesitation.")

when officers and men are not given specific duties,

(Tu Mu explains: "Neither the officers nor the soldiers have any set routines.")

and when the troops are assembled in a careless and disorganized manner, the result is complete chaos.

When a general fails to properly assess the enemy's strength and sends a smaller force against a much larger one, or orders a weak unit to engage a stronger force without placing the best soldiers at the front, the outcome will be a disastrous defeat.

(Chang Yu explains this by saying: "Whenever there is fighting, the most determined soldiers should be placed at the front, both to inspire confidence in our own troops and to intimidate the enemy." This concept aligns with Caesar's use of the primi ordines in "De Bello Gallico," V. 28, 44, and elsewhere.)

These are six ways to invite defeat, and they must be carefully observed by any general who holds a position of responsibility.

(See earlier discussion in § 13.)

The natural landscape is the soldier's greatest ally;

(Ch'en Hao notes: "The advantages of weather and timing are not as significant as those related to the terrain.")

but the ability to assess the enemy, control the factors that lead to victory, and accurately judge difficulties, dangers, and distances is what defines a truly great general.

He who knows these principles and in fighting puts his knowledge into practice, will win his battles. He who knows them not, nor practises them, will surely be defeated.

If fighting is sure to result in victory, then you must fight, even though the ruler forbids it; if fighting will not result in victory, then you must not fight even at the ruler's bidding.

(Chang Yu also quotes the saying: "Decrees from the Son of Heaven do not penetrate the walls of a camp." Huang Shih-kung of the Ch'in dynasty, who is said to have been the patron of Chang Liang and to have written the San Lueh, has these words attributed to him: "The responsibility of setting an army in motion must devolve on the general alone; if advance and retreat are controlled from the Palace, brilliant results will hardly be achieved. Hence the god-like ruler and the enlightened monarch are content to play a humble part in furthering their country's cause [literally, kneel down to push the chariot wheel]." This means that "in matters lying outside the zenana, the decision of the military commander must be absolute.")

The general who advances without coveting fame and retreats without fearing disgrace,

(It was Wellington, I think, who said that the hardest thing of all for a soldier is to retreat.)

whose only thought is to protect his country and do good service for his sovereign, is the jewel of the kingdom.

(A noble presentiment, in few words, of the Chinese "happy warrior." Such a man, says Ho Shih, "even if he had to suffer punishment, would not regret his conduct.")

Regard your soldiers as your children, and they will follow you into the deepest valleys; look on them as your own beloved sons, and they will stand by you even unto death.

(Cf. I. § 6. In this connection, Tu Mu draws for us an engaging picture of the famous general Wu Ch'i, from whose treatise on war I have frequently had occasion to quote: "He wore the same clothes and ate the same food as the meanest of his soldiers, refused to have either a horse to ride or a mat to sleep on, carried his own surplus rations wrapped in a parcel, and shared every hardship with his men. One of his soldiers was suffering from an abscess, and Wu Ch'i himself sucked out the virus. The soldier's mother, hearing this, began wailing and lamenting. Somebody asked her, saying: 'Why do you cry? Your son is only a common soldier, and yet the commander-in-chief himself has sucked the poison from his sore.' The woman replied, 'Many years ago, Lord Wu performed a similar service for my husband, who never left him afterwards, and finally met his death at the hands of the enemy. And now that he has done the same for my son, he too will fall fighting I know not where.'")

Li Ch'uan mentions the Viscount of Ch'u, who invaded the small state of Hsiao during the winter. The Duke of Shen said to him: "Many of the soldiers are suffering severely from the cold." So he made a round of the whole army, comforting and encouraging the men; and straightway they felt as if they were clothed in garments lined with floss silk.

If, however, you are lenient but unable to assert your authority; kind-hearted but unable to enforce your commands; and also incapable of maintaining order, then your soldiers will be like spoiled children—they will be useless in any real situation.

[Li Ching once said that if you could make your soldiers fear you, they wouldn't be afraid of the enemy. Tu Mu recounts a strict example of military discipline from 219 A.D., when Lu Meng was holding the town of Chiang-ling. He had ordered his army not to bother the local people or take anything from them by force. However, one officer under his command, who happened to be from the same town, took a bamboo hat from a villager to wear over his helmet in the rain. Despite being a fellow townsman, Lu Meng didn't excuse the breach of discipline. He ordered the officer's execution, though tears fell down his face as he gave the command. This strict action instilled a healthy sense of fear in the army, and from that point on, even items left in the road were not touched.]

If we know our own men are ready to attack but don't know that the enemy is not vulnerable to attack, we've only come halfway to victory.

[As Ts'ao Kung says, "in this case, the outcome is uncertain."]

If we know the enemy is vulnerable but don't realize that our own men aren't ready to attack, we've again only come halfway to victory.

If we know the enemy is vulnerable, and we know our men are ready to attack, but we don't realize that the terrain makes fighting impossible, we're still only halfway to victory.

Hence, the seasoned soldier, once on the move, is never confused; once he breaks camp, he is never lost.

[According to Tu Mu, this is because he has planned everything so thoroughly that victory is ensured before any action is taken. Chang

Yu adds, "He doesn't act rashly, so when he does move, he makes no mistakes."]

Thus the saying goes: If you know the enemy and know yourself, you won't have to worry about the outcome of a hundred battles; if you know both Heaven and Earth, your victory will be complete.

[Li Ch'uan concludes: "If you understand three things—the affairs of men, the seasons of Heaven, and the natural advantages of Earth—, you will always win your battles."]

Chapter 11 - The Nine Situations

Sun Tzu said: The art of war recognizes nine types of ground: (1) Dispersive ground; (2) facile ground; (3) contentious ground; (4) open ground; (5) ground of intersecting highways; (6) serious ground; (7) difficult ground; (8) hemmed-in ground; (9) desperate ground.

When a leader is fighting in his own territory, it is called dispersive ground. This is because the soldiers, being near their homes and eager to see their wives and children, are likely to seize the opportunity of a battle to scatter in every direction. As Tu Mu explains, "They will lack the desperation needed to fight with full valor, and when they retreat, they will find places of refuge."

When the army has crossed into enemy territory, but not deeply, it is called facile ground. Li Ch'uan and Ho Shih say this is because retreat is still easy, and other commentators give similar explanations. Tu Mu adds, "When your army has crossed the border, you should burn your boats and bridges to show everyone there is no turning back."

Ground that offers great advantage to either side is called contentious ground. Tu Mu defines this as ground "worth fighting for." Ts'ao Kung says it is ground "on which the few and weak can defeat the many and strong," such as "the neck of a pass," which Li Ch'uan mentions as an example. Thermopylae fits this description because holding it for even a short time delayed an entire invading army, providing invaluable time. As Wu Tzu says in his writings: "When facing odds of one against ten, there is nothing better than a narrow pass."

When Lu Kuang was returning from his successful expedition to Turkestan in 385 A.D., and had reached I-ho with many spoils, Liang Hsi, the administrator of Liang-chou, took advantage of the death of Fu Chien, King of Ch'in, to plot against him. Yang Han, governor of Kao-ch'ang, advised him, saying, "Lu Kuang has just won victories in the west, and his soldiers are strong and confident. If we face him in the desert sands, we will not stand a chance. Instead, let's take control of the defile at the mouth of the Kao-wu pass. By cutting off his water supply, we can wait until his troops are weakened by thirst and then dictate our terms. Or, if that pass is too far, we could confront him at the I-wu pass, which is closer. Even a skilled strategist like Tzŭ-fang could not overcome the strength of these two positions." Liang Hsi, however, refused this advice and was overwhelmed and defeated by the invader.

Ground where both sides can move freely is called open ground.

[There are different interpretations of the word used for this type of ground. Ts'ao Kung says it means "ground covered with roads, like a chessboard." Ho Shih suggests it means "ground where communication is easy."]

Ground that forms the key to three neighboring states is ground of intersecting highways.

[Ts'au Kung defines this as "our country next to the enemy's, with a third country adjoining both." Meng Shih uses the example of Cheng, a small state bordered by Ch'i to the northeast, Chin to the west, and Ch'u to the south.]

Whoever takes control of this area first has a strategic advantage over most of the region.

[The one who holds this important position can force many neighboring states to become allies.]

When an army has moved deep into enemy territory, leaving fortified cities behind, it is on serious ground.

[Wang Hsi says it is called serious ground because "the army's situation becomes serious when it reaches this point."]

Mountain forests, steep terrain, marshes, and fens—all areas that are difficult to pass—are called difficult ground.

Ground that is reached through narrow gorges, where retreat can only happen through winding paths, and where a small enemy force could easily defeat a large army, is called hemmed-in ground.

Ground where the only way to avoid destruction is to fight immediately is called desperate ground.

[The situation, as described by Ts'ao Kung, is much like hemmed-in ground but worse, with no way out: "A tall mountain in front, a large river behind, no way to advance, no way to retreat." Ch'en Hao says being on desperate ground is "like sitting in a sinking boat or standing in a burning house." Tu Mu shares a vivid description from Li Ching of an army caught in this type of trap: "Imagine an army in enemy territory with no local guides. The army stumbles into a deadly trap, at the enemy's mercy. A ravine on the left, a mountain on the right, and a path so dangerous that horses must be tied together and chariots lifted with slings. There's no way forward, and retreat is blocked. The soldiers move in single file, barely forming ranks before an overwhelming enemy force appears. There's no time to rest, no escape. We try to fight, but there's no space; we try to defend ourselves, but there's no respite. Staying put means wasting time, but any move invites enemy attacks from the front and rear. The land is wild, with no food or water. The soldiers are exhausted, the horses worn out, and every effort seems hopeless. The path is so narrow that one person could stop an army of ten thousand. The enemy controls all the advantages, while we have lost all our options. Even with the bravest soldiers and sharpest weapons, how could they possibly be effective?" Students of Greek history may recall the tragic end of the

Sicilian expedition and the suffering of the Athenians under Nicias and Demosthenes. [See Thucydides, VII. 78 sqq.]]

Do not fight on ground where you're scattered. Do not stop on easy ground. Do not attack when there's a lot of opposition.

[Instead, focus all your energy on getting the upper hand first. So says Ts'ao Kung. However, Li Ch'uan and others believe this means the enemy has already beaten us to it, so attacking would be foolish. In the Sun Tzŭ Hsu Lu, when the King of Wu asks what to do in this situation, Sun Tzŭ responds: "The rule for contested ground is that whoever holds the ground first has the advantage. If the enemy has secured this type of position, do not attack. Trick them into moving by pretending to flee—show your flags and beat your drums—rush to other spots they can't afford to lose—drag branches and kick up dust—confuse their senses—send your best troops to secretly ambush them. Then your enemy will rush out to save the situation."]

On open ground, don't try to block the enemy's path.

[Because it would be pointless and would put the blocking force in danger. There are two interpretations here. I follow Chang Yu's view. The other is found in Ts'ao Kung's short note: "Come closer together"—which means making sure part of your army isn't cut off.]

On ground with crossing roads, join up with your allies.

[Or perhaps, "make alliances with neighboring states."]

On serious ground, take what you need.

[Li Ch'uan adds an interesting note: "When an army moves deep into enemy territory, it's important not to anger the local people by treating them unfairly. Follow the example of the Han Emperor Kao Tsu, who during his march into Ch'in territory didn't harm women or steal valuables. [Note: this was in 207 B.C., a lesson that could embarrass Christian armies that marched into Peking in 1900 A.D.] This is how he won the hearts of the people. In this passage, I think the right reading is not 'take what you need,' but 'don't take what you don't need.' Sadly, the commentator's emotions may have clouded his judgment. Tu Mu, at least, isn't under any such illusions. He says: 'When camped on serious ground, where there's no reason to advance and no chance to retreat, one should prepare for a long defense by gathering supplies from all around, while keeping a close watch on the enemy.'"]

In tough terrain, keep moving steadily forward.

[Or, in the words of VIII. § 2, "don't stop and make camp."]

When trapped, use a clever strategy.

[Ts'ao Kung says, "Try something unusual or unexpected," and Tu Yu adds, "In such situations, you must come up with a plan that fits the moment. If you can trick the enemy, you might escape the danger." This is exactly what happened when Hannibal was trapped in the mountains on the road to Casilinum, seemingly caught by the dictator Fabius. Hannibal came up with a clever trick, similar to one used by T'ien Tan 62 years earlier. [See IX. § 24, note.] At nightfall, they tied bundles of twigs to the horns of around 2,000 oxen and set them on fire. The terrified animals were driven towards the mountain passes held by the enemy. The sight of these fast-moving lights frightened the Romans, causing them to retreat, and Hannibal's army safely passed through the narrow pass. [See Polybius, III. 93, 94; Livy, XXII. 16, 17.]]

When in desperate situations, fight.

[As Chia Lin notes, "If you fight with everything you've got, you have a chance to survive. But if you just stay in your corner, death is certain."]

In the past, skilled leaders knew how to divide the enemy's front from their rear;

[In more exact terms, "They would make sure the front and rear were no longer in touch with each other."]

They knew how to stop the enemy's big and small divisions from working together, and how to prevent strong troops from saving the weak, and officers from rallying their soldiers.

When the enemy's troops were scattered, they made sure the enemy couldn't regroup. Even when the enemy's forces were united, they still managed to keep them disorganized.

When it was to their advantage, they moved forward; if not, they stayed put.

[Mei Yao-ch'en links this to the previous point: "After successfully disrupting the enemy, they would advance to secure any advantage; if there was no advantage, they would stay where they were."]

If asked how to handle a large, organized enemy force about to launch an attack, I would say: "Start by capturing something your opponent values; this will force him to act according to your will."

[There are different views on what Sun Tzŭ meant here. Ts'ao Kung thinks it refers to "some strategic advantage the enemy relies on." Tu Mu says: "The three things an enemy is eager to do, and on which his success depends, are: (1) to capture our key positions; (2) to destroy our farmlands; and (3) to protect his own supply lines." Our goal should be to disrupt his plans in these three areas, rendering him powerless. [Cf. III. § 3.] By boldly seizing the initiative, you force the enemy into a defensive position.]

Speed is the essence of war.

[Tu Mu explains, "This is a summary of the main principles of warfare," and adds, "These are the deepest truths of military science, and the general's most important duty." The following stories, told by Ho Shih, show how important speed was to two of China's greatest generals. In 227 A.D., Meng Ta, governor of Hsin-ch'eng under the Wei Emperor Wen Ti, was planning to defect to the House of Shu, and had begun communicating with Chu-ko Liang, the Prime Minister of that state. The Wei general Ssu-ma I, who was then the military governor of Wan, heard about Meng Ta's treachery and immediately set out with an army to stop him, after having tricked him with a friendly message. Ssu-ma's officers suggested that they should investigate more thoroughly before making a move. Ssu-ma I replied, "Meng Ta is an unreliable man, and we should go and punish him right away, while he is still uncertain and before he has fully betrayed us." Then, with a series of forced marches, he brought his army to the walls of Hsin-ch'eng in just eight days. Now, Meng Ta had earlier written in a letter to Chu-ko Liang: "Wan is 1,200 li from here. When news of my revolt reaches Ssu-ma I, he will inform the emperor, but it will take a whole month before any action is taken. By that time, my city will be well fortified. Besides, Ssu-ma I is not likely to come himself, and the generals that will be sent are not worth worrying about." But his next letter was full of panic: "Though only eight days have passed since I revolted, an army is already at the gates. What incredible speed!" Two weeks later, Hsin-ch'eng fell, and Meng Ta was executed. [See Chin Shu, ch. 1, f. 3.] In 621 A.D., Li Ching was sent from K'uei-chou in Ssu-ch'uan to defeat the rebel Hsiao Hsien, who had declared himself Emperor in the modern-day Ching-chou Fu in Hupeh. It was autumn, and the Yangtze River was in flood, so Hsiao Hsien did not expect Li Ching to risk coming down through the gorges, and as a result made no preparations. But Li Ching immediately prepared his army and was about to set off when the other generals begged him to delay his departure until the river was less dangerous to navigate. Li Ching replied, "For a soldier, overwhelming speed is of the utmost importance, and he must never miss an opportunity. Now is the time to strike, before Hsiao Hsien even knows we have gathered an army. If we attack while the river is in flood, we will reach his capital with such unexpected speed, like thunder that is heard before you have time to cover your ears." [See VII. § 19, note.] This is a key principle of war. Even if Hsiao Hsien hears of our approach, he will have to raise his soldiers in such a rush that they will not be fit to fight us. This way, we will secure total victory." Everything happened as predicted, and Hsiao Hsien was forced to surrender, nobly asking that his people be spared and he alone face death.]

Take advantage of the enemy's lack of readiness, move by unexpected routes, and attack where they are not guarded.

Here are the principles for an invading force to follow: The deeper you go into a country, the stronger the unity among your troops will become, and the defenders will struggle to defeat you.

Make raids in fertile lands to provide your army with food.

[Cf. § 13. Li Ch'uan does not provide a note here.]

Pay close attention to the well-being of your soldiers,

[By "well-being," Wang Hsi means, "Take good care of them, indulge them, make sure they have enough food and drink, and generally keep them in good condition."]

and do not overwork them. Focus your energy and save your strength.

[Ch'en recalls the approach used in 224 B.C. by the brilliant general Wang Chien, whose leadership was key to the First Emperor's success. He invaded the Ch'u State, where a mass mobilization had been raised against him. However, uncertain about the mood of his troops, he refused to engage in battle and stayed strictly on the defensive. The Ch'u general tried repeatedly to provoke a fight, but day after day, Wang Chien remained inside his fortifications. Instead of rushing into battle, he focused on winning the trust and loyalty of his soldiers. He ensured they were well-fed, even sharing meals with them, provided opportunities for bathing, and used every possible method to keep them content and united. After some time, he sent people to check on how his soldiers were spending their free time. The report came back that they were competing in activities like weightlifting and long jumping. When Wang Chien heard this, he knew their morale was high, and they were ready for battle. By then, the Ch'u army, frustrated by their unanswered challenges, had marched away to the east. At that moment, Wang Chien broke camp and pursued them. In the battle that followed, the Ch'u forces were crushed, and shortly after, the entire state of Ch'u was conquered by Ch'in, with their king, Fu-ch'u, taken captive.]

Keep your army constantly on the move,

[So the enemy never knows where you are. However, it has occurred to me that the true meaning might be "link your army together."]

and develop plans that are impossible for the enemy to understand.

Put your soldiers in positions where there is no escape, and they will choose death over retreat. If they are ready to face death, there is nothing they cannot accomplish.

[Chang Yu quotes Wei Liao Tzŭ (ch. 3): "If a single man ran wild with a sword in a marketplace, and everyone else fled from him, it wouldn't mean that he alone was brave and the rest were cowards. The truth is, a man with nothing to lose and a man who values his life are not in the same position."]

Both officers and soldiers will give their full strength.

[Chang Yu says: "If they find themselves in a difficult situation together, they will definitely combine their strength to get out of it."]

When soldiers are in desperate situations, they lose all sense of fear. If they have nowhere to run, they will stand firm. If they are deep in enemy territory, they will fight with determination. If there is no other option, they will fight fiercely.

Thus, without needing to be organized, soldiers will always be alert; without needing to be asked, they will follow your orders.

[Literally, "Without asking, you will receive."]

Without strict rules, they will stay loyal; without needing commands, they can be trusted.

Ban the taking of omens, and eliminate superstitious doubts. Then, until the moment of death, no disaster will be feared.

[Superstition and fear can turn men into cowards who "die many times before their deaths." Tu Mu quotes Huang Shih-kung: "Spells and incantations should be strictly forbidden, and no officer should inquire about the fate of the army through divination, as this can unsettle the soldiers' minds." He continues, "If all doubts and superstitions are cast aside, your soldiers will remain resolute until the very end."]

If our soldiers are not burdened with wealth, it is not because they dislike riches; if their lives are not overly long, it is not because they do not want longevity.

[Chang Yu explains this well: "Wealth and long life are natural desires for all men. So, if soldiers burn or throw away valuables and give up their lives, it is not because they hate them, but because they have no choice." Sun Tzŭ hints that since soldiers are only human, it is the general's responsibility to make sure they are not tempted to avoid battle and seek riches instead.]

On the day your soldiers are ordered to battle, they may cry,

[The word used here is "snivel," which suggests deeper sorrow than just tears.]

some of them sitting up and soaking their clothes with tears, while others lying down let the tears roll down their faces.

[This isn't because they are afraid, but because, as Ts'ao Kung says, "they have all made a firm decision to fight to the death." We can also remember that the heroes of the Iliad were similarly open in showing their emotions. Chang Yu references the sad farewell at the I River between Ching K'o and his friends, when Ching K'o was sent to assassinate the King of Ch'in (who would later become the First Emperor) in 227 B.C. As he said goodbye, tears flowed like rain, and he recited these lines: "The wind blows sharp, the river is cold; Your hero goes forth—never to return."]

But when they are cornered, they will show the courage of a Chu or a Kuei.

[Chu was the personal name of Chuan Chu, a native of the Wu State and a contemporary of Sun Tzǔ. He was hired by Kung-tzu Kuang, also known as Ho Lu Wang, to assassinate the king Wang Liao with a dagger hidden inside a fish at a banquet. He succeeded, but was immediately cut down by the king's guards. This happened in 515 B.C. The other hero, Ts'ao Kuei (also known as Ts'ao Mo), became famous 166 years earlier, in 681 B.C. After Lu had been defeated three times by Ch'i, they were about to sign a treaty giving up a large part of their territory. At that moment, Ts'ao Kuei grabbed Huan Kung, the Duke of Ch'i, at the altar and held a dagger to his chest. None of the Duke's men dared move, and Ts'ao Kuei demanded that all of Lu's territory be returned, arguing that Lu was unfairly treated because it was smaller and weaker. Fearing for his life, Huan Kung agreed. Ts'ao Kuei then calmly put away his dagger and sat back down, showing no fear. Although the Duke wanted to break the agreement later, his wise counselor Kuan Chung advised him that it would be unwise to go back on his word. As a result, Lu regained all the land they had lost in the three battles.]

A skilled strategist can be compared to the shuai-jan. The shuai-jan is a snake found in the Ch'ang mountains.

["Shuai-jan" means "suddenly" or "rapidly," and the snake got this name because of how quickly it moves. Over time, the term came to refer to military maneuvers.]

If you strike at its head, its tail will attack you; if you strike at its tail, its head will attack you; if you strike at its middle, both head and tail will attack you together.

If asked whether an army can be made to act like the shuai-jan,

[As Mei Yao-ch'en says, "Is it possible to make the front and rear of an army respond quickly to an attack on the other, just as if they were parts of one living body?"]

I would answer, Yes. The men of Wu and the men of Yüeh are enemies;

[Cf. VI. § 21.]

yet if they are crossing a river in the same boat and a storm strikes, they will help each other, just as the left hand helps the right.

[The meaning is: If two enemies will cooperate when faced with a shared danger, how much more should two parts of the same army, bound together by shared interests and camaraderie, work together? Still, it is well known that many campaigns have been lost because of a lack of cooperation, especially when allied armies are involved.]

Therefore, it is not enough to rely on tethering horses or burying chariot wheels in the ground to keep an army from fleeing.

[These strange methods, meant to stop soldiers from running away, remind us of the Athenian hero Sophanes, who carried an anchor into battle at Plataea and used it to tie himself to one spot. [See Herodotus, IX. 74.] Sun Tzŭ is saying that merely making flight impossible through such mechanical means is not enough. You will only succeed if your men have strong willpower, unity of purpose, and, most importantly, a spirit of cooperation. This is the lesson we can learn from the shuai-jan.]

The way to manage an army is to set one standard of courage that everyone must meet.

[Literally, "make the courage of all equal as if it were that of one." If the ideal army is to act as one cohesive unit, then the determination and spirit of its members must be of the same quality, or at least not below a certain level. Wellington's comment about his army at Waterloo, calling it "the worst he had ever commanded," was likely a reflection of its lack of this essential trait—unity of courage and spirit. If he hadn't anticipated the Belgian defections and kept those troops in the background, he almost certainly would have lost the battle.]

How to make the best use of both strong and weak soldiers is a matter of how you use the terrain.

[Mei Yao-ch'en explains: "The way to erase the differences between strong and weak and make both useful is by using the natural features of the ground." Weaker troops, if placed in strong defensive positions, can hold out as effectively as better troops on more vulnerable ground. A good position can make up for a lack of stamina and courage. Col. Henderson comments: "With all due respect to textbooks and standard tactics, I believe the study of terrain is often neglected, and that too little attention is given to the selection of positions and the great benefits that come from using natural features, whether attacking or defending." [2]]

Thus, the skillful general leads his army as easily as if he were leading a single person by the hand, whether they want to follow or not.

[Tu Mu says: "The comparison refers to how easily this is done."]

A general must stay calm to ensure secrecy and be upright and just to maintain order.

He must be able to confuse his officers and soldiers with false reports and deceptive appearances,

[Literally, "to deceive their eyes and ears."]

so that they remain in complete ignorance of his true plans.

[Ts'ao Kung gives a wise saying: "Troops should not be allowed to know your plans at the beginning; they may only share in your success when it is achieved." One of the key principles of war is "to mystify, mislead, and surprise the enemy." But how about deceiving your own troops? Those who think Sun Tzŭ overstates this would benefit from reading Col. Henderson's comments on Stonewall Jackson's Valley campaign: "The great care Jackson took to hide his movements, intentions, and thoughts, even from his most trusted staff officers, would have been seen as unnecessary by a less meticulous commander." [3] In 88 A.D., according to ch. 47 of the Hou Han Shu, Pan Ch'ao led 25,000 men from Khotan and other Central Asian states to attack Yarkand. The King of Kutcha sent his commander with 50,000 troops from Wen-su, Ku-mo, and Wei-t'ou to defend it. Pan Ch'ao called a war council with his officers and the King of Khotan and said, 'We are outnumbered and cannot defeat the enemy directly. The best plan is to split up and go in different directions. The King of Khotan will march east, and I will head west. We will leave after the evening drum sounds.' Pan Ch'ao secretly released some prisoners, who informed the King of Kutcha of these plans. Feeling confident, the King of Kutcha took 10,000 horsemen to block Pan Ch'ao's retreat in the west, while the King of Wen-su led 8,000 cavalry east to intercept the King of Khotan. Once Pan Ch'ao knew the enemy leaders had left, he quickly reunited his troops and launched a surprise attack at dawn on Yarkand's camp. The enemy fled in confusion, and Pan Ch'ao pursued them, killing over 5,000 and seizing many horses, cattle, and other valuables. After Yarkand surrendered, Kutcha and the other states withdrew their forces. From then on, Pan Ch'ao's influence dominated the western regions." In this case, the Chinese general not only kept his officers in the dark about his real plans, but also used the bold tactic of splitting his army to deceive the enemy.]

By altering his tactics and changing his plans,

[Wang Hsi believes this means not using the same strategy twice.]

he keeps the enemy unsure and without clear information.

[Chang Yu, in a quote from another work, says: "The idea that war is based on deception doesn't only apply to tricking the enemy. You must also deceive your own soldiers. Make them follow you without letting them know the reasons behind your decisions."]

By shifting his camp and taking indirect routes, he prevents the enemy from predicting his intentions.

At the crucial moment, the leader of an army acts like someone who has climbed a high wall and then kicks away the ladder behind him. He takes his soldiers deep into enemy territory before revealing his true plans.

[Literally, "releases the spring" (see V. § 15), meaning that he takes a decisive action that makes retreat impossible—similar to Hsiang Yu, who sank his ships after crossing a river. Ch'en Hao, followed by Chia Lin, interprets this less clearly as "uses every trick at his disposal."]

He burns his boats and destroys his cooking pots; like a shepherd driving a flock of sheep, he directs his soldiers this way and that, and no one knows where they are headed.

[Tu Mu says: "The army only understands orders to advance or retreat; it doesn't know the true goals of attacking or conquering."]

To gather his forces and lead them into danger—this is the duty of a general.

[Sun Tzŭ means that once the army is mobilized, there should be no delay in striking at the enemy's core. Note how he returns to this idea again and again. In the warring states of ancient China, desertion was likely a much more immediate and serious threat than in today's armies.]

The different strategies suitable for the nine types of ground;

[Chang Yu says: "One should not rigidly apply the rules for the nine types of ground."]

the need for either aggressive or defensive tactics, and the basic laws of human nature: these are things that must absolutely be studied.

When invading hostile territory, the general principle is that penetrating deeply creates unity, while penetrating only a little leads to division.

[Cf. § 20.]

When you leave your homeland and lead your army into neighboring lands, you are on critical ground.

This kind of ground is mentioned earlier, but it is not listed among the Nine Situations or the Six Calamities in another chapter. At first glance, you might think it means "distant ground," but according to commentators, this is not correct. Mei Yao-ch'en explains that it's ground that is neither far enough to be called "easy" nor close enough to be "scattered." It is somewhere in between. Wang Hsi says that it is ground separated from home by a state whose territory we had to cross to reach it, so it is important to finish our task there quickly. He adds that this situation is rare, which is why it is not included among the Nine Situations.

When you have roads in all directions, it is ground of intersecting highways.

When you go deep into enemy territory, it is serious ground. When you advance only a little, it is easy ground.

When the enemy's strongholds are behind you, and narrow paths are in front, it is hemmed-in ground. When there is no place to retreat, it is desperate ground.

Therefore, on scattered ground, I would unite my men under a common goal.

To achieve this, Tu Mu suggests staying on the defensive and avoiding battle.

On easy ground, I would keep all parts of my army closely connected.

Tu Mu explains that this is to prevent two dangers: the possibility of soldiers deserting or a sudden enemy attack. Mei Yao-ch'en adds that during the march, the troops should stay close together, and in camp, the fortifications should be continuous.

On contested ground, I would hurry to bring up my rear forces.

Ts'ao Kung offers this view, and Chang Yu agrees, saying that the head and tail of the army must reach their destination together without straggling. Mei Yao-ch'en suggests another view: If the enemy hasn't yet reached the desired position and we are behind them, we should move quickly to claim it. Ch'en Hao takes another approach, thinking the enemy may have already chosen their ground.

He quotes a passage where Sun Tzŭ warns against attacking when exhausted. If a favorable position lies ahead, Ch'en Hao advises sending a strong unit to secure it, and if the enemy tries to fight for it, the main force can strike their rear, leading to victory.

On open ground, I would stay alert and defend carefully. On ground of intersecting highways, I would strengthen my alliances.

On serious ground, I would make sure to maintain a steady flow of supplies.

Commentators believe this refers to gathering forage and plunder, not maintaining a connection with home, as you might expect.

On difficult ground, I would keep moving forward.

On hemmed-in ground, I would block any escape routes.

Meng Shih explains that this would make it seem like I am defending the position, but my real plan is to break through the enemy's lines unexpectedly. Mei Yao-ch'en adds that this would make my soldiers fight with desperation. Wang Hsi suggests that this would prevent my men from being tempted to flee. Tu Mu points out that this is the opposite of a previous situation, where it is the enemy who is surrounded. An example of this is from 532 A.D., when Kao Huan, who later became Emperor, was surrounded by a much larger army led by Erh-chu Chao and others. Despite his smaller force, which included only 2000 horsemen and fewer than 30,000 foot soldiers, Kao Huan blocked all remaining escape routes by driving oxen and donkeys into the gaps. When his officers and men saw there was no escape, they fought with extraordinary bravery and broke through the enemy ranks with fierce determination.

On desperate ground, I would tell my soldiers there is no hope of survival.

Tu Yu suggests making it clear to the soldiers that survival is impossible by burning their baggage, throwing away supplies, blocking wells, and destroying cooking stoves. The only way to live is to fight as if they expect to die. Mei Yao-ch'en adds that their only chance of survival is to abandon all hope of it.

This concludes what Sun Tzŭ says about "grounds" and their corresponding "variations." Reviewing these passages, it is clear that the subject is treated in a somewhat scattered and unstructured manner. Sun Tzŭ begins by listing a few variations before discussing "grounds" but only mentions five variations, which are later expanded. Some types of ground are addressed earlier, while chapter X introduces six new types of ground, each with a variation to match. However, none of these six types are revisited, and one closely resembles a type of ground described later. In chapter XI, we encounter the Nine Grounds, followed by a list of their variations. By sections 43-45, new definitions for several of these grounds are provided, as well as for another type not previously mentioned. Finally, the nine variations are listed again, though many of them differ from earlier versions.

Although we cannot definitively explain the current state of Sun Tzŭ's text, a few interesting observations stand out: (1) Chapter VIII is titled "Nine Variations," but only five are listed. (2) This chapter is unusually short. (3) Chapter XI is called "The Nine Grounds," but some of the grounds are defined more than once, and two separate lists of variations are given. (4) This chapter is much longer than any other, except chapter IX. While no specific conclusions can be drawn from these facts, it seems likely that Sun Tzŭ's work has not reached us exactly as he originally wrote it. Chapter VIII appears incomplete and possibly out of place, while chapter XI contains material that may have been added later or misplaced from another part of the text.

For it is the soldier's nature to offer a determined resistance when surrounded, to fight fiercely when there is no way out, and to follow orders quickly when faced with danger. Chang Yu refers to the actions of Pan Ch'ao's loyal followers in 73 A.D. The story is found in the Hou Han Shu, chapter 47: "When Pan Ch'ao arrived at Shan-shan, the king, Kuang, initially treated him with great politeness and respect;

but soon after, his attitude changed abruptly, and he became negligent and indifferent. Pan Ch'ao spoke of this to the officers with him: 'Have you noticed,' he said, 'that Kuang's courtesy is fading? This must mean that envoys from the Northern barbarians have arrived, leaving him uncertain about which side to support. That is surely the reason. The wise man, we are told, can foresee events before they happen; how much more easily can he observe what is already taking place!' Then he called one of the locals assigned to his service and set a trap by asking, 'Where are those envoys from the Hsiung-nu who arrived a few days ago?' The man, startled and afraid, quickly revealed the whole truth. Pan Ch'ao, having secured the man, then summoned a meeting with his officers, thirty-six in all, and began drinking with them. As the wine took effect, he encouraged their spirits further by saying: 'Gentlemen, here we are in a remote region, eager to achieve riches and honor through a great deed. Recently, an ambassador from the Hsiung-nu has arrived, and because of this, the respectful treatment we've received from the king has faded. If this envoy persuades him to capture us and deliver us to the Hsiung-nu, our bones will be left for the wolves of the desert. What are we to do?' The officers, as one, replied, 'With our lives at risk, we will follow you through life and death.' The rest of this story can be found in chapter twelve, section one."

We cannot form alliances with neighboring rulers until we understand their intentions. We are not fit to lead an army on the march unless we know the landscape—its mountains and forests, its traps and cliffs, its marshes and swamps. We cannot make use of the land's advantages unless we employ local guides. These three statements are repeated from chapter seven to stress their importance, according to the commentators. However, I believe they are placed here as a lead-in to the next statements. Regarding local guides, Sun Tzŭ might have added that there is always a risk of error, either due to their betrayal or through misunderstanding. Livy, for instance, recounts a case where Hannibal ordered a guide to take him near Casinum, where an important pass was to be secured; but Hannibal's

Carthaginian accent, not well-suited to Latin names, led the guide to mishear Casilinum instead of Casinum. The mistake was not discovered until the army had nearly reached the wrong location.

To be ignorant of any one of the following four or five principles is unworthy of a warlike leader.

When a prince who is ready for war attacks a strong nation, his skill as a leader comes from stopping the enemy from gathering their forces. He intimidates his opponents, and their allies are scared off from uniting against him.

[Mei Tao-ch'en offers one of the logical chains of thought that the Chinese are fond of: "When attacking a strong state, if you can separate its forces, you gain the advantage in strength; if you have the advantage in strength, you can intimidate the enemy; if you intimidate the enemy, neighboring states will become fearful; and if neighboring states are fearful, the enemy's allies will be stopped from joining her." The following interpretation gives an even stronger meaning: "If the powerful state is defeated before they can call on their allies, then the smaller states will hesitate and avoid bringing their forces together." Ch'en Hao and Chang Yu understand this in a very different way. Ch'en Hao says: "Even though a prince may be strong, if he attacks a large state, he won't have enough troops and will have to rely on outside help. If he ignores this and, with too much confidence in his own strength, tries to scare the enemy, he will certainly lose." Chang Yu explains it this way: "If we recklessly attack a large state, our own people will be unhappy and hesitant. And if our military power is clearly weaker than the enemy's, other leaders will be too scared to join us."]

So, he does not try to form alliances with everyone, nor does he help other states become stronger. He carries out his secret plans, keeping his enemies in fear.

[Li Ch'uan explains the thinking like this: Confident that his enemies won't join forces, "he can afford to turn down risky alliances and just focus on his own secret plans, with his reputation allowing him to do without external friendships."]

In this way, he can capture their cities and bring down their kingdoms.

[Even though this paragraph was written long before the state of Ch'in became a serious threat, it sums up well the strategy that the Six Chancellors used to pave the way for Ch'in's final victory under Shih Huang Ti. Chang Yu, expanding on his earlier note, thinks that Sun Tzŭ is criticizing this cold, selfish, and isolated approach.]

Bestow rewards without regard to rules,

[Wu Tzŭ, less wisely, says: "Let advancement be richly rewarded and retreat be heavily punished."]

issue orders

[Literally, "hang" or post them up.]

without regard to previous arrangements;

["In order to prevent treachery," says Wang Hsi. The general meaning is made clear by Ts'ao Kung's quotation from the Ssu-ma Fa: "Give instructions only upon sighting the enemy; give rewards when you see worthy deeds." Ts'ao Kung paraphrases: "The final instructions you give to your army should not match those that were previously posted." Chang Yu simplifies this to "your plans should not be revealed in advance." And Chia Lin adds: "There should be no fixed rules in your arrangements." Not only is there risk in letting your plans be known, but war often requires reversing them at the last moment.]

and you will be able to manage a whole army as though you were dealing with just one man.

[Cf. supra, § 34.]

Confront your soldiers with the action itself; never let them know your plan.

[Literally, "do not tell them words," meaning do not give reasons for any order. Lord Mansfield once told a junior colleague to "give no reasons" for his decisions, and this rule applies even more to a general than to a judge.]

When the situation looks promising, show it to them; but when the outlook is bleak, tell them nothing.

Place your army in deadly peril, and it will survive; throw it into desperate situations, and it will come out safely.

[These words of Sun Tzŭ were once quoted by Han Hsin to explain the tactics he used in one of his most brilliant battles, mentioned earlier. In 204 B.C., Han Hsin was sent against the army of Chao, halting ten miles from the Ching-hsing pass, where the enemy had gathered in full strength. At midnight, he sent out 2000 light cavalry, each equipped with a red flag. Their orders were to pass through narrow defiles and secretly observe the enemy. "When the men of Chao see me retreating in full flight," Han Hsin said, "they will abandon their defenses and chase us. This will be your signal to rush in, pull down the Chao banners, and raise the red flags of Han instead." He then told his other officers: "The enemy holds a strong position and won't attack us until they see the standard and drums of the commander-in-chief, fearing I might retreat through the mountains." With this, he sent out a division of 10,000 men, ordering them to form a line of battle with their backs to the River Ti. Upon seeing this maneuver, the entire Chao army burst into laughter. By morning, Han Hsin raised his general's flag and marched out of the pass with drums beating, quickly engaging the enemy. A fierce battle followed, lasting for some time, until Han Hsin and his colleague, Chang Ni, left the drums and flag on the battlefield and fled to the division by the river, where another intense fight was underway. The enemy rushed after them to claim the trophies, leaving their defenses exposed, but the two generals managed to join their army, which was fighting desperately. Now it was time for the 2000 horsemen to act. When they saw the men of Chao pursuing the fleeing forces, they galloped behind the abandoned fortifications, tore down the enemy's flags, and replaced them with the banners of Han. When the Chao army looked back during the chase and saw the red flags, they were struck with terror. Convinced that the Hans had overpowered their king, they panicked and scattered, despite their leader's attempts to stop them. Then the Han forces attacked from both sides, completely routing the Chao army, killing many and capturing the rest, including King Ya himself. After the battle, some of Han Hsin's officers approached him and said: "In the Art of War, we are taught to position troops with a hill or mound on the right rear and a river or marsh on the left front. Yet you ordered us to draw up with the river at our backs. How did you manage to win under such conditions?" The general replied: "I'm afraid you haven't studied the Art of War carefully enough. Does it not say, 'Plunge your army into desperate straits, and it will come off in safety; place it in deadly peril, and it will survive'? Had I followed the usual methods, I wouldn't have been able to bring my colleague around. As the Military Classic says, 'Swoop down on the marketplace and drive the men off to fight.' If I hadn't placed my troops where they had no choice but to fight for their lives, and instead allowed them to act freely, they would have scattered, and we couldn't have accomplished anything." The officers acknowledged the wisdom of his argument and said: "These are tactics beyond our own abilities."]

For it is precisely when a force finds itself in danger that it becomes capable of striking a blow for victory.

[Danger has a motivating effect.]

Success in warfare is achieved by carefully adapting to the enemy's intentions.

[Ts'ao Kung says: "Feign ignorance" by appearing to comply with the enemy's wishes. Chang Yu explains: "If the enemy shows a desire to advance, encourage him to do so; if he wishes to retreat, delay deliberately to allow him to carry out his plan." The goal is to make him overconfident and careless before launching our attack.]

By constantly keeping pressure on the enemy's flank,

[I understand this to mean "moving alongside the enemy in the same direction." Ts'ao Kung says: "Unite the troops and advance towards the enemy." But such a rearrangement of words is not defensible.]

we will eventually succeed,

[Literally, "after a thousand li."]

in killing the enemy's commander.

[This was always a significant aim in Chinese warfare.]

This is what it means to achieve something through sheer strategy.

On the day you take command, block the frontier passes, destroy the official tallies,

[These were tablets of bamboo or wood, half of which was used as a permit by an official. When returned within a set period, the gate could be opened for the traveler.]

and stop all communication,

[Whether to or from the enemy's territory.]

Be firm in the council-chamber,

[Show no weakness, and ensure your plans are approved by the ruler.]

so that you can maintain control over the situation.

[Mei Yao-ch'en interprets this to mean: Take the strictest measures to maintain secrecy in your discussions.]

If the enemy leaves an opening, you must charge through it.

Outsmart your opponent by seizing what he values most,

[See earlier, § 18.]

and subtly manipulate the timing of his arrival at the battlefield.

[Ch'en Hao explains: "If I seize a favorable position but the enemy doesn't show up, the advantage gained is meaningless. To control an important position, you must create a kind of 'appointment' with the enemy, tricking him into arriving there as well." Mei Yao-ch'en says this "appointment" can be made by using the enemy's own spies, who will bring back only the information we want them to have. Once we've cunningly revealed our plans, we can make sure, by starting after the enemy, that we arrive before him (VII. § 4). Starting later forces him to move there; arriving first allows us to capture the position without resistance. This supports Mei Yao-ch'en's reading of § 47.]

Walk the path guided by strategy,

[Chia Lin says: "Victory is all that matters, and this cannot be won by strictly following conventional rules." Unfortunately, this interpretation relies on weak authority, though it makes much more sense. As we know, Napoleon, according to the veterans of the old school whom he defeated, won his battles by breaking all the traditional rules of warfare.]

and adapt to the enemy until the moment comes for a decisive battle.

[Tu Mu says: "Follow the enemy's tactics until a favorable moment arises; then engage in a battle that will be conclusive."]

At first, show the reserve of a shy maiden until the enemy gives you an opening; then strike with the speed of a running hare, and it will be too late for the enemy to resist you.

[Though the hare is known for its timidity, Sun Tzŭ was clearly referring to its speed. The words have sometimes been interpreted to mean fleeing from the enemy as fast as a hare, but Tu Mu rightly rejects this idea.]

Chapter 12 - The Attack by Fire

Sun Tzŭ said: There are five ways to attack using fire. The first is to set fire to soldiers in their camp.

[Tu Mu agrees. Li Ch'uan adds: "Set the camp on fire, and kill the soldiers as they try to escape from the flames." Pan Ch'ao, on a diplomatic mission to the King of Shan-shan, found himself in great danger when an envoy from the Hsiung-nu, China's mortal enemies, unexpectedly arrived. During a meeting with his officers, he declared: "Nothing ventured, nothing gained! Our only option now is to attack the barbarians with fire under the cover of night, when they won't be able to see how many we are. Taking advantage of their panic, we can wipe them out, discourage the King, and achieve glory, ensuring the success of our mission." The officers suggested discussing the plan with the Intendant first, but Pan Ch'ao was outraged: "Today is the day our fate will be decided! The Intendant is a mere civilian and will be too scared when he hears our plan, leading to its exposure. Dying ingloriously is not the fate for brave warriors." The officers then agreed to follow his lead. That night, Pan Ch'ao and his small group approached the barbarian camp. A strong wind was blowing. Pan Ch'ao ordered ten men to hide behind the enemy barracks with drums, ready to make a loud noise when they saw the fire. The rest of his men, armed with bows and crossbows, were placed in ambush at the camp's gate. Pan Ch'ao set the camp on fire from the windward side, and immediately, the drums began to beat, and shouts filled the air. The Hsiung-nu ran out in panic. Pan Ch'ao personally killed three of them, while his men beheaded the envoy and thirty others. More than a hundred of the enemy perished in the flames. The next day, Pan Ch'ao, aware of the Intendant's concerns, assured him, "Although you didn't join us last night, I won't take sole credit for the success." This satisfied Kuo Hsun, and Pan Ch'ao presented the head of the barbarian envoy to the King of Shan-shan, causing fear throughout the kingdom. Pan Ch'ao calmed the situation by issuing a public proclamation, took the king's sons as hostages, and then reported his success to Tou Ku." *Hou Han Shu,* ch. 47, ff. 1, 2.]

The second is to burn stores.

[Tu Mu says: "Food, fuel, and fodder." During the Sui dynasty, to subdue the rebellious population of Kiangnan, Kao Keng advised Emperor Wen Ti to make periodic raids and burn their grain stores, a strategy that ultimately succeeded.]

The third is to burn baggage trains.

[An example is Ts'ao Ts'ao's destruction of Yuan Shao's wagons and supplies in 200 A.D.]

The fourth is to burn arsenals and magazines.

[Tu Mu explains that arsenals and magazines contain the same items, listing weapons, bullion, and clothing. See VII. § 11 for comparison.]

The fifth is to hurl fire into the enemy's camp.

[Tu Yu mentions in the *T'ung Tien*: "To drop fire into the enemy camp, dip arrowheads into a brazier to set them alight and then shoot them from powerful crossbows into the enemy's lines."]

In order to carry out an attack, we must have the necessary means available.

[T'sao Kung believes this refers to "traitors in the enemy's camp." However, Ch'en Hao more likely means: "We must have favorable circumstances in general, not just rely on traitors." Chia Lin adds: "We should take advantage of wind and dry weather."]

The material for raising fire should always be kept ready.

[Tu Mu suggests materials for starting a fire like "dry vegetation, reeds, brushwood, straw, grease, oil, etc." This is the material cause. Chang Yu adds: "Containers for hoarding fire and things for lighting fires."]

There is a proper season for making attacks with fire and specific days for starting a blaze.

The proper season is during very dry weather, and the specific days are when the moon is in the constellations of the Sieve, the Wall, the Wing, or the Cross-bar;

[These correspond roughly to the 7th, 14th, 27th, and 28th of the Twenty-eight Stellar Mansions, which are Sagittarius, Pegasus, Crater, and Corvus.]

because these four are all days when the wind rises.

When attacking with fire, you must be prepared for five possible outcomes:

(1) When fire breaks out inside the enemy's camp, immediately launch an attack from outside.

(2) If a fire starts but the enemy's soldiers remain calm, wait and do not attack.

[The main goal of attacking with fire is to create confusion among the enemy. If that doesn't happen, it means the enemy is prepared for you. Therefore, caution is necessary.]

(3) When the flames reach their peak, follow up with an attack if possible; if not, stay where you are.

[Ts'ao Kung advises: "If you see an opportunity, advance; but if the difficulties seem too great, retreat."]

If it is possible to make an assault with fire from the outside, do not wait for it to break out within, but launch your attack at a favorable moment.

[Tu Mu explains that the previous sections referred to fire breaking out inside the enemy's camp, either by accident or through arson. He adds: "But if the enemy is camped in a waste area filled with grass, or if he has set up camp in a location that can easily be burned, we should attack with fire at any good opportunity instead of waiting for a fire to start within. Otherwise, the enemy might burn the surrounding vegetation themselves, rendering our efforts useless." The famous Li Ling once outsmarted a leader of the Hsiung-nu this way. The latter, taking advantage of a favorable wind, attempted to set fire to the Chinese general's camp, but found that all combustible vegetation had already been burned down. On the other hand, Po-ts'ai, a general of the Yellow Turban rebels, was badly defeated in 184 A.D. for neglecting this basic precaution. While leading a large army, he was besieging Ch'ang-she, which was defended by Huang-fu Sung. Although the garrison was small and nervous, Huang-fu Sung called his officers together and said: "In war, there are various indirect ways to attack, and numbers are not everything." [Here the commentator quotes Sun Tzŭ, V. §§ 5, 6, and 10.] "The rebels have set up camp in thick grass that will easily catch fire when the wind blows. If we set fire to it at night, they will panic, and we can attack from all sides, just like T'ien Tan did." [See page 90.] That night, a strong breeze arose, so Huang-fu Sung ordered his soldiers to bind reeds into torches and guard the city walls. Then, he sent out a group of brave men who sneaked through the enemy lines and started the fire with loud shouts and yells. At the same time, a bright light flared up from the city walls, and Huang-fu Sung, sounding the drums, led a swift charge, throwing the rebels into confusion and sending them fleeing." *Hou Han Shu,* ch. 71.]

When you start a fire, make sure you are upwind from it. Do not attack from the downwind side.

[Chang Yu, following Tu Yu, explains: "When you start a fire, the enemy will retreat away from it; if you block their retreat and attack, they will fight desperately, which will not lead to your success." Tu Mu offers a simpler explanation: "If the wind is blowing from the east, begin burning to the east of the enemy and follow up your attack from that direction. If you start the fire on the east side and attack from the west, both you and the enemy will suffer."]

A wind that rises during the day lasts long, but a night breeze dies down quickly.

[Lao Tzŭ says: "A violent wind does not last the space of a morning." (Tao Te Ching, chap. 23.) Mei Yao-ch'en and Wang Hsi explain: "A daytime breeze fades at nightfall, and a night breeze ends at daybreak. This is usually the case." While this observation may be accurate, how this applies in the context is not immediately clear.]

In every army, the five developments related to fire must be understood, the movements of the stars calculated, and attention paid to the proper days.

[Tu Mu says: "We must calculate the paths of the stars and watch for the days when wind will rise before launching a fire attack." Chang Yu seems to interpret the text differently, suggesting: "We must not only know how to attack our opponents with fire but also guard against similar attacks from them."]

Those who use fire as a tool for attacking show intelligence, while those who use water as a tool for attacking gain additional strength.

By means of water, an enemy may be intercepted, but not stripped of all his possessions.

[Ts'ao Kung comments: "We can only obstruct the enemy's path or divide his forces, but we cannot wipe out all his stores." Water can be helpful, but it lacks the overwhelming destructive power of fire. This, Chang Yu concludes, is why water is dismissed in just a few lines, while fire attacks are discussed in detail. Wu Tzŭ (ch. 4) remarks: "If an army is camped on low-lying marshy ground, where water can't drain away, and where rainfall is heavy, it may be flooded. If an army is camped in wild marshlands overgrown with weeds and brambles, and frequently visited by gales, it may be wiped out by fire."]

Unhappy is the fate of one who tries to win his battles and succeed in his attacks without fostering a spirit of initiative; for the result is wasted time and general stagnation.

[This is one of the most puzzling passages in Sun Tzŭ. Ts'ao Kung says: "Rewards for good service should not be delayed even for a single day." Tu Mu adds: "If you don't seize the opportunity to advance and reward those who deserve it, your subordinates will not follow your orders, and disaster will follow." However, I prefer the interpretation suggested by Mei Yao-ch'en, whose words I will quote: "Those who want to ensure success in their battles and attacks must seize favorable opportunities when they arise and not shy away from bold measures. That means they must use such means of attack as fire, water, and the like. What they must avoid, which will lead to failure, is sitting still and merely holding on to the advantages they have already gained."]

Hence the saying: The enlightened ruler plans well in advance; the capable general builds up his resources.

[Tu Mu quotes from the *San Lueh,* ch. 2: "The warlike prince controls his soldiers through his authority, unites them through trust, and makes them serve through rewards. If trust fades, there will be disorder; if rewards are insufficient, orders will not be obeyed."]

Move not unless you see an advantage; use not your troops unless there is something to be gained; fight not unless the position is critical.

[Sun Tzŭ may seem overly cautious at times, but he never goes as far as the passage in the *Tao Te Ching,* ch. 69: "I dare not take the initiative but prefer to act defensively; I dare not advance an inch but prefer to retreat a foot."]

No ruler should send troops into the field merely to satisfy personal anger; no general should fight a battle out of resentment.

If it benefits you, make a forward move; if not, stay where you are.

[This repeats from XI. § 17. It feels like an interpolation here because § 20 clearly follows from § 18.]

Anger may eventually turn into gladness; frustration may be replaced by contentment.

But a kingdom once destroyed can never be restored;

[The Wu State serves as a sad example of this saying.]

nor can the dead ever be brought back to life.

Therefore, the enlightened ruler is cautious, and the wise general is full of care. This is the way to keep a country at peace and an army intact.

["Unless you enter the tiger's lair, you cannot catch its cubs."]

Chapter 13 - The Use of Spies

Sun Tzŭ said: Raising an army of a hundred thousand men and marching them over long distances causes heavy losses to the people and drains the State's resources. The daily cost will amount to a thousand ounces of silver.

[Cf. II. §§ 1, 13, 14.]

There will be unrest both at home and abroad, and men will collapse from exhaustion along the highways.

[Cf. *Tao Te Ching,* ch. 30: "Where troops have been stationed, thorns and brambles spring up." Chang Yu notes: "We are reminded of the saying: 'On serious ground, gather in plunder.' So why does transport cause such exhaustion on the highways?—The answer lies in the fact that it is not just food but all sorts of munitions that must be transported to the army. Additionally, the command to 'forage on the enemy' means that, when deeply engaged in enemy territory, food shortages must be anticipated. Therefore, while not entirely dependent on the enemy for supplies, we must forage to ensure a continuous flow. Moreover, in places like salt deserts, where provisions are unavailable, supplies from home become indispensable."]

As many as seven hundred thousand families will be hindered in their work.

[Mei Yao-ch'en comments: "There will be a shortage of men to work the fields." The reference is to the system of dividing land into nine parts, with the central plot farmed for the State by the tenants of the other eight plots. It was here, as Tu Mu notes, that the families built their cottages and shared a common well. [See II. § 12, note.] During wartime, one family had to serve in the army, while the other seven provided support. Therefore, when 100,000 men were conscripted (with one able-bodied soldier per family), the agricultural work of 700,000 families would be affected.]

Hostile armies may face each other for years, striving for a victory that is decided in a single day. Given this, to remain ignorant of the enemy's condition simply because one begrudges the cost of a hundred ounces of silver for rewards and payments

["For spies" is implied here, though it is not explicitly mentioned to maintain the effect of this elaborate introduction.] is the height of inhumanity.

[Sun Tzŭ's argument is quite clever. He starts by acknowledging the immense misery and staggering cost in lives and resources that war brings. If you remain uninformed about the enemy's situation and fail to strike at the right moment, a war can drag on for years. The only way to get this information is by employing spies, and reliable spies cannot be found unless they are well paid. It is false economy to begrudge such a small amount when each additional day of war costs vastly more. This burden falls hardest on the poor, so neglecting the use of spies is, in Sun Tzŭ's view, nothing less than a crime against humanity.]

One who acts in this way is no leader of men, no true support to his sovereign, and no master of victory.

[This notion, that the ultimate goal of war is peace, has deep roots in the Chinese national temperament. Even as far back as 597 B.C., Prince Chuang of the Ch'u State said: "The [Chinese] character for 'prowess' is formed by the characters for 'to stay' and 'a spear' (the cessation of hostilities). Military prowess is seen in the suppression of cruelty, the laying down of weapons, upholding the mandate of Heaven, establishing merit, bringing happiness to the people, promoting harmony among the princes, and spreading wealth."]

Thus, what enables the wise sovereign and the good general to strike and conquer, achieving things beyond the reach of ordinary men, is foreknowledge.

[That is, understanding the enemy's plans and intentions.]

Now, this foreknowledge cannot be gained from spirits; it cannot be derived from experience,

[Tu Mu explains: "[Knowledge of the enemy] cannot be obtained by reasoning from similar cases."]

nor can it be deduced through calculation.

[Li Ch'uan notes: "Quantities like length, breadth, distance, and magnitude can be determined mathematically, but human actions cannot be calculated in the same way."]

Knowledge of the enemy's plans can only be obtained from other men.

[Mei Yao-ch'en adds an interesting point: "Divination can provide knowledge of the spirit-world; inductive reasoning can reveal truths in natural science; and mathematical calculation can verify the laws of the universe. But the enemy's plans can only be learned through spies, and spies alone."]

Hence the use of spies, of whom there are five types: (1) Local spies; (2) inward spies; (3) converted spies; (4) doomed spies; (5) surviving spies.

When all five types of spies are working together, no one can unravel the secret system. This is called "divine manipulation of the threads." It is the sovereign's most valuable skill.

[Cromwell, one of the greatest and most practical cavalry leaders, had officers called 'scout masters,' whose task was to gather all possible intelligence regarding the enemy through scouts and spies. Much of his success in warfare was due to the prior knowledge of the enemy's movements gained in this way.]

Having local spies means using the inhabitants of a region.

[Tu Mu advises: "In the enemy's country, win people over through kind treatment and use them as spies."]

Having inward spies means using officials of the enemy.

[Tu Mu lists several groups likely to be useful in this regard: "Worthy men who have been disgraced, criminals who have been punished, favorite concubines greedy for gold, men frustrated with being in subordinate positions or passed over for promotions, others hoping for their side's defeat so they can showcase their talents, and turncoats who always try to keep a foot in both camps. Officials of these types should be secretly approached and won over with rich gifts. In this way, you can discover the state of affairs in the enemy's country, learn their plans, and also cause discord between the ruler and his ministers." However, dealing with inward spies requires extreme caution, as illustrated by an incident related by Ho Shih: "Lo Shang, Governor of I-Chou, sent his general Wei Po to attack the rebel Li Hsiung of Shu in his stronghold at P'i. After several victories and defeats on both sides, Li Hsiung employed the services of a certain P'o-t'ai, a native of Wu-tu. He had P'o-t'ai whipped until blood flowed, then sent him to deceive Lo Shang by pretending to cooperate from inside the city and promising to light a fire signal for a coordinated assault. Lo Shang trusted these promises, sent out his best troops, and ordered Wei Po and others to attack when P'o-t'ai signaled. Meanwhile, Li Hsiung's general, Li Hsiang, prepared an ambush along their path. P'o-t'ai then raised long scaling ladders against the city walls and lit the signal fire. Wei Po's men rushed in upon seeing the signal, climbed the ladders, and were pulled up by ropes. More than a hundred of Lo Shang's soldiers entered the city, where they were immediately beheaded. Li Hsiung then charged with his full forces, both inside and outside the city, and completely routed the enemy." This occurred in 303 A.D. Though Ho Shih does not provide his source, it is not mentioned in the biographies of Li Hsiung or his father, Li T'e, in *Chin Shu,* ch. 120, 121.]

Having converted spies means capturing the enemy's spies and using them for our own purposes.

[This involves offering them large bribes and making generous promises to turn them against their original side, so they will send false information back to the enemy and spy on their own people. Another approach, mentioned by Hsiao Shih-hsien, is to pretend that we haven't caught on to the spy, allowing him to leave with a false understanding of what is happening. Some commentators accept this as an alternative interpretation, but it's not what Sun Tzŭ intended, as shown by his later comments on treating the converted spy well. Ho Shih gives three examples of successful use of converted spies: (1) T'ien Tan in his defense of Chi-mo, (2) Chao She on his march to O-yu, and (3) Fan Chu in 260 B.C., when Lien P'o was conducting a defensive campaign against Ch'in. The King of Chao, unhappy with Lien P'o's slow and cautious methods, listened to reports from spies who had secretly switched sides and were already being paid by Fan Chu. The spies said, "The only concern Ch'in has is if Chao Kua becomes general. They see Lien P'o as an easy target who will be defeated eventually." Chao Kua, the son of the famous general Chao She, had been obsessed with war and strategy since childhood, believing no one could defeat him. His father, worried about his arrogance, warned that if Kua ever became a general, he would ruin the army of Chao. Despite warnings from his mother and the statesman Lin Hsiang-ju, Chao Kua was appointed to replace Lien P'o. He proved no match for the skilled general Po Ch'i and the mighty Ch'in army. His army was split, his supply lines were cut, and after a 46-day resistance, during which his starving soldiers resorted to cannibalism, he was killed by an arrow, and his entire force, reportedly 400,000 men, was slaughtered.]

Having doomed spies means openly doing certain things to deceive the enemy and letting our own spies know about it so they can report back.

[Tu Yu explains it best: "We deliberately do things to fool our own spies into thinking they've uncovered real secrets. When they are caught by the enemy, they will give false reports, causing the enemy to prepare for something that won't happen." Once the enemy realizes the deception, the spies will be executed. Ho Shih gives the example of prisoners released by Pan Ch'ao during his campaign against Yarkand. He also mentions T'ang Chien, who was sent by T'ai Tsung in 630 A.D. to lull the Turkish Kahn Chieh-li into a false sense of security until Li Ching could launch a surprise attack. Some say the Turks killed T'ang Chien in revenge, but both the old and new T'ang histories record that he escaped and lived until 656. Li I-chi played a similar role in 203 B.C., when sent by the King of Han to negotiate with Ch'i. Li I-chi may be a more fitting example of a doomed spy, as the King of Ch'i, feeling betrayed after an unexpected attack by Han Hsin, had Li I-chi boiled alive.]

Surviving spies are those who return with information from the enemy's camp.

[These are the typical spies, forming a regular part of the army. Tu Mu says: "A surviving spy must be intelligent but appear foolish; he should look shabby on the outside but possess a strong will. He must be active, tough, physically strong, and brave; accustomed to doing dirty work, able to endure hunger and cold, and capable of handling shame and humiliation." Ho Shih tells a story about Ta'hsi Wu of the Sui dynasty: "When he was governor of Eastern Ch'in, Shen-wu of Ch'i launched an attack on Sha-yuan. Emperor T'ai Tsu sent Ta'hsi Wu to spy on the enemy, accompanied by two others. They rode on horseback, wearing the enemy's uniform. After nightfall, they dismounted a few hundred feet from the enemy's camp and sneaked closer to listen. They managed to overhear the army's passwords. Then they got back on their horses and, pretending to be night watchmen, boldly rode through the camp. Several times, they even punished soldiers who were breaking the rules, beating them as if they were enforcing discipline! This way, they gathered detailed information about the enemy's position and returned to report. The Emperor was so impressed by their intelligence that he used it to achieve a major victory over the enemy."]

Hence, none in the entire army should be more closely connected with than spies.

[Tu Mu and Mei Yao-ch'en note that spies have the privilege of entering even the general's private tent.]

No one should be rewarded more generously, and no other work should be kept more secret.

[Tu Mu adds that all communication with spies should be done "mouth-to-ear," in utmost secrecy. The following advice on spies can be quoted from Turenne, who used them more than any previous commander: "Spies work for those who pay them the most. A commander who pays poorly will never be well-served. They should remain unknown to others, and they should not know one another. When they propose something important, secure their loyalty by holding them or their families as hostages for their faithfulness. Only share with them what is absolutely necessary for them to know."]

Spies cannot be effectively used without a certain intuitive sagacity.

[Mei Yao-ch'en says: "To use them well, you must be able to distinguish truth from lies and recognize honesty from deceit." Wang Hsi interprets this more as "intuitive perception" and "practical intelligence." Tu Mu, however, strangely attributes these qualities to the spies themselves: "Before employing spies, we must confirm their integrity and assess their experience and skills." But he adds: "A bold face and a cunning mind are more dangerous than mountains or rivers; it takes a genius to see through them." This leaves some uncertainty as to his true view of the passage.]

They cannot be properly managed without benevolence and straightforwardness.

[Chang Yu says: "After attracting spies with good offers, you must treat them with complete sincerity, so they will serve you with full dedication."]

Without subtle ingenuity, one cannot be sure of the accuracy of their reports.

[Mei Yao-ch'en warns: "Beware of the possibility that spies might defect to the enemy."]

Be subtle! Be subtle! And use your spies for all kinds of tasks.

If a spy leaks a secret before the time is right, he must be executed along with the person who received the information.

[The literal translation is: "If spy matters are heard before [our plans] are carried out," etc. Sun Tzŭ's point is that the spy is executed as punishment for revealing the secret, while the other person is killed, as Ch'en Hao explains, "to keep his mouth shut" and prevent further leaks. If the information has already been shared with others, this would be ineffective. Sun Tzŭ's advice may seem harsh, though Tu Mu defends it, saying the recipient deserves punishment because he must have pressured the spy into revealing the secret.]

Whether the goal is to defeat an army, storm a city, or assassinate a leader, it is crucial to start by learning the names of the attendants, aides-de-camp,

[Literally "visitors," referring to those who supply the general with information, requiring regular meetings with him.]

the doorkeepers, and sentries of the general in command. Our spies must be assigned to find out these details.

[This would be the first step toward determining whether any of these key figures can be bribed.]

The enemy's spies who come to spy on us must be identified, tempted with bribes, and then won over and treated well. This way, they become converted spies and can work for us.

It is through the information provided by the converted spy that we can recruit and use local and inward spies.

[Tu Yu explains: "By converting the enemy's spies, we learn the true state of the enemy." Chang Yu adds: "We must entice the converted spy into our service because he knows which local inhabitants are greedy for profit and which officials are open to corruption."]

It is also through the converted spy's information that we can use doomed spies to send false reports to the enemy.

[Chang Yu says, "The converted spy knows the best ways to deceive the enemy."]

Finally, the converted spy's information allows us to use the surviving spy on special occasions.

The ultimate purpose of all five types of spies is to gain knowledge of the enemy; and this knowledge primarily comes from the converted spy.

[As outlined in §§ 22-24. The converted spy not only provides direct information but also makes it possible to effectively employ the other types of spies.]

Therefore, it is crucial to treat the converted spy with the greatest generosity.

Of old, the rise of the Yin dynasty

[Sun Tzŭ is referring to the Shang dynasty, founded in 1766 B.C., which was later renamed Yin by P'an Keng in 1401.]

was due to I Chih

[Also known as I Yin, the famous general and statesman who played a key role in Ch'eng T'ang's campaign against Chieh Kuei.]

126

who had served under the Hsia. Likewise, the rise of the Chou dynasty was due to Lü Ya

[Lü Shang, who rose to prominence under the tyrant Chou Hsin, later helped to overthrow him. He is widely known as T'ai Kung, a title given to him by Wen Wang, and is said to have authored a treatise on war, though it has been wrongly identified with the *Liu T'ao.*]

who had served under the Yin.

[The Chinese wording here is less precise than this translation, and the commentaries are not clear. However, in the context, it seems likely that Sun Tzŭ is presenting I Chih and Lü Ya as examples of converted spies or something similar. His point is that the Hsia and Yin dynasties fell because these former ministers had intimate knowledge of their weaknesses, which they shared with the opposing side. Mei Yao-ch'en objects to this interpretation, saying: "I Yin and Lü Ya were not traitors. The Hsia dynasty failed to employ I Yin, so the Yin did. The Yin dynasty failed to employ Lü Ya, so the Chou did. Their great deeds were for the benefit of the people." Ho Shih is also offended: "How could divinely inspired men like I and Lü have been mere spies? Sun Tzŭ is not suggesting that they were spies, but rather that using spies requires the highest level of intelligence, which people like I and Lü possessed. That is why they are mentioned here." Ho Shih believes they are referenced for their wisdom in using spies, but this interpretation is weak.]

Hence, only the enlightened ruler and the wise general will use the highest intelligence in the army for spying, and by doing so, they achieve great results.

[Tu Mu concludes with a note of caution: "Just as water, which can carry a boat across a river, can also sink it, so relying on spies can bring great success but also lead to disaster."]

Spies are a crucial part of warfare because the movement of the army depends on them.

The Prince

Niccollo Macchiavelli

Chapter 1
How Many Kinds of Principalities There Are, And by What Means They Are Acquired

All states, all powers that have governed or currently govern people, are either republics or principalities.

Principalities can be hereditary, where the ruling family has been established for a long time, or they can be new.

New principalities can be completely new, as Milan was to Francesco Sforza, or they can be added to an existing hereditary state, like the kingdom of Naples, which was added to the kingdom of the King of Spain.

These newly acquired territories are either used to living under a prince or accustomed to living in freedom. They are acquired either by the ruler's own military force, by the arms of others, or by fortune or personal skill.

Chapter 2
Concerning Hereditary Principalities

I will set aside any discussion on republics, since I have written about them extensively elsewhere, and will focus only on principalities. In doing so, I will follow the order outlined above and explain how such principalities can be governed and maintained.

I state right away that it is easier to maintain control over hereditary states, where the people are long accustomed to the family of their prince, than over new states. This is because it is generally enough for a hereditary prince to follow the traditions of his ancestors and to act wisely when new situations arise. A prince of even average ability can hold onto his state unless he is overthrown by an exceptionally powerful force. Even if he is removed, when misfortune befalls the usurper, the prince is likely to regain his power.

As an example from Italy, consider the Duke of Ferrara. He would not have been able to withstand the Venetians' attacks in 1484 or those of Pope Julius in 1510 if he had not been securely established in his dominions. A hereditary prince has fewer reasons and less need to offend his subjects, which makes it more likely that he will be loved. Unless extraordinary vices cause him to be hated, it is reasonable to expect that his subjects will naturally be inclined to support him. The longer a prince's rule endures, the more the reasons and motivations for change are forgotten, because one change always sparks a desire for another.

Chapter 3
Concerning Mixed Principalities

But the difficulties arise in a new principality. First, if the principality is not completely new, but instead a part of a larger state—what can be called a composite state—the challenges primarily stem from a common problem inherent in all new principalities. People often willingly change their rulers, hoping to improve their situation, and this hope drives them to rise up against the current ruler. However, they are frequently deceived, as they later find through experience that they have gone from bad to worse. This issue is further complicated by a natural and common occurrence: a new prince must place burdens on the people who have submitted to him. He must station his soldiers there and impose countless other difficulties on his new territory in order to secure his position.

In this way, the new prince makes enemies of those he has harmed in seizing power, and at the same time, he cannot hold onto the support of those who helped him, because he is unable to meet their expectations. Moreover, he cannot take decisive action against them because he feels obligated to them. Even if a prince has a strong military, when entering a new province, he will always require the goodwill of the local population.

For these reasons, Louis XII, King of France, quickly captured Milan but just as quickly lost it. In the first instance, it was enough for Duke Lodovico's own forces to drive him out, because the people who had opened their gates to Louis, feeling betrayed in their hopes for future benefits, could not tolerate the mistreatment from the new prince. It is true, though, that once rebellious provinces are regained a second time, they are not as easily lost. This is because the prince, without hesitation, uses the rebellion as an opportunity to punish wrongdoers, remove those he cannot trust, and strengthen his position in weaker areas. Thus, to make France lose Milan the first time, it was enough for Duke Lodovico to incite unrest along the borders. But to make France lose Milan a second time, it required the combined efforts of the entire world against Louis, and his armies had to be defeated and expelled from Italy. These results occurred due to the reasons I've mentioned.

Nevertheless, France lost Milan both the first and second time. The general reasons for the first loss have already been discussed, so now we must turn to the reasons for the second and consider what resources Louis had, and what anyone in his situation would need to secure such a conquest more effectively than the King of France did.

I now say that territories which are acquired and added to an ancient state, by the one who conquers them, either share the same language and culture as the existing state or they do not. When they do, it is much easier to maintain control, especially if the new territory is not accustomed to self-governance. In such cases, to hold onto the new state securely, it is enough to eliminate the ruling family of the previous prince. The two peoples, being alike in most other respects, will live peacefully together. An example of this can be seen in Brittany, Burgundy, Gascony, and Normandy, which have been part of France for a long time. Even if there are some differences in language, the customs are similar enough that the people can live together without much difficulty. The ruler who has annexed these territories should keep two things in mind: first, he must ensure that the family of the former ruler is completely eliminated, and second, he must make sure that neither their laws nor their taxes are changed. If he does this, in a short time, the new territory will be fully integrated with the old principality.

But when a state is acquired in a region with a different language, customs, or laws, the challenges are much greater, and maintaining control requires a combination of good fortune and strong effort. One of the best ways to secure such a territory is for the prince to go and reside there. This step greatly increases the stability and longevity of the prince's rule, as it did for the Turk in Greece. Despite all the other measures he took to hold onto that state, the Turk would not have been able to keep it had he not gone to live there. By being present in the territory, the prince can observe problems as they arise and address them quickly. When a prince is not present, these issues only come to light once they have grown more serious and are more difficult to resolve. In addition, by residing there, the local officials cannot exploit the country, and the people can appeal directly to the prince for help. This not only makes the subjects more likely to remain loyal, but also gives them more reason to love the prince if he acts justly, or to fear him if they intend to rebel. Furthermore, as long as the prince resides in the new territory, any external enemy seeking to conquer it will find the task much more difficult.

Another good method for maintaining control over a new state is to establish colonies in one or two strategic locations. These colonies act as strongholds or keys to the territory. This approach is either necessary or a large number of cavalry and infantry must be kept there. Colonies, however, are much less expensive to maintain. A prince can send them out with little or no cost, and they will offend only a small portion of the local population—the ones whose lands and homes are taken to give to the new settlers. Those who are harmed in this way are left poor and scattered, so they cannot organize any serious resistance. Meanwhile, the majority of the population, who are not affected, will remain quiet and be careful not to make mistakes, fearing they could suffer the same fate as those who lost their property. In conclusion, colonies are inexpensive, loyal, and cause less harm, while those harmed by them are too weak and dispersed to seek revenge. It should be noted that men must either be treated well or crushed, because they can take revenge for minor injuries, but not for severe ones. Therefore, if a prince needs to harm someone, it should be in such a way that no fear of retaliation remains.

On the other hand, maintaining a standing army in the new territory, instead of establishing colonies, is much more costly. The entire revenue of the state must be spent on the garrison, turning the acquisition into a financial burden. Additionally, a much larger portion of the population is angered, since the presence of the garrison affects everyone. As the soldiers move throughout the territory, all the inhabitants experience hardship, and they become hostile. These people are enemies who, even if defeated in battle, can still cause damage. For all these reasons, keeping a standing garrison in the new territory is far less effective than establishing colonies.

Furthermore, a prince who controls a state with a different language, customs, or laws should make himself the leader and protector of the weaker neighboring states while weakening the stronger ones. He must also ensure that no foreign power as strong as himself gains a foothold in the region, because this often happens when dissatisfied locals invite foreign intervention due to their ambition or fear. This has occurred many times throughout history, such as when the Romans were brought into Greece by the Aetolians. In every case where foreign powers gained control, it was because local factions invited them in. The typical pattern is that when a powerful foreigner enters a territory, all the weaker states rally to him, motivated by their hatred for the ruling power. As a result, the foreigner gains their support with little effort. However, the prince must ensure that these states do not gain too much power, and with his own forces and their support, he can easily keep the more powerful factions in check, allowing him to remain the dominant ruler in the territory.

If the prince does not handle these matters effectively, he will soon lose the territory he has gained, and even while he holds onto it, he will face constant difficulties and challenges.

The Romans, whenever they annexed new territories, always paid very close attention to how they managed those lands. They sent settlers to create colonies and made sure to maintain friendly relations with smaller powers. However, they were careful not to make these smaller powers stronger than they already were. At the same time, they kept the larger, more powerful nations in check, and they never allowed any strong foreign powers to gain too much control. I think Greece offers a perfect example of this. The Romans managed to keep the Achaeans and Aetolians as allies, but they never let them become too powerful. They brought down the kingdom of Macedonia and forced Antiochus to retreat. Yet, even though the Achaeans and Aetolians had been good allies to Rome, the Romans still didn't allow them to expand their influence. And no matter how hard Philip tried to win the friendship of the Romans, they would only agree to be his allies after humbling him. As for Antiochus, no amount of influence he possessed could convince the Romans to let him hold any real power over the land. The Romans acted in these ways because they followed what every smart and cautious ruler should do—rulers who look not only at the problems right in front of them but also at potential future troubles. They understood that they needed to prepare for these future challenges with all their energy because, when you can see a problem coming, it's much easier to address it. But if you wait too long and let the issue get closer, it will already be too late to fix because the problem will have grown so much that it becomes impossible to solve. This is very similar to what doctors say about hectic fever: when the illness first starts, it's easy to cure but hard to notice. However, if too much time passes and the illness isn't treated, it becomes very obvious but extremely hard to cure. The same thing happens with matters of state—if you foresee a problem early on (which only wise leaders can do), you can address it quickly and easily. But if you let that problem grow without addressing it, it will eventually become so big that everyone can see it, and by that point, it will be much harder to fix. That's why the Romans, when they saw potential problems in the future, dealt with them right away. They didn't wait for the problems to escalate because they knew that trying to avoid a small conflict now would only lead to a bigger conflict later, which would work in their enemies' favor. The Romans preferred to handle conflicts early, even if it meant smaller battles, because they knew that war was inevitable. They believed that postponing war would only benefit others. They also wanted to fight Philip and Antiochus in Greece, rather than later facing them in Italy. The Romans could have avoided both conflicts, but they chose not to because they knew that avoiding war wasn't an option—it would only delay the inevitable and give their enemies more of an advantage. The Romans didn't subscribe to the popular idea we often hear today, that you should "enjoy the benefits of the present moment." Instead, they focused on reaping the benefits that came from their own courage and careful planning. They understood that time pushes everything forward, bringing both good and bad, just as fortune can bring both success and failure.

Now, let's take a look at France and see if they followed any of these same principles. I'll focus on King Louis XII (rather than Charles VIII), because Louis held power in Italy for a longer period, and his actions are more relevant. You'll see that Louis made many mistakes by doing the exact opposite of what he should have done to maintain control over a state made up of many different regions and people.

King Louis was brought into Italy by the ambition of the Venetians, who hoped to use him to help them gain control over half of Lombardy. I don't blame the king for taking this course of action, because when he wanted to establish a foothold in Italy, he didn't have any friends there. The actions of Charles VIII had closed every door to him. So, Louis had no choice but to accept the alliances that were available to him. He could have succeeded in his plans very quickly if he hadn't made some critical mistakes along the way. After conquering Lombardy, Louis immediately regained the authority that Charles had lost. Genoa surrendered to him, and the Florentines became his allies. The Marquess of Mantua, the Duke of Ferrara, the Bentivogli family, my lady of Forli, the rulers of Faenza, Pesaro, Rimini, Camerino, Piombino, Lucca, Pisa, and Siena—all of them approached Louis, seeking to become his allies. At that moment, the Venetians realized how reckless their decision had been. In their attempt to gain control of two towns in Lombardy, they had allowed Louis to become the ruler of two-thirds of Italy.

Let's now consider how easily Louis could have maintained his position in Italy if he had followed the principles we've already discussed. He had many allies, and even though they were numerous, they were all weak and fearful—some feared the Church, while others were scared of the Venetians. As a result, they would have always relied on Louis for support. With their help, he could have strengthened his position and protected himself against any remaining powerful forces in Italy. But instead of securing his position, as soon as he took control of Milan, Louis made the opposite mistake. He helped Pope Alexander VI take over the Romagna, and in doing so, he failed to realize that he was weakening himself. By supporting Alexander's ambitions, he lost the allies who had placed their trust in him, while at the same time strengthening the Church by giving it even more political power. This action allowed the Church to gain greater authority. After making this huge mistake, Louis had no choice but to continue down the wrong path. He soon found himself in a position where, in order to stop Alexander's growing ambitions and prevent the Pope from gaining control over Tuscany, Louis was forced to return to Italy to deal with the situation himself.

As if it weren't enough that he had empowered the Church and lost his allies, Louis, in his desire to gain control of Naples, decided to divide the kingdom with the King of Spain. By doing this, he went from being the dominant ruler in Italy to just one of many competing powers. This gave ambitious nobles in Italy and discontented individuals in France a place to turn to for refuge and support. Louis could have placed a ruler loyal to him in Naples, but instead, he removed this ruler and replaced him with someone who would eventually turn against him and drive him, Louis, out of Italy.

It's only natural for rulers to desire more power, and they are often praised for gaining it. However, when a ruler tries to seize power in ways beyond their capabilities, they are seen as foolish and open to criticism. So, if France had the strength to conquer Naples on its own, it should have done so. But if it didn't have that strength, then dividing the kingdom was a major mistake. While Louis's decision to divide Lombardy with the Venetians could be justified because it allowed him to gain a foothold in Italy, the same cannot be said for his decision to divide Naples.

Louis made five major errors: he destroyed the smaller powers in Italy, he increased the strength of one of the major powers (the Church), he brought a foreign power (Spain) into Italy, he failed to establish a lasting presence in the country, and he didn't send colonies to secure his control. These five mistakes alone wouldn't have completely ruined him, but then Louis made a sixth error by weakening the Venetians. If Louis hadn't strengthened the Church or brought Spain into Italy, it would have made sense to weaken the Venetians. But after making those earlier mistakes, Louis should have left the Venetians strong enough to keep other powers from meddling in Lombardy. The Venetians wouldn't have allowed anyone to take Lombardy from France just to give it to them, and no other power would have dared to challenge France's hold on Lombardy if it meant giving it to the Venetians.

And if someone tries to argue that "King Louis gave the Romagna to Pope Alexander and the kingdom of Naples to Spain in order to avoid war," my response would be that, as I've already explained, making mistakes to avoid war is never wise. War cannot be avoided; it can only be postponed, and postponing it will only work to your disadvantage. If someone else argues that Louis had promised the Pope to help him in exchange for dissolving his marriage and giving the Archbishop of Rouen a cardinal's hat, I will address that issue later when discussing the importance of keeping promises.

In the end, King Louis lost Lombardy because he didn't follow the principles that successful rulers have used to gain and maintain control over new territories. There's no mystery or miracle in what happened to Louis—his downfall was predictable and completely natural. I discussed this issue with Cardinal Rouen at Nantes when Cesare Borgia (also known as Valentino), the son of Pope Alexander, had taken control of the Romagna. Cardinal Rouen remarked to me that Italians didn't understand warfare, and I responded by saying that the French didn't understand statecraft. If they had, they wouldn't have allowed the Church to grow so powerful. In fact, it's clear that France's downfall in Italy was caused by the very powers they helped strengthen—the Church and Spain.

From this, we can draw a general rule that almost always holds true: when you help someone else gain power, you are often the one who ends up being ruined. This happens because the person who rises to power, whether through cleverness or strength, no longer trusts the one who helped them get there.

Chapter 4

Why the Kingdom of Darius, Conquered by Alexander, Did Not Rebel Against the Successors of Alexander at His Death

When thinking about the struggles people face when trying to keep control of a newly conquered state, some might wonder why, after Alexander the Great took control of Asia in just a few years and then died before he could fully settle it, the empire didn't immediately rebel. It would seem natural that such a large empire would fall apart, yet his successors managed to hold on to power, and the only real problems they faced were those created by their own ambitions.

The reason for this is that there are generally two ways that principalities, or territories ruled by princes, are governed. In one system, the prince is helped by a group of servants or ministers who only have power because the prince allows them to. In the second system, the prince rules alongside barons who gained their power through family ties, not because the prince granted it to them. These barons have their own lands and subjects, who recognize them as their rightful lords and feel a natural loyalty toward them. In the first type of government, where the prince and his servants hold power, the prince is much more respected because no one else in the country is seen as his equal. If people obey anyone else, they do so because that person is the prince's official, not because they truly feel loyal to him.

In modern times, we can see examples of both types of government by looking at the Turkish Empire and the Kingdom of France. In the Turkish Empire, the sultan is the only ruler, and everyone else is his servant. He divides his kingdom into provinces, called sanjaks, and sends different governors to rule over them. These governors can be replaced or moved whenever the sultan chooses. On the other hand, in France, the king rules alongside many lords who have been in power for a long time and are respected by their own subjects. The French lords have their own privileges, and the king cannot take those away without risking serious trouble.

When you compare these two systems, it becomes clear that conquering the Turkish Empire would be difficult, but once it's taken, it would be relatively easy to hold on to. The difficulty in conquering the Turkish Empire comes from the fact that the ruler's power is so centralized. No local princes can be persuaded to help an invader, and the sultan's ministers are loyal to him, not to their own people. Because these ministers are essentially slaves to the sultan, it's very hard to bribe or corrupt them. Even if they were bribed, they wouldn't be able to turn the people against the sultan because the people don't feel any loyalty toward them. So, if you attack the Turkish Empire, you need to rely on your own military strength rather than expecting help from the inside. However, once you've defeated the sultan in battle and his army is destroyed, there's little left to worry about. As long as the sultan's family is wiped out, there's no one else with the authority to rally the people against you, since all the sultan's officials only held power because of him.

In contrast, conquering a kingdom like France is much easier because you can gain the support of some of the local lords who are unhappy with the king. There are always people who want change and are willing to help an invader in exchange for power. These lords can help you take over the kingdom fairly easily. But holding on to it after you've conquered it is much harder. You will face challenges from both the people who helped you and those you defeated. It's not enough to simply eliminate the royal family, because the remaining lords will continue to resist you and may lead rebellions. You can't satisfy or completely eliminate all these lords, so the kingdom will eventually be lost as soon as an opportunity arises for them to strike back.

If you look at the government of Darius, the Persian ruler, you'll see that it was similar to the system used by the Turks. This is why Alexander the Great only had to defeat Darius in battle to take over his kingdom. Once Darius was killed, Alexander was able to secure the territory without much trouble for the same reasons mentioned earlier. If Alexander's successors had stayed united, they could have ruled the kingdom without difficulty because no internal rebellions would have threatened them, except those they caused themselves.

On the other hand, kingdoms like France, which have many powerful lords, are much harder to control. This is why, during Roman times, there were frequent rebellions in places like Spain, France, and Greece. These regions were filled with many principalities, and as long as the memory of these local rulers remained, the Romans could never feel completely secure in their rule. However, after the Roman Empire had ruled these places for a long time, people began to forget about their old rulers, and the Romans were finally able to maintain control without fear of rebellion. Later on, when the Roman Empire itself started to weaken, the regions were divided up among those who had gained power there, and the only rulers recognized by the people were the Romans, since the old ruling families had been eliminated.

When we consider these facts, it becomes clear why Alexander the Great was able to hold onto his empire in Asia with relative ease, while others, like Pyrrhus, struggled to maintain their conquests. It wasn't because Alexander was more skilled or capable than these other rulers, but because the structure of the territories he conquered made it easier for him to maintain control.

Chapter 5
Concerning the Way to Govern Cities or Principalities Which Lived Under Their Own Laws Before They Were Annexed

When a state that has been acquired is used to living under its own laws and enjoying freedom, there are three main ways to keep control of it. The first way is to destroy it completely. The second option is for the ruler to go and live there in person. The third way is to allow the state to keep its own laws but collect taxes from them and set up an oligarchy that will be loyal to the new ruler. This kind of government, having been put in place by the ruler, knows it cannot survive without his help and will do everything to support him. So, if a ruler wants to keep control of a city that's used to freedom, it's often easier to do so by using the city's own people to help govern rather than any other method.

Consider the example of the Spartans and the Romans. The Spartans controlled Athens and Thebes by establishing oligarchies there, but they still lost control of them. On the other hand, the Romans completely destroyed Capua, Carthage, and Numantia, and they never lost them. The Romans tried to keep control of Greece the same way the Spartans did—by allowing it to remain free and letting it keep its own laws—but they were unsuccessful. In the end, they had to destroy many cities in Greece to maintain control. The truth is, there's no safer way to keep control of a state that's used to freedom than by completely destroying it. If someone takes control of a city that is accustomed to freedom and doesn't destroy it, they can expect that city to eventually rise up and destroy them. A city like that will always use the idea of liberty and its old privileges as a rallying cry for rebellion. No amount of time or benefits will ever make them forget their former freedoms. No matter what a ruler does to prevent it, the people will never forget their past or their rights unless they become divided or scattered. They will seize any opportunity to fight for their freedom again, as Pisa did after being under the control of Florence for a hundred years.

However, when a city or state has always been ruled by a prince and the ruling family is wiped out, the people, having been used to obeying and now without their old prince, often find it hard to agree on a new leader among themselves. They don't know how to govern themselves, which makes them much slower to rebel. In such cases, it's easier for a new ruler to take control and keep them in line. But in republics, there is more energy, more hatred, and a stronger desire for revenge, which means they will never let go of the memory of their former liberty. Because of this, the safest way to handle them is either to destroy them completely or to live there and rule them directly.

Chapter 6

Concerning New Principalities Which Are Acquired by One's Own Arms and Ability

No one should be surprised if, when discussing completely new principalities, I refer to the greatest examples of both princes and states. The reason is simple: people, for the most part, walk along paths that others have already paved. They follow the footsteps of those who came before them, and though they try to imitate the actions of these predecessors, they are not always able to stick closely to their ways or match their achievements. A wise person, however, should always strive to follow in the steps of great men and emulate the best examples of leadership. Even if this person's abilities do not fully measure up to the greatness of those they are imitating, they will still come closer to success simply by aiming higher. It's like skilled archers who aim for a target that seems out of reach. Knowing the limits of their bow, they aim higher than the target, not because they expect to hit that higher point, but because aiming high allows them to reach their true target.

I say, then, that when it comes to ruling entirely new principalities, where the prince is new to his position, the difficulty of maintaining control will depend on the abilities of the person who has acquired the state. If someone rises from being a private citizen to becoming a ruler, whether through personal skill or through fortune, the challenges they face will vary according to their level of competence. Luck, or fortune, can ease some of the difficulties, but a ruler who relies less on fortune and more on their own abilities is always in a stronger position. Additionally, it is easier for a prince who doesn't rule over another state to maintain control of their own domain, because they are forced to live within their own state and focus entirely on its governance.

Let's look now at those who became princes through their own talents and abilities, rather than relying on fortune. In this regard, I would say that the most excellent examples are Moses, Cyrus, Romulus, Theseus, and others like them. Even though Moses is often regarded as simply carrying out the will of God, he should still be admired because of the favor that allowed him to speak directly with God. Setting Moses aside for a moment, when we consider Cyrus and other leaders who founded or acquired kingdoms, we find that their deeds are no less worthy of admiration. If we closely examine their lives and actions, we see that they owed very little to fortune beyond the opportunities they encountered. Without those opportunities, their talents might have gone unnoticed. Similarly, without their extraordinary abilities, the opportunities they came across would have been wasted.

For instance, it was necessary for Moses to find the people of Israel enslaved in Egypt, oppressed and longing for freedom, so that they would be ready to follow him. It was essential for Romulus to be abandoned at birth and not remain in Alba, because only by being in such a situation could he rise to become the King of Rome and the founder of his nation. Cyrus needed to find the Persians unhappy under the rule of the Medes, while the Medes themselves had grown soft and weak from too many years of peace. Theseus, in turn, could not have demonstrated his leadership abilities had he not found the Athenians scattered and in disarray. In each of these cases, the opportunity presented itself, but it was their great abilities that allowed them to seize that opportunity and bring honor to their nations.

Those who rise to power through their own valor, like these men, often face tremendous challenges in gaining their position, but once they have succeeded, they find it much easier to maintain their rule. The difficulties they face in acquiring power often stem from the new rules and systems they must introduce to ensure the stability and security of their government. It's important to remember that nothing is harder to manage, more dangerous to carry out, or more uncertain in its success than introducing a new system of government. The reason for this is that those who benefited from the old system will naturally oppose the change, while those who stand to gain from the new system often offer only half-hearted support. This lack of strong support arises partly from fear of those who oppose the change, as they have the law on their side, and partly because people are generally resistant to accepting new things until they have had a long time to experience them.

As a result, when the enemies of change have the opportunity to attack, they do so with great determination, while the supporters defend the new system weakly, thus putting the ruler in danger. This is why, when discussing this topic in full, we need to ask whether these innovators can rely on themselves or if they must depend on others. In other words, do they achieve their goals through persuasion, or do they have the ability to use force if necessary? Those who rely solely on persuasion often fail because their efforts lack the strength to enforce their ideas. But those who can rely on their own strength and use force when needed face far fewer risks. This is why all armed prophets have succeeded, while unarmed ones have failed.

Beyond this, we must also understand that people are naturally inconsistent. It is easy to persuade them of something, but it's much harder to keep them convinced over time. For this reason, a ruler must be prepared to use force to maintain control when persuasion alone no longer works. If Moses, Cyrus, Theseus, and Romulus had not been armed, they would not have been able to establish and enforce their laws for long. This was the downfall of Fra Girolamo Savonarola, a man from our own time who tried to introduce a new order of things. As soon as people stopped believing in him, he had no way to maintain his followers' support or to bring back those who had turned against him.

Therefore, rulers who seek to introduce new systems face significant challenges, and most of their dangers arise during the process of gaining power. However, those with the necessary abilities can overcome these difficulties. Once they have triumphed over their adversaries and neutralized the threats against them, they will become secure, respected, and powerful, ensuring their success for the future.

In addition to these great examples, I want to mention a lesser-known one that still bears a resemblance to the others. This is the case of Hiero of Syracuse. Although his story may not be as grand as those of Moses or Romulus, it is still significant. Hiero rose from being an ordinary citizen to becoming the ruler of Syracuse. He did not owe his rise to fortune, but rather to opportunity, as the people of Syracuse, feeling oppressed, chose him as their leader. Later, they made him their prince. Hiero possessed such great skill, even before he became ruler, that someone once said he only needed a kingdom to become a king. After gaining power, he reorganized the military, replaced old alliances with new ones, and built a solid foundation for his rule. With his own soldiers and allies, he was able to maintain his power with ease. Though he faced great challenges in rising to power, he found it relatively easy to hold onto once he had achieved it.

Chapter 7

Concerning New Principalities Which Are Acquired Either by The Arms of Others or By Good Fortune

Those who become princes solely through good fortune, starting as private citizens, find it easy to rise but struggle to stay in power. They face few difficulties on their way up because they ascend so quickly, but they encounter many challenges once they reach the top. These are the people who gain control of a state through money or by the favor of someone else, like many in Greece who were made princes in the cities of Ionia and the Hellespont by Darius. He made them rulers to secure the cities for his own safety and glory. The same happened with emperors who, through the corruption of soldiers, rose from being private citizens to emperors. These individuals rely only on the goodwill and luck of the person who raised them to power—two of the most unreliable and unstable foundations to stand on. They also lack the necessary experience for their position because, unless they are extremely capable, it is not reasonable to expect them to know how to lead, having always lived as ordinary citizens. Additionally, they cannot maintain their power because they don't have loyal and dependable forces.

States that rise suddenly, like many things in nature that are born and grow rapidly, often fail to establish strong foundations or lasting relationships with other states. As a result, when the first storm hits, they are easily overthrown. This is what happens to people who become princes unexpectedly. Unless they are very capable and understand that they need to quickly prepare to hold onto the power fortune has handed them, their reign will be short-lived. The strong foundations that other rulers lay before becoming princes must be laid afterward by those who rise suddenly.

To illustrate the two methods of becoming a prince, through either ability or fortune, I will give two examples from recent memory: Francesco Sforza and Cesare Borgia. Francesco, through his abilities and wise actions, rose from being a private citizen to becoming Duke of Milan, and he held onto his power with ease after working so hard to obtain it. On the other hand, Cesare Borgia, who was called Duke Valentino, gained power through his father's influence, but when his father's power declined, he lost his own position. This happened even though he did everything a wise and capable person should do to firmly secure the states that were handed to him by others' efforts and fortune.

As mentioned before, if someone has not already laid their foundations, they might be able to do so later with great skill, but it will be much harder for them, and there will always be a risk of failure. If we consider the actions taken by Duke Valentino, we can see that he laid solid foundations for his future power, and I don't think it's a waste of time to discuss his efforts. In fact, I believe there is no better example to offer a new prince than the actions he took. If his plans ultimately failed, it wasn't because of any fault of his own, but rather due to an extraordinary and unpredictable stroke of bad luck.

Alexander the Sixth, Cesare Borgia's father, wanted to elevate his son's power, but he faced many difficulties, both immediate and in the long term. First, he couldn't figure out how to make his son the ruler of any state that wasn't already part of the Church. Even if he had been willing to take land from the Church, the Duke of Milan and the Venetians would never have agreed to it because Faenza and Rimini were already under the Venetians' protection. Moreover, the military forces in Italy, which could have helped Cesare, were in the hands of people who feared the Pope's growing power, like the Orsini and the Colonna families and their followers. Therefore, the Pope needed to disrupt this balance of power and create conflicts to gain control of some of their lands. Fortunately for him, he found that the Venetians, for other reasons, wanted to bring the French back into Italy. The Pope didn't oppose this; instead, he made it easier by annulling King Louis's previous marriage. As a result, the French king entered Italy with the support of the Venetians and the Pope. Once King Louis took Milan, the Pope gained soldiers from him for his campaign in the Romagna, which quickly surrendered to Cesare because of the king's reputation.

After Cesare conquered the Romagna and defeated the Colonna family, he wanted to hold onto his new territories and expand further. However, he was faced with two major problems. First, his forces didn't seem entirely loyal to him, and second, he couldn't be sure of France's continued support. In particular, he feared that the Orsini family, whose forces he was using, might not remain loyal. Not only might they prevent him from expanding, but they could also seize the territories he had already taken. He had already seen a sign of this when, after taking Faenza and attacking Bologna, the Orsini troops showed little enthusiasm for continuing the fight. As for the king of France, Cesare realized his intentions when, after he took the Duchy of Urbino, he began to move against Tuscany, only for the king to order him to stop. This led Cesare to decide that he could no longer rely on the armies or luck of others.

To address the first problem, Cesare weakened the power of the Orsini and Colonna families in Rome by gaining the loyalty of their supporters. He made these nobles his own by paying them well and giving them honors and offices. In this way, he turned their loyalty away from their former factions and toward himself. Within a few months, all their loyalty had shifted. After dealing with their supporters, Cesare waited for the right moment to crush the Orsini family itself, having already scattered the followers of the Colonna family. His opportunity came quickly, and he took full advantage of it. The Orsini family, realizing that Cesare's rise to power and the strengthening of the Church were their downfall, organized a meeting in Magione in Perugia. This led to the rebellion in Urbino and uprisings throughout the Romagna, which put Cesare in great danger. However, with the help of the French, he managed to restore his authority.

Once his power was restored, Cesare knew he couldn't leave his future to chance or trust in the help of either the French or any other foreign forces. He turned to cunning and strategy, hiding his true intentions so well that, with the help of Signor Pagolo, he tricked the Orsini into a false sense of security. He gave Pagolo money, clothes, and horses, and through these efforts, the Orsini were lulled into reconciliation, which led them right into Cesare's trap at Sinigaglia. After eliminating their leaders and winning over their followers, Cesare laid a strong foundation for his power. He now controlled all of Romagna and the Duchy of Urbino, and the people, seeing the prosperity he brought, came to support him. Since this is an important and instructive point, I believe it is worth noting for others to follow.

When the duke took control of the Romagna, he found the region under the governance of weak rulers who did not lead their people properly. Instead of ruling fairly, they exploited their subjects and caused more division than unity. The land was full of thieves, conflicts, and widespread violence. To restore peace and order, and to ensure that authority was respected again, the duke realized that a strong governor was necessary. He decided to appoint Messer Ramiro d'Orco, a man known for being swift and ruthless, giving him absolute power to do whatever was needed. In a short period, Ramiro managed to bring peace and unity to the region with great success. However, the duke soon realized that it was dangerous to allow someone to hold such immense power for too long. Ramiro had become unpopular due to his severity. To address this, the duke established a court of justice with an excellent judge presiding, giving each city representation in the court. Understanding that the harsh actions of the past might have caused the people to resent him, the duke wanted to show them that if any cruelty had been committed, it wasn't his fault, but rather the nature of the minister he had appointed. In order to clear his own name and win the people over, he took action. One morning, he had Ramiro arrested, executed, and left his body on display in the town square of Cesena with the chopping block and bloody knife beside him. The shock of this brutal scene left the people both satisfied and terrified, achieving the duke's goal of maintaining control while distancing himself from the harshness of Ramiro's rule.

Now, let's return to the situation as it was. The duke, feeling confident in his power, had armed himself and weakened the forces nearby that might have been a threat to his rule. He had dealt with the immediate dangers surrounding him and had strengthened his position. However, he now had to turn his attention to France. The duke understood that the king of France, having realized too late the mistakes he had made, would no longer support him. From that moment on, the duke began looking for new alliances and strategies to manage the French, who were involved in a campaign in Naples against the Spaniards, who had laid siege to Gaeta. The duke's goal was to secure himself against these powers, and he likely would have succeeded had Pope Alexander VI lived longer.

This was how the duke handled the present challenges, but he also had to think about the future. One of his biggest concerns was that the next pope might not be favorable to him and could try to take away the lands Alexander had given him. To prepare for this, the duke devised a four-part strategy. First, he aimed to eliminate the families of the lords he had overthrown, so the new pope couldn't use them as a reason to act against him. Second, he sought to win the loyalty of all the nobles of Rome, so he could use them to keep the pope in check. Third, he worked to build influence within the College of Cardinals. Fourth, he wanted to build enough power before the pope's death to withstand any challenges that might arise afterward. By the time Alexander died, the duke had already achieved three of these goals. He had eliminated many of the dispossessed lords, secured the loyalty of the Roman nobles, and had the largest faction within the College of Cardinals on his side. As for the fourth goal, gaining more power, he was on the way to achieving that as well. He had set his sights on controlling Tuscany, since he already held Perugia and Piombino, and Pisa was under his protection. With France no longer a threat, because the French had been driven out of Naples by the Spaniards, both sides needed his favor. He decided to make his move on Pisa. Soon after, both Lucca and Siena also fell in line, partly because of their hatred of the Florentines and partly out of fear. The Florentines would have had no way to stop him if he had continued his campaign, as he was in a strong position when Alexander died. The duke had built up so much power and reputation that he could have stood on his own, without relying on the fortune or forces of others, depending only on his own abilities.

But Alexander died just five years after the duke first took up arms. This left the duke with Romagna as the only fully consolidated part of his territory, while the rest was still up in the air. He found himself caught between two powerful enemy armies, and to make things worse, he was gravely ill. Even under these challenging circumstances, the duke's boldness and skill were evident. He knew exactly how to win over people or defeat them if necessary, and the foundations he had built in such a short time were so strong that, had it not been for the armies pressing against him or his illness, he likely would have overcome all his challenges. It was clear that the foundations he had laid were solid, as the people of Romagna waited for him for over a month. In Rome, even while severely weakened, he remained secure. Despite the presence of the Baglioni, Vitelli, and Orsini in Rome, they could do nothing to undermine him. Even though he couldn't ensure the election of the pope he wanted, he was strong enough to prevent the election of someone he opposed. If only he had been in better health at the time of Alexander's death, everything could have turned out differently. On the day Julius II was elected, the duke confided in me, saying that he had planned for every possible scenario following his father's death, and had prepared solutions for each one. The only thing he hadn't anticipated was that, when his father died, he himself would be on the verge of death.

In reviewing all of the duke's actions, I find no reason to criticize him. On the contrary, I believe that he provides an example worthy of imitation for anyone who gains power through the fortune and arms of others. The duke had a grand vision and vast ambitions, and he acted in the only way he could have to achieve them. It was not his fault that he was thwarted by the short life of Alexander and his own illness. For anyone who wishes to secure themselves in a new principality, to win friends, defeat enemies by force or deceit, be loved and feared by the people, respected by the soldiers, eliminate those who can harm them, change the old order to create something new, be both severe and gracious, and maintain alliances with other rulers so they only help with care and harm with reluctance, there is no better example to follow than the actions of this man.

The only mistake the duke made was in allowing Julius II to be elected as pope. This was a poor choice because, although he couldn't ensure the election of a pope favorable to him, he could have prevented the election of someone who would be hostile to him. He should have never permitted anyone he had wronged or who had a reason to fear him to ascend to the papacy. People harm others either out of fear or hatred. Those he had wronged, such as San Pietro ad Vincula, Colonna, San Giorgio, and Ascanio, had every reason to be concerned if they became pope. The exceptions were Rouen and the Spaniards, due to their connections and obligations to the duke.

Above all, the duke should have ensured that a Spaniard was elected pope, and if that wasn't possible, he should have supported Rouen instead of San Pietro ad Vincula. Anyone who thinks that new favors can make people forget old injuries is mistaken. This is where the duke went wrong, and this misstep led to his ultimate downfall.

Chapter 8
Concerning Those Who Have Obtained a Principality by Wickedness

Although a prince may rise from a private station in two different ways, neither of which can be completely attributed to fortune or to individual ability, it is clear to me that I must not remain silent on them. Even though one of these paths could be explored in greater depth when I discuss republics, these methods still deserve attention. The two ways are: first, when someone rises to power through wicked and immoral means, and second, when a private person becomes the prince of his country through the favor of his fellow citizens. In regard to the first method, I will illustrate it with two examples—one from ancient times and one from modern times—and without delving too deeply into the subject, I am confident these examples will provide sufficient insight for anyone who might find themselves compelled to follow such a path to power.

Agathocles of Sicily became King of Syracuse not only from a private station but from a particularly humble and lowly background. Born the son of a potter, Agathocles lived an infamous life through all the shifts in his fortune. Despite his many crimes and misdeeds, he combined his wicked acts with such skill, both in mind and body, that after dedicating himself to a military career, he rose steadily through the ranks. He eventually attained the position of Praetor of Syracuse. Once firmly established in that position and determined to make himself prince, Agathocles decided to seize power through force, relying on no one but himself. To this end, he formed an alliance with

Amilcar, a Carthaginian general who was already engaged in war in Sicily. One morning, Agathocles summoned the people and senate of Syracuse to what appeared to be a discussion of matters concerning the Republic. But at a prearranged signal, his soldiers killed all the senators and the wealthiest citizens of the city. Once these individuals were eliminated, Agathocles took control of the city without any civil unrest or opposition from the populace.

Although Agathocles was defeated twice by the Carthaginians and eventually besieged, he managed not only to defend the city but also, after leaving part of his forces behind to guard it, led the rest of his army to launch an offensive against Africa. In a relatively short period of time, he was able to raise the siege of Syracuse and force the Carthaginians, now reduced to a state of extreme desperation, to come to terms. As a result, Agathocles gained control of Sicily while the Carthaginians were forced to content themselves with retaining control of Africa.

Anyone who closely examines the actions and mind of Agathocles will see that very little, if anything, in his rise to power can be attributed to luck. As mentioned above, Agathocles achieved prominence not through the favor of anyone else but through his advancement in the military profession, step by step, despite countless hardships and dangers. After gaining power, he was able to maintain his rule through bold, decisive actions, regardless of the dangers involved. However, it would not be right to call Agathocles' methods true talent, as they involved the murder of fellow citizens, the betrayal of friends, and a complete lack of faith, mercy, or religious belief. These methods might bring about the acquisition of power, but they will never bring lasting glory. Still, when considering Agathocles' bravery in both entering into and extricating himself from dangerous situations, as well as his strength in enduring and overcoming hardships, it is difficult to see why he should not be ranked among the greatest military leaders. Nevertheless, his extreme cruelty, barbarous nature, and endless wickedness prevent him from being celebrated among the most excellent and admired men. What he accomplished cannot be attributed to fortune or true genius, but rather to ruthless persistence.

In more recent times, during the rule of Pope Alexander VI, Oliverotto da Fermo provides another example of this kind of rise to power. Orphaned at a young age, Oliverotto was raised by his maternal uncle, Giovanni Fogliani. In his youth, Oliverotto was sent to serve under Pagolo Vitelli, with the aim of learning the military profession and hopefully achieving distinction. After Pagolo died, Oliverotto fought under Pagolo's brother, Vitellozzo, and quickly distinguished himself due to his intelligence and physical vigor. In a short time, he became one of the foremost men in his profession. However, feeling it was beneath him to serve under others, Oliverotto resolved to seize power for himself. With the support of several citizens of Fermo, who valued the servitude of their city more than its freedom, and with the backing of the Vitelli family, he devised a plan to take control of Fermo.

Oliverotto wrote to his uncle Giovanni, expressing his desire to visit after many years away and to see his patrimony once again. He claimed that, although he had only gained honor from his time away, he wanted to show the citizens that he had not wasted his years of service. To make his return more impressive, he planned to arrive with a hundred horsemen, friends, and followers, and he asked Giovanni to arrange an honorable reception for him. Giovanni spared no effort in fulfilling his nephew's wishes. He ensured that Oliverotto was received with honor by the people of Fermo and even hosted him in his own home. After spending several days there and carefully planning his scheme, Oliverotto invited Giovanni and the leading citizens of Fermo to a grand banquet. Once the meal and festivities were finished, Oliverotto began discussing the greatness of Pope Alexander and his son Cesare and their numerous achievements. The guests engaged in this conversation, but Oliverotto soon suggested that such important matters should be discussed in private. He led them into a separate chamber, and as soon as they were seated, armed soldiers appeared from hiding and killed Giovanni and the others.

Following these murders, Oliverotto mounted his horse, rode through the streets of the city, and laid siege to the palace where the chief magistrate resided. The terrified people were forced to submit to his rule, and Oliverotto established a new government, with himself as prince. He ruthlessly killed anyone who opposed him and solidified his control with new civil and military policies. During the year he held power, he not only secured his position in Fermo but also became feared by all his neighbors. His downfall would have been as difficult as Agathocles' had he not been deceived by Cesare Borgia, who captured him, along with the Orsini and Vitelli, at Sinigaglia. One year after committing this parricide, Oliverotto was strangled, along with Vitellozzo, who had led him in both valor and wickedness.

Some might wonder how men like Agathocles and Oliverotto, despite their countless acts of treachery and cruelty, were able to live securely in their own countries, defend themselves from external enemies, and avoid being overthrown by their own citizens. Meanwhile, other rulers who employed cruelty have never been able to hold onto power, even in times of peace, let alone in the face of war. I believe the difference lies in how cruelty is used—whether it is used effectively or poorly. Cruelty can be considered well-used—if such a thing can be said—when it is executed all at once and is necessary for securing power. Once the initial harm is done, it should not be repeated unless it benefits the people. On the other hand, cruelty is poorly used when, although it may start small, it gradually increases over time instead of being reduced. Those who use cruelty well are able, with the help of God or man, to soften its impact on their subjects, as Agathocles did. But those who misuse cruelty will never be able to maintain their power.

Thus, it is important to note that when a ruler takes over a state, he must carefully consider all the harm he needs to inflict and do it all at once, so that he does not have to repeat it every day. By inflicting harm in a single stroke, the ruler can avoid unsettling the people repeatedly, and after the initial violence, he can win their loyalty through later acts of kindness and generosity. A ruler who acts otherwise, either out of fear or due to bad advice, will be forced to keep the knife in his hand constantly, never able to trust his subjects, and they will never be able to fully trust him due to the continual harm he causes. Cruel actions should be carried out all at once so that the people experience less of the pain, while acts of kindness should be distributed gradually, allowing the people to savor them over time.

Above all, a prince must live among his people in such a way that no sudden change in fortune, whether good or bad, forces him to alter his behavior. Because if he waits until times of trouble to act, it will be too late for harsh measures to succeed, and any acts of kindness will be seen as forced and insincere. In such circumstances, no one will feel obligated to support him, and his actions will fail to inspire loyalty or gratitude.

Chapter 9
Concerning A Civil Principality

Now, turning to the other case—where a leading citizen becomes the prince of his country not through wickedness or unbearable violence, but by the favor of his fellow citizens—this is what we can call a civil principality. To achieve this, neither genius nor fortune is entirely necessary, but rather a cleverness that comes from good judgment. I would say that such a principality is gained either with the help of the people or with the help of the nobles. In all cities, there are these two distinct groups, and from this division, it naturally happens that the people do not want to be ruled or oppressed by the nobles, while the nobles want to rule and oppress the people. From these conflicting desires, one of three outcomes arises in cities: a principality, self-government, or anarchy.

A principality can be created either by the people or by the nobles, depending on who has the opportunity. When the nobles see that they cannot defeat the people, they elevate one of their own to the position of prince, so that they can use his power to fulfill their ambitions. On the other hand, when the people realize they cannot resist the power of the nobles, they will raise up one of their own as a prince, so that they can be protected by his authority. However, it is more difficult for someone who gains power through the support of the nobles to maintain his rule than it is for someone who rises with the support of the people. This is because a prince backed by the nobles finds himself surrounded by many who see themselves as his equals, making it harder for him to control them. In contrast, a prince who rises with the support of the people finds himself more alone, with few or no individuals around him who are not willing to obey him.

Additionally, it is nearly impossible to satisfy the nobles through honest means without harming others, but you can satisfy the people because their desires are more reasonable than those of the nobles. The nobles want to oppress, while the people simply want to avoid being oppressed. Moreover, a prince can never fully protect himself from a hostile population, as they are too numerous, but he can defend himself against hostile nobles, as they are fewer in number. The worst a prince can expect from an angry people is that they will abandon him. However, when it comes to hostile nobles, the prince has to worry not only about their abandonment but also about their active opposition. The nobles, being more cunning and farsighted in such matters, will always act in time to save themselves and seek favor with whoever they think will win. Furthermore, a prince must always live among the people, while he can easily do without the same group of nobles, as he can elevate or demote them at will, giving and taking away authority as he pleases.

To make this point clearer, I would say that the nobles should be considered in two main ways. First, some nobles will attach themselves entirely to your fortune and follow your lead. These nobles should be honored and loved. Second, there are those who do not attach themselves to you, and they can be handled in one of two ways. Some fail to do so because of a natural lack of courage or fearfulness. These nobles can still be useful, especially those who offer good advice. You can honor them when things are going well, and during difficult times, you don't have to fear them. However, when nobles avoid aligning with you out of ambition and self-interest, it is a sign that they are thinking more about themselves than about your success. In this case, the prince must be cautious of them and treat them as potential enemies because, in times of adversity, they will likely work toward his downfall.

Thus, a prince who gains power through the favor of the people must keep them on his side, which is relatively easy because they only ask not to be oppressed. On the other hand, a prince who rises to power with the support of the nobles, despite the people's opposition, must make it his top priority to win over the people. This can be done easily if the prince takes the people under his protection. When people receive good from a prince whom they expected to harm them, they become even more loyal to him. In such cases, the people will quickly become more dedicated to the prince than if he had originally gained power through their support. A prince can win the favor of the people in many ways, but since these ways vary depending on the circumstances, it's difficult to set hard and fast rules for this. However, I will repeat that it is crucial for a prince to maintain the people's goodwill, because without it, he has no security in difficult times.

Nabis, the prince of Sparta, successfully defended his country and his rule against the combined forces of all of Greece and a victorious Roman army. He was able to overcome this peril by ensuring he had secured the loyalty of a few key individuals. This would not have been possible had the people been against him. Some might argue using the well-known saying, "He who builds on the people, builds on mud," but this is only true for private citizens who rely on the people to save them from their enemies or from government authorities. Such people often find themselves deceived, as happened to the Gracchi in Rome and to Giorgio Scali in Florence. But a prince who has established his power, who is able to command respect, who is courageous, and who does not lose his nerve in tough times will not find himself deceived by the people. It will become clear that he has built his foundations well.

These types of principalities are at risk when they transition from a civil government to an absolute one. Princes may rule either directly or through magistrates. When a prince rules through magistrates, his government is weaker and more vulnerable because it relies on the goodwill of the citizens who hold these offices. These citizens, especially in times of unrest, can easily undermine the government through conspiracy or open defiance. During such times, the prince may not be able to exercise full authority, because the people, having become accustomed to taking orders from the magistrates, may be unwilling to obey the prince in moments of confusion. In these challenging times, the prince may also find it difficult to trust anyone around him. The loyalty he sees during peaceful times, when people depend on the state, will not necessarily be present when the state needs its citizens. In quiet times, everyone agrees with the prince, they all make promises, and when death seems far away, they are all willing to die for him. However, in times of crisis, when the state requires their help, the prince often finds very few willing to act. This makes the situation even more dangerous because it can only be tested once.

Therefore, a wise prince must ensure that his citizens, in all situations, will always need both the state and him. If he can achieve this, he will always find them loyal and faithful to him.

Chapter 10

Concerning the Way in Which the Strength of All Principalities Ought to Be Measured

It's important to consider another factor when examining these types of principalities: whether a prince has enough power to rely on his own resources in times of need, or if he will always require the help of others. To make this clear, I believe that those princes can rely on their own resources who, through an abundance of men or money, can raise a sufficient army to face any enemy who attacks them. On the other hand, there are those who will always need the assistance of others because they cannot meet the enemy in open battle and must instead defend themselves by hiding behind their city walls.

We have already discussed the first scenario, but I will revisit it if necessary. In the second scenario, there is little more to say than to encourage such princes to strengthen and provision their cities well, and avoid trying to defend the countryside. Any prince who properly fortifies his town and manages the affairs of his subjects as we have already discussed and will continue to emphasize, will rarely be attacked without careful consideration by his enemies. This is because men generally avoid undertaking tasks that appear difficult, and it is clear that attacking a well-fortified city, ruled by a prince who is not hated by his people, is not an easy venture.

For example, the cities of Germany are almost entirely independent, owning little land outside their walls, and they obey the emperor only when it suits them. They do not fear the emperor or any neighboring power because they are so well fortified. Each city has proper defenses, such as deep ditches and strong walls, and they maintain enough artillery. Furthermore, they always store enough provisions—food, drink, and firewood—to last a year. Beyond this, they keep their people busy with work that benefits the city, providing the labor that strengthens their community and supports its economy. These cities also value military training, and they have many laws and regulations in place to keep everything running smoothly.

Therefore, a prince who has a strong, well-fortified city and has not made himself hated by his people will not be easily attacked. And even if someone does try to attack, they will likely be met with failure and shame. Moreover, because the affairs of the world are so unpredictable, it's nearly impossible for an army to remain in the field for a full year without facing some kind of disruption. If anyone argues that the people, upon seeing their property outside the city burned and destroyed, will not remain patient and will eventually forget their loyalty to the prince during a long siege, I would respond by saying that a brave and wise prince will be able to handle these challenges. He can assure his people that the hardships will not last long, instill fear of the enemy's cruelty when necessary, and skillfully manage any subjects who seem too bold or rebellious.

Additionally, the enemy will most likely burn and devastate the countryside immediately upon arrival, while the spirits of the people are still high and ready for defense. This means the prince should hesitate even less, because by the time the initial excitement has worn off and people's spirits have cooled, the damage will already have been done, and there will be no way to undo the harm. By then, the people are more likely to unite with their prince, feeling a stronger connection to him since their homes and belongings have been destroyed in the prince's defense. After all, it is human nature to feel tied to others not only by the benefits one receives but also by the benefits one gives.

Therefore, when all things are carefully considered, a wise prince will not find it difficult to maintain the loyalty of his citizens from the beginning of a siege to the end, as long as he remains steadfast in supporting and defending them.

Chapter 11
Concerning Ecclesiastical Principalities

Now we turn to the topic of ecclesiastical principalities. All difficulties concerning them arise before one acquires such a state because these types of principalities are gained either through skill or fortune. However, once acquired, they can be maintained without either of those qualities. These states are supported by the long-standing rules of religion, which are so powerful and influential that these principalities can be maintained regardless of how their princes behave. These princes are unique because they have states but do not need to defend them, and they have subjects they do not need to rule.

Even though their states are not guarded, they are not taken from them, and even though their subjects are not actively governed, they do not mind. Neither do the people have the desire or the ability to separate themselves from the rule of these princes. These principalities are secure and prosperous. Since they are upheld by forces beyond human understanding, I will say no more about them, as their exalted position is maintained by God, and it would be arrogant and rash to discuss them further.

However, if anyone asks how it is that the Church has gained such great temporal power, especially considering that before the time of Alexander VI, Italian rulers, including even the smallest barons and lords, paid little attention to the Church's secular power—yet now even a king of France fears it—it would not be unnecessary to revisit this in some detail.

Before Charles VIII, King of France, invaded Italy, the country was divided among several powers: the Pope, the Venetians, the King of Naples, the Duke of Milan, and the Florentines. These rulers had two main concerns: first, that no foreign power should invade Italy, and second, that none among themselves should gain more territory. Of all these powers, the Pope and the Venetians were the most concerning. It took the united efforts of the others to restrain the Venetians, such as during the defense of Ferrara. To keep the Pope's power in check, they relied on the barons of Rome, who were divided into two factions, the Orsini and the Colonnesi. These factions were constantly at odds, and with arms always in hand, they caused unrest right under the Pope's nose, which kept the papacy weak. Even when a courageous Pope, such as Sixtus IV, came to power, neither fortune nor wisdom could free him from these challenges. Another factor that contributed to the weakness of the papacy was the short tenure of each Pope. On average, a Pope ruled for about ten years, which was not enough time to weaken one faction fully. For example, even if one Pope nearly destroyed the Colonnesi, the Orsini would rise up, and the cycle of factional rivalry would continue. This is why, in Italy, the temporal power of the Pope was not highly regarded.

Then came Alexander VI, a Pope who showed, more than any other, how powerful a Pope could become when he had both money and military strength. Through his partnership with Duke Valentino (Cesare Borgia) and the involvement of the French, Alexander was able to accomplish many things, as I have already discussed regarding the actions of the duke. Although Alexander's primary goal was to increase the power of his son, the Duke, his efforts also ended up strengthening the Church. After Alexander's death and the fall of the Duke, the Church inherited all of his efforts and became much more powerful.

Pope Julius II followed Alexander and found the Church in a strong position. It had gained control of all of Romagna, the barons of Rome had been weakened, and the factions that had once caused so much disorder were nearly destroyed, thanks to Alexander's actions. In addition, Julius found a new way to raise money that had not been practiced before Alexander's time. Julius not only continued Alexander's policies but also improved upon them. His ambitions included conquering Bologna, defeating the Venetians, and driving the French out of Italy. Julius was successful in all these endeavors, and his achievements are even more commendable because he worked solely to strengthen the Church, rather than to benefit any private individual. He also kept the Orsini and Colonnesi factions under control. Although there were still some who wanted to cause trouble, Julius maintained two key advantages: first, the great power of the Church, which he used to intimidate the factions; and second, he did not allow them to have their own cardinals, who were often the cause of disorder. When these factions have their own cardinals, they rarely remain quiet because the cardinals stir up trouble both in Rome and outside of it, and the barons are forced to support them. Thus, the ambitions of these high-ranking church officials create disorder among the barons.

For these reasons, Pope Leo X inherited a powerful papacy. If his predecessors made the Church great through military strength, it is to be hoped that Leo will make it even greater and more revered through his kindness, goodness, and many other virtues.

Chapter 12

How Many Kinds of Soldiery There Are, And Concerning Mercenaries

Having now thoroughly examined the characteristics of principalities as I initially set out to do, and having delved into the reasons why some are good and others bad, as well as the strategies through which many have acquired and maintained them, it is time to discuss the broader means of offense and defense that apply to each of them.

We have already observed how vital it is for a prince to have strong foundations. Without a solid base, a prince will inevitably face downfall. The key foundations of all states, whether new, old, or composite, are good laws and strong arms. However, since good laws cannot exist where the state is poorly armed, it naturally follows that where there are strong arms, there will also be good laws. Although laws are essential, I shall leave them aside for the moment and focus primarily on the topic of arms.

The arms with which a prince defends his state can be categorized into several types: they are either his own, or they are mercenaries, auxiliaries, or a combination of these. Of these, mercenaries and auxiliaries are not only unreliable but downright dangerous. A state that is defended by these forces will never stand firm or secure. Mercenaries are disloyal, disunited, undisciplined, and often more concerned with their own gain than with the safety of the state. They might appear brave among friends, but they will prove cowardly before enemies. They have neither the fear of God nor loyalty to their fellow men. Their destruction is merely delayed, as it is only postponed until the enemy decides to strike. In peacetime, mercenaries rob you of security, and in wartime, they abandon you to the mercy of your enemies. Their only motivation is a meager stipend, which is never enough to make them willing to sacrifice their lives for you. These soldiers are happy to serve you when there is no conflict, but as soon as war breaks out, they desert or flee from the enemy. It is not difficult to prove this point, as Italy's ruin can be traced directly to her reliance on mercenary forces for many years. While these mercenaries once put on a display of bravery among themselves, they quickly revealed their cowardice when foreign invaders arrived. This is why Charles, King of France, was able to seize Italy with "chalk in hand." The person who claimed that our sins were the reason for Italy's downfall spoke the truth, but it was not the sins they believed. It was, in fact, the failures of our princes. Since these faults lay with the rulers, they are the ones who have paid the price.

I would like to further illustrate the shortcomings of mercenary forces. Mercenary captains are either capable or they are not. If they are skilled, you cannot trust them, because they will always strive to increase their own power, often by oppressing you, their employer, or acting against your will and attacking others. If the captain is not competent, then the state will fall as expected in the usual way.

One might argue that anyone, whether a mercenary or a native soldier, will behave similarly once armed. However, I would reply that when a state must rely on arms, whether it is a prince or a republic, the prince should personally lead his army. In the case of a republic, it should send its own citizens. If one commander proves unworthy, he can be recalled, and if another proves capable, the state can secure him through laws to ensure his continued loyalty. Both history and experience have shown that states relying on their own arms have thrived, whereas those relying on mercenaries have suffered greatly. It is far easier to bring a state that is armed with foreign soldiers under the control of an ambitious individual than it is to subjugate one that is armed with its own people. Rome and Sparta, for example, remained armed and free for centuries. Similarly, the Swiss today are fully armed and completely free.

Looking back at ancient times, one of the most famous examples of mercenary soldiers is the case of the Carthaginians, who were nearly destroyed by their mercenaries after their first war with the Romans, even though the Carthaginians had placed their own citizens in command. After the death of Epaminondas, the Thebans chose Philip of Macedon as their military leader, but after securing victory for them, he stripped them of their liberty.

When Duke Filippo died, the Milanese hired Francesco Sforza to fight against the Venetians. After defeating the Venetians at Caravaggio, Sforza allied himself with them and turned against his original employers, the Milanese. Likewise, his father, Sforza, had been hired by Queen Johanna of Naples, but he abandoned her, forcing her to turn to the King of Aragon for help in order to save her kingdom. If we look to the Venetians and Florentines, they were fortunate in their use of mercenaries during their early expansions, as their commanders did not seek to overthrow them and make themselves princes. But this was more due to luck than wisdom. In the case of the Florentines, many capable captains whom they might have feared were either unsuccessful, opposed by rivals, or had ambitions elsewhere. For example, Giovanni Acuto, a notable commander, did not achieve victory, so his loyalty was never put to the test. However, it is universally accepted that had he succeeded, the Florentines would have been at his mercy. Francesco Sforza always had the Bracceschi opposing him, keeping both factions in check. Francesco set his sights on Lombardy, while Braccio focused on the Church and the Kingdom of Naples.

Let us now consider more recent events. The Florentines appointed Pagolo Vitelli, a man of great wisdom and renown, as their captain. He had risen from humble beginnings to great fame. Had he taken the city of Pisa, the Florentines would have had no choice but to align themselves with him, for they would have had no way to resist him if he chose to turn against them. If they supported him, they would have had to submit entirely to his will. The Venetians, on the other hand, acted wisely and with glory as long as they relied on their own citizens to fight their wars. Both their noblemen and commoners fought with great courage during that time. However, this was before they began seeking to expand their territories on land. Once they did, they abandoned their earlier virtues and adopted the flawed practices common in Italy.

At the beginning of their land expansion, the Venetians had little territory and an outstanding reputation, so they had little to fear from their captains. However, as they grew, they began to experience the consequences of relying on mercenary forces, particularly under the leadership of Carmignuola. Although Carmignuola had been a valiant and capable commander who led them to victory against the Duke of Milan, his growing indifference to the war made them fear he would no longer deliver further victories. They found themselves unable to dismiss him, nor could they afford to continue relying on him. To avoid losing what they had already gained, they were forced to take extreme measures and have him killed. Later, they appointed other captains, such as Bartolomeo da Bergamo, Roberto da San Severino, and the Count of Pitigliano. However, under these leaders, the Venetians experienced more losses than gains, as was evident in the Battle of Vaila, where they lost in one battle what had taken them eight hundred years to acquire. This occurred because conquests achieved through mercenary forces are slow and painstaking, while losses, when they come, are sudden and catastrophic.

With these examples now bringing us to Italy, which has been governed for many years by mercenaries, I find it necessary to delve more thoroughly into their role. By gaining a deeper understanding of their rise and how they came to dominate, we can better prepare to counteract the negative influence they've had. It's crucial to grasp that Italy recently began rejecting the authority of the empire. At the same time, the Pope gained more control over temporal power, and Italy became fragmented into numerous smaller states. This fragmentation happened because many of the large cities had taken up arms against their nobles, who, with the emperor's favor, had been oppressing them. Meanwhile, the Church was helping these cities in order to extend its own influence over political matters. In other cities, citizens themselves rose to become the rulers. Because of these shifts, Italy gradually fell partly into the hands of the Church and various republics. But since the Church was made up of clergy and the republics were run by citizens unused to warfare, both turned to hiring foreign soldiers to defend themselves.

The first to bring recognition to this practice of hiring mercenaries was Alberigo da Conio, a man from Romagna. From his military school came prominent figures such as Braccio and Sforza, who, during their lifetimes, became the most powerful military leaders in Italy. After them came a long list of commanders who have directed Italy's military affairs up until now. However, despite their supposed military prowess, the outcome of their actions has been disastrous. Italy has been trampled by Charles, plundered by Louis, ravaged by Ferdinand, and humiliated by the Swiss. The main strategy these commanders followed was to undermine the importance of infantry, solely to increase their own influence. They did this because they lived off their wages and didn't own land, which meant they couldn't support large armies. A small number of infantry soldiers didn't give them enough power, so they began to rely more on cavalry, which allowed them to maintain their influence while commanding fewer troops. As a result, Italy's armies became imbalanced, with fewer than 2,000 foot soldiers in armies of 20,000.

In addition to this, they employed various strategies to avoid both exertion and danger for themselves and their men. Rather than killing in battle, they preferred to capture their enemies and then release them without demanding ransom. They avoided night attacks on towns, and in return, garrisons didn't launch surprise raids on camps during the night. Their camps were left unfortified, without ditches or defensive barriers, and they avoided engaging in campaigns during the winter months. All of these practices were part of their military guidelines and were specifically designed to minimize effort and risks, as I've previously mentioned. Through these tactics, they have ultimately weakened Italy, leading it into slavery and earning the contempt of other nations. Their avoidance of real warfare and refusal to engage in the hardships of battle have left Italy vulnerable, both militarily and politically, to foreign powers that now dominate and exploit the region without resistance.

Chapter 13

Concerning Auxiliaries, Mixed Soldiery, And One's Own

Auxiliaries, which are another type of unreliable military force, are used when a ruler enlists the troops of another sovereign to aid in his defense, much like Pope Julius II did in recent times. When Julius embarked on his campaign against Ferrara and saw that his mercenaries were not performing well, he turned to auxiliaries, negotiating with Ferdinand, King of Spain, to provide soldiers and weapons. Although these troops may be skilled and effective in their own right, they are always a disadvantage for the ruler who relies on them. If they lose, the ruler faces defeat. If they win, the ruler becomes their prisoner, bound by their success.

There are numerous examples throughout history that illustrate this point, but I would like to highlight this recent instance with Pope Julius II, as it clearly shows the risks involved. Julius, in his eagerness to capture Ferrara, placed his entire trust in foreign troops. However, fortune intervened, bringing about an unexpected outcome that saved him from the full consequences of his poor decision. His auxiliary forces were defeated at the Battle of Ravenna, but soon after, the Swiss unexpectedly rose up and drove out the conquerors. This turn of events allowed Julius to avoid becoming a prisoner, either to his enemies or to the auxiliaries he had depended on for victory.

The Florentines made a similar mistake when they, having no army of their own, called in 10,000 French soldiers to help them capture Pisa. This decision put them in greater danger than at any other time during their troubles.

Likewise, the Emperor of Constantinople, facing threats from his neighbors, brought 10,000 Turkish troops into Greece for protection. But when the war ended, these troops refused to leave, marking the beginning of Greece's long period of subjugation to foreign rule.

Thus, any ruler who does not wish to be conquered should avoid relying on auxiliary forces. These troops pose a much greater risk than mercenaries because they come as a unified force, loyal to their original sovereign, not the ruler who hires them. Mercenaries, though dangerous, are scattered and are paid by the ruler, meaning that the person in command of them does not immediately gain enough power to overthrow the ruler. In short, the greatest risk with mercenaries is that they may be cowardly, while with auxiliaries, the danger lies in their strength and potential to overpower. Therefore, a wise ruler should always avoid relying on such forces and should instead depend on his own troops. Even if defeat is a possibility, it is better to face it with one's own army, as a victory gained with another's troops is not a true victory.

I feel compelled to mention Cesare Borgia and his actions here as an illustrative example. When Cesare first entered the Romagna, he relied on auxiliaries, specifically French troops, to capture the towns of Imola and Forli. However, it wasn't long before Cesare realized these forces were unreliable, so he switched to mercenaries, hiring the Orsini and Vitelli families. Yet, after testing these forces, he found them to be treacherous, untrustworthy, and dangerous. He eventually eliminated them and shifted entirely to using his own troops. The difference between these forces and their impact on his power and reputation can be clearly seen. When Cesare relied on foreign troops, his control was shaky. When he employed mercenaries, it was still fraught with risk. But when he depended solely on his own forces, his power grew, his reputation flourished, and his position became much more secure. He was never more respected than when people saw that he commanded his own forces and did not rely on the help of others.

Although I intended to limit my examples to recent Italian events, I cannot help but mention Hiero of Syracuse, who offers another example of the wisdom of using one's own troops. As I mentioned earlier, Hiero was placed in command of the Syracusan army, but he quickly realized that mercenaries—much like the Italian condottieri of his day—were ineffective and dangerous. Recognizing that he could neither dismiss them nor safely keep them, he had them all killed. Afterward, he waged his wars with soldiers from his own people rather than foreign troops.

I also want to recall an example from the Old Testament. When David offered to fight Goliath, the Philistine giant, King Saul gave him his own armor and weapons to use. But David, after trying them on, rejected them, saying he couldn't fight with weapons he wasn't familiar with. He chose instead to face Goliath with his own sling and stones, tools he knew well. This story perfectly illustrates the danger of relying on the arms or forces of others: they are either ill-fitting or will fail you at the critical moment.

Another notable example comes from Charles VII of France, the father of Louis XI. After Charles successfully liberated France from English control through his own efforts and good fortune, he realized the importance of having a strong, self-reliant military force. He established a system of men-at-arms and infantry, which helped secure his kingdom. However, his son Louis XI made the critical mistake of disbanding the infantry and turning to Swiss mercenaries. This decision, along with other similar errors, put France in great danger. By relying too heavily on the Swiss, Louis diminished the strength and independence of his own forces. Over time, the French became so dependent on Swiss soldiers that they could no longer fight effectively without them.

As a result, the French military became a mixed force, combining national troops and mercenaries. While this was still better than relying solely on mercenaries or auxiliaries, it was far weaker than an army composed entirely of the kingdom's own soldiers. The example of France clearly shows that if Charles VII's reforms had been continued and expanded, the kingdom would have been much more secure and potentially unconquerable.

Sadly, human wisdom often fails when dealing with situations that seem promising on the surface. People fail to recognize the hidden dangers, much like how the early symptoms of a disease can go unnoticed until it's too late to treat. This is exactly what happened to the Roman Empire. Its decline began when it started relying on foreign troops, like the Goths, to defend its territories. From that point on, the empire's strength and resilience weakened, and the power that had once made Rome great began to pass into the hands of others.

In conclusion, no state can ever be truly secure without its own military forces. Any state that relies on the soldiers of others is at the mercy of fortune and lacks the strength to defend itself when challenges arise. Wise leaders have always recognized that power based on foreign support is unstable and prone to collapse. A ruler's own forces should be made up of his own subjects, citizens, or loyal followers. Mercenaries and auxiliaries should be avoided as much as possible. The path to building a strong, self-reliant military can be found by following the principles I have laid out and by reflecting on the examples of great leaders like Philip of Macedon (the father of Alexander the Great) and the many republics and princes who have successfully armed and organized themselves. To these examples, I leave my final advice.

Chapter 14

That Which Concerns a Prince on The Subject of The Art of War

A prince should focus on nothing else but war, its rules, and its discipline. This is the most important skill for someone who rules because it not only helps those born into royalty to stay in power but also allows ordinary men to rise to greatness. On the other hand, history shows that princes who become too comfortable and neglect the art of war end up losing their kingdoms. The main reason for losing a state is ignoring this skill, while the key to acquiring one is mastering it. Francesco Sforza became the Duke of Milan through his military abilities, while his sons, who avoided the hardships of war, lost their power and became commoners. Among the many dangers that come with being unarmed, the greatest is being despised. This is a humiliation that a prince should avoid at all costs, as we will see later. There is simply no balance between those who are armed and those who are not. It's unreasonable to expect an armed man to willingly obey someone who is unarmed, or for an unarmed leader to feel safe around armed servants. There will always be distrust from one side and disrespect from the other, which makes it impossible for them to work well together. As a result, a prince who doesn't understand the art of war will not only face other misfortunes but will also fail to earn the respect of his soldiers or be able to rely on them.

Therefore, a prince should never stop thinking about war, and in times of peace, he should devote even more time to practicing it than he does during war. He can do this in two main ways: through action and through study.

As for action, the prince should keep his soldiers organized and well-trained. He should also regularly go hunting, which helps his body get used to the physical demands of war. This activity also teaches him about the lay of the land, allowing him to understand how mountains rise, how valleys spread out, where plains lie, and the nature of rivers and marshes. This knowledge is valuable in two ways. First, it helps the prince defend his own country more effectively. Second, by knowing his land well, he can easily understand other territories, since the hills, valleys, rivers, and plains of one place often resemble those of another. This understanding of geography is a crucial skill for any military leader, as it enables him to plan surprise attacks, set up camps, lead troops, organize battles, and lay siege to towns in a strategic way.

Philopoemen, the leader of the Achaeans, is praised by historians for always thinking about war, even in times of peace. Whenever he was out in the countryside with his friends, he would often stop and discuss battle scenarios with them. He would ask, "If the enemy were on that hill and we were down here with our army, who would have the advantage? How should we advance to keep our troops in order? If we needed to retreat, how could we do it effectively?" He would explore every possible situation that could happen in a battle, listen to his friends' opinions, and share his own ideas, backing them up with solid reasoning. By constantly engaging in these discussions, Philopoemen made sure that no situation in war could ever catch him off guard.

In addition to physical practice, a prince should exercise his mind by studying history. He should read about the actions of great leaders from the past to see how they conducted themselves in battle, examining what led to their victories or defeats. By doing so, the prince can learn from their mistakes and follow their successful strategies. He should also find a historical figure to model himself after, much like Alexander the Great admired and imitated Achilles, or how Julius Caesar looked up to Alexander. Similarly, Scipio followed the example of Cyrus the Great, as written about by Xenophon, and he gained glory for emulating Cyrus's virtues, such as kindness, affability, humanity, and generosity.

A wise prince should follow these examples and never allow himself to become idle during peaceful times. Instead, he should work diligently to improve his resources and prepare for any challenges that may arise in the future. This way, if fortune brings adversity, the prince will be ready to face it, having already equipped himself with the necessary skills and knowledge to defend his state.

Chapter 15
Concerning Things for Which Men, And Especially Princes, Are Praised or Blamed

Now we need to consider how a prince should behave toward his subjects and friends. Although many have written on this topic, I know I may seem bold to address it again, especially since I intend to depart from the traditional views. However, my goal is to offer practical advice to those who are willing to understand it, and for this reason, I prefer to focus on the truth of the matter rather than on idealized versions of it. Many people have imagined republics and principalities that have never truly existed because the way people live is often far removed from how they should live. Anyone who tries to live up to a completely virtuous standard in such a flawed world will quickly face ruin rather than survival.

A prince, therefore, who wishes to maintain power must learn how to do wrong when necessary and know when to apply it or refrain from doing so based on the situation. Instead of imagining how a prince ought to behave, we must consider how a prince actually behaves. When people, especially princes, are discussed, they are often judged by qualities that either bring them praise or criticism. For instance, one prince might be considered generous, while another is seen as miserly. Some are viewed as bold and brave, while others appear cowardly and effeminate. Some are seen as compassionate, while others are considered cruel. One prince may be regarded as faithful and sincere, while another is known to be cunning and deceitful. These traits can go on: one may be chaste, another lascivious; one may be religious, another impious.

I understand that everyone would agree it would be praiseworthy for a prince to possess all of these good qualities. But because it is nearly impossible for a ruler to have or follow all of them, human nature being what it is, a prince must be wise enough to avoid the vices that would cause him to lose his state. He should also aim to avoid those that don't necessarily threaten his rule if he can, but when it's not possible, he should be less worried about indulging in those particular vices. In fact, a prince should not be troubled if he is criticized for certain flaws that are essential to saving his state.

Ultimately, if a prince carefully considers everything, he will see that something that appears to be virtuous may lead to his downfall, while actions that seem to be vices may actually result in his security and success. In this way, what is often viewed as a vice can sometimes be more beneficial than a perceived virtue.

Chapter 16
Concerning Liberality and Meanness

Starting with the first quality I mentioned earlier, I will say that it is indeed desirable for a prince to be known as generous. However, if generosity is practiced in a way that doesn't earn a reputation for it, it can harm more than help. If a prince is truly generous in the proper sense of the word, his efforts might not be noticed, and he could still be criticized for being the opposite. To maintain a reputation for generosity, a prince would need to spare no expense in lavish displays, leading him to exhaust his resources. In time, to maintain this image, he would be forced to burden his people with taxes or find other ways to obtain money, which would eventually make him unpopular among his subjects. As his wealth dries up, he would lose respect, and the number of people he offends would far outnumber those he rewards. The moment any crisis arises, he will be vulnerable because of his generosity, and as soon as he tries to correct his course, he risks being labeled as miserly.

Therefore, if a prince cannot be generous without harming himself, he should not fear being seen as stingy. With careful management of his resources, he can provide for his state, defend against enemies, and embark on new endeavors without burdening his people. This will earn him the respect of many because, while he is only perceived as miserly by a small number of those who expect gifts, the broader population—whom he does not tax—will appreciate his restraint. In fact, all the great achievements we've witnessed have been accomplished by those who were considered frugal, not by those who were thought of as liberal with their wealth.

Take Pope Julius II, for instance. He gained the papacy partly because he was seen as generous, but once he secured his position, he no longer needed to uphold that image. When he went to war with the King of France, he financed these wars without imposing extra taxes on his subjects, relying instead on the wealth he had saved through careful spending. Similarly, the current King of Spain has been able to undertake and succeed in many ventures because he has not been viewed as wastefully generous. Therefore, as long as a prince doesn't need to exploit his subjects, can defend his realm, avoid poverty, and stay clear of the temptation to be greedy, he should not worry too much about being labeled as miserly. In fact, it is a vice that can help him govern successfully.

Some may argue that Caesar rose to power through his generosity, and that many others have achieved great things by being liberal with their wealth. To this, I respond: it depends on whether you are already a prince or seeking to become one. If you are already a ruler, generosity can be risky, but if you are working to rise to power, then it is crucial to be seen as generous. Caesar, for instance, sought to become the most powerful figure in Rome, and his liberality helped him achieve that goal. But had he lived longer and not reined in his spending, he would have eventually destroyed his rule.

Others might point to the fact that some princes who have led great armies and accomplished major feats have been known for their generosity. However, I would clarify that a prince either spends his own wealth, his people's wealth, or someone else's. If a prince is spending his own or his subjects' wealth, he must be frugal. But if he is spending what belongs to others, especially during military campaigns where he funds his army through looting or conquest, then generosity is useful. In these cases, being liberal with the spoils of others' wealth will make the soldiers follow him. Figures like Cyrus, Caesar, and Alexander were able to be generous without harming themselves because they were using the wealth of others. Spending what isn't yours can enhance your reputation, while spending your own wealth can diminish it.

Nothing drains resources faster than generosity, because even as you practice it, you lose the ability to continue doing so. This can lead to either poverty or a loss of respect. And if you try to avoid poverty by raising funds through unfair means, you will become hated. Above all, a prince must guard against being despised or hated, and generosity can lead to both outcomes. Therefore, it is much safer to accept a reputation for frugality, which may lead to minor criticism but without hatred, than to pursue a reputation for generosity that could lead to financial ruin and, ultimately, being seen as greedy and hated.

Chapter 17

Concerning Cruelty and Clemency, And Whether It Is Better to Be Loved Than Feared

Turning now to the other qualities I have mentioned, I say that every prince should desire to be considered kind-hearted rather than cruel. However, it is crucial that he does not misuse this kindness. Cesare Borgia was viewed as cruel, yet his cruelty brought the Romagna under control, unified it, and restored it to peace and loyalty. When this is properly considered, one will see that Borgia was far more merciful than the Florentine people, who, in order to avoid being called cruel, allowed Pistoia to be destroyed. Therefore, a prince, as long as he keeps his subjects united and loyal, should not worry about being called cruel; because, through just a few decisive examples, he will be seen as more merciful than those who, by showing too much mercy, allow disorders to arise, leading to murders and robberies.

Such acts of violence harm the entire population, while executions ordered by a prince harm only a few individuals.

For a new prince in particular, it is impossible to avoid the accusation of cruelty, as new states are full of dangers. This is why Virgil, speaking through the character Dido, justifies the harshness of her rule because her reign was new, saying: "The harshness of circumstances and the newness of my reign compel me to take such measures and protect my borders with guards far and wide." However, a prince should be cautious in believing accusations and slow in acting, avoiding fear and proceeding with calmness, wisdom, and humanity. He must ensure that overconfidence does not make him reckless and that excessive distrust does not make him unbearable.

This brings us to the question: is it better to be loved than feared, or feared than loved? Ideally, a prince should be both, but since it is difficult to unite them in one person, it is much safer to be feared than loved when one must choose. For we can say this in general about men: they are ungrateful, fickle, false, cowardly, and greedy. As long as you succeed, they are entirely yours; they will offer you their blood, property, lives, and children, as I mentioned earlier, when the need is distant. But when it comes closer, they will turn against you. The prince who relies solely on their promises and neglects other precautions will be ruined. Friendships that are bought with money and not earned through respect and greatness of character may indeed be gained but are not secure, and when you need them, they will not support you. Men are less likely to offend someone they fear than someone they love, for love is maintained by a bond of obligation, which, due to men's selfishness, is broken whenever it benefits them; but fear is maintained by a dread of punishment, which never fails.

However, a prince must ensure that he inspires fear in such a way that he avoids hatred, because being feared while not hated is something he can endure. This is guaranteed as long as he abstains from seizing the property or women of his subjects. When a prince needs to act against someone's life, he must have clear justification and a proper reason, but above all, he must avoid taking away the property of others. People are quicker to forget the death of their father than the loss of their inheritance. Furthermore, reasons for taking away property are never lacking, for a prince who has started living by theft will always find reasons to seize what belongs to others. But reasons for taking life are harder to find and less frequent. When a prince is leading his army, and he has many soldiers under his control, it becomes absolutely necessary for him to ignore the reputation for cruelty. Without that reputation, he could never keep his army united or prepared for battle.

Among Hannibal's many great deeds, one that stands out is his ability to lead a massive army made up of men from different nations, waging war in foreign lands, without causing any rebellion against him. This was due to nothing other than his extreme cruelty, which, combined with his boundless courage, made him both feared and respected by his soldiers. Without this cruelty, his other virtues would not have been enough to achieve this. Some short-sighted writers admire his achievements but condemn the main reason for his success. That his other virtues alone would not have sufficed is clear when we compare him to Scipio, the most outstanding man of his time or perhaps of any time. Yet, Scipio's army rebelled against him in Spain, not because he lacked ability, but because of his excessive leniency, which allowed his soldiers more freedom than was compatible with military discipline. For this, he was reprimanded by Fabius Maximus in the Senate and labeled the corrupter of the Roman army. When Scipio's legate ravaged the Locrians, they were not avenged, nor was the legate punished, all due to Scipio's overly gentle nature. In fact, someone in the Senate, trying to defend Scipio, remarked that some men are better at avoiding mistakes than correcting the mistakes of others. Had Scipio's easy-going nature continued unchecked, it would eventually have ruined his fame and glory. But since he was under the control of the Senate, this weakness was concealed and even added to his renown.

Returning to the question of whether it is better to be feared or loved, I conclude that, because men love at their own will but fear at the will of the prince, a wise prince should build his foundation on what is within his control, and not on what depends on others. He should aim to avoid hatred, as I have explained.

Chapter 18
Concerning the Way in Which Princes Should Keep Faith

Everyone recognizes how praiseworthy it is for a prince to keep his word and live honestly, showing integrity in his actions. This is what most people expect of a ruler. However, history and experience tell a different story. The most successful princes, the ones who have accomplished the greatest feats, have not always been those who strictly kept their promises or were honest in all their dealings. Instead, they knew how to cleverly deceive others when necessary, and through this cunning, they outmaneuvered and defeated those who blindly relied on the prince's promises. This is not to say that deceit is always the first course of action, but it has often proven effective when handled correctly.

There are two main ways of engaging in conflict, as seen throughout history: one is through law, and the other is through force. The law is the proper domain of men, while force belongs to beasts. Yet, there are times when the law is insufficient, and a prince must rely on force. Therefore, a wise ruler must know how to use both methods—being able to act as both a man and a beast. This concept is illustrated in ancient stories where princes like Achilles were entrusted to the care of the Centaur Chiron, who was half man and half beast. The symbolic meaning of these tales is that a prince must learn to combine the wisdom of man with the cunning of the beast in order to rule successfully. Relying on one without the other is a sure path to failure.

In particular, when a prince is forced to adopt the ways of the beast, he should aim to be both a fox and a lion. The lion is powerful and can fend off wolves, but he is vulnerable to traps. The fox, on the other hand, is clever and can avoid traps but is defenseless against wolves. Therefore, a prince must be as shrewd as a fox to recognize traps and as strong as a lion to scare off the wolves. Those rulers who rely solely on the lion's strength are often reckless and fail to recognize dangers that could have been avoided with more subtlety.

A prince should not feel bound by his word if keeping it would harm him, especially when the reasons for making the promise no longer exist. If all men were good and trustworthy, this rule would not apply. But since people are generally untrustworthy and self-serving, a prince has no obligation to be bound by promises when others do not keep faith with him. In fact, breaking a promise when circumstances change or when keeping it would be detrimental is often necessary for survival. There will always be legitimate reasons for a prince to justify not keeping his word, and history is full of examples where rulers who were adept at deception thrived while those who naively kept their promises lost their power.

One of the most recent examples of this is Pope Alexander VI. He was known for constantly deceiving others, and he made no attempt to hide this habit. He always found people willing to believe him, and despite his endless falsehoods, his schemes succeeded time and time again. He never kept his word, yet his manipulations worked because he understood human nature very well. People are simple in many ways and often prioritize their immediate needs, which makes them easy targets for deception. Alexander was particularly skilled at taking advantage of this simplicity, and his repeated success shows just how effective a well-executed strategy of deceit can be.

Therefore, it is not necessary for a prince to actually possess all the good qualities that people expect of a ruler, but it is essential for him to appear to have them. It is often more dangerous for a prince to fully embody virtues like mercy, honesty, or faithfulness, as adhering strictly to these principles can make him vulnerable. Instead, a prince should appear to be merciful, honest, faithful, humane, and religious, and in most cases, he should act that way. However, he must also be prepared to do the opposite when the situation demands it. A successful ruler knows how to adapt to changing circumstances while maintaining the appearance of virtue. This is especially important for a new prince, who will face more challenges in consolidating his power. If a prince wants to keep his state, he must be willing to act against virtues like honesty, loyalty, and kindness when necessary, though he should return to these virtues when it is safe to do so.

A prince must never let anything escape his lips that would suggest he is not all of these things—merciful, faithful, humane, upright, and religious—because his subjects and rivals alike will judge him based on what they see and hear. Appearances are critical because most people only see the surface and do not know the true intentions of their ruler. Only a few people will know a prince's real character, but they will not dare challenge the majority's opinion, which is shaped by appearances and protected by the authority of the state. This is why it is so important for a prince to cultivate an image of virtue, even if he does not always practice it in reality.

In the actions of princes, and indeed in the actions of all men, people tend to judge by the results. If a ruler is successful in maintaining power and achieving his goals, his methods will be justified, and people will praise him for his accomplishments. The means by which he achieved success will be forgotten or excused. The common people, who make up the vast majority, are more impressed by appearances and outcomes than by the details of how those outcomes were achieved. The opinions of the few who might know the full story do not matter unless they can sway the masses, and that is rarely possible.

One modern prince, whose name I will not mention, is known for constantly preaching peace and good faith. Yet, in reality, he is an enemy to both. If he had faithfully practiced what he preached, he would have lost his kingdom and reputation many times over. This shows that maintaining appearances and adapting to the realities of power are more important for a prince than strict adherence to the ideals of honesty and integrity. A wise prince understands this and uses it to his advantage, securing his rule by any means necessary while maintaining the illusion of virtue.

Chapter 19

That One Should Avoid Being Despised and Hated

Now, regarding the other traits that I mentioned earlier, I've already gone over the most important ones. For the rest, I'll address them briefly under one general rule: a prince must be mindful of avoiding actions that would make him hated or disrespected. If he manages to avoid these, he has done his part well and doesn't need to worry much about other criticisms that might come his way.

The surest way for a prince to become hated is by being greedy, taking the property of his people, or dishonoring their women. A ruler must steer clear of these behaviors. As long as their property and honor are left untouched, most people will be content. In that case, the prince only has to deal with the ambitions of a few people, which he can handle easily in several ways.

On the other hand, a prince becomes disrespected if he's seen as inconsistent, frivolous, weak, or indecisive. These are dangerous traits for any ruler, and he should avoid them as one would avoid a deadly threat. Instead, he should demonstrate boldness, strength, seriousness, and resolve in his actions. In his personal dealings with his people, he should be firm and decisive, establishing a reputation that he is not easily fooled or taken advantage of.

A prince who shows these qualities will earn the respect of his people, and a respected prince is much harder to conspire against. If people see him as a capable and strong leader, they will be less likely to rise against him. For this reason, a ruler must focus on two main areas of concern: the potential threats from his own subjects and external threats from foreign powers. He can protect himself from foreign threats by maintaining a strong military and forming good alliances. If he is well-armed, he will have strong friends, and his internal affairs will remain calm as long as his external situation is stable. Even if external conflicts arise, a prince who has prepared himself properly and followed good practices, as described earlier, will be able to withstand any attack, just as Nabis, the Spartan, did.

When it comes to his subjects, the prince should only fear secret conspiracies when things outside his kingdom are unstable. But a ruler can protect himself from these plots by avoiding hatred and contempt and by keeping his people satisfied. As I mentioned before, this is one of the most important things a prince can do. The best defense against conspiracies is to ensure that the people do not hate or despise the ruler. After all, those who plot against a prince often believe that they will win favor with the people by removing him from power. But if they know that the people support the prince, they will lack the courage to follow through, as the risks of conspiring are enormous.

History shows that conspiracies are plentiful, but very few actually succeed. This is because a conspirator cannot act alone, and must involve others. As soon as he shares his plan with another person, he puts himself at risk. The person he confides in may turn him in to the authorities in exchange for rewards or favors, because doing so is often safer and more rewarding than following through with the plot. The risks of a conspiracy are great, and only a very determined enemy or a rare, loyal friend would go through with it.

In short, the conspirator has little to motivate him aside from fear, jealousy, or anger, while the prince has many advantages on his side. The prince has the authority of his position, the laws, loyal friends, and the support of the state. When he has the goodwill of the people on top of all this, it is almost impossible for anyone to conspire successfully against him. In general, the conspirator is most fearful before carrying out his plan, but in this case, he must also fear what will happen afterward because the people will turn against him if he succeeds. The risks are simply too high.

There are countless examples of this, but I will focus on one that happened within living memory. Messer Annibale Bentivogli, the ruler of Bologna, was murdered by the Canneschi, a group of conspirators. After his death, only his young relative, Messer Giovanni, survived. However, as soon as Annibale was killed, the people of Bologna rose up and killed all the Canneschi. This was due to the loyalty the people felt towards the Bentivogli family. Even though no one from the family was left to take over, the people of Bologna learned that another Bentivogli, who had been raised in Florence and was thought to be the son of a blacksmith, was still alive. They sent for him and put him in charge of their city until Giovanni Bentivogli grew up and could rule.

From this, we can see that a prince has little to fear from conspiracies when he is loved by the people. But if the people hate him, he must fear everyone and everything. Wise rulers and well-organized states have always worked to avoid pushing the nobles into despair and have made efforts to keep the people content and satisfied. This is one of the most crucial objectives a prince can pursue.

One of the best-governed kingdoms of our time is France, which has many institutions that safeguard the king's power and security. The most important of these is the authority of the parliament. The founder of the French kingdom recognized that the nobility was ambitious and bold, and he knew they needed to be controlled. At the same time, he understood that the people feared and disliked the nobles, so he created a system to protect the people without making it seem like the king was choosing sides. He appointed a separate body to handle these issues, which allowed him to avoid accusations of favoring either the nobles or the people. This system has provided great security for both the king and the kingdom. From this, we can conclude that princes should delegate unpopular tasks to others while keeping the more rewarding actions for themselves.

Finally, I would argue that a prince should maintain good relations with the nobility, but never in a way that causes him to lose the favor of the people.

Now, some might think that the lives and deaths of Roman emperors show examples that contradict my ideas. Many of these emperors lived nobly, showing great strength of character, yet they still lost their power or were killed by conspiracies led by their own subjects. To address these concerns, I'll look at the lives of some of these emperors and explain that their downfalls happened for the reasons I've already mentioned. I will point out the key lessons to be learned from their reigns for those who want to understand the nature of leadership during those times.

To illustrate this, let's examine all the emperors who ruled after Marcus Aurelius up to Maximinus: they include Marcus Aurelius himself, his son Commodus, Pertinax, Julian, Severus, his son Caracalla, Macrinus, Heliogabalus, Alexander, and Maximinus. The main thing to note is that, while other rulers only had to deal with the ambition of the nobles or the temper of the people, Roman emperors faced an additional challenge: the cruelty and greed of their soldiers. This problem proved to be a stumbling block for many emperors, as it was difficult to satisfy both the soldiers and the people. The people preferred peaceful rulers who did not seek conflict, while the soldiers favored those who were warlike, cruel, and greedy, as these qualities allowed them to receive higher pay and plunder the people. As a result, emperors who lacked strong authority were frequently overthrown, especially those who were new to the throne. These rulers often found it easier to cater to the soldiers, even if it meant hurting the people, because they believed it was more dangerous to be hated by the soldiers than by the people. However, whether this approach succeeded or failed depended on the emperor's ability to maintain control over the soldiers.

Marcus Aurelius, Pertinax, and Alexander were all known for their modest lifestyles, love of justice, and opposition to cruelty. While Marcus Aurelius managed to live and die with honor, the other two did not fare so well. Marcus Aurelius succeeded because he inherited the throne and had the respect of both the soldiers and the people due to his many virtues. He kept both groups in check and was neither hated nor despised during his reign. However, Pertinax was made emperor against the wishes of the soldiers, who were used to the indulgent rule of Commodus and did not want to be reined in by Pertinax's strict policies. The soldiers hated him for trying to restore discipline, and, adding contempt for his old age to this hatred, they quickly overthrew him at the start of his rule.

This leads to an important lesson: a ruler can become hated not only through bad actions but also through good ones. As I mentioned earlier, a prince who wants to hold on to power is often forced to do things that may seem bad. When those who help maintain the prince's rule—whether it's the people, the soldiers, or the nobles—are corrupt, the ruler must give in to their desires. In such cases, doing what is morally right can actually be harmful.

Now, let's consider Alexander, a man of such great kindness that one of the highest praises he received was that, during the fourteen years of his reign, he never executed anyone without a fair trial. However, this very kindness led to his downfall. He was seen as weak and overly influenced by his mother, which caused him to lose the respect of the army. Eventually, the soldiers conspired against him and killed him.

On the other hand, if we look at emperors like Commodus, Severus, Caracalla, and Maximinus, we find men who were cruel and greedy. They did not hesitate to harm the people in order to please the soldiers. With the exception of Severus, all of these emperors met a bad end. Severus, however, was able to maintain power because of his remarkable strength and courage. Even though the people suffered under him, his military prowess earned him the admiration of both the soldiers and the people. The people were in awe of him, while the soldiers were kept happy. Severus serves as a prime example of how a ruler must imitate both the fox and the lion, as I discussed earlier.

Severus was cunning enough to manipulate the army into believing that they should avenge the death of Pertinax, who had been killed by the praetorian soldiers. Under this pretense, Severus led the army to Rome, claiming not to seek the throne. However, upon his arrival, the Senate, out of fear, named him emperor and executed Julian, who had been ruling at the time. After this, Severus faced two main challenges: one in Asia, where Niger had proclaimed himself emperor, and another in the West, where Albinus also sought the throne. Severus decided to deceive Albinus, pretending to share power with him by sending him the title of Caesar. Meanwhile, he focused on defeating Niger. Once he had conquered Niger and settled affairs in the East, Severus returned to Rome and accused Albinus of treachery. He eventually pursued Albinus to France, where he defeated him and seized control.

Severus exemplified both the strength of a lion and the cunning of a fox. He was feared and respected by all, yet he managed to avoid the hatred of the army. His success as a new ruler was due to his extraordinary reputation, which shielded him from any resentment the people might have felt toward his harsh rule.

Severus's son, Antoninus (Caracalla), was similarly admired for his military skills and his ability to endure hardship, which made him beloved by the soldiers. However, his extreme cruelty alienated both the people and those around him. After many acts of violence, including the slaughter of countless citizens in Rome and Alexandria, he became hated by all. Eventually, he was killed by a centurion within his own army. This demonstrates a key point: deliberate and desperate assassinations like this one are nearly impossible for a ruler to prevent, especially when carried out by someone with nothing to lose. However, such occurrences are rare, and a prince can reduce the risk by avoiding serious harm to those close to him, particularly those in his service. Antoninus failed in this regard, having previously killed the centurion's brother and threatened the centurion himself, yet he foolishly kept him in his bodyguard—leading to his own downfall.

Lastly, let's turn to Commodus, who could have easily maintained power by following in the footsteps of his father, Marcus Aurelius. However, Commodus was naturally cruel and corrupt. He focused on pleasing the soldiers and indulging their worst tendencies while exploiting the people. He undermined his own dignity by participating in gladiator fights and other demeaning activities, actions unworthy of the emperor's position. As a result, he lost the respect of the soldiers and the people, and ultimately, he was killed in a conspiracy.

Let's now talk about Maximinus. He was a very warlike man, and after the soldiers grew tired of the soft nature of Alexander, whom we've already mentioned, they killed him and made Maximinus the emperor. However, he didn't hold onto power for long, as two things made him both hated and despised. First, everyone knew he had once been a shepherd in Thrace, which people saw as humiliating. Second, after gaining control of the empire, he delayed his journey to Rome to officially take his seat, which made people view him with suspicion. On top of that, he was known for extreme cruelty, which he enforced through his officials both in Rome and other parts of the empire. This led to widespread anger because of his low birth and his brutal behavior. As a result, Africa was the first region to rebel, followed by the Senate, the people of Rome, and eventually all of Italy. His own army even turned against him when they encountered difficulties besieging the city of Aquileia. Disgusted by his cruelty and seeing that many others were against him, they ultimately killed him.

I won't go into detail about Heliogabalus, Macrinus, or Julian, as they were quickly eliminated due to their complete lack of worthiness, but I will conclude by saying that in modern times, princes don't face the same issue of needing to excessively satisfy their soldiers. Though princes still have to indulge them to some degree, this is a much smaller issue than it was in the past. Nowadays, no prince commands armies like those of the Roman Empire, which were seasoned and held great power over provinces. Back then, it was often more important to keep the soldiers happy than the people. Today, however, for almost all rulers—except for the Turkish sultan and the Egyptian sultan—it is more crucial to win over the people than the soldiers, as the people hold more influence.

The reason I exclude the Turkish sultan is that he keeps around him a permanent force of 12,000 infantry and 15,000 cavalry, and his kingdom's safety and strength depend on them. Therefore, he must focus on keeping these soldiers loyal to him, not worrying much about the general population. The same is true for the Egyptian sultan, whose power also depends entirely on his soldiers. In both of these cases, the rulers don't need to worry about pleasing the people; their soldiers are the key to maintaining their rule. But you should note that the structure of the Egyptian sultanate is different from other types of principalities because it resembles the system of the Christian papacy. It isn't exactly hereditary, nor is it a newly established principality. The sons of the previous ruler do not inherit the throne, as someone is elected to that position by those who have authority. The sons of former rulers remain nobles but don't become rulers themselves. Since this is an ancient custom, it doesn't bring the challenges that come with new principalities. Even though the prince is new, the state's framework is old, and it's designed to receive a new leader as if he had always been the rightful heir.

Returning to the subject at hand, anyone who thinks about it will see that the downfall of the emperors I've mentioned was caused either by hatred or contempt. You will also notice that, although some emperors acted one way and others acted differently, only one in each group managed to have a good outcome, while the rest met unfortunate ends. For example, it would have been a mistake for new rulers like Pertinax or Alexander to imitate Marcus Aurelius, who inherited his position. At the same time, it would have been disastrous for rulers like Caracalla, Commodus, or Maximinus to imitate Severus, as they lacked the strength and skills needed to follow in his footsteps. Therefore, a prince who is new to power should not try to copy Marcus Aurelius, but he doesn't need to imitate Severus entirely either. Instead, he should adopt the parts of Severus's approach that will help him establish his rule, while also taking from Marcus the qualities that help maintain a stable and secure state.

Chapter 20
Are Fortresses, And Many Other Things to Which Princes Often Resort, Advantageous or Hurtful?

Some princes, in order to securely hold their states, have disarmed their subjects, while others have kept their subject cities divided by encouraging factions. Some have nurtured enemies against themselves, while others have worked to win over those they distrusted at the beginning of their rule. Some princes have built fortresses, while others have torn them down. Although it's difficult to make a final judgment on all of these strategies without knowing the specifics of the states involved, I will address the topic as broadly as possible.

No new prince has ever disarmed his subjects. In fact, when new princes find their subjects unarmed, they arm them instead. By doing this, they make those arms their own, turning the people who were once untrusted into loyal followers. Those who were already loyal will remain so, and all of the prince's subjects will feel tied to him. Even though not all of the prince's subjects can be armed, those who are given arms will feel privileged. As a result, those who aren't armed won't resent the prince because they'll understand why others deserve to be trusted with weapons. However, when a prince disarms his subjects, he immediately offends them because it shows he doesn't trust them. This either suggests he believes them to be cowards or disloyal, and both interpretations create hatred. Since a prince can't remain without an armed force, he then has to rely on mercenaries. But as I've already shown, mercenaries are unreliable, and even if they were skilled, they wouldn't be enough to protect a prince from powerful enemies and dissatisfied subjects. Thus, a new prince in a new state should always give arms to his people. History is full of examples supporting this point. On the other hand, when a prince acquires a new territory, which becomes an addition to his existing state, he should disarm the people of that new land, except for those who helped him take control. Over time, even those allies should be softened and made less dangerous, and the prince should make sure that the only soldiers in the state are those from his original territory, who live close to him.

Our ancestors, who were considered wise, believed it was necessary to control cities like Pistoia by encouraging internal divisions, while maintaining control over Pisa through fortresses. They fostered divisions in their tributary cities to make it easier to manage them. This strategy may have worked in their time, when Italy's power structure was more balanced, but I don't think it applies today. Factions and divisions are never helpful. In fact, when a city is divided and an enemy attacks, the weaker faction will often side with the invader, making it easier for the enemy to take control. Meanwhile, the stronger faction won't be able to resist on its own. The Venetians, for instance, allowed the Guelph and Ghibelline factions to exist in their subject cities. They kept these factions from causing bloodshed but let their disputes continue, thinking this would keep the cities from uniting against them. However, this tactic backfired after their defeat at the Battle of Vaila, when one faction seized control of the state. This shows that encouraging factions indicates a prince's weakness. Divisions might help in times of peace, but in war, they are disastrous.

Princes, especially new ones, gain greatness when they overcome challenges and obstacles. Fortune often raises enemies against a new prince so that he has the chance to defeat them and strengthen his reputation. Many believe that a wise prince, when given the chance, should intentionally create animosity against himself, so that by overcoming it, his renown will grow even more.

New princes have often found that those they initially distrusted end up being more loyal and helpful than those they trusted from the start. For example, Pandolfo Petrucci, who ruled Siena, relied more on those he had distrusted than on others to maintain control of his state. However, this doesn't apply universally and varies depending on the circumstances. I'll only say that when a prince wins over those who were originally his enemies, they are often the ones who serve him most faithfully. They know they need to prove their loyalty and erase the bad impression they once gave. These individuals are usually more reliable than those who serve the prince with too much confidence and may become complacent. A prince who gains power through secret favors must be cautious. If the people who helped him rise did so because they were unhappy with the previous government, rather than out of genuine loyalty to him, it will be difficult to keep them on his side. If we look at examples from both ancient and modern history, we'll find that it's often easier for a prince to win over people who were content with the old government but initially opposed him, rather than those who were dissatisfied and helped him seize power.

Many princes have built fortresses to secure their rule. These fortresses can serve as protection from potential uprisings and as safe retreats in times of attack. I praise this strategy because it has been used effectively in the past. However, in modern times, we've seen princes destroy fortresses to maintain control. For example, Niccolò Vitelli demolished two fortresses in Città di Castello to keep his hold on power. Similarly, when Duke Guido Ubaldo reclaimed Urbino from Cesare Borgia, he destroyed all the fortresses in the province to reduce the threat of rebellion. The Bentivoglio family made the same decision when they returned to Bologna. Fortresses can be either useful or harmful, depending on the situation. If they help in one way, they may hurt in another. Here's how we can think about it: A prince who fears his people more than foreign enemies should build fortresses. However, a prince who fears foreign enemies more than his own people should avoid building them. For instance, the castle built by Francesco Sforza in Milan has caused more problems for his descendants than any other issue in the state. Ultimately, the best fortress a prince can have is the support of his people. Even if a prince has many fortresses, they won't protect him if his people hate him. There will always be foreign forces willing to help a population that rises up against its ruler. In modern times, fortresses have rarely been useful to any prince, except perhaps to the Countess of Forlì when her husband was killed. Fortresses helped her hold off a popular attack and wait for help from Milan, allowing her to regain control of her state. However, when Cesare Borgia attacked her, and the people sided with him, the fortresses were of little use. It would have been safer for her not to be hated by her people, rather than rely on fortresses for protection.

All things considered, I can praise both the decision to build fortresses and the decision not to. However, I criticize any prince who believes fortresses can save him while ignoring the hatred of his people.

Chapter 21

How A Prince Should Conduct Himself so as To Gain Renown

Nothing earns a prince more respect than taking on great projects and setting a good example. A good example of this in our time is Ferdinand of Aragon, the current King of Spain. He can almost be considered a new prince because, through his fame and achievements, he went from being a minor king to becoming the most powerful king in all of Christendom. If you look at his actions, you'll find that they've all been significant, and some have been extraordinary. Early in his reign, he set his sights on conquering Granada, and this goal became the foundation of his power. He carried it out quietly at first, without fear of interference, because he kept the barons of Castile focused on the war, preventing them from noticing any changes he was making. As a result, they didn't realize that, through these efforts, he was gaining more power and authority over them. He funded his armies with money from the Church and the people, and through that long war, he built the military skill that would later define him.

Additionally, Ferdinand always used religion as an excuse to take on bigger projects. For example, he ruthlessly expelled the Moors from his kingdom, claiming it was for a religious cause. This was an admirable and rare example of using piety to justify cruelty. Using this same religious excuse, he then launched campaigns in Africa, moved into Italy, and eventually set his sights on France. His achievements and goals have always been significant, keeping the people in awe and focused on what he would do next. His actions followed one after the other in such a way that no one ever had time to oppose him.

It's also important for a prince to set remarkable examples in domestic affairs, just like Messer Bernabo da Milano did. Whenever someone did something extraordinary—whether good or bad—he would make sure to reward or punish them in a way that got people talking. A prince should always try to earn a reputation as a great and remarkable man through his actions.

A prince also gains respect when he either openly supports or opposes something. In other words, he should make it clear whether he is a true ally or a firm enemy. It's always better to take a side than to remain neutral because this will ultimately work out better. If two of your powerful neighbors start fighting, you'll need to either fear the winner or not, depending on the situation. In either case, it's always better to declare where you stand and fight hard. If you stay neutral, the winner will likely see you as an enemy, and the loser won't trust you because you didn't help. The victorious side doesn't want uncertain allies who won't help in times of need, and the losing side won't trust someone who didn't share in their struggle.

Antiochus, for instance, went to Greece at the request of the Aetolians to fight the Romans. He sent ambassadors to the Achaeans, who were Roman allies, asking them to stay neutral. The Romans, on the other hand, urged the Achaeans to join the fight. In the Achaean council, Antiochus's representative argued for neutrality. In response, the Roman representative said, "It's a mistake to think that neutrality is better for your state, because if you stay out of the fight, you'll end up as the spoils of the victor." This proves that when someone isn't your friend, they will often ask you to stay neutral, while your true allies will urge you to take a stand.

Indecisive princes tend to follow the path of neutrality to avoid immediate danger, but this often leads to their downfall. However, when a prince boldly declares support for one side, if that side wins, the victor may have the power to harm the prince but will still feel a sense of obligation and gratitude. People are rarely so ungrateful that they will turn on someone who helped them. Victory isn't always so complete that the winner can afford to ignore the need for justice. If the prince's ally loses, they may still protect him as much as they can, and together, they can wait for a chance to rise again.

In the second situation, when the outcome of the conflict doesn't concern the prince because either side winning isn't a threat, it's even wiser to pick a side. In this case, the prince will be helping one side defeat the other, which would have saved the defeated side if they had been more careful. By ensuring one side's victory, the prince can gain control over them. However, a prince should be careful not to ally with someone more powerful than himself when attacking others unless it's absolutely necessary, as I've mentioned before. If that more powerful ally wins, the prince will be at their mercy. Princes should avoid being at someone else's mercy whenever possible.

The Venetians made this mistake when they allied with France against the Duke of Milan, and this alliance led to their downfall. But when it's impossible to avoid choosing a side, as was the case when the Pope and Spain sent armies to attack Lombardy, a prince should support one of the parties for the reasons I've given.

No government can choose a perfectly safe path. Instead, they should expect to face risky decisions. In general, you can't avoid one problem without running into another, so wisdom lies in being able to choose the lesser evil.

A prince should also present himself as a supporter of talent and honor those who excel in any field. He should encourage his citizens to practice their trades without fear, whether they are involved in business, farming, or anything else. No one should be afraid to improve their property out of fear that it will be taken from them, and no one should hesitate to expand their trade out of fear of taxes. Instead, the prince should offer rewards to those who benefit the state in any way and bring honor to their city.

Furthermore, a prince should entertain the people with festivals and public spectacles at the right times of the year. Every city is usually divided into guilds or societies, and the prince should hold these groups in high regard. He should also associate with them from time to time and show them courtesy and generosity. However, he must always maintain the dignity of his position and never lower himself in any way that could undermine his authority.

In this way, a prince can gain the respect of his people while still maintaining his power and majesty.

Chapter 22

Concerning the Secretaries of Princes

Choosing good servants is very important for a prince, and whether they are good or bad depends on the prince's judgment. The first impression people have of a prince and his intelligence comes from looking at the people he surrounds himself with. If his servants are capable and loyal, the prince will always be considered wise because he knew how to pick the right people and keep them loyal. But if the servants are bad, people will have a poor opinion of the prince because his first mistake was choosing them in the first place.

Anyone who knew Messer Antonio da Venafro, the servant of Pandolfo Petrucci, the Prince of Siena, would think Pandolfo was very smart for having Venafro as his servant. This is because there are three types of minds: one that understands things on its own, one that can appreciate what others understand, and one that cannot understand anything, either by itself or from others. The first is the best, the second is good, and the third is useless. So, even if Pandolfo wasn't in the first category, he was at least in the second, because he had the ability to recognize what was good or bad when he saw or heard it. Even if he didn't come up with ideas himself, he could still see what was good or bad in his servant, praising the good and correcting the bad. This way, his servant could not deceive him and was kept honest.

There is one reliable way for a prince to judge his servant: when you see the servant caring more about his own interests than the prince's and always looking to benefit himself, that man will never be a good servant, and the prince will never be able to trust him. A servant who manages someone else's affairs should never think of himself but always of his prince, and should never focus on things that don't concern the prince.

On the other hand, to keep his servant honest, a prince should treat him well—honor him, make him wealthy, show him kindness, and share both honors and responsibilities with him. At the same time, the prince should make sure that the servant knows he cannot stand on his own. The servant shouldn't desire more honors or wealth than he already has, and the many responsibilities should make him careful about taking risks. When both the servant and the prince are like this towards each other, they can trust one another. But when things are different, it will always end badly for one or both of them.

Chapter 23
How Flatterers Should Be Avoided

I don't want to overlook an important part of this subject, which is a serious risk for princes unless they are very careful and thoughtful. This is the danger of flatterers, who are everywhere in royal courts. People tend to be pleased with themselves and are often misled by their own affairs, making it hard to avoid falling for flattery. If a prince tries to defend himself against it, he risks being seen as contemptuous. The only way to protect oneself from flatterers is by making it clear that telling the truth does not offend you. However, if everyone feels free to speak the truth, it can lead to a loss of respect.

Therefore, a wise prince should take a middle path. He should select wise men from his state and give them permission to speak the truth to him, but only about the matters he asks them about, and nothing else. He should question them about everything, listen to their opinions, and then make his own decisions. He should behave in such a way that each adviser knows the more openly they speak, the more he will value them. But beyond these trusted advisers, the prince should not listen to anyone else. Once a decision is made, he should stick to it firmly. A prince who does not do this is either manipulated by flatterers or swayed by too many differing opinions, causing him to lose respect.

I would like to bring up a modern example to illustrate this. Fra Luca, who worked for Emperor Maximilian, said that the emperor consulted no one but never got what he wanted. This happened because Maximilian did the opposite of what I recommend. He was secretive and didn't share his plans with anyone or ask for advice. However, as his plans unfolded and became known, those around him obstructed them. Because Maximilian was easily swayed, he abandoned his plans. As a result, he would undo today what he had done yesterday, leaving everyone confused about his intentions and making it impossible for anyone to trust his decisions.

A prince should always seek counsel, but only when he wants it, not when others want to give it. He should discourage unsolicited advice, but when he does ask for it, he should be a careful and patient listener. If he finds out that someone has lied to him, he should let his anger be known.

Some people think that a prince only seems wise because of the good advisers around him, but that's a mistake. There's a rule that always holds true: a prince who isn't wise on his own will never be able to take good advice. The only exception is if the prince hands over all his decisions to a single, very smart person, in which case things might go well for a while. But even then, it wouldn't last long, because eventually that adviser would take control of the state for himself.

On the other hand, if a prince who lacks experience tries to get advice from several people, he will end up with conflicting opinions and won't know how to manage them. Every adviser will look out for their own interests, and the prince won't be able to understand or manage them properly. People will always be unfaithful unless they are kept honest by force. Therefore, it should be concluded that good advice comes from the wisdom of the prince, not the other way around—the prince's wisdom doesn't come from good advice.

Chapter 24
Why the Princes of Italy
Have Lost Their States

The previous advice, when followed carefully, will allow a new prince to quickly establish himself and become more secure and stable in his position than even a ruler who has been on the throne for a long time. The actions of a new prince are scrutinized more closely than those of a hereditary one, and if they are seen to be competent, they will attract more followers and gain stronger loyalty than old family ties ever could. People are drawn to what is happening now rather than what happened in the past. When they find that the present ruler is doing well, they are satisfied and look no further. If the prince continues to meet their expectations in other areas, they will defend him fiercely. Thus, a new prince can earn double the glory by founding a principality and strengthening it with good laws, a strong military, reliable allies, and by setting a good example. On the other hand, it would be a double disgrace for a prince born into power to lose his state because of a lack of wisdom.

If we examine the rulers who have lost their states in Italy in recent times, such as the King of Naples, the Duke of Milan, and others, we will find that they all had one main weakness in terms of military power, which has been discussed in detail earlier. Additionally, some of these rulers had alienated their people, while others, who may have had the support of the people, failed to secure the loyalty of the nobles. Without these weaknesses, states that have enough strength to maintain an army would not be lost.

Take Philip of Macedon, not the father of Alexander the Great, but the one who was defeated by Titus Quintius. Although Philip did not control much territory compared to the vast power of the Romans and the Greeks who attacked him, he was a skilled warrior who knew how to win over the people and secure the loyalty of the nobles. Because of this, he was able to sustain the war against his enemies for many years. While he eventually lost control of some cities, he still managed to keep his kingdom.

Therefore, our modern-day princes should not blame fortune for the loss of their principalities after having ruled for many years. Instead, they should blame their own laziness, for in peaceful times they never considered that a change might come. It is a common flaw in human nature to fail to prepare for difficulties during calm times. When trouble finally arrived, instead of defending themselves, they thought of fleeing and hoped that the people, tired of the arrogance of the conquerors, would call them back. This strategy might work when all else has failed, but it is a poor choice to neglect every other option in favor of it. No ruler should put themselves in a position where they fall and have to hope that someone will come along later to restore them to power. That kind of rescue is neither secure nor reliable. Only those actions that depend on your own strength and courage will be trustworthy, certain, and lasting.

Chapter 25

What Fortune Can Effect in Human Affairs and How to Withstand Her

I know that many people have believed, and still believe, that the events of the world are so governed by fortune and by divine will that human wisdom cannot direct them, and that no one can help them. As a result, they argue that it is unnecessary to work hard in managing affairs and instead leave everything to chance. This belief has gained more support in recent times due to the unpredictable changes we witness every day, beyond any human foresight. Sometimes, after reflecting on this, I find myself somewhat inclined to agree with this view. However, without disregarding free will, I hold that fortune controls about half of our actions, but the other half, or perhaps a little less, is left to us to direct.

I liken fortune to a river that floods and overflows, sweeping away everything in its path—trees, buildings, and even the earth itself. Its force is so overwhelming that no one can stand against it. Yet, despite its destructive nature, this does not mean that people cannot take precautions when the weather is calm, building defenses and barriers so that, when the river rises again, its waters can be channeled safely and its force reduced. In the same way, fortune shows its power where people have not prepared to resist it, and it strikes hardest where there are no barriers or defenses to restrain it.

If you consider Italy, the epicenter of so many changes, you will see that it is an open country, lacking any true defenses. Had Italy been properly fortified and defended, like Germany, Spain, or France, the great changes that have swept through it might not have occurred or would have been less severe. This is enough to say about resisting fortune in general.

Now, narrowing the focus, we often see a prince who is successful today and ruined tomorrow without having changed his character or behavior. This, I believe, happens for reasons already discussed: a prince who relies entirely on fortune will fall when fortune changes. I also believe that a prince will succeed if his actions align with the spirit of the times, while he will fail if his actions do not. People pursue glory and wealth through different methods—some with caution, others with speed; some through strength, others through cunning; some with patience, others with urgency. Each approach can lead to success. For example, two cautious men may pursue the same goal, with one succeeding and the other failing; similarly, two men using opposite methods, one cautious and the other reckless, might both succeed. This all depends on whether their actions fit the times.

The rise and fall of rulers often result from this principle. A cautious and patient prince may thrive when circumstances suit his careful approach, but if the times change and he fails to adapt, he will be ruined. Most people cannot adapt easily, either because their nature inclines them toward a particular way of acting, or because they have always succeeded by following one method and cannot be convinced to change it. Thus, when a cautious man needs to become bold, he may not know how, and as a result, he will fail. But if he had adjusted his behavior to the times, fortune would not have abandoned him.

Pope Julius II was always impetuous in his actions, and circumstances favored this approach, so he succeeded in all his ventures. Consider his first campaign against Bologna when Messer Giovanni Bentivogli was still alive. The Venetians and the King of Spain opposed his plans, and he was still negotiating with the King of France. Despite this, Julius acted boldly, leading the campaign himself, which caused the Venetians to hesitate and the Spanish to remain passive, with the latter focused on reclaiming Naples. Even the King of France, recognizing Julius's resolve, could not refuse him because he wanted the Pope as an ally to weaken the Venetians. Julius's impetuousness achieved what no other pope could have accomplished through cautious planning. Had he waited in Rome to organize everything carefully, the French king would have found many excuses, and others would have raised many objections.

All of Julius's actions followed this same pattern, and they were all successful because he was fortunate to die before facing any contrary circumstances. Had times arisen that required a more cautious approach, Julius would likely have met with failure because he could never have changed his nature.

In conclusion, fortune is ever-changing, while human beings tend to remain fixed in their habits. As long as a person's actions are in harmony with the times, they will succeed; but when times change, and they do not, failure follows. I believe it is better to be bold than cautious because fortune, like a woman, must be controlled with force and audacity. Fortune is more likely to be commanded by those who act boldly and decisively than by those who proceed with caution. Like a woman, fortune favors the young, who are less cautious, more daring, and more aggressive in their pursuit of her.

Chapter 26

An Exhortation to Liberate Italy from The Barbarians

Having carefully considered the subject of the above discourses, and wondering within myself whether the present times were propitious to a new prince, and whether there were elements that would give an opportunity to a wise and virtuous one to introduce a new order of things which would do honour to him and good to the people of this country, it appears to me that so many things concur to favour a new prince that I never knew a time more fit than the present.

And if, as I said, it was necessary that the people of Israel should be captive so as to make manifest the ability of Moses; that the Persians should be oppressed by the Medes so as to discover the greatness of the soul of Cyrus; and that the Athenians should be dispersed to illustrate the capabilities of Theseus: then at the present time, in order to discover the virtue of an Italian spirit, it was necessary that Italy should be reduced to the extremity that she is now in, that she should be more enslaved than the Hebrews, more oppressed than the Persians, more scattered than the Athenians; without head, without order, beaten, despoiled, torn, overrun; and to have endured every kind of desolation.

Although lately some spark may have been shown by one, which made us think he was ordained by God for our redemption, nevertheless it was afterwards seen, in the height of his career, that fortune rejected him; so that Italy, left as without life, waits for him who shall yet heal her wounds and put an end to the ravaging and plundering of Lombardy, to the swindling and taxing of the kingdom and of Tuscany, and cleanse those sores that for long have festered. It is seen how she entreats God to send someone who shall deliver her from these wrongs and barbarous insolencies. It is seen also that she is ready and willing to follow a banner if only someone will raise it.

Nor is there to be seen at present one in whom she can place more hope than in your illustrious house,[1] with its valour and fortune, favoured by God and by the Church of which it is now the chief, and which could be made the head of this redemption. This will not be difficult if you will recall to yourself the actions and lives of the men I have named. And although they were great and wonderful men, yet they were men, and each one of them had no more opportunity than the present offers, for their enterprises were neither more just nor easier than this, nor was God more their friend than He is yours.

[1] Giuliano de Medici. He had just been created a cardinal by Leo X. In 1523 Giuliano was elected Pope, and took the title of Clement VII.

With us there is great justice, because that war is just which is necessary, and arms are hallowed when there is no other hope but in them. Here there is the greatest willingness, and where the willingness is great the difficulties cannot be great if you will only follow those men to whom I have directed your attention. Further than this, how extraordinarily the ways of God have been manifested beyond example: the sea is divided, a cloud has led the way, the rock has poured forth water, it has rained manna, everything has contributed to your greatness; you ought to do the rest. God is not willing to do everything, and thus take away our free will and that share of glory which belongs to us.

And it is not to be wondered at if none of the above-named Italians have been able to accomplish all that is expected from your illustrious house; and if in so many revolutions in Italy, and in so many campaigns, it has always appeared as if military virtue were exhausted, this has happened because the old order of things was not good, and none of us have known how to find a new one. And nothing honours a man more than to establish new laws and new ordinances when he himself was newly risen. Such things when they are well founded and dignified will make him revered and admired, and in Italy there are not wanting opportunities to bring such into use in every form.

Here there is great valour in the limbs whilst it fails in the head. Look attentively at the duels and the hand-to-hand combats, how superior the Italians are in strength, dexterity, and subtlety. But when it comes to armies they do not bear comparison, and this springs entirely from the insufficiency of the leaders, since those who are capable are not obedient, and each one seems to himself to know, there having never been any one so distinguished above the rest, either by valour or fortune, that others would yield to him. Hence it is that for so long a time, and during so much fighting in the past twenty years, whenever there has been an army wholly Italian, it has always given a poor account of itself; the first witness to this is Il Taro, afterwards Allesandria, Capua, Genoa, Vaila, Bologna, Mestri.[2]

[2] The battles of Il Taro, 1495; Alessandria, 1499; Capua, 1501; Genoa, 1507; Vaila, 1509; Bologna, 1511; Mestri, 1513.

If, therefore, your illustrious house wishes to follow these remarkable men who have redeemed their country, it is necessary before all things, as a true foundation for every enterprise, to be provided with your own forces, because there can be no more faithful, truer, or better soldiers. And although singly they are good, altogether they will be much better when they find themselves commanded by their prince, honoured by him, and maintained at his expense. Therefore it is necessary to be prepared with such arms, so that you can be defended against foreigners by Italian valour.

And although Swiss and Spanish infantry may be considered very formidable, nevertheless there is a defect in both, by reason of which a third order would not only be able to oppose them, but might be relied upon to overthrow them. For the Spaniards cannot resist cavalry, and the Switzers are afraid of infantry whenever they encounter them in close combat. Owing to this, as has been and may again be seen, the Spaniards are unable to resist French cavalry, and the Switzers are overthrown by Spanish infantry. And although a complete proof of this latter cannot be shown, nevertheless there was some evidence of it at the battle of Ravenna, when the Spanish infantry were confronted by German battalions, who follow the same tactics as the Swiss; when the Spaniards, by agility of body and with the aid of their shields, got in under the pikes of the Germans and stood out of danger, able to attack, while the Germans stood helpless, and, if the cavalry had not dashed up, all would have been over with them. It is possible, therefore, knowing the defects of both these infantries, to invent a new one, which will resist cavalry and not be afraid of infantry; this need not create a new order of arms, but a variation upon the old. And these are the kind of improvements which confer reputation and power upon a new prince.

This opportunity, therefore, ought not to be allowed to pass for letting Italy at last see her liberator appear. Nor can one express the love with which he would be received in all those provinces which have suffered so much from these foreign scourings, with what thirst for revenge, with what stubborn faith, with what devotion, with what tears. What door would be closed to him? Who would refuse obedience to him? What envy would hinder him? What Italian would refuse him homage? To all of us this barbarous dominion stinks. Let, therefore, your illustrious house take up this charge with that courage and hope with which all just enterprises are undertaken, so that under its standard our native country may be ennobled, and under its auspices may be verified that saying of Petrarch:

Chapter 27

Description of The Methods Adopted by The Duke Valentino When Murdering Vitellozzo Vitelli, Oliverotto Da Fermo, The Signor Pagolo, And the Duke Di Gravina Orsini

Duke Valentino had just returned from Lombardy, where he went to clear his name with the King of France. The Florentines had accused him of stirring up rebellion in Arezzo and other towns in the Val di Chiana. He arrived at Imola, where he planned to gather his army and march against Giovanni Bentivogli, the tyrant of Bologna. He wanted to bring Bologna under his control and make it the center of his Romagnian duchy.

When the Vitelli and Orsini, along with their followers, learned of this, they became worried that the duke was gaining too much power. They feared that after taking Bologna, he would try to destroy them to become the supreme ruler of Italy. So, they called a meeting at Magione, in the district of Perugia. The meeting was attended by Cardinal Pagolo and Duke di Gravina Orsini, Vitellozzo Vitelli, Oliverotto da Fermo, Gianpagolo Baglioni, the tyrant of Perugia, and Messer Antonio da Venafro, who represented Pandolfo Petrucci, the

Prince of Siena. They discussed how strong and ambitious the duke was and decided they had to stop him before his power threatened them all. They resolved not to abandon Bentivogli and to try to win the support of the Florentines. They sent messengers to different places, offering help to one group and encouragement to others to unite against their common enemy. News of this meeting spread quickly across Italy, giving hope to those discontented with the duke, including the people of Urbino, who began planning a rebellion.

Because of this unrest, some men in Urbino decided to seize the fortress of San Leo, which was under the duke's control. They did so by watching the castellan as he fortified the rock and brought timber to the fortress. When the beams were being carried across the bridge, making it impossible for those inside to raise the bridge, the conspirators seized their chance. They jumped onto the bridge and then into the fortress. After they captured it, the whole region rebelled and brought back their old duke. They were encouraged not only by the capture of the fort but also by the Diet at Magione, from whom they expected to get support.

When others heard of the rebellion in Urbino, they saw an opportunity. They quickly gathered their forces to take control of any towns that still remained loyal to the duke. They sent another message to Florence, urging the republic to join them in overthrowing their common enemy. They argued that the risk was smaller now, and they shouldn't wait for another chance.

However, the Florentines, who hated the Vitelli and Orsini for several reasons, refused to join the rebellion. Instead, they sent their secretary, Nicolo Machiavelli, to offer protection and help to the duke against his enemies. The duke, who was in Imola, was full of fear because, to everyone's surprise, his soldiers had quickly switched sides and joined the enemy. This left him unarmed and vulnerable, with war at his doorstep. But after receiving support from the Florentines, he regained his courage. He decided to delay the battle, with the few soldiers he had left, and to negotiate for peace while also seeking reinforcements. He managed to get help in two ways: by asking the King of France for more men and by recruiting soldiers and turning them into cavalry. He paid them all with money.

Despite this, his enemies moved closer to him, advancing toward Fossombrone, where they encountered some of the duke's men and, with the help of the Orsini and Vitelli, defeated them. After this occurred, the duke immediately resolved to see if he could end the conflict through offers of reconciliation. Being a master of deception, he didn't fail to make the insurgents believe that he wished for everyone who had gained something to keep it. He acted as if it was enough for him to have the title of prince, while others could hold the lands.

The duke succeeded so well in this effort that they sent Signor Pagolo to him to negotiate peace, and they brought their army to a halt. However, the duke did not stop his own preparations. He carefully ensured that he had both cavalry and infantry, and to keep these preparations hidden from others, he sent his troops in small groups to different parts of Romagna. Meanwhile, five hundred French lancers arrived to support him. And even though he found himself strong enough to seek revenge on his enemies through open war, he thought it safer and more advantageous to deceive them. For this reason, he did not stop the peace negotiations.

To ensure this, the duke made peace with them, confirming their previous agreements. He immediately gave them four thousand ducats and promised not to harm the Bentivogli. He also formed an alliance with Giovanni, and, moreover, he agreed not to force them to appear before him unless they wished to. On the other hand, they promised to return the duchy of Urbino and other places they had seized, to serve him in all his campaigns, and not to wage war or make alliances with anyone without his permission.

After this reconciliation was completed, Guido Ubaldo, the Duke of Urbino, fled once more to Venice, but not before he destroyed all the fortresses in his territory. Trusting in the loyalty of his people, he didn't want the fortresses, which he believed he couldn't defend, to fall into enemy hands, as they could then be used against his friends. However, Duke Valentino, after concluding this agreement and spreading his forces throughout Romagna, set out for Imola at the end of November, accompanied by his French cavalry. From there, he went to Cesena, where he stayed for some time to negotiate with the envoys of the Vitelli and Orsini, who had gathered their men in the duchy of Urbino to discuss their next undertaking. But since no decision was reached, Oliverotto da Fermo was sent to propose that, if the duke wished to launch an attack on Tuscany, they were ready. If not, they would besiege Sinigalia. To this, the duke replied that he did not wish to go to war with Tuscany and thus turn against the Florentines, but he was quite willing to proceed with the siege of Sinigalia.

It happened not long after that the town surrendered, but the fortress still refused to yield because the castellan insisted that he would only hand it over to the duke himself. So, they urged the duke to come in person. This seemed like a perfect chance for the duke, as being invited by them rather than coming by his own decision would not raise any suspicion. To further ease their concerns, he allowed all the French men-at-arms who had been with him in Lombardy to leave, except for the hundred lancers under the command of Mons. di Candales, his brother-in-law. He departed from Cesena around the middle of December and went to Fano. With great cunning, he managed to convince the Vitelli and Orsini to wait for him at Sinigalia, arguing that any reluctance to do so might cast doubt on the sincerity and lasting nature of their reconciliation. He assured them that he was a man who valued the arms and counsel of his friends. Still, Vitellozzo remained highly suspicious, as the death of his brother had warned him against offending a prince and then trusting him again. However, he was eventually persuaded by Pagolo Orsini, whom the duke had corrupted with gifts and promises, to stay and wait.

Before the duke departed from Fano on the 30th of December, 1502, he shared his plans with eight of his most trusted followers, including Don Michele and Monsignor d'Euna, who would later become a cardinal. He instructed them that once Vitellozzo, Pagolo Orsini, the Duke di Gravina, and Oliverotto arrived, his followers were to pair up and each pair would take responsibility for one of the leaders. These pairs were to keep their assigned men occupied until they reached Sinigalia, where the leaders were to be held under strict watch until they could be taken to the duke's quarters, where they would be seized.

The duke then commanded that all his cavalry and infantry, more than two thousand horsemen and ten thousand foot soldiers, gather at daybreak near the Metauro River, about five miles from Fano, and wait for him there. On the last day of December, the duke arrived at the Metauro with his forces. He sent a group of about two hundred horsemen ahead, followed by the rest of the infantry, which he accompanied along with the remaining men-at-arms.

Fano and Sinigalia are two cities located in La Marca, along the Adriatic Sea, about fifteen miles apart. As one approaches Sinigalia from Fano, the mountains are on the right, with the sea touching their base in some places. The city of Sinigalia sits slightly more than a bow-shot away from the base of the mountains and about a mile from the shore. On the opposite side of the city runs a small river, which flows along the part of the city walls facing Fano and the main road. Anyone approaching Sinigalia travels for a good distance along the mountainside and reaches the river that passes by the city. If they turn left along the riverbank and continue for about a bow-shot's distance, they come to a bridge that crosses the river. At this point, they are almost directly in line with the gate leading into Sinigalia, though not in a straight path, but at an angle. Before this gate, there is a cluster of houses and a square, bordered on one side by the riverbank.

The Vitelli and Orsini, having received orders to wait for the duke and honor him in person, sent their troops to several castles about six miles away from Sinigalia to make room for the duke's forces. They left only Oliverotto and his band, which included one thousand infantry and one hundred fifty horsemen, quartered in the suburb mentioned earlier. With everything arranged, Duke Valentino left for Sinigalia. When the leaders of the cavalry reached the bridge, they didn't cross it. Instead, after opening it, one group turned towards the river and the other towards the countryside, leaving a path in the middle for the infantry to enter the town without stopping.

Vitellozzo, Pagolo, and the Duke di Gravina, riding on mules and accompanied by a few horsemen, headed toward the duke. Vitellozzo, unarmed and wearing a green-lined cape, appeared deeply troubled, as if he knew his death was near. His mood, given his abilities and previous successes, caused some surprise. It is said that when he parted from his men before leaving for Sinigalia to meet the duke, he acted as if it were his final farewell. He entrusted his household and its fortune to his captains, reminding his nephews that it was not their family's fortune, but their fathers' virtues, that should be remembered. The three men came before the duke, saluted him with respect, and were received by him with apparent goodwill. They were immediately placed under the watch of those assigned to guard them.

However, the duke noticed that Oliverotto, who had stayed in Sinigalia with his troops, was missing. Oliverotto was in the square near the river, organizing and drilling his men. The duke signaled with his eyes to Don Michele, who was responsible for Oliverotto, to make sure he didn't escape. Don Michele then rode over to Oliverotto and told him that it wasn't proper to keep his men out of their quarters, as they might be taken by the duke's forces. He advised Oliverotto to send his men to their quarters and come himself to meet the duke. Oliverotto took this advice and went to see the duke. When the duke saw him, he called to him, and after Oliverotto bowed, he joined the others.

The entire group then entered Sinigalia, dismounted at the duke's quarters, and followed him into a private chamber, where the duke had them imprisoned. He then mounted his horse and gave orders for Oliverotto's and the Orsini's men to be disarmed. Oliverotto's men, being close by, were quickly dealt with. But the Orsini and Vitelli's forces, stationed farther away and sensing the doom of their leaders, had time to prepare. Remembering the strength and discipline of the Orsini and Vitelli families, they gathered themselves and successfully defended against the local forces, saving themselves.

The duke's soldiers, after stripping Oliverotto's men of their weapons, began to sack Sinigalia. Had the duke not put a stop to the looting by executing some of his soldiers, they would have completely ransacked the city. Once night fell and the chaos subsided, the duke prepared to execute Vitellozzo and Oliverotto. He led them into a room and had them strangled. Neither of them spoke in a way fitting their past lives. Vitellozzo prayed for permission to ask the pope's full pardon for his sins, while Oliverotto begged for mercy, blaming Vitellozzo for all the wrongs committed against the duke.

Pagolo and the Duke di Gravina Orsini were kept alive until the duke received word from Rome that the pope had captured Cardinal Orsino, the Archbishop of Florence, and Messer Jacopo da Santa Croce. After hearing this, on January 18, 1502, at the castle of Pieve, Pagolo and the Duke di Gravina Orsini were also strangled in the same manner.

Chapter 28

The Life of Castruccio Castracani of Lucca

Written By Nicolo Machiavelli

And Sent to His Friends Zanobi Buondelmonti And Luigi Alamanni.

Castruccio Castracani 1284-1328

It seems, dearest Zanobi and Luigi, an extraordinary thing to those who have thought about it, that nearly all the men who have achieved great things in the world and surpassed others in their time have come from lowly or obscure beginnings, or have been harshly mistreated by Fortune. Some have been abandoned to wild animals, or have had such humble origins that, out of shame, they claimed to be the sons of Jupiter or some other god. It would be tedious to list who these men were, as they are well-known to everyone, and such stories wouldn't offer much benefit to readers, so they are left out. I believe these humble beginnings of great men happen because Fortune wants to show the world that such men owe their success to her, rather than to wisdom, since she steps in when wisdom has little or no role to play in their rise, making all their accomplishments appear to be the result of her influence. Castruccio Castracani of Lucca was one such man who performed great deeds, considering the time and place in which he lived. However, like many others, he was neither fortunate nor distinguished by birth, as this story will demonstrate. It seems worthwhile to bring his memory back to light, because I've noticed in him examples of courage and fortune that make him a model for others to follow. I also believe that you should take note of his actions, as I know that of all men, you both take the greatest pleasure in noble deeds.

The Castracani family was once counted among the noble families of Lucca, but by the time of this story, their status had somewhat declined, as often happens in life. A son named Antonio was born into this family, and he became a priest in the Order of San Michele of Lucca, earning the title of Messer Antonio. He had only one sister, who had been married to Buonaccorso Cenami. After Buonaccorso's death, she became a widow, and not wishing to remarry, she went to live with her brother. Messer Antonio's house had a vineyard behind it, surrounded by gardens, making it easily accessible from various sides.

One morning, just after sunrise, Madonna Dianora, as Messer Antonio's sister was called, went into the vineyard as usual to gather herbs for the day's meal. While she was there, she heard a faint rustling among the vine leaves. Turning to look, she heard a sound resembling a baby's cry. Curious and slightly afraid, but filled with compassion, she approached and found a baby lying hidden among the leaves, its tiny hands and face visible, crying as if it were calling for its mother.

Moved by the sight, she picked the baby up, brought it into the house, washed and dressed it in clean linen as was customary, and showed it to Messer Antonio when he returned home.

Messer Antonio was just as surprised and moved as his sister when he saw the child and heard how she had found it. They discussed what should be done, and since he was a priest and she was childless, they decided to raise the baby themselves. They hired a nurse to care for the infant, and they loved and raised it as their own. They baptized the child and gave him the name Castruccio, after their father.

As the years passed, Castruccio grew to be very handsome, showing signs of intelligence and good judgment. He quickly learned the lessons that Messer Antonio taught him, far beyond what was expected for his age. Messer Antonio had intended to make Castruccio a priest, planning to eventually induct him into his canonry and other church positions. All of his teachings were directed towards that goal, but Antonio soon realized that Castruccio's nature was entirely unsuited for the priesthood.

By the time Castruccio reached the age of fourteen, he had started to ignore the reprimands of Messer Antonio and Madonna Dianora and no longer feared them. He abandoned the study of religious books and instead focused on playing with weapons, finding nothing more enjoyable than learning how to use them. He also loved running, jumping, and wrestling with other boys. In all physical activities, he greatly outshone his peers, both in courage and strength. And when he did turn to books, the only ones that interested him were those that told of wars and heroic deeds. Messer Antonio watched all of this with frustration and sadness.

In the city of Lucca lived a gentleman from the Guinigi family, named Messer Francesco. He was a man of arms and stood above all others in Lucca in wealth, physical strength, and courage. He had fought many times under the command of the Visconti of Milan and, as a Ghibelline, was the esteemed leader of that faction in Lucca.

Messer Francesco resided in Lucca and often gathered with others in the mornings and evenings under the balcony of the Podesta, located at the top of the San Michele square, the finest square in Lucca. He frequently saw Castruccio playing with other street children in the games I previously mentioned. Observing that Castruccio excelled far beyond the other boys, and that he seemed to hold a kind of royal authority over them, being loved and obeyed by them, Messer Francesco became eager to know more about him. After learning of Castruccio's background and how he had been raised, his desire to have the boy near him only grew stronger.

One day, he called Castruccio and asked him whether he would prefer living in the house of a gentleman, where he would learn to ride horses and handle weapons, or in the house of a priest, where he would learn only masses and church services. Messer Francesco could see that Castruccio's eyes lit up at the mention of horses and weapons, though the boy stood silent, blushing modestly. Encouraged by Messer Francesco to speak, Castruccio replied that if his master approved, nothing would please him more than to abandon his priestly studies and embrace the life of a soldier. This answer delighted Messer Francesco, and soon after, he obtained the consent of Messer Antonio. Antonio, knowing the boy's true nature and fearing he could no longer keep him in the priestly path, reluctantly agreed.

Thus, Castruccio left the house of Messer Antonio the priest and entered the home of Messer Francesco Guinigi, the soldier. It was remarkable how quickly Castruccio showed all the qualities and behavior of a true gentleman. He first became an accomplished horseman, easily mastering even the most spirited horses. In all jousts and tournaments, despite his youth, he stood out above the others. He excelled in all physical exercises, demonstrating both strength and skill. What made his talents even more admirable was his charming modesty, which allowed him to avoid offending anyone in either action or speech. He showed respect to those of high rank, modesty with his equals, and kindness to those beneath him. These virtues made him beloved not only by the entire Guinigi family but by the people of Lucca as well.

When Castruccio turned eighteen, the Ghibellines were driven out of Pavia by the Guelphs, and Messer Francesco was sent by the Visconti to support the Ghibellines. Castruccio accompanied him, leading a part of his forces. During this expedition, Castruccio proved his wisdom and bravery, earning a greater reputation than any other commander. His name and fame spread not only in Pavia but throughout all of Lombardy.

Castruccio, having returned to Lucca with a far higher reputation than when he left, did not fail to use every possible means to gain as many friends as he could, neglecting none of the strategies necessary for this purpose. Around this time, Messer Francesco passed away, leaving behind a thirteen-year-old son named Pagolo, and appointing Castruccio as his son's tutor and the administrator of his estate. Before he died, Francesco called Castruccio to his side, asking him to show the same goodwill to Pagolo that he, Francesco, had always shown to Castruccio, and to repay the father's kindness by looking after the son. Upon Francesco's death, Castruccio became the governor and tutor of Pagolo, which greatly increased his power and status. However, this rise in prominence also sparked envy in Lucca, replacing the universal goodwill he had once enjoyed, as many suspected him of harboring ambitions for tyranny. The most prominent among these was Giorgio degli Opizi, the head of the Guelph party.

Giorgio, after Messer Francesco's death, had hoped to become the leading figure in Lucca, but it seemed to him that Castruccio, with his already apparent great abilities and his position as governor, was robbing him of this opportunity. Thus, Giorgio began to plant seeds of distrust, aiming to undermine Castruccio's influence. At first, Castruccio dismissed these efforts with contempt, but later he became alarmed, fearing that Messer Giorgio might succeed in turning the deputy of King Ruberto of Naples against him, which could result in his expulsion from Lucca.

At that time, Pisa was ruled by Uguccione della Faggiuola of Arezzo, who had initially been elected as their captain but had later become their lord. Some exiled Ghibellines from Lucca were living in Pisa, and Castruccio communicated with them, seeking their help in restoring them to their homeland with Uguccione's support. Castruccio also enlisted the support of his friends in Lucca who resented the authority of the Opizi. Once the plan was set, Castruccio carefully fortified the tower of the Onesti family, stocking it with provisions and arms to withstand a siege for a few days if necessary.

On the night agreed upon with Uguccione, who had positioned his forces between the mountains and Pisa, the signal was given. Without being detected, Uguccione advanced to the gate of San Piero and set fire to the portcullis. Inside the city, Castruccio raised a great uproar, calling the people to arms and forcing open the gate from his side. Uguccione and his men poured into the town, and they killed Messer Giorgio along with his entire family and many of his friends and followers. The governor was driven out, and the government was reshaped according to Uguccione's wishes, to the detriment of the city. It was reported that over one hundred families were exiled during this time. Some of those who fled sought refuge in Florence, while others went to Pistoia, a stronghold of the Guelph party, making the city highly hostile towards Uguccione and the people of Lucca.

As it now seemed to the Florentines and the other members of the Guelph party that the Ghibellines had gained too much power in Tuscany, they decided to restore the exiled Guelphs to Lucca. They gathered a large army in the Val di Nievole and seized Montecatini. From there, they advanced to Montecarlo to secure an open passage into Lucca. In response, Uguccione gathered his Pisan and Lucchese forces, along with a number of German cavalry that he had brought down from Lombardy, and moved to confront the Florentine camp. Upon seeing the enemy approach, the Florentines withdrew from

Montecarlo and set up a position between Montecatini and Pescia. Uguccione then camped near Montecarlo, about two miles away from the Florentines, and daily skirmishes between the cavalry of both armies ensued.

Due to Uguccione's illness, the Pisans and Lucchese delayed engaging the enemy in a full battle. As Uguccione's condition worsened, he retreated to Montecarlo for treatment, leaving command of the army in the hands of Castruccio. This change turned out to be disastrous for the Guelphs, who, assuming that the enemy army had lost its leadership with Uguccione's departure, grew overconfident. Castruccio noticed this and allowed several days to pass, giving the Guelphs time to strengthen their belief that the opposing forces were leaderless. He also made gestures of hesitation and didn't allow any camp supplies to be used, further giving the impression of fear.

On the Guelph side, their arrogance increased as they observed what they believed to be signs of weakness in Castruccio's army. Every day, they drew up in battle formation before his troops, challenging him. Once Castruccio saw that the enemy had become sufficiently emboldened and had understood their tactics, he decided it was time to engage them. He addressed his soldiers with words of encouragement, assuring them of certain victory if they obeyed his commands.

Castruccio had observed that the Guelphs had placed their best troops in the center of their line and their weaker forces on the flanks. In response, he arranged his army in the opposite manner, positioning his strongest soldiers on the wings and moving the less reliable men to the center. Following this strategy, he led his army out and quickly brought them within sight of the enemy, who, as usual, had lined up in their boastful manner. Castruccio ordered his central units to advance slowly, while the wings moved forward rapidly. When the battle began, only the flanks of the two armies engaged, while the central battalions on both sides remained apart, too distant to assist one another.

This tactic ensured that Castruccio's strongest troops were pitted against the enemy's weaker ones, while the best forces of the Florentines remained idle in the center, unable to help their comrades on the wings. Castruccio quickly routed the enemy's flanks, and when the Guelph center realized they were vulnerable to attack without having fought, they too fled. The defeat was total, with a heavy loss of life on the Guelph side. Over ten thousand men were killed, including many officers and knights of the Guelph party in Tuscany, as well as several princes who had come to their aid. Among the fallen were Piero, the brother of King Ruberto, Carlo, his nephew, and Filippo, the lord of Taranto.

On Castruccio's side, the loss was minimal, with fewer than three hundred men killed. Among the dead was Francesco, Uguccione's son, who, being young and reckless, was slain in the first charge.

This victory greatly enhanced Castruccio's reputation, so much so that Uguccione became jealous and suspicious of him. It seemed to Uguccione that the victory had brought him no increase in power, but rather diminished it. With this in mind, Uguccione only waited for the right moment to act. The opportunity came with the murder of Pier Agnolo Micheli, a well-known and capable man in Lucca. The murderer fled to Castruccio's house for protection. When the sergeants of the captain came to arrest him, they were driven away by Castruccio, allowing the murderer to escape. This incident reached Uguccione, who was then in Pisa, and he saw it as the perfect moment to punish Castruccio.

Uguccione sent for his son, Neri, who was the governor of Lucca, and instructed him to capture Castruccio at a banquet and have him killed. Castruccio, suspecting no ill will, went to Neri in good faith, enjoyed supper, and was then thrown into prison. However, Neri hesitated to kill him, fearing that the people would rise in anger. He decided to wait for further instructions from his father. Uguccione, enraged by his son's hesitation and cowardice, set out immediately from Pisa to Lucca with four hundred horsemen to finish the matter himself. However, before he reached Lucca, the Pisans rebelled, killed his deputy, and appointed Count Gaddo della Gherardesca as their lord. Upon hearing the news of Pisa's revolt, Uguccione chose not to turn back, fearing that the people of Lucca, inspired by Pisa's example, might close their gates against him.

Meanwhile, the citizens of Lucca, aware of what had occurred in Pisa, seized the opportunity to demand Castruccio's release, despite Uguccione's presence in the city. The matter was first discussed in private gatherings, but soon it became public, with people openly demanding Castruccio's freedom in the streets and squares. Armed and determined, the people confronted Uguccione and demanded Castruccio's release. Fearing that the situation could escalate, Uguccione freed Castruccio from prison. Castruccio then gathered his supporters, and, with the help of the people, attacked Uguccione. Seeing no option but to flee, Uguccione escaped with his followers to Lombardy, where he sought refuge with the lords of Scala and eventually died in poverty.

Castruccio, having gone from being a prisoner to almost a prince in Lucca, handled his newfound power with such discretion that he was appointed captain of the army for one year. With this position, and eager to gain fame through military exploits, Castruccio planned to recover several towns that had rebelled after Uguccione's departure. With the help of the Pisans, with whom he had forged a treaty, he marched on Sarzana. To capture the town, he built a fort against it, which is still called Zerezzanello today. After two months, Castruccio took Sarzana. Buoyed by this success, he quickly captured Massa, Carrara, and Lavenza, and in a short time, had overrun the entire Lunigiana region.

To secure the pass between Lombardy and Lunigiana, Castruccio laid siege to Pontremoli and took it from Messer Anastagio Palavicini, who was its lord. After this victory, he returned to Lucca, where he was greeted with great celebration by the people. By now, Castruccio, seeing that it was unwise to delay any longer, sought to become the prince of Lucca. With the help of Pazzino del Poggio, Puccinello dal Portico, Francesco Boccansacchi, and Cecco Guinigi—all of whom he had corrupted—he had himself appointed lord of Lucca. He was then solemnly and officially elected prince by the people.

Around this time, Frederick of Bavaria, the King of the Romans, came to Italy to claim the Imperial crown. Castruccio, seeking to ally himself with Frederick, met him at the head of five hundred horsemen. In his absence, Castruccio left Pagolo Guinigi as his deputy in Lucca. Pagolo was highly respected because of the people's affection for the memory of his father. Frederick received Castruccio with great honor and granted him many privileges, appointing him the emperor's lieutenant in Tuscany.

At this time, the Pisans were greatly afraid of Gaddo della Gherardesca, whom they had expelled from Pisa. They turned to Frederick for assistance, and he, in turn, appointed Castruccio as the lord of Pisa. The Pisans, fearing the Guelphs and particularly the Florentines, were forced to accept Castruccio as their lord.

Frederick, having appointed a governor in Rome to manage his Italian affairs, returned to Germany. All the Tuscan and Lombard Ghibellines, who followed the imperial cause, sought Castruccio's counsel and aid, promising him governance over their regions if he could help them reclaim them. Among these exiles were Matteo Guidi, Nardo Scolari, Lapo Uberti, Gerozzo Nardi, and Piero Buonaccorsi, all Florentine Ghibellines. Castruccio secretly aimed to become the master of all Tuscany with the help of these men and his own forces. To strengthen his position, he allied himself with Messer Matteo Visconti, the Prince of Milan, and organized his city's forces and surrounding districts. Lucca had five gates, and Castruccio divided his territories into five regions, equipping each with arms and placing them under captains. This organization allowed him to quickly mobilize twenty thousand soldiers, in addition to those he could call upon from Pisa.

While Castruccio was consolidating his power, Messer Matteo Visconti was attacked by the Guelphs of Piacenza, who had expelled the Ghibellines with the help of a Florentine army and King Ruberto. Matteo called on Castruccio to invade Florentine territory, forcing them to withdraw their forces from Lombardy to defend their homeland. Castruccio invaded the Valdarno, capturing Fucecchio and San Miniato, and causing great devastation. The Florentines recalled their army, but Castruccio, dealing with other matters, was forced to return to Lucca before they could fully engage.

There lived in the city of Lucca the Poggio family, who were so influential that they had the power not only to elevate Castruccio but also to help him attain the title of prince. However, feeling that they had not been sufficiently rewarded for their services, they began to incite other families to rebel and to overthrow Castruccio. One morning, they seized their opportunity, armed themselves, and attacked the lieutenant Castruccio had left in charge, killing him. They attempted to rouse the people to revolt, but Stefano di Poggio, an elderly, peaceable man who had taken no part in the rebellion, intervened. Using his authority, he compelled them to lay down their arms, offering to act as their mediator with Castruccio to secure what they desired. The rebels, lacking better judgment, disarmed just as easily as they had taken up arms.

When Castruccio heard the news of the events in Lucca, he immediately placed Pagolo Guinigi in command of his army and hurried home with a troop of cavalry. To his surprise, he found the rebellion already quelled. Nonetheless, he stationed his soldiers in the most strategic positions throughout the city. Stefano, believing that Castruccio owed him a great debt of gratitude, sought him out. Without pleading for himself, as he saw no need, he asked Castruccio to pardon the other members of his family, citing their youth, their past friendship, and the many obligations Castruccio owed to their house.

Castruccio responded graciously, assuring Stefano that he was more pleased to find the rebellion ended than he had ever been troubled by its beginning. He encouraged Stefano to bring his family before him, saying that he thanked God for the chance to demonstrate his clemency and generosity. Trusting in Castruccio's words, Stefano convinced his family to surrender. However, once they did, they, along with Stefano, were immediately imprisoned and executed.

Meanwhile, the Florentines had reclaimed San Miniato, and Castruccio, feeling that his position in Lucca was not yet secure enough to leave, thought it wise to seek peace. He approached the Florentines with a proposal for a truce, which they were quick to accept, as they were weary of the war and eager to reduce its costs. A two-year treaty was agreed upon, allowing both sides to retain the territories they had conquered.

Freed from external troubles, Castruccio turned his attention to Lucca's internal affairs. Determined not to face similar dangers again, he methodically eliminated anyone whose ambition might challenge his rule. Under various pretexts and justifications, he wiped out every potential rival—exiling some, confiscating their property, and executing those he had captured, declaring that his experience had taught him none of them could be trusted. To further ensure his security, he constructed a fortress in Lucca using stones from the towers of those he had killed or driven from the state.

While Castruccio made peace with the Florentines and strengthened his rule in Lucca, he missed no chance, short of open warfare, to increase his influence elsewhere. He believed that gaining control of Pistoia would give him a foothold in Florence, which was his ultimate goal. To this end, he formed alliances with the mountaineers and worked matters in Pistoia so cleverly that both factions in the city entrusted him with their secrets. Pistoia was, as always, divided between two factions: the Bianchi, led by Bastiano di Possente, and the Neri, led by Jacopo da Gia. Both men were secretly in communication with Castruccio, each hoping to drive the other out of the city. After many threats, open conflict finally broke out between them. Jacopo fortified himself near the Florentine gate, while Bastiano took control of the Lucchese gate. Both sides trusted Castruccio more than they trusted the Florentines, believing that he was more willing and ready to fight. They both sent to him for help.

Castruccio gave promises to both. He told Bastiano that he would come personally, and assured Jacopo that he would send his student, Pagolo Guinigi. At the agreed-upon time, Castruccio sent Pagolo through Pisa, while he himself went directly to Pistoia. At midnight, both met outside the city and were admitted as friends. Once inside, and at a signal from Castruccio, one of them killed Jacopo da Gia, while the other killed Bastiano di Possente. Their followers were either captured or slain. With little further resistance, Pistoia fell into Castruccio's hands. He forced the Signoria to leave the palace and made the people swear obedience to him, offering them many promises and forgiving their old debts. The surrounding countryside flocked to the city to see their new prince, and all were filled with hope and quickly settled under his rule, much influenced by his reputation for great valor.

Around this time, great disturbances arose in Rome due to the high cost of living, which was caused by the absence of the pope, who was residing in Avignon. Enrico, the German governor, was widely blamed for the unrest, as murders and riots occurred daily without his ability to stop them. Enrico grew anxious, fearing that the Romans might call on Ruberto, the King of Naples, who could drive out the Germans and bring the pope back to the city. With no closer ally to turn to, Enrico sent a request to Castruccio, asking for both his assistance and his personal presence in Rome. Castruccio, considering that it was in his interest to support the emperor, agreed. He believed his own safety would be at risk if the emperor lost control of Rome.

Leaving Pagolo Guinigi in charge of Lucca, Castruccio set out for Rome with six hundred horsemen.

Upon his arrival, he was received with the highest honors by Enrico. Castruccio's presence quickly restored respect for the emperor's authority, and without bloodshed or violence, peace was restored in the city. A large part of this success was due to Castruccio, who sent large supplies of grain from the area around Pisa by sea, thus relieving the food shortage that had caused much of the trouble. After disciplining some of the Roman leaders and warning others, order was voluntarily restored to Enrico's rule. Castruccio was showered with honors and was made a Roman senator. This title was bestowed upon him with great ceremony. He wore a richly brocaded toga, embroidered on the front with the words: "I am what God wills," and on the back: "What God desires shall be."

During this time, the Florentines, angered that Castruccio had taken Pistoia during the truce, began to devise ways to incite the city to rebel, believing it would be easy to achieve in his absence. Among the exiled Pistoians living in Florence were two prominent men, Baldo Cecchi and Jacopo Baldini, both of whom were willing to face danger. These men maintained contact with their friends in Pistoia, and with the help of the Florentines, they entered the city by night. After expelling some of Castruccio's officials and partisans, and killing others, they succeeded in restoring Pistoia's independence.

When Castruccio received this news, he was furious. He quickly took leave of Enrico and hastened toward Pistoia. Upon hearing of his return, the Florentines, aware that he would waste no time, decided to intercept him in the Val di Nievole. They believed that by doing so, they could block his route to Pistoia. Gathering a large army of Guelph supporters, the Florentines marched into Pistoian territory. Meanwhile, Castruccio reached Montecarlo with his army. Learning of the Florentines' position, he chose not to engage them in the plains of Pistoia or wait for them in the plains of Pescia. Instead, he planned a bold attack in the Pass of Serravalle. He believed that, despite having only twelve thousand men compared to the Florentines' thirty thousand, success would guarantee his victory. Although he trusted in his own abilities and the bravery of his troops, he hesitated to meet the Florentines in open battle, fearing they might overwhelm him with their numbers.

Serravalle is a castle located between Pescia and Pistoia, positioned on a hill that blocks the Val di Nievole. It lies just beyond the pass, which is narrow and steep in some areas, while generally rising gently but still remaining narrow, especially at the summit where the waters divide. Here, twenty men side by side could hold the pass. The lord of Serravalle, Manfred, a German, had been allowed to remain in possession of the castle even before Castruccio became lord of Pistoia. The castle was considered neutral territory, unclaimed by either the Lucchese or the Pistoians, as neither side wished to displace Manfred as long as he remained neutral and made no commitments to anyone. The castle was well fortified, and Manfred had maintained his position there for these reasons.

Castruccio saw that possessing this castle would give him a significant advantage in his conflict with Florence. Knowing this, and having a close friendship with a resident inside the castle, Castruccio arranged for four hundred of his men to be secretly admitted the night before the attack on the Florentines, with the castellan to be killed.

Castruccio, having prepared everything, needed to ensure that the Florentines continued with their plan to move the war away from Pistoia into the Val di Nievole. Thus, he did not move his army from Montecarlo, allowing the Florentines to proceed. They hurried on and set up camp beneath Serravalle, planning to cross the hill the next morning. Meanwhile, Castruccio had seized the castle during the night, and, marching his army silently from Montecarlo at midnight, reached the base of Serravalle. At dawn, both Castruccio's forces and the Florentines began ascending the hill simultaneously.

Castruccio sent his infantry up the main road and dispatched a troop of four hundred horsemen along a path to the left toward the castle. The Florentines, unaware that Castruccio had seized the hill and the castle, sent forward four hundred cavalry ahead of their main army. To their complete surprise, they encountered Castruccio's infantry. So close were they upon the enemy that they barely had time to lower their visors before being attacked. The Florentines, unprepared and caught off guard, faced a well-prepared enemy who assaulted them with such vigor that they struggled to hold their position, although a few managed to break through.

When the sounds of battle reached the Florentine camp below, confusion erupted. The narrow pass caused the cavalry and infantry to become entangled, and the captains could not move their men either forward or backward. Amid the chaos, no one knew what should or could be done. In short order, the Florentine cavalry engaged with Castruccio's infantry were either scattered or killed. Due to their unfortunate position, they were unable to defend themselves effectively, despite their desperate resistance. Retreat was impossible, as the mountains flanked them on both sides, their enemies blocked their way ahead, and their own forces pressed from behind.

Seeing that his forces had not yet dealt a decisive blow, Castruccio sent one thousand infantry to join the four hundred horsemen stationed at the castle, ordering them to strike the Florentine flank. They carried out the attack with such ferocity that the Florentines were unable to withstand it. Soon, they broke ranks and fled in full retreat, defeated more by the difficult terrain than by the strength of their enemy. Those in the rear fled toward Pistoia, spreading across the plains, each man seeking only his own safety.

The defeat was total and bloody. Many captains were taken prisoner, including Bandini dei Rossi, Francesco Brunelleschi, and Giovanni della Tosa, all prominent Florentine nobles. Many Tuscans and Neapolitans who had fought alongside the Florentines, sent by King Ruberto to support the Guelphs, were also captured. When news of the defeat reached Pistoia, the citizens expelled the Guelph supporters and surrendered the city to Castruccio.

Castruccio did not stop at Pistoia. He took control of Prato and all the castles on both sides of the Arno plains. He then advanced his army to the plains of Peretola, just two miles from Florence. There, he stayed for several days, dividing the spoils of war and celebrating his victory with feasts, games, horse races, and foot races for both men and women. To commemorate the Florentines' defeat, he even minted medals.

During this time, Castruccio attempted to bribe some citizens of Florence to open the city gates at night, but the conspiracy was uncovered. Those involved in the plot, including Tommaso Lupacci and Lambertuccio Frescobaldi, were captured and beheaded. The Florentines, deeply anxious after their defeat and despairing of preserving their liberty, sent envoys to King Ruberto of Naples, offering him control of the city. Recognizing the immense importance of maintaining Guelph power, Ruberto accepted their offer. He agreed to receive a yearly tribute of two hundred thousand florins from Florence and sent his son, Carlo, to the city with four thousand horsemen.

Shortly after this, the Florentines experienced some relief from the pressure of Castruccio's army, as he was forced to abandon his positions near Florence and march on Pisa to suppress a conspiracy. This rebellion was led by Benedetto Lanfranchi, one of the most prominent men in Pisa, who could not tolerate seeing his homeland under the control of the Lucchese. Lanfranchi had planned to seize the citadel, kill Castruccio's supporters, and expel the garrison. However, in any conspiracy, secrecy requires few participants, while execution requires many, and in seeking more supporters, Lanfranchi approached someone who betrayed the plot to Castruccio. This betrayal cannot go without harsh condemnation of Bonifacio Cerchi and Giovanni Guidi, two Florentine exiles living in Pisa, who were involved in the plot's exposure.

As a result, Castruccio captured Benedetto and had him executed, along with many other noble citizens, whose families he sent into exile.

Castruccio now realized that both Pisa and Pistoia were deeply disaffected, and he dedicated considerable thought and effort to securing his hold on these cities. This preoccupation gave the Florentines an opportunity to regroup their army and await the arrival of Carlo, the son of the King of Naples. Once Carlo arrived, they decided to act swiftly, assembling a massive army of over thirty thousand infantry and ten thousand cavalry, having called upon every Guelph in Italy for assistance. They deliberated whether to attack Pistoia or Pisa first and concluded that Pisa was the better target, especially considering the recent conspiracy. They believed that once Pisa fell, Pistoia would quickly follow.

In early May 1328, the Florentines launched their campaign, swiftly capturing Lastra, Signa, Montelupo, and Empoli, before advancing to San Miniato. When Castruccio learned of the enormous army the Florentines were sending against him, he remained unshaken. He believed that Fortune was now preparing to grant him control of Tuscany, confident that his enemies would fare no better than they had at Pisa or Serravalle. Castruccio gathered twenty thousand infantry and four thousand cavalry and marched to Fucecchio, while he sent Pagolo Guinigi to Pisa with five thousand infantry.

Fucecchio was strategically stronger than any other town in the Pisan region, situated between the Arno and Gusciana rivers and slightly elevated above the surrounding plains. The Florentines would be unable to prevent supplies from reaching it without splitting their forces. Furthermore, they could not approach the town either from Lucca or Pisa without putting themselves at a disadvantage. If they attempted to attack Castruccio, they would find themselves caught between his two armies, the one under his own command and the other under Pagolo's. Alternatively, they would need to cross the Arno to engage directly with his forces, a risky maneuver.

To tempt the Florentines into this dangerous course of action, Castruccio withdrew his men from the riverbanks and positioned them beneath the walls of Fucecchio, leaving a wide stretch of land between his army and the river.

The Florentines, after taking San Miniato, convened a war council to decide whether to attack Pisa or engage Castruccio's army. After weighing the challenges of both options, they chose to face Castruccio. At that time, the Arno River was low enough to be fordable, though the water still reached the shoulders of the infantrymen and the saddles of the cavalry. On the morning of June 10, 1328, the Florentines initiated the battle, sending forward several cavalry units and ten thousand infantrymen. Castruccio, who had already formulated his plan and knew exactly what to do, immediately attacked the Florentines with five thousand infantry and three thousand cavalry, not allowing them to emerge from the river before charging them. He also sent one thousand light infantry up the riverbank and another thousand down the Arno.

The Florentine infantry, weighed down by their armor and hindered by the water, struggled to scale the riverbanks. Meanwhile, the cavalry, having crossed in small numbers, made the crossing more difficult for others by disturbing the riverbed, which became bogged down with mud. Many horses toppled over with their riders, and others became stuck, unable to move. Seeing the difficulties their troops were facing, the Florentine captains pulled their men back and moved them further up the river, hoping to find a less treacherous crossing point and more suitable banks for landing.

However, when they reached the bank, they were met by the forces Castruccio had already dispatched, who, armed lightly with bucklers and javelins, unleashed a fierce barrage of projectiles at the faces and bodies of the Florentine cavalry. The horses, spooked by the noise and wounds, fell into confusion, trampling each other in the chaos. A fierce and desperate battle erupted between Castruccio's men and the Florentines who managed to cross. The Florentines fought to establish a foothold on the banks to make room for their comrades still in the water, while Castruccio's troops strove to drive them back into the river. Both sides fought with equal determination, encouraged by their captains. Castruccio rallied his men by reminding them that these were the same enemies they had defeated at Serravalle, while the Florentine captains scolded their troops, urging them not to let the many be defeated by the few.

The battle dragged on, with heavy losses and exhaustion on both sides. Recognizing that the fight had lasted long and both sides were near their breaking point, Castruccio sent a fresh unit of infantry to the rear of his engaged forces. He then ordered his front lines to open their ranks as if they were retreating, with one part turning to the right and the other to the left. The Florentines, thinking they had gained an advantage, rushed forward to occupy the space. However, exhausted from battle, they could not hold their ground when they encountered Castruccio's reserves and were soon driven back into the river.

Meanwhile, the cavalry on both sides had yet to gain any decisive advantage, as Castruccio, aware of his disadvantage in cavalry numbers, had instructed his commanders to focus on defense rather than offense. He knew that once he defeated the Florentine infantry, he would be able to quickly deal with the cavalry. His strategy worked. When he saw the Florentine army pushed back into the river, he ordered the rest of his infantry to attack the enemy cavalry. His forces, armed with lances and javelins, along with their own cavalry, launched a furious assault on the Florentine cavalry, quickly routing them.

The Florentine captains, seeing how difficult it was for their cavalry to cross the river, had attempted to send their infantry lower down the river to flank Castruccio's army. However, the steep banks were already fortified by Castruccio's men, making this maneuver futile. The Florentines were completely defeated at all points, and barely a third of their forces escaped. Castruccio once again emerged victorious and covered in glory.

Many Florentine captains were taken prisoner, while Carlo, the son of King Ruberto, along with Michelagnolo Falconi and Taddeo degli Albizzi, the Florentine commissioners, fled to Empoli. Although the spoils of war were significant, the slaughter was far greater, as is often the case in such battles. Of the Florentines, 20,231 men were killed, while Castruccio lost only 1,570 men.

But Fortune, envious of Castruccio's glory, took his life at the very moment when she should have preserved it, thereby ruining all the plans he had worked so long to bring to fruition—plans that only death could have stopped. Castruccio had been fully engaged in the battle all day, and when it ended, despite being exhausted and overheated, he stood at the gate of Fucecchio to welcome his returning soldiers and personally thank them for their efforts. Ever vigilant, he also watched for any signs of the enemy attempting to recover from their defeat, believing it was the duty of a good general to be the first to mount his horse and the last to dismount.

While standing there, Castruccio was exposed to a wind that often rises at midday along the banks of the Arno, a wind notorious for being unhealthy. Though he felt chilled, he paid little attention to it, as he was used to enduring such discomforts. However, this chill would prove fatal. That night, he was struck with a high fever, which worsened so quickly that the doctors realized it would be the cause of his death. Knowing his end was near, Castruccio called Pagolo Guinigi to his side and spoke to him as follows:

"If I had known that Fortune would cut me off in the midst of my path to the glory promised by all my successes, I would have worked less, and left you, if not a larger state, at least one with fewer enemies and dangers. I would have been content with ruling Lucca and Pisa alone. I wouldn't have subjugated the Pistoians or provoked the Florentines with so many offenses. Instead, I would have made both peoples my allies. I might not have lived longer, but I would have lived more peacefully, and I would have left you a state that, while smaller, would have been more secure and established on a stronger foundation.

But Fortune, who governs human affairs, did not grant me the foresight to recognize this from the beginning, nor the time to correct it. You've heard, as many have told you, and I have never hidden it, how I entered your father's house as a boy—without the ambitions that every noble heart should possess—and how he raised me and loved me as if I were his own son. Under his guidance, I learned to be valiant and to seize every opportunity Fortune offered me, as you yourself have witnessed. When your good father passed away, he entrusted you and all his possessions to me. I have cared for you with love and expanded your estate with the devotion I owed him.

In order that you would inherit not only the estate your father left but also what my fortune and abilities have gained, I never married. I didn't want the love for my own children to conflict with the loyalty I owed to your father's. So, I leave you a vast estate, of which I am proud, but I am deeply concerned because I leave it to you unsettled and insecure.

You now have Lucca, but its people will never be satisfied under your rule. You also have Pisa, where the people are fickle and unreliable. Though they may submit to control for a time, they will always resist serving under someone from Lucca. Pistoia, too, is disloyal, torn by factions and still bitter towards your family due to the wrongs we recently inflicted on them. You are surrounded by the Florentines, whom we have harmed in countless ways but not entirely defeated. They will rejoice more at the news of my death than they would if they gained all of Tuscany.

You cannot rely on the Emperor or the princes of Milan—they are distant, slow to act, and their help comes far too late. So, you must depend on your own abilities, the memory of my valor, and the prestige this latest victory has brought you. If you use it wisely, it will help you make peace with the Florentines, who, after suffering this major defeat, should be more willing to negotiate. While I sought to make them my enemies, believing that war would bring me power and glory, you have every reason to make them your allies. Their friendship will provide you with both security and advantages.

In this world, it is crucial for a man to know himself and understand the limits of his own strength and resources. A man who knows he is not suited for war must learn to govern through the arts of peace. It would be wise for you to follow my counsel, and in doing so, you will enjoy the fruits of my life's work and the dangers I have endured. You will succeed easily if you learn to trust what I have told you is true. And you will owe me a double debt, for I have not only left you this realm but also taught you how to keep it."

After this, the citizens of Pisa, Pistoia, and Lucca who had fought alongside Castruccio came to him. As he recommended Pagolo to them and had them swear their loyalty to Pagolo as his successor, Castruccio passed away. He left behind a cherished memory among those who knew him, and no prince of that time was ever loved with such devotion as he was. His funeral was marked by every sign of mourning, and he was buried in San Francesco in Lucca. Fortune did not favor Pagolo Guinigi as she had favored Castruccio, for Pagolo lacked the abilities of his predecessor. Not long after Castruccio's death, Pagolo lost Pisa, then Pistoia, and struggled to retain control over Lucca. This city remained under the Guinigi family until the time of Pagolo's great-grandson.

From what has been related, it is clear that Castruccio was a man of exceptional abilities, measured not only against the men of his own time but also those of earlier eras. He was taller than average, perfectly proportioned, and of a gracious presence. He greeted people with such charm and warmth that few ever left his company displeased. His hair was reddish, and he wore it short above the ears, going without a hat regardless of rain or snow. Castruccio was delightful among friends but formidable to his enemies, just to his subjects, and cunning with those who betrayed him. He was willing to defeat others through deceit if necessary, believing that it was victory, not the means of achieving it, that brought glory. No one was bolder in facing danger, and few were more prudent in extracting themselves from difficult situations.

Castruccio often said that men should attempt everything and fear nothing, claiming that God favored the strong, as the weak are always punished by the strong. He was known for his sharp wit, often biting but always courteous in his responses. Just as he didn't expect indulgence in his way of speaking, he didn't take offense when others spoke sharply to him. Many times, he calmly listened when others were bold with him. For example, when he once paid a ducat for a partridge and was criticized by a friend, Castruccio responded, "You wouldn't have paid more than a penny." The friend agreed, and Castruccio replied, "A ducat means much less to me than a penny does to you." Another time, he spat on a flatterer to show his contempt. The flatterer, unbothered, remarked, "Fishermen endure the sea's waters to catch a few small fish, and I let myself be drenched in spittle to catch a whale." Castruccio heard this with patience and even rewarded the man.

Once, a priest told Castruccio that living so lavishly was a sin. Castruccio replied, "If that's a vice, then you shouldn't indulge so extravagantly at the feasts of our saints." On another occasion, he saw a young man blush as he left a brothel and said, "You should be ashamed when you go in, not when you come out." When a friend handed him a complicated knot to untie, Castruccio quipped, "Fool, do you think I want to undo something that was tied with so much difficulty?" He also remarked to someone who claimed to be a philosopher, "You're like dogs, always chasing after those who will feed you the best." The philosopher responded, "We're more like doctors, going where we're most needed."

Once, while traveling by boat from Pisa to Leghorn, Castruccio was alarmed by a sudden storm. Someone with him mocked his fear, saying they weren't afraid at all.

Castruccio, known for his sharp wit, once responded to someone mocking his fear of a storm by saying, "I'm not surprised you aren't afraid—every man values his soul according to what it's worth." When asked what one should do to gain respect, he advised, "When you go to a banquet, be sure not to seat one piece of wood upon another," suggesting that one should avoid acting foolishly. To someone boasting about having read many things, Castruccio replied, "A wise man knows better than to boast about remembering much." When another bragged that he could drink heavily without getting drunk, Castruccio quipped, "An ox can do the same."

Castruccio had an intimate relationship with a woman, and when a friend criticized him for being taken in by her, he replied, "She hasn't taken me in—I've taken her." Similarly, when scolded for enjoying fine foods, he asked, "Do you spend as much as I do?" When the critic admitted spending less, Castruccio retorted, "Then you're more miserly than I am gluttonous."

At a supper hosted by Taddeo Bernardi, a wealthy citizen of Lucca, Castruccio was shown into a beautifully adorned room. He spat on the floor, and when Taddeo was disturbed, Castruccio calmly said, "I didn't know where else to spit to offend you less." When asked how Caesar died, he replied, "God willing, I will die the same way."

One evening, while dancing and socializing with ladies, a friend remarked that it was beneath someone of his rank to behave so. Castruccio responded, "He who is considered wise by day won't be thought a fool at night." A man once threw himself to the ground in a desperate plea for a favor. When Castruccio rebuked him, the man replied, "You force me to act this way, for your ears are in your feet." Amused, Castruccio granted him double the favor he had requested.

Castruccio often said that the path to hell was easy since it was downhill and traveled blindfolded. When asked for a favor by someone using too many words, he said, "Next time, send someone else to make your request." After enduring a long-winded oration, the speaker apologized, saying, "Perhaps I have tired you." Castruccio replied, "Not at all, I didn't listen to a word."

Of a man who had been a beautiful child and grew into a fine adult, Castruccio remarked, "He's dangerous—he first took husbands from their wives, and now he takes wives from their husbands." To an envious man who laughed, Castruccio asked, "Do you laugh because you're successful, or because someone else is unfortunate?"

While under the care of Messer Francesco Guinigi, a companion asked Castruccio, "What will you give me if I let you strike me on the nose?" Castruccio answered, "A helmet." When criticized for executing a citizen of Lucca who had helped him rise to power, Castruccio responded, "People misunderstand—I didn't kill an old friend, I killed a new enemy." Castruccio often praised men who intended to marry but then decided against it, comparing them to sailors who planned to set sail but wisely chose not to when the time came. He was always surprised that while men would tap and inspect an earthen or glass vase to check its quality before buying, they would choose a wife based only on her appearance.

When asked how he wished to be buried after his death, Castruccio replied, "With my face downwards, because I know that once I'm gone, this country will be turned upside down." On another occasion, someone asked if he had ever considered becoming a friar to save his soul. He responded that the thought had never crossed his mind, as he found it odd that someone like Fra Lazerone could end up in Paradise while Uguccione della Faggiuola would go to Hell.

Once, when asked when a man should eat to maintain his health, Castruccio said, "If the man is rich, he should eat when he is hungry; if he is poor, then whenever he can." Observing one of his gentlemen being laced up by a family member, Castruccio remarked, "I pray God you let him feed you as well."

Upon seeing a house with a Latin inscription that read, "May God preserve this house from the wicked," Castruccio quipped, "Then the owner must never go inside." While passing by a small house with a disproportionately large door, he commented, "That house will fly through the door."

In a discussion with the ambassador of the King of Naples about the property of exiled nobles, a disagreement arose. The ambassador asked Castruccio if he feared the king. Castruccio replied, "Is your king a bad man or a good one?" When the ambassador said the king was a good man, Castruccio responded, "Then why should I fear a good man?"

I could recount many more stories of his sayings, both witty and profound, but I believe the examples already given are enough to demonstrate his remarkable qualities. He lived for forty-four years and, in every sense, was a true prince. Though surrounded by the many signs of his good fortune, Castruccio also wished to keep reminders of his hardships close by. The manacles that once bound him in prison can still be seen today, fixed to the tower of his residence, placed there by him as a lasting testament to the days of his adversity.

In his lifetime, Castruccio was not inferior to figures like Philip of Macedon, the father of Alexander, or Scipio of Rome. He died at the same age as they did, and without question, had Fortune placed him in Macedonia or Rome instead of Lucca, he would have surpassed them both.

Meditations

Marcus Aurelius

Introduction

I. Biography of Marcus Aurelius

Marcus Aurelius, one of history's most revered philosopher-emperors, was born on April 26, 121 AD, in Rome. His birth name was Marcus Annius Verus, reflecting his noble lineage. The Annii Verus family was well-established and influential within the Roman aristocracy, known for their wealth and connections to the imperial court. Marcus's father, Annius Verus, held the esteemed position of a praetor, a senior official in the Roman Republic, but he passed away when Marcus was only three years old. Raised primarily by his grandfather, Marcus Annius Verus, a revered figure in Roman society, young Marcus was imbued with a sense of duty and moral fortitude from an early age.

His upbringing was characterized by the highest standards of Roman education, emphasizing rhetoric and philosophy, the cornerstones of intellectual development in the ancient world. This background laid the foundation for his later philosophical pursuits and writings. Marcus was betrothed at a young age to the daughter of Lucius Aelius Caesar, the first adopted heir of Emperor Hadrian, aligning him closely with the line of succession.

Rise to Power and Role as Roman Emperor

Marcus Aurelius's path to power was paved by the foresight of Emperor Hadrian, who saw potential in the young nobleman. After the death of Aelius Caesar, Hadrian adopted Antoninus Pius as his successor, with the condition that Antoninus would, in turn, adopt Marcus and Lucius Verus, the son of Aelius Caesar. This arrangement placed Marcus directly in line for the imperial throne.

In 138 AD, upon Hadrian's death, Antoninus Pius ascended to the throne and took on the role of a mentor and father figure to Marcus. Marcus's political and philosophical education continued under Antoninus's guidance, preparing him for future leadership.

During this period, he became deeply engaged with Stoic philosophy, profoundly influencing his thinking and governance approach.

Marcus's reign as emperor began in 161 AD, following Antoninus Pius's death. Uniquely, he shared this role with his adoptive brother, Lucius Verus, marking the first instance of co-emperors in Roman history. However, Marcus was recognized as the senior partner, entrusted with greater authority and responsibilities. His reign was marked by a series of military conflicts, most notably the Marcomannic Wars against Germanic tribes along the Danube frontier and the Parthian War in the East. Despite these challenges, Marcus remained committed to the principles of Stoicism, which emphasized rationality, self-control, and the importance of duty.

As emperor, Marcus Aurelius strove to balance his philosophical ideals with the demands of leadership. His writings, now known as the Meditations, reflect his internal struggles and dedication to self-improvement amidst the pressures of ruling a vast empire. The text offers timeless wisdom on resilience, virtue, and the human condition, making it as relevant today as it was in antiquity.

Marcus Aurelius passed away in 180 AD, leaving a legacy as both a philosopher and a ruler who sought to harmonize the complexities of power with the pursuit of ethical living. His life and works continue to inspire those who seek to navigate the challenges of modern life with wisdom and integrity.

Historical Context

The Roman Empire during the reign of Marcus Aurelius was a vast and complex entity, stretching from the Atlantic Ocean in the west to the Euphrates River in the east. At its height, the empire included regions that are now parts of over 40 modern countries, encompassing diverse cultures, languages, and economies. Governed from Rome, this massive realm was held together by a sophisticated network of roads, a shared legal system, and the might of the Roman legions.

Marcus Aurelius ascended to the throne in 161 AD, a time when the Roman Empire was the preeminent power in the Western world. The city of Rome, with its monumental architecture, bustling markets, and teeming population, served as the heart of this empire. Roman society was highly stratified, with a rigid class system, yet it was also a melting pot of peoples and ideas, influenced by centuries of conquest and trade.

Despite its grandeur, the empire faced numerous challenges. The economy relied heavily on agriculture, supplemented by trade with far-flung regions. The social fabric was underpinned by slavery, which fueled the empire's economy and infrastructure but also posed moral and practical dilemmas. Culturally, the empire was a mosaic of traditions, as Roman religion and customs intertwined with those of conquered peoples.

During Marcus's reign, the empire maintained its prosperity but was also stretched to its limits. The sheer size of the empire made it difficult to govern effectively, with distant provinces often acting semi-autonomously. This complexity required a delicate balance of power and diplomacy, alongside military might, to keep the empire stable.

The reign of Marcus Aurelius was marked by significant events and challenges that tested the resilience of the Roman Empire and its leader.

The Marcomannic Wars

One of the primary challenges Marcus faced was the Marcomannic Wars, a series of battles against Germanic tribes and other barbarian groups along the Danube frontier. These wars spanned much of his reign, from 166 to 180 AD, and required constant vigilance and military engagement. The conflicts were driven by pressures from migrating tribes displaced by other groups farther north and the empire's attempts to secure its borders.

The Marcomannic Wars were not just a test of military strategy but also of Marcus's leadership. As a Stoic philosopher, he struggled to reconcile his duties as a warrior emperor with his philosophical ideals of peace and rationality. The wars strained the empire's resources and highlighted the fragility of its frontiers, forcing Marcus to adopt new military tactics and fortify the empire's defenses.

The Parthian War

Another significant challenge during Marcus Aurelius's reign was the Parthian War, which began shortly after he ascended to the throne in 161 AD. The conflict arose when the Parthian Empire, Rome's rival in the East, invaded the Roman client state of Armenia, a strategic buffer region between the two empires. The Parthian King Vologases IV sought to expand his influence, prompting a Roman military response.

The Parthian War demanded significant resources and military attention. Marcus appointed his co-emperor Lucius Verus to oversee the campaign, which involved a series of complex military operations across the eastern provinces. Despite initial setbacks, the Roman forces ultimately succeeded in repelling the Parthian advance, capturing the Parthian capital, Ctesiphon, and re-establishing Roman authority in the region.

The war was a testament to the strategic acumen of Roman military leaders and the resilience of the Roman army. However, it also revealed the strains on the empire's resources, as the cost of sustaining such distant military campaigns was immense. Marcus's ability to manage these military operations while addressing other challenges underscores his effectiveness as a leader who balanced military necessity with philosophical reflection.

The Antonine Plague

In addition to military conflicts, Marcus Aurelius's reign was plagued—quite literally—by a devastating pandemic known as the Antonine Plague. This epidemic, believed to have been smallpox or measles, struck the empire in 165 AD and continued for over a decade, causing widespread mortality and economic disruption.

The plague significantly impacted the Roman military, reducing the number of available soldiers and weakening the empire's defensive capabilities. It also affected civilian populations, leading to labor shortages and a decline in agricultural productivity. The social and economic ramifications of the plague were profound, contributing to a sense of instability and uncertainty within the empire.

Marcus Aurelius's response to these challenges demonstrated his commitment to duty and resilience. He worked tirelessly to support the empire's recovery, overseeing relief efforts and implementing measures to stabilize the economy. Despite personal losses, including the death of his co-emperor Lucius Verus, Marcus maintained a stoic resolve, viewing the trials as opportunities for personal and philosophical growth.

Political and Economic Struggles

Throughout his reign, Marcus Aurelius also contended with internal political and economic challenges. The Roman economy was heavily reliant on agriculture and trade, both of which were disrupted by the ongoing military conflicts and the Antonine Plague. To address financial shortfalls, Marcus took measures such as debasing the currency, which temporarily alleviated fiscal pressures but also contributed to long-term economic difficulties.

Politically, Marcus faced challenges in maintaining the loyalty and cooperation of the Roman Senate and provincial governors. His reign saw occasional uprisings and conspiracies, which he addressed through a combination of clemency and strategic governance. Marcus's leadership style was characterized by his emphasis on justice, reason, and the importance of leading by example.

Domestic Reforms and Legal Contributions

During his reign, Marcus Aurelius undertook several domestic reforms aimed at improving governance and addressing social issues within the empire. His legal reforms reflected his commitment to justice and equity, as he sought to ensure that Roman law was fair and accessible to all citizens.

Marcus introduced measures to protect the rights of slaves and orphans, reflecting his Stoic belief in the inherent worth of all individuals. He also worked to improve the administration of justice, emphasizing the importance of legal integrity and reducing corruption among provincial governors.

These reforms were consistent with his philosophical ideals, as Marcus believed that a just and equitable society was essential for the well-being of its citizens. His legal contributions helped shape Roman law, leaving a legacy that influenced legal systems in later Western civilizations.

The Rise of Christianity

The rise of Christianity posed another challenge during Marcus Aurelius's reign. As a new religious movement, Christianity was often viewed with suspicion by Roman authorities, who perceived it as a threat to traditional Roman religious practices and social order.

While Marcus Aurelius is not known to have actively persecuted Christians, his reign saw instances of local persecutions, as Christian communities were often scapegoated for societal problems. The tension between traditional Roman values and the growing Christian faith reflected broader cultural and religious shifts within the empire.

Marcus's philosophical writings, while not directly addressing Christianity, emphasize tolerance and understanding, values that resonate with contemporary discussions on religious freedom and coexistence. His emphasis on rationality and virtue provided a framework for navigating the complex religious landscape of his time.

The Succession and Legacy

One of the enduring challenges for Roman emperors was ensuring a stable succession. Marcus Aurelius faced the difficult task of securing the future of the empire beyond his reign. Unlike his predecessors, Marcus chose to appoint his son Commodus as his successor, a decision that proved contentious.

Commodus's rule, marked by autocracy and instability, contrasted sharply with his father's philosophical and principled leadership. The transition highlighted the inherent risks in dynastic succession and the challenges of maintaining imperial stability. Despite the difficulties of his son's reign, Marcus Aurelius's legacy as a philosopher-emperor endured, with his writings continuing to inspire future generations.

II. The Duality of Marcus Aurelius

Philosopher and Emperor

Marcus Aurelius is celebrated as both a philosopher and an emperor, two roles that may seem fundamentally at odds with one another. His life presents a fascinating duality, as he was tasked with wielding immense political power while simultaneously pursuing the introspective path of a philosopher. This intersection of roles makes Marcus a compelling figure in history and philosophy.

As a philosopher, Marcus Aurelius was deeply influenced by Stoicism, a school of thought that emphasized reason, self-discipline, and the pursuit of virtue as the highest good. Stoicism taught that the key to a fulfilling life was living in harmony with nature and accepting the things beyond one's control. Marcus's philosophical journey was driven by a relentless pursuit of self-improvement and wisdom, as he sought to align his actions with the Stoic ideals of rationality and virtue.

Conversely, as emperor of Rome, Marcus faced the practical demands of governance, leading a vast empire fraught with challenges such as military conflicts, political intrigue, and economic pressures. His role required decisive action and strategic thinking to maintain the stability and prosperity of the Roman Empire. Balancing these demands with his philosophical aspirations created a profound tension in his life.

Exploration of the Tension Between His Philosophical Pursuits and Imperial Duties

As a Stoic, Marcus believed in the importance of rational thought and virtuous living. However, as an emperor, he was often required to engage in warfare and make difficult decisions that could seem at odds with Stoic principles.

This tension is evident in his personal writings, where Marcus frequently reflects on the challenges of maintaining his philosophical integrity while fulfilling his imperial responsibilities. The Meditations reveal his internal struggles with anger, fear, and the burdens of leadership. He grappled with the idea of duty versus desire, questioning how to remain true to his philosophical beliefs while effectively governing an empire.

One of the key challenges Marcus faced was reconciling the Stoic ideal of peace with the necessity of war. The Marcomannic Wars required him to take on the role of a military leader, directing campaigns against invading tribes to protect the empire's borders. Despite his personal distaste for conflict, Marcus viewed these actions as necessary to fulfill his duty to Rome. He approached these decisions with a sense of Stoic detachment, striving to act in accordance with reason and the greater good.

Contrast Between His Public Role and Private Philosophical Reflections

The contrast between Marcus Aurelius's public and private lives is striking. As emperor, he was the most powerful man in the world, responsible for the welfare of millions of people. Yet, his Meditations reveal a private individual who was introspective, self-critical, and often doubtful of his own abilities.

In public, Marcus was expected to project confidence and authority, maintaining the image of a strong and capable ruler. He was seen as a wise and just leader, dedicated to the well-being of his subjects. However, his personal writings reveal a different side—a man who continually questioned his own motives and actions, seeking to improve himself in the face of life's challenges.

His writings are a testament to Marcus's commitment to self-reflection and personal growth. They offer insight into his efforts to reconcile his public responsibilities with his private philosophical aspirations. Through his writings, Marcus sought to hold himself accountable, using Stoic philosophy as a guide to navigate the complexities of his dual role.

In this way, Marcus Aurelius serves as a timeless example of the struggle to balance personal ideals with external demands. His life and writings demonstrate the enduring relevance of philosophy in providing guidance and perspective in the face of life's challenges. For contemporary readers, Marcus's duality offers valuable lessons on how to integrate philosophical principles into everyday life, even amidst the pressures of modern society.

III. Philosophical Background

Stoicism is a philosophical school that emerged in Athens during the early 3rd century BC. Founded by Zeno of Citium, it gained prominence in the Hellenistic world and later found a home in Rome, where it deeply influenced thinkers like Seneca, Epictetus, and Marcus Aurelius. Stoicism offers a practical guide for living a virtuous life, emphasizing the development of personal wisdom and self-control as pathways to true happiness.

At its core, Stoicism teaches that the universe is governed by a rational and divine order, often referred to as "Logos." This belief in a rational cosmos shaped the Stoics' understanding of human nature and their emphasis on living in harmony with this natural order. For the Stoics, philosophy was not merely a theoretical pursuit but a way of life that required continuous practice and reflection.

Marcus Aurelius, as a Stoic philosopher, was deeply influenced by these teachings. His writings reflect his efforts to apply Stoic principles to his daily life and challenges, offering timeless insights into the human condition.

Core Principles of Stoicism

The philosophy of Stoicism is built upon several core principles that guide individuals toward a life of virtue and tranquility. Understanding these principles provides a foundation for exploring Marcus Aurelius's Meditations and their relevance to modern life.

1. The Dichotomy of Control

One of the fundamental tenets of Stoicism is the distinction between what is within our control and what is not. The Stoics taught that we should focus on our thoughts, intentions, and actions, as these are within our control. External events, the opinions of others, and the outcomes of our efforts are beyond our control and should be accepted with equanimity. This principle encourages individuals to cultivate inner peace by letting go of concerns about things they cannot change.

2. Living in Accordance with Nature

Stoicism emphasizes living in harmony with nature, which means aligning our actions with the rational order of the universe. This principle involves understanding and accepting our place in the world, recognizing that we are all part of a larger whole. Living in accordance with nature also means acknowledging our human nature, which is characterized by reason and social interconnectedness.

3. The Pursuit of Virtue

For the Stoics, virtue is the highest good and the only true source of happiness. Virtue encompasses qualities such as wisdom, courage, justice, and temperance. By cultivating these virtues, individuals can achieve a state of moral excellence and live a fulfilling life. The Stoics believed that external goods, such as wealth and fame, are indifferent and do not contribute to genuine happiness.

4. The Practice of Mindfulness and Reflection

Stoicism encourages regular self-examination and mindfulness as tools for personal growth. By reflecting on one's thoughts and actions, individuals can identify areas for improvement and reinforce their commitment to living virtuously. This practice of self-awareness helps cultivate resilience and adaptability in the face of life's challenges.

5. The Acceptance of Fate

The Stoics taught the importance of accepting the unfolding of events with grace and composure. This principle, often referred to as "amor fati" or love of fate, involves embracing life's circumstances, both good and bad, as part of the natural order. By accepting fate, individuals can maintain their inner tranquility and focus on what truly matters: their response to life's challenges.

6. Universal Brotherhood

Stoicism emphasizes the interconnectedness of all human beings. The Stoics believed that we are all part of a universal community and have a responsibility to care for one another. This principle encourages empathy, compassion, and cooperation, promoting a sense of shared humanity that transcends individual differences.

These core principles form the foundation of Stoic philosophy and offer a practical framework for navigating the complexities of life. Marcus reflects on his engagement with these ideas, providing a timeless guide for those seeking wisdom and resilience in a rapidly changing world. By embracing Stoic principles, contemporary readers can find guidance and inspiration to lead more meaningful and virtuous lives.

Influence of Stoic Philosophy on Marcus Aurelius

Stoicism offered Marcus a framework for understanding the world and his place within it. It provided him with the tools to navigate the complexities of leadership and personal development.

1. Stoicism as a Guide to Leadership

For Marcus Aurelius, Stoicism was more than an abstract philosophy; it was a practical guide to governance and leadership. The Stoic emphasis on virtue and ethical conduct informed his approach to these responsibilities, guiding him to prioritize justice, fairness, and the common good.

Marcus's adherence to Stoic principles helped him maintain a sense of balance and perspective amidst the challenges of his reign. The Stoic idea of focusing on what is within one's control and accepting what is not enabled him to remain composed and effective in the face of external pressures, such as wars, political intrigue, and natural disasters.

2. Personal Resilience and Inner Strength

Stoicism taught Marcus the importance of cultivating inner strength and resilience, qualities that were crucial for his personal development and effectiveness as a ruler. The philosophy's focus on self-discipline and emotional regulation helped Marcus manage his reactions to the inevitable difficulties and frustrations of life.

Marcus reflects on his efforts to practice Stoic exercises, such as self-examination and mindfulness. These practices allowed him to maintain a sense of inner peace and clarity, even when confronted with adversity. By striving to align his thoughts and actions with Stoic principles, Marcus was able to build a foundation of personal integrity and resilience.

3. The Pursuit of Virtue

Central to Marcus's philosophical journey was the pursuit of virtue, which the Stoics regarded as the highest good. Stoicism taught him that true happiness and fulfillment come from living a life in accordance with virtue, rather than seeking external rewards such as wealth or fame.

Marcus's commitment to this ideal is evident throughout the book He continually emphasizes the importance of wisdom, courage, justice, and temperance as guiding principles for his conduct. These virtues served as a moral compass, helping him navigate the complexities of imperial rule and personal challenges.

4. Acceptance and Tranquility

The Stoic concept of "amor fati," or love of fate, profoundly influenced Marcus Aurelius's outlook on life. Stoicism encourages acceptance of the natural order and the unfolding of events, teaching that peace of mind comes from embracing life as it is, rather than how one wishes it to be.

Marcus applied this principle to his role as emperor, striving to accept the burdens and responsibilities that came with his position. By practicing acceptance, he was able to maintain a sense of tranquility and purpose, even when faced with the uncertainties of leadership and the transience of life.

5. A Legacy of Stoic Thought

The influence of Stoicism on Marcus Aurelius is perhaps most clearly reflected in the legacy of his writings. They serve as a timeless testament to the practical wisdom of Stoic philosophy, offering insights that continue to resonate with readers today.

Through his engagement with Stoic principles, Marcus Aurelius exemplified the possibility of integrating philosophy into everyday life. His reflections encourage contemporary readers to consider how Stoic teachings can inform their own pursuit of a virtuous and meaningful existence.

IV. The Meditations

Purpose and Nature of the Text

The Meditations is a remarkable work of philosophical reflection and personal introspection. Unlike typical philosophical treatises of the time, it was not intended for public consumption or scholarly debate. Instead, it serves as a private journal where Marcus recorded his thoughts, struggles, and insights as he endeavored to live according to Stoic principles.

Personal Reflections

Written during the last decade of his life, the text was crafted during military campaigns on the frontiers of the Roman Empire. This setting highlights the personal and practical nature of the work, as Marcus wrote in stolen moments of solitude, often in the midst of hardship and uncertainty. The text is composed of twelve books, each a collection of thoughts and reflections that offer a glimpse into Marcus's inner life and philosophical journey.

The primary purpose of this textwas self-improvement. Marcus Aurelius used his writings as a tool for self-examination, aiming to reinforce his commitment to Stoic ideals and cultivate personal virtue. By reflecting on his experiences and challenges, he sought to better understand himself and align his actions with his philosophical beliefs. In this sense, the text serves as a manual for personal development, guiding the reader—both Marcus and modern readers—toward a life of wisdom and integrity.

Not a Public Philosophical Treatise

Unlike the works of other philosophers such as Plato or Aristotle, Meditations was not intended as a systematic exposition of philosophical doctrines. It lacks the formal structure and argumentative rigor typical of philosophical texts. Instead, the work is characterized by its fragmented and spontaneous nature, reflecting the fact that it was written for Marcus's eyes alone.

Marcus's writings are deeply personal and candid, revealing his vulnerabilities, doubts, and aspirations. The text does not seek to instruct or persuade others; rather, it is a record of Marcus's ongoing dialogue with himself as he grapples with the challenges of being both a philosopher and an emperor. This introspective quality makes it unique among ancient texts, offering a rare insight into the personal application of Stoic philosophy.

A Timeless Guide for Self-Reflection

While Meditations was written as a private journal, its insights and reflections have transcended time, offering timeless guidance to those seeking to lead a life of virtue and purpose. The text's appeal lies in its universality; Marcus's reflections on the human condition, the nature of happiness, and the pursuit of wisdom resonate with readers across cultures and eras.

For contemporary readers, this book serves as a powerful reminder of the value of self-reflection and the importance of living in accordance with one's principles. The text encourages individuals to examine their own lives, confront their weaknesses, and strive for personal growth. In an age where external distractions and pressures abound, the book invites readers to turn inward, fostering a deeper understanding of themselves and their place in the world.

Relevance for Today

The enduring relevance of Meditations is a testament to the universal nature of its themes. In a fast-paced and often chaotic world, Marcus's reflections on inner peace, resilience, and the pursuit of virtue offer a source of inspiration and guidance. His writings remind us that true fulfillment comes not from external achievements but from living a life aligned with our deepest values.

Contemporary readers can explore the transformative power of Stoic philosophy, gaining insights into how to navigate life's challenges with grace and wisdom. Marcus Aurelius's personal reflections continue to illuminate the path to self-improvement, encouraging us to cultivate the qualities that define a meaningful and virtuous life.

Structure and Style

Overview of the Organization of the Text

Meditations is organized into twelve books, each containing a series of reflections, aphorisms, and philosophical musings.

Each book varies in length and content, reflecting the episodic nature of Marcus's reflections. The entries are not organized thematically but are rather a spontaneous outpouring of his inner dialogue. This structure highlights the deeply personal nature of the work, as Marcus uses writing as a tool for self-examination and personal growth.

Despite the lack of formal organization, certain themes and topics recur throughout the text, such as the pursuit of virtue, the transience of life, and the importance of rationality and self-discipline. These themes provide a unifying thread, connecting Marcus's reflections across different contexts and periods.

Literary Style and Use of Language

Meditations is written in a direct and unadorned style, reflecting Marcus Aurelius's commitment to clarity and sincerity. The language is often concise and pointed, capturing the essence of his philosophical reflections with minimal embellishment. This straightforward style aligns with Stoic values, emphasizing the importance of truth and simplicity.

The text is rich in metaphor and imagery, using vivid language to illustrate philosophical concepts. Marcus often employs analogies drawn from nature, daily life, and the military to convey his insights. For example, he likens the soul to a citadel, emphasizing the importance of inner strength and resilience against external challenges.

The use of the second person is a distinctive feature of the text, as Marcus frequently addresses himself directly. This creates an intimate and introspective tone, inviting readers to engage with his reflections as a form of personal dialogue. By writing in this manner, Marcus underscores the self-directed nature of his philosophical practice, encouraging readers to apply similar introspection in their own lives.

The text also incorporates elements of rhetorical questioning and paradox, challenging readers to think critically about their assumptions and beliefs. Marcus's style reflects his philosophical rigor and his desire to provoke thoughtful reflection.

A Living Document

The literary style is marked by its variability, ranging from meticulously crafted passages to fragmented and cryptic notes. This variability reflects the conditions under which the text was written—often during military campaigns and moments of solitude—and the dynamic nature of Marcus's thought process.

The text is best understood as a living document, capturing the evolution of Marcus's philosophical understanding over time. This fluidity allows readers to witness his struggles and growth, making it a powerful testament to the ongoing journey of self-improvement.

V. Themes and Content of Meditations

Key Themes

Meditations explores a rich tapestry of themes that delve into the nature of the human experience and the quest for a virtuous life. Written as a series of personal reflections, these themes reflect Marcus's struggle to reconcile his philosophical beliefs with the demands of his role as Roman Emperor. Despite the centuries that separate us from his time, the insights Marcus offers remain profoundly relevant, providing guidance on how to navigate the complexities of modern life.

The Pursuit of Virtue and Self-Improvement

Central is the Stoic ideal of virtue as the highest good. Marcus Aurelius constantly emphasizes the importance of living in accordance with virtue, which encompasses wisdom, courage, justice, and temperance. For Marcus, the pursuit of virtue is not just an abstract goal but a practical guide for everyday conduct.

His reflections encourage readers to cultivate self-discipline and strive for personal improvement. He believed that by consistently practicing virtue, individuals could achieve a state of inner harmony and fulfillment. This pursuit requires continuous self-examination and the willingness to confront one's weaknesses, making virtue a dynamic and lifelong journey.

Marcus's dedication to self-improvement is evident in his commitment to Stoic exercises and practices. These exercises, which include mindfulness, reflection, and the repetition of core principles, serve as tools to strengthen his resolve and maintain focus on what truly matters. By sharing these practices, Marcus provides a roadmap for readers to follow in their quest for personal growth and ethical living.

The Nature of Death and Impermanence

Another significant theme is the contemplation of death and the transient nature of life. Marcus Aurelius often reflects on the inevitability of death, viewing it as a natural part of the human experience. For the Stoics, acceptance of mortality is crucial for living a meaningful life, as it encourages individuals to focus on the present moment and prioritize their values.

Marcus's writings offer a sober yet empowering perspective on death. By accepting the impermanence of life, he argues, we can free ourselves from the fear of death and the anxieties that come with it. This acceptance allows us to appreciate the fleeting nature of existence and inspires us to live each day with intention and purpose.

For contemporary readers, Marcus's reflections on death serve as a reminder to cherish life's fleeting moments and to align our actions with our core values. His insights encourage us to let go of trivial concerns and focus on what is truly important, fostering a sense of gratitude and mindfulness in our daily lives.

The Insignificance of Fame and External Validation

Marcus frequently contemplates the futility of seeking fame and external validation. As emperor, he was acutely aware of the transient nature of power and the superficiality of public acclaim. He urges readers to recognize that true fulfillment comes from within, rather than from the fleeting approval of others.

Marcus's reflections challenge us to question the societal emphasis on status, wealth, and recognition. He encourages us to pursue intrinsic values, such as integrity and authenticity, rather than relying on external measures of success. By shifting our focus away from external validation, we can cultivate a deeper sense of self-worth and contentment.

In today's world, where social media and external pressures often dictate our self-image, Marcus's insights are particularly relevant. His writings invite us to reevaluate our priorities and seek fulfillment through personal growth and self-acceptance, rather than through the opinions of others.

Dealing with Anger and Maintaining Composure

A recurring theme is the challenge of managing anger and maintaining composure in the face of adversity. Marcus Aurelius candidly acknowledges his struggles with anger and frustration, particularly in his role as a leader. He draws upon Stoic principles to navigate these emotions, emphasizing the importance of reason and self-control.

Marcus encourages readers to adopt a detached perspective, viewing challenges and setbacks as opportunities for growth rather than sources of distress. By practicing patience and understanding, we can cultivate resilience and respond to difficult situations with grace and equanimity.

His reflections remind us that anger is a natural human emotion but one that must be managed to maintain inner peace. By practicing mindfulness and cultivating a rational mindset, we can transform anger into a catalyst for personal development and positive change.

Stoic Practices and Exercises

Marcus Aurelius not only reflects on Stoic philosophy but also demonstrates how to integrate its principles into daily life through practical exercises. These Stoic practices are designed to cultivate self-awareness, resilience, and personal growth, offering valuable tools for navigating the complexities of modern life. By engaging in these exercises, Marcus sought to strengthen his character and live in harmony with his philosophical ideals.

1. Daily Reflection and Journaling

One of the most prominent practices in Meditations is the use of daily reflection and journaling as a means of self-examination. Marcus Aurelius utilized writing as a tool for introspection, recording his thoughts, challenges, and aspirations. This exercise allowed him to evaluate his actions, assess his adherence to Stoic principles, and identify areas for improvement.

For contemporary readers, daily reflection and journaling can serve as powerful tools for personal development. By setting aside time each day to write about our thoughts and experiences, we can gain clarity, foster self-awareness, and reinforce our commitment to living in accordance with our values.

2. The Dichotomy of Control

A fundamental Stoic exercise practiced by Marcus is the dichotomy of control, which involves distinguishing between what is within our control and what is not. By focusing on our thoughts, intentions, and actions—elements within our control—we can cultivate inner peace and resilience. Marcus frequently reminded himself to accept external events and outcomes, understanding that they are beyond his control.

This exercise encourages modern readers to let go of anxiety and frustration over things they cannot change, allowing them to concentrate on their responses and attitudes. By embracing the dichotomy of control, we can develop a sense of empowerment and tranquility in the face of life's uncertainties.

3. Mindfulness and Presence

Mindfulness, or the practice of being present in the moment, is another key Stoic exercise. Marcus emphasized the importance of living in the present, avoiding distractions from the past and future. He believed that by fully engaging with the present moment, individuals could act with intention and purpose.

For today's readers, mindfulness can be a transformative practice, helping to reduce stress and enhance focus. By cultivating presence and awareness, we can make more deliberate choices and appreciate the richness of our experiences.

4. Negative Visualization

Negative visualization, or premeditatio malorum, is a Stoic exercise that involves contemplating potential challenges and setbacks in advance. Marcus used this practice to prepare himself mentally for difficulties, reducing their impact when they occurred. By envisioning possible obstacles, he was able to develop strategies for coping and maintaining a sense of equanimity.

This exercise can be valuable for contemporary readers as a means of building resilience and adaptability. By anticipating potential challenges, we can reduce fear and anxiety, allowing us to respond to adversity with greater confidence and composure.

5. Practicing Virtue

Central to Marcus's practice was the active pursuit of virtue, which the Stoics considered the highest good. Marcus continually sought to embody qualities such as wisdom, courage, justice, and temperance in his daily life. He believed that by practicing virtue, individuals could achieve true fulfillment and happiness.

For modern readers, focusing on the cultivation of virtue can provide a meaningful framework for personal growth. By striving to embody these qualities, we can develop a strong moral character and live a life aligned with our deepest values.

6. Reflection on Mortality

Marcus frequently reflected on the impermanence of life and the inevitability of death, using this awareness to inspire a sense of urgency and purpose. This exercise encouraged him to prioritize meaningful actions and relationships, reminding him of the preciousness of each moment.

Contemplating mortality can help contemporary readers clarify their priorities and make choices that align with their core values. By embracing the finite nature of life, we can focus on what truly matters and cultivate gratitude for the present.

VI. The Legacy of Marcus Aurelius

Meditations has resonated with readers for centuries, influencing a wide range of philosophers, writers, and leaders. Its appeal lies in its practical wisdom and deeply personal reflections, which provide a window into the mind of a ruler grappling with the challenges of leadership and life.

Throughout history, it has inspired prominent figures in philosophy, literature, and politics. During the Renaissance, the revival of classical learning brought renewed interest in Stoic philosophy, with Meditations serving as a key text for thinkers seeking to integrate Stoic ideals into their own work. Renaissance humanists, such as Erasmus and Montaigne, drew upon Marcus's reflections to explore themes of virtue, reason, and self-governance.

In the modern era, the text has continued to influence philosophers like Friedrich Nietzsche, who admired Marcus's ability to maintain philosophical ideals while fulfilling his duties as emperor. The existentialists, including Jean-Paul Sartre and Albert Camus, also found resonance in Marcus's reflections on meaning, choice, and the human struggle for authenticity.

Beyond philosophy, Meditations has inspired leaders seeking to apply Stoic principles to the complexities of governance and decision-making. Figures such as Thomas Jefferson and Theodore Roosevelt found guidance in Marcus's writings, using his insights to navigate the challenges of leadership with integrity and wisdom.

A Timeless Guide to Leadership and Ethics

For those in positions of leadership, Meditations provides a timeless guide to ethical decision-making and the cultivation of moral character. Marcus's reflections on justice, courage, and empathy offer valuable insights for leaders seeking to navigate the complexities of modern governance with integrity and compassion.

In a world where ethical leadership is increasingly important, Marcus's example serves as a reminder of the power of philosophy to shape not only personal conduct but also the governance of society. His writings encourage leaders to prioritize the common good, act with wisdom and fairness, and remain true to their principles in the face of adversity.

Inspiration for Personal and Collective Resilience

Finally, Meditations inspires both personal and collective resilience, offering guidance on how to confront life's challenges with courage and grace. Marcus's reflections on the impermanence of life and the importance of accepting fate resonate with readers seeking to find meaning and purpose in an uncertain world.

By embracing the Stoic ideals, individuals and communities can cultivate a deeper sense of connection, purpose, and resilience. Marcus Aurelius's legacy continues to inspire and guide those who seek to lead lives of virtue and meaning, demonstrating the enduring power of philosophy to transform both individuals and society.

VII. Personal Reflections

This book offers an extraordinary glimpse into the mind of a philosopher-king, providing insights into his lifelong quest for wisdom and virtue. As you embark on this journey through Meditations, I invite you to explore the text as a source of guidance and inspiration for your own personal development. Marcus Aurelius's reflections offer a wealth of wisdom that can help you navigate the complexities of modern life with grace and resilience. His teachings remind us of the importance of cultivating self-discipline, embracing challenges as opportunities for growth, and living in accordance with our values.

In a world that often emphasizes external achievements and validation, the text encourages us to turn inward, fostering a deeper understanding of ourselves and our place in the world. By engaging with Marcus's reflections, you can develop a greater sense of self-awareness and clarity, empowering you to make more deliberate choices and lead a more fulfilling life.

Consider using the book as a tool for daily reflection, drawing upon its insights to guide your actions and decisions. Allow the Stoic exercises and principles outlined in the text to inspire your own journey of self-improvement, helping you cultivate a mindset of mindfulness and resilience.

Ultimately, the wisdom of Marcus Aurelius offers a timeless reminder that true fulfillment comes not from external success but from living a life of virtue and authenticity. Let the journey be an invitation to explore the richness of Stoic philosophy and its potential to illuminate the path toward a life well-lived. As you read and reflect on Marcus Aurelius's words, may you find inspiration to cultivate the qualities that define a virtuous and meaningful existence.

Book 1

From my grandfather Verus, I learned to be a good person and control my temper.

From my father's reputation and memory, I learned how to be humble and act like a man.

From my mother, I learned to be religious, generous, and to avoid not only bad actions but even bad thoughts. I also learned to live simply, far from the habits of the rich.

From my great-grandfather, I learned not to attend public schools and to have good teachers at home, knowing that it's worth spending money on education.

From Diognetus, I learned not to care about trivial things and not to believe in magic or people who claim to banish demons. I learned not to get obsessed with things like raising quails for fighting. I learned to accept free speech and became interested in philosophy, attending lectures first of Bacchius, then Tandasis and Marcianus, and to write dialogues when I was young. I also learned to desire a simple bed and lifestyle, following Greek customs.

From Rusticus, I learned that my character needed improvement and discipline. He taught me not to get caught up in the love of fancy arguments, not to write about things just to show off, not to give little moral speeches, or to pretend I was someone who practiced a lot of self-discipline or did good deeds just to look impressive. I also learned to stay away from using fancy words, writing poems, or trying to sound too sophisticated. He showed me not to walk around the house in formal clothes or do anything similar. I learned to write letters in a simple and straightforward way, like the letter Rusticus wrote to my mother from Sinuessa. He also taught me to be quick to make peace with those who have wronged me as soon as they show they want to make up. From him, I learned to read carefully and not be satisfied with just a shallow understanding of a book, and not to agree too quickly with people who talk a lot. I owe it to him that I got to know the discourses of Epictetus, which he shared with me from his own collection.

From Apollonius, I learned to have freedom of will and unwavering steadiness of purpose. He taught me to focus on nothing else, not even for a moment, except reason. He showed me how to stay the same person, whether in sharp pain, during the loss of a child, or in long illness. He was a clear example of how the same man can be both determined and flexible, and he was never irritable when teaching. He considered his experience and skill in explaining philosophical ideas as the least of his talents. From him, I also learned how to accept favors from friends without feeling humbled by them or letting them go unnoticed.

From Sextus, I learned to have a kind disposition and the example of a family led by a fatherly figure. He taught me the idea of living according to nature and to have dignity without being pretentious. He showed me how to carefully look after the interests of friends and to tolerate ignorant people and those who form opinions without thinking. He was able to adapt easily to everyone, making interactions with him more pleasant than any flattery. At the same time, he was highly respected by those who knew him. He had the ability to discover and organize the important principles of life intelligently and methodically. He never showed anger or any other strong emotion, remaining completely free from passion, yet he was very affectionate. He could express approval without making a big show and had a lot of knowledge without being boastful.

From Alexander the grammarian, I learned not to find fault with others, and not to scold those who used incorrect or strange expressions in a harsh way. Instead, he would skillfully introduce the correct expression that should have been used, either by answering, confirming, or engaging in a discussion about the thing itself, rather than focusing on the word, or by some other fitting suggestion.

From Fronto, I learned to understand what envy, deceit, and hypocrisy are in a tyrant, and that generally, those among us who are called Patricians often lack paternal affection.

From Alexander the Platonic, I learned not to frequently or unnecessarily say to anyone, or write in a letter, that "I am toobusy". He also taught me not to constantly excuse neglecting the duties required by our relationships with others by claiming urgent business.

From Catulus, I learned not to be indifferent when a friend criticizes me, even if the criticism seems unreasonable, but to try to restore the friend to their usual good feelings. He also taught me to be ready to speak well of my teachers, as is said of Domitius and Athenodotus, and to truly love my children.

From my brother Severus, I learned to love my family, to love truth, and to love justice. Through him, I came to know Thrasea, Helvidius, Cato, Dion, and Brutus. From him, I received the idea of a government in which there is the same law for everyone, a government that respects equal rights and freedom of speech. I also learned from him the idea of a monarchy that values the freedom of its people above all. He taught me consistency and unwavering steadiness in my commitment to philosophy. He showed me how to be generous, to give to others readily, to hold on to good hopes, and to believe that I am loved by my friends. I noticed in him that he never hid his opinions about those he disapproved of, and his friends never had to guess what he wanted or did not want—it was always clear.

From Maximus, I learned self-control and not to be easily led astray by anything. He showed me how to be cheerful in all circumstances, even in illness. His character was a perfect blend of gentleness and dignity. He did whatever was required of him without complaining. I observed that everyone believed he thought as he spoke, and that in everything he did, he never had any bad intentions. He never showed amazement or surprise, was never in a hurry, and never put off doing something. He was never confused or dejected, nor did he ever laugh to hide his irritation, and he was never passionate or suspicious. He was used to doing kind acts, was always ready to forgive, and was free from all falsehood. He appeared to be someone who couldn't be turned away from doing the right thing, rather than someone who had to be improved. I also observed that no one ever thought they were looked down upon by Maximus or dared to think they were better than him. He had a pleasant sense of humor in an agreeable way.

In my (adoptive) father, I observed a mild temper and unchangeable determination in the things he decided after careful thought. He had no vanity in those things that men call honors. He had a love for hard work and perseverance, and he was always ready to listen to those who had something to suggest for the common good. He was unwavering in giving everyone what they deserved. He had knowledge from experience about when to take vigorous action and when to be lenient. I noticed that he had overcome any desire for young boys and saw himself as no better than any other citizen. He released his friends from any obligation to dine with him or to accompany him when he went abroad. Those who couldn't join him because of urgent circumstances always found him the same. I also observed his habit of careful inquiry in all matters of decision-making, and his persistence. He never stopped investigating a matter just because he was satisfied with the first impression. He was loyal to his friends and was not quick to tire of them, nor was he extravagant in his affection. He was satisfied in all situations and cheerful. He could foresee things far ahead and took care of the smallest details without making a show of it. He immediately checked popular applause and all flattery. He was always watchful over the things necessary for running the empire, and he was a good manager of expenses. He patiently endured the criticism he received for such conduct. He was not superstitious with respect to the gods, nor did he try to win over men by giving them gifts, by trying to please them, or by flattering the public. He showed sobriety in all things and firmness, never having any mean thoughts or actions, nor a love of novelty. The things that contributed to the comfort of life, which fortune gave him in abundance, he used without arrogance and without excuses. When he had them, he enjoyed them without showing off, and when he didn't have them, he didn't miss them. No one could ever say that he was either a sophist or a flippant servant or a pedant. Everyone recognized him as a man mature, perfect, beyond flattery, capable of managing his own and other people's affairs. He also honored those who were true philosophers and did not criticize those who pretended to be philosophers, nor was he easily swayed by them. He was easy in conversation, and he made himself pleasant without any offensive affectation. He took reasonable care of his health, not because he was attached to life, nor out of concern for his appearance, nor in a careless way, but so that through his own attention, he very seldom needed a doctor or medicine or external treatments. He was most ready to give without envy to those who had any special skill, such as eloquence or knowledge of the law or morals or anything else, and he gave them his help so that each might enjoy the reputation they deserved. He always acted according to the traditions of his country without pretending to do so. He was not fond of change nor was he unsteady. He liked to stay in the same places and to focus on the same things. After his headaches, he would return immediately fresh and vigorous to his usual activities. His secrets were very few and rare, and only about public matters. He showed prudence and economy in arranging public spectacles and in constructing public buildings, in his donations to the people, and in other such things. He was a man who looked at what needed to be done, not at the reputation that might come from doing it. He didn't take baths at odd hours. He wasn't interested in building houses, or curious about what he ate, or about the texture and color of his clothes, or about the beauty of his slaves. His clothes came from Lorium, his villa on the coast, and from Lanuvium generally. We know how he behaved toward the toll-collector at Tusculum who asked his pardon. All his behavior was like this. There was nothing harsh, implacable, or violent in him. You could say that he never broke a sweat. He examined everything one by one as if he had all the time in the world, without confusion, in an orderly way, energetically and consistently. The saying about Socrates could be applied to him: that he was able both to abstain from and to enjoy those things which many are too weak to abstain from and cannot enjoy without excess. But to be strong enough both to bear one and to be moderate in the other is the mark of a man who has a perfect and invincible soul, as he showed in the illness of Maximus.

I owe to the gods that I had good grandfathers, good parents, a good sister, good teachers, good relatives, and friends—almost everything good. I also owe it to the gods that I was not pushed into any offense against any of them, though I had a nature which, if the opportunity had come, might have led me to do something wrong. But through their favor, there was never such a combination of circumstances as put me to the test. I am also thankful to the gods that I was not raised for a long time with my grandfather's concubine, that I kept the flower of my youth, and that I did not prove my manhood before the proper time, but even delayed it. I was subjected to a ruler and a father who was able to take away all pride from me and to bring me to the realization that it is possible for a man to live in a palace without wanting guards, fancy dresses, torches, statues, and other such showy things. A man in such a position can bring himself very close to living like an ordinary person, without being any lower in thought or more careless in action with respect to the things that must be done for the public good in a way that fits a ruler. I thank the gods for giving me such a brother who was able, by his moral character, to make me watchful over myself, and who at the same time pleased me with his respect and affection. I am thankful that my children have not been stupid or deformed in body. I am grateful that I didn't make more progress in rhetoric, poetry, and other studies, in which I might have been completely absorbed if I had seen that I was improving in them. I am glad that I quickly placed those who brought me up in the position of honor that they seemed to desire, without making them wait with the hope that I would do it later because they were still young. I am thankful that I knew Apollonius, Rusticus, and Maximus, and that I received clear and frequent impressions about living according to nature and what kind of life that is. So far as it depended on the gods, their gifts, help, and inspirations, nothing stopped me from living according to nature, though I still fall short of it because of my own fault and because I don't pay attention to the warnings of the gods, and, I may almost say, their direct instructions. I am grateful that my body has held out so long in such a life. I am thankful that I never touched either Benedicta or Theodotus, and that, after falling into romantic passions, I was cured. Even though I was often upset with Rusticus, I never did anything that I had reason to regret. I am thankful that, even though it was my mother's fate to die young, she spent the last years of her life with me. Whenever I wanted to help someone in need, or on any other occasion, I was never told that I didn't have the means to do it. I am also grateful that I never had to receive anything from another. I am thankful that I have such an obedient, affectionate, and simple wife. I am thankful that I had many good teachers for my children. I am also grateful that remedies have been shown to me by dreams, both for other things and for spitting blood and dizziness. I am thankful that when I wanted to study philosophy, I didn't fall into the hands of any sophist, and that I didn't waste my time on writers of histories, or in resolving complex arguments, or in studying appearances in the heavens. All these things required the help of the gods and fortune.

These reflections were written while I was among the Quadi, near the Granua River.

Book 2

Begin each morning by reminding yourself: today, I will meet people who are nosy, ungrateful, arrogant, deceitful, jealous, and unfriendly. They behave this way because they don't understand what is truly good or bad. But I know that the nature of good is what is right, and the nature of bad is what is wrong. I understand that those who do wrong are related to me, not just by blood, but because we share the same intelligence and divine spark. Therefore, they cannot truly harm me, nor can I be angry or hate them, for we are meant to work together, like feet, hands, eyelids, or the rows of upper and lower teeth. To fight against each other is against our nature, just as it is to be annoyed or to turn away from one another.

Remember that you are made up of a little flesh, some breath, and a guiding mind. Let go of distractions, like books, and focus on your true self. You don't have time to waste as if you were on the edge of death. Disregard the flesh—it is just blood and bones, a network of nerves, veins, and arteries. Consider your breath, too—it is just air, which is constantly expelled and drawn in. The most important part is the guiding mind: remember that you are aging and should not allow it to be controlled by unsocial impulses or be dissatisfied with life or fearful of the future.

Everything from the gods is full of purpose. What comes from fortune is connected with nature and is part of the divine plan. Everything flows from this source, including necessity and what benefits the entire universe, of which you are a part. What is good for every part of nature is what maintains and supports it. The universe is preserved by the changing elements and the transformation of things made from these elements. Let these principles be your foundation, and hold them as unshakeable truths. Set aside your desire for books so that you may die content and grateful to the gods.

Remember how long you've been delaying, how often the gods have given you opportunities, yet you've not taken them. It is time to understand which universe you are part of and recognize the divine source from which you come. There is limited time for you to clear your mind of confusion, and if you don't use it, it will be gone and will not return.

In every moment, act as a Roman and a human being by doing your tasks with dignity, kindness, freedom, and justice. Let go of all other thoughts by acting as if each task were your last. Let go of carelessness, resistance to reason, hypocrisy, selfishness, and dissatisfaction with your life. Notice how few things are needed to live a life that flows with peace and resembles the existence of the gods. The gods require nothing more from someone who follows these principles.

My soul, don't harm yourself any longer; you may not have another chance to honor yourself. Every person's life is complete, yet yours is nearly over, and you have not yet respected your own soul, instead seeking happiness in others' opinions.

Do external distractions bother you? Give yourself time to learn new and good things and stop being whirled around. But avoid being led astray by trivial activities that leave you without a purpose or clear thoughts.

People rarely become unhappy by not knowing what's in another person's mind, but those who don't understand their own minds will inevitably be unhappy.

Always keep in mind the nature of the whole universe and your nature and how they relate. No one can stop you from doing and saying things that align with your true nature.

The philosopher Theophrastus said that offenses driven by desire are worse than those caused by anger. When someone is angry, they may act against reason with pain and impulse, but someone driven by desire is controlled by pleasure and acts without self-control. He rightly said that actions driven by pleasure are more blameworthy than those driven by pain. Someone who acts out of anger may feel wronged, but someone who acts out of desire is driven to do wrong by their impulses.

Since you could leave this life at any moment, act and think as if this were true. Leaving this world shouldn't frighten you if the gods exist, for they wouldn't harm you. And if they don't exist, or don't care for human affairs, then why should it matter to live in a world without gods or purpose? But the gods do exist, and they do care for humans, and they've given us the means to avoid true evils. If there were real evils, they would ensure that we wouldn't fall into them. What doesn't make a person worse can't make their life worse. The universe hasn't overlooked this, nor made mistakes by letting good and bad happen randomly. Death, life, honor, dishonor, pain, and pleasure all happen to both good and bad people, and they don't make us better or worse, so they are neither good nor bad.

All things quickly fade: bodies disappear, and even their memories vanish. The nature of all things that bring pleasure or cause fear or are celebrated by fame are worthless and fleeting. It is up to our mind to observe this. We should also notice who gives us a reputation and understand death. When analyzed, death is just a natural process, and to fear it is childish. It is not only a natural process but also serves nature's purposes. Consider how humans are close to the divine, and what part of us connects with it when we are aligned with nature.

There is nothing more miserable than a person who is constantly running around in circles, trying to figure out everything. Like the poet said, they dig deep into the earth, searching for signs to guess what others are thinking. They don't realize that it's enough to focus on the divine spirit within themselves and serve it sincerely. This service means keeping it free from passion, trivial thoughts, and dissatisfaction with what happens, whether it comes from gods or men. What comes from the gods should be respected for its goodness, and what comes from men should be accepted because of our kinship. Sometimes, we may even feel pity for people due to their ignorance of what is good and bad, which is as serious a flaw as not being able to tell the difference between light and dark.

Even if you were going to live for three thousand years or even ten times that, remember that no one loses any life other than the one they are living now, nor lives any life other than the one they are losing. So, the longest and the shortest lives end up the same. The present moment is the same for everyone, though what is passing is different. Therefore, what is lost seems like just a brief moment. No one can lose either the past or the future, because how could someone take away what you don't have?

Remember these two things: First, everything has been the same from eternity and will keep coming back in a cycle, so it doesn't matter if a person sees the same things for a hundred years, two hundred, or forever. Second, both the longest-lived and the one who dies soonest lose the same thing—the present moment. This is the only thing we can be deprived of because it's the only thing we truly have, and we cannot lose what we don't have.

Remember that everything is just as we think it is. The Cynic philosopher Monimus pointed this out, and it's clear that his saying is useful if we take what is true from it.

The soul harms itself first when it becomes like a sore or tumor on the universe, as much as it can. To be upset by anything that happens is to separate ourselves from nature, of which we are all a part. Second, the soul harms itself when it turns away from another person or moves toward them with the intention of harming them, as with those who are angry. Third, the soul harms itself when it is overpowered by pleasure or pain. Fourth, when it acts insincerely, saying or doing anything false. Fifth, when it allows any action of its own to be without a purpose, acting thoughtlessly without considering what it's doing. Even the smallest things should be done with a goal in mind. The goal for rational beings is to follow reason and the law of the oldest and most respected state—the Universe.

In human life, time is just a moment, everything is in flux, our perception is dull, our bodies are rotting, our minds are spinning, fortune is hard to predict, and fame is lacking in judgment. To sum it up, everything related to the body flows away like a river, everything related to the soul is like a dream and vapor, life is a battle and a temporary stay in a strange land, and after fame comes oblivion. What, then, can guide us? One thing, and one thing only—philosophy. This means keeping the divine spirit within us free from harm and violence, superior to pleasure and pain, acting with purpose, truthfully and without hypocrisy, and not needing others to act or refrain from acting. It also means accepting everything that happens and everything that is allotted to us as coming from the same place from which we ourselves came. Finally, it means waiting for death with a cheerful mind, knowing that death is nothing more than the dissolution of the elements of which every living being is made. If the elements themselves are not harmed by constantly changing into each other, why should we fear the change and dissolution of all the elements? This is according to nature, and nothing that follows nature is evil.

This was written during my time in Carnuntum.

Book 3

Written in Carnuntum.

We should think about how our life is getting shorter every day, and how we have less and less time left. But there's something else to consider too: even if we live longer, we can't be sure that our mind will stay sharp enough to understand things the way we do now, and to keep thinking about both the divine and human things. If our mind starts to weaken, things like breathing, eating, imagining, and desiring will still work, but our ability to use our mind properly, to understand what we need to do, to separate truth from lies, and to decide if it's time to leave this life, all of these important abilities will be gone. So, we must act quickly, not just because we're getting closer to death every day, but also because our understanding and clarity of thought will fade away before our life does.

We should also notice that even the little things that happen in nature have their own kind of beauty. For example, when bread is baking, it sometimes cracks open on the top. These cracks might seem like a mistake, but they actually look nice and make us want to eat the bread. When figs are fully ripe, they split open, and even though this might look like they're about to rot, it still makes them look beautiful. The same goes for ripe olives and many other things in nature. If you look at these things by themselves, they might not seem beautiful, but because they happen naturally, they add beauty to the whole. So, if someone understands how nature works, they will find beauty in almost everything, even in things that might not look nice at first. Such a person can even enjoy the sight of wild animals, not just the paintings or sculptures of them. They can see beauty in an old woman or man, and even in young people, they will see beauty in a pure and respectful way. But this kind of appreciation is not for everyone, only for those who truly understand and love nature and its works.

Hippocrates, a famous doctor who cured many diseases, eventually got sick and died himself. The Chaldeans, who were known for predicting the future, couldn't avoid their own fates. Great leaders like Alexander, Pompey, and Julius Caesar, who destroyed entire cities and killed many soldiers, eventually died too. Heraclitus, who spent his life thinking about the universe, died from an illness that filled him with water. Democritus was killed by lice, and Socrates was also killed by vermin. What does all this mean? It means that life is like a journey on a ship—you board, you sail, and then you reach the shore. When you get there, it's time to leave. If there's another life after this one, the gods will be there too. But if there's nothing after, you'll stop feeling pain and pleasure, and you'll no longer be a slave to your body, which is just made of earth and blood, while your mind is something divine.

Do not waste the rest of your life by thinking about what others are doing unless it is relevant to some common good. When you spend time thinking about what someone else is doing, why they are doing it, what they are saying, what they are thinking, or what they are planning, you lose the chance to focus on your own mind. We should stop any thoughts that have no purpose and are useless, especially those that are overly curious or harmful. A person should train themselves to think only about things that, if someone suddenly asked, "What are you thinking about now?" you could answer immediately and honestly, "This or that." Your answer should show that everything in your mind is simple, kind, and fitting for a social being. Your thoughts should not be about pleasure or indulgence, rivalry, envy, suspicion, or anything else that would make you ashamed to admit what you are thinking.

A person like this, who no longer delays becoming one of the best, is like a priest and servant of the gods, using the divine spirit within them. This makes the person pure, unaffected by pleasure, unharmed by pain, untouched by insults, and free from feeling wronged. Such a person fights the noblest fight, one where no passion can overpower them. They are deeply just, accepting with all their soul everything that happens and is given to them as their share. They rarely, and only when absolutely necessary for the common good, think about what others are saying, doing, or thinking. They focus only on their own actions and the part of life that has been assigned to them. They make sure their own actions are good and believe that their own portion of life is good. Each person's destiny is part of them, and they move forward together with it.

They also remember that every rational being is a relative, and that caring for others is part of human nature. However, they do not hold on to the opinions of everyone, only of those who clearly live according to nature. As for those who do not live this way, they always remember what kind of people they are, both in private and in public, both day and night, and the kind of company they keep. Therefore, they do not value the praise of such people because those people are not even satisfied with themselves.

Do not work unwillingly, selfishly, or without careful thought, or while being distracted. Do not try to make your thoughts sound fancy, and do not be a person who talks too much or tries to do too many things. Additionally, let the divine spirit within you be the protector of a person who is mature, manly, involved in public affairs, Roman, and a leader. Be someone who is ready to leave life when the signal comes, without needing oaths or other people's approval. Be cheerful, and do not seek help from outside or rely on the peace that others can give. A person must stand upright, not be held up by others.

If you find anything in human life better than justice, truth, temperance, fortitude, and, in short, anything better than your own mind's satisfaction in doing what is right according to reason, and in accepting the life given to you without your own choice, then turn to that with all your soul and enjoy what you have found to be the best. But if nothing seems better than the divine spirit within you, which controls all your desires, carefully examines all your thoughts, and, as Socrates said, separates itself from the influence of the senses and submits to the gods while caring for mankind, then do not give any space to anything else. If you let anything else take its place, you will not be able to focus without distraction on the good that is truly yours.

It is not right that anything else, like praise from others, power, or enjoyment of pleasure, should compete with what is rational and truly good. These other things may seem to fit with what is better in a small way, but they quickly take control and lead us away. So, I say, simply and freely choose the better and stick to it.

What is useful is the better. If it is useful to you as a rational being, then keep to it; but if it is only useful to you as an animal, say so and stick to your judgment without arrogance. Just be sure that you make this decision carefully.

Never consider anything good for yourself that would force you to break a promise, lose your self-respect, hate anyone, be suspicious, curse, act dishonestly, or desire anything that requires secrecy. The person who puts their intelligence, spirit, and worship of what is excellent above everything else does not act tragically, does not groan, and does not need either solitude or large crowds. Most importantly, they live without either chasing after or running away from death. Whether they live with the soul inside their body for a long time or a short time, they do not care at all. Even if they must leave immediately, they will do so as readily as they would perform any other action that can be done with decency and order. Throughout life, they only make sure that their thoughts do not stray from what belongs to an intelligent animal and a member of a community.

In the mind of someone who is disciplined and pure, you will find no corruption, no festering wounds, and no sores that are just covered up. Their life does not feel incomplete when fate comes for them, just as an actor does not leave the stage before finishing the play. There is nothing servile, fake, overly attached, or detached in them, nothing that deserves blame, and nothing that seeks to hide.

Respect the ability that forms your opinions. Everything depends on whether your opinions agree with the nature and constitution of a rational being. This ability promises freedom from rash judgments, friendship towards others, and obedience to the gods.

Therefore, hold on to these few things and let go of everything else. Remember that every person lives only in the present moment, which is a small, indivisible point in time, and that the rest of their life is either in the past or uncertain. The time each person lives is short, the part of the earth where they live is small, and even the longest-lasting fame is short and will be passed on by people who will soon die and who do not even know themselves, much less someone who died long ago.

To the aids that have been mentioned, add this one: Make for yourself a clear description of whatever comes to your mind so that you can see clearly what kind of thing it is in its true form, completely and entirely, and tell yourself its proper name, the names of its parts, and what it will become. Nothing is more effective in elevating the mind than being able to examine each thing you encounter in life methodically and truthfully. Always look at things in a way that allows you to see what kind of universe this is, what role everything plays in it, what value everything has for the whole, and what value it has for a person, who is a citizen of the highest city, of which all other cities are like families. Consider what each thing is, what it is made of, how long it will last, and what virtue you need to face it, such as gentleness, courage, truthfulness, loyalty, simplicity, or contentment. On every occasion, a person should say, "This comes from God," or "This is according to the plan of destiny," or "This is from someone who is like me, a relative, but who does not know what is truly natural." But I know, and for this reason, I behave towards them with kindness and justice, following the natural law of fellowship. At the same time, in things that are indifferent, I try to determine their true value.

If you work on what is in front of you, following right reason seriously, vigorously, calmly, and without letting anything distract you, while keeping your divine part pure as if you had to give it back immediately, if you hold on to this, expecting nothing, fearing nothing, and being satisfied with your present actions according to nature, and if you speak the truth in every word and action, you will live happily. And no one can prevent this.

Just as doctors always have their instruments and knives ready for emergencies, you should always have principles ready for understanding both divine and human things and for doing everything, even the smallest task, with an awareness of the bond that unites the divine and human. You will not do anything well that belongs to humans without also referring to the divine, and the same is true in reverse.

No longer wander aimlessly; you will not read your own memoirs, nor the acts of the ancient Romans and Greeks, nor the selections from books that you were saving for old age. Hurry then to the goal before you, and, abandoning idle hopes, help yourself if you care for yourself while it is still possible.

They do not know how many things are signified by the words stealing, sowing, buying, staying quiet, or seeing what needs to be done, for this is not done by the eyes, but by a different kind of vision.

Body, soul, and mind: the body perceives through the senses, the soul has desires, and the mind has principles. Receiving sensory impressions is something even animals do; being driven by desires is common to both wild beasts and men who have become weak, and to tyrants like Phalaris and Nero. Having the mind to guide what seems appropriate is also found in those who do not believe in the gods, betray their country, and commit immoral acts in secret. If everything else I mentioned is shared by many, then what remains unique to a good person is being pleased and content with what happens, and with the fate assigned to them, not polluting the divine spirit within, and not disturbing it with a flood of images. Instead, they keep it calm, following it obediently as a god, never saying anything untrue or doing anything unjust. If everyone doubts that this person lives a simple, modest, and content life, he is not angry with them, nor does he stray from the path that leads to the end of life, which he should reach pure, calm, ready to leave, and in complete acceptance of his fate.

Book 4

The ruling part within us, when aligned with nature, adapts easily to whatever happens and is presented to it. It doesn't need specific materials but works toward its purpose under certain conditions. It creates its own path from obstacles, just as fire consumes what falls into it, making it grow stronger and higher.

Let every action have a purpose and align with the perfect principles of the art of life. People seek retreats for themselves—houses in the country, by the sea, or in the mountains—and you might desire such things too. But this is common thinking, for you can retreat into yourself anytime you choose. Nowhere can a person find more quiet or freedom from trouble than within his own soul, especially when he has thoughts that bring immediate tranquility. I affirm that tranquility is nothing more than the proper ordering of the mind. Constantly give yourself this retreat and renew yourself. Let your guiding principles be brief and fundamental, so they can cleanse your soul and free you from discontent with the world.

What are you upset about? Is it because of the bad behavior of others? Remember this: rational creatures are made to help each other, and being patient with others is part of being just. People don't do wrong on purpose. Think about how many people have fought, hated, and hurt each other, only to end up dead and turned to ashes. So calm yourself. Or maybe you're unhappy with what life has given you. Then remember this choice: either there is a higher plan guiding everything, or everything happens by chance. Or think about the arguments that prove the world is like a big community, and find peace in that.

But maybe physical things still bother you. In that case, remember that your mind is separate from the body, whether the body is calm or troubled. Once your mind realizes its own power, it doesn't need to be affected by the body. Also, think about everything you've learned about dealing with pain and pleasure, and find peace.

Or maybe you're worried about fame. Think about how quickly people forget everything and how endless time stretches out before and after us. Fame is empty, and the opinions of those who praise you are often unreliable. The space in which people praise you is so small, and the people who do it are so few and insignificant.

So, retreat into your own mind and be free. Don't let yourself be distracted or stressed. Look at things as a human being, as a citizen, and as someone who is mortal. Keep two ideas in mind: first, that things outside of you don't really touch your soul; they remain outside and can't move you unless you let them. Second, that all the things you see are constantly changing and will soon be gone. Remember how many changes you've already seen. The universe is always changing, and life is shaped by our opinions.

If our minds are shared, then so is the reason that makes us rational beings. If that's true, then the reason that tells us what to do and what not to do is also shared. If that's true, then we share a common law. If that's true, then we are fellow citizens. If that's true, then we are part of a community. And if that's true, then the world is like a single city. What other community could all humans be members of? And from this shared community comes our very mind, our reason, and our sense of law. Where else could they come from? Just as my body comes from the earth, and the water in me comes from some source, and the heat in me from another, so too my mind must come from some source.

Death is just like birth—a mystery of nature. It's the same elements being combined and then separated. It's nothing to be ashamed of because it's not unnatural for a rational being, and it's not against the reason we are made with.

It's natural for certain people to act a certain way, and it's unavoidable. If you wish it were different, it's like wanting figs to stop producing juice. But remember that in a short time, both you and the person who bothers you will be dead, and soon after, not even your names will be remembered.

If you take away your opinion that you've been hurt, then the hurt itself disappears. And if you take away the feeling that you've been harmed, then there is no harm.

Whatever doesn't make a person worse in themselves doesn't make their life worse either. It can't hurt them from the outside or the inside.

The nature of what is beneficial had to act this way.

Think about it: everything that happens, happens justly. If you look closely, you'll see this is true, not just in how events follow each other, but in the sense that everything happens as it should, as if someone were assigning each thing its place. So keep observing, and in whatever you do, aim to be good and to act as a good person should in every situation.

When someone wrongs you, don't see things the way they do or the way they want you to see them. Instead, see things as they truly are.

Always keep these two principles ready: first, to do only what reason and fairness suggest is good for people. Second, to be willing to change your opinion if someone convinces you that you're wrong. But this change should only come from a clear understanding of what is just or beneficial, not just because it feels good or brings approval.

Do you have reason? Yes, you do. So why not use it? If reason is doing its job, what else could you want?

You have existed as part of the Whole. You will disappear into what made you, but really, you will be taken back into the source that created everything.

Many grains of incense are placed on the same altar. One burns away first, another later, but it doesn't matter.

In just a few days, you could seem like a god to the people who now see you as an animal or a fool—if you return to your principles and the worship of reason.

Don't act as if you're going to live for ten thousand years. Death hangs over you. While you live, while it's in your power, be good.

Think about how much peace you gain when you don't worry about what your neighbor says, does, or thinks, but focus only on making sure your own actions are just and pure. Or as Agathon said, don't look around at the bad behavior of others, but keep your path straight.

If you're obsessed with posthumous fame, consider this: everyone who remembers you will soon be dead too. Then those who come after them will also die, until all memory of you is extinguished. Even if people remember you forever, what does that matter to you? I don't mean just to the dead, but to the living—what's the point of praise, except if it has some practical benefit? By focusing on fame, you are rejecting the gift of nature and clinging to something else.

Everything that is beautiful is beautiful in itself and is complete in itself. Praise is not part of what makes it beautiful. Whether or not it's praised, it's neither better nor worse. This is true even of things commonly considered beautiful, like material objects or works of art. Something that is truly beautiful doesn't need anything else, not more than law, not more than truth, not more than kindness or modesty. Which of these things becomes beautiful because it is praised or is ruined by being blamed? Is an emerald less valuable if no one praises it? What about gold, ivory, purple, a lyre, a knife, a flower, or a bush?

If souls continue to exist, how does the air hold all of them from the beginning of time? But how does the earth hold all the bodies that have been buried since time began? Just as the earth eventually breaks down these bodies to make room for others, so too the air transforms souls, making room for new ones. This could be one explanation if we believe that souls live on. But we should also think about the number of animals eaten every day by us and other creatures—an enormous number, yet the earth still has room for them because they transform into blood and other elements.

How do we seek the truth in this matter? By separating what is material from what is the cause of form.

Don't let yourself be swept away. In every action, keep justice in mind, and in every thought, stick to what is certain.

Everything that happens is in harmony with you, O Universe. Nothing is too early or too late if it happens at the right time for you. Everything that comes to me is like fruit from your seasons, O Nature. From you come all things, in you are all things, and to you, all things return. The poet says, "Dear city of Cecrops," and should you not say, "Dear city of Zeus"?

Keep yourself occupied with few things, says the philosopher, if you want to be calm. But consider if it wouldn't be better to do only what is necessary, what reason and the social nature of humans demand, and to do it in the way that reason requires. This brings both the peace that comes from doing good and the peace that comes from doing few things. Most of what we say and do is unnecessary. If you can remove unnecessary things, you will have more time and less stress. So on every occasion, ask yourself, "Is this one of the unnecessary things?" And don't just remove unnecessary actions, but unnecessary thoughts too, so that unnecessary actions won't follow.

Try living the life of a good person—someone who is satisfied with their place in the world and with their own just actions and kind disposition.

Have you seen these things? Then look at them again. Don't upset yourself. Be simple. Does someone do wrong? They do wrong to themselves. Has something happened to you? Well, everything that happens has been arranged by the universe from the beginning and has been given to you as part of your destiny. In short, life is short. Use the present moment wisely with reason and justice. Be calm and relaxed.

Either the universe is well-organized, or it's a chaotic mix of elements, but still a universe. But can there be order within you if there is disorder in the whole? Especially when all things are connected and influence each other.

A black character, a weak character, a stubborn character, a beastly character, a childish character, a foolish character, a false character, a cruel character, a deceitful character, a tyrannical character.

If someone doesn't understand what's in the universe, they are a stranger in it. If they don't understand what's happening in it, they are also a stranger. They are like someone running away if they reject social reason. They are blind if they close their mind's eye. They are poor if they depend on others and don't have everything they need within themselves. They are a tumor on the universe if they separate themselves from the common nature through dissatisfaction with what happens because the same nature produces everything, including them. They are torn away from the community if they separate their soul from the soul of all rational beings, which is one.

One philosopher has no shirt, another has no book. Here is someone else who is half-naked: "I have no bread," he says, "but I stick to reason." But I have all the food of learning, and yet I am not faithful.

Love the art you have learned, and take comfort in it. Go through the rest of your life with sincere commitment to the gods, never making yourself a tyrant or a slave to anyone.

Consider, for example, the time of Vespasian. You will see the same things happening: people marrying, having children, getting sick, dying, fighting, feasting, trading, farming, flattering, being arrogant, suspecting others, plotting, wishing for others to die, complaining about their lot, falling in love, gathering wealth, wanting political power. And now, that life is gone. Look at the time of Trajan. Again, the same things happened, and that life too is gone. Similarly, look at the histories of other times and nations, and see how many lives, after much effort, quickly fell apart and returned to the elements. But most importantly, remember those you have known yourself, who distracted themselves with empty things and neglected to live according to their true nature, to hold on to it firmly and find contentment in it. And remember that the attention you give to each action should be in proportion to its importance. This way, you won't be dissatisfied if you only devote as much time as necessary to less important matters.

Words that were common long ago are now outdated, and so too are the names of people who were once famous—like Camillus, Caeso, Volesus, Dentatus, and later Scipio and Cato, then Augustus, and then Hadrian and Antoninus. All things quickly fade and turn into mere stories, and complete oblivion soon buries them. And I'm talking about those who shone with great brilliance. For the rest, as soon as they breathe their last, they are gone, and no one talks about them. And in the end, what is even an eternal memory? It's nothing. So what should we focus on? Only this: just thoughts, social actions, honest words, and a disposition that gladly accepts everything that happens as necessary, understandable, and coming from a reasonable source.

Willingly submit yourself to Clotho, one of the Fates, allowing her to spin your thread into whatever she chooses.

Everything is fleeting—both the memory of things and the things themselves.

Constantly observe how everything changes and get used to the idea that the universe loves nothing more than to change old things into new ones. Everything that exists is like a seed of what will come next. But you might be thinking only of seeds that are planted in the earth or a womb. That's a very simple way of thinking.

You will soon die, and you are not yet calm, free from disturbances, unafraid of external harm, kind to all people, or convinced that acting justly is the only wisdom.

Look into the minds of others, even those who are wise, and see what they avoid and what they pursue.

What is evil to you does not exist in the mind of another, nor in any change of your body. Where is it, then? It is in your own mind, in the part that forms opinions about what is evil. Let this part not form such opinions, and all will be well. Even if your body is hurt, burned, or decays, let the part of you that judges these things remain calm. It should understand that nothing is truly bad or good that can happen equally to both bad and good people. For what happens equally to those who live according to nature and those who live against nature is neither in line with nature nor against it.

Always think of the universe as one living being, made of one substance and one soul. Notice how everything is connected to one understanding, how everything works together, and how all things are part of everything else. Observe the continuous weaving of the threads and the interconnection of the web.

You are a small soul carrying a dead body, as Epictetus used to say.

It's not bad for things to change, and it's not good for things to stay the same because of change.

Time is like a river of events, a powerful stream. As soon as one thing appears, it's swept away, and another takes its place, and this too will be carried away.

Everything that happens is as natural and expected as roses in spring and fruit in summer—like disease, death, slander, and betrayal, and all the things that either delight or trouble foolish people.

In the chain of events, those that come after always fit with those that came before. This chain is not just a list of disconnected things but a rational connection. Just as everything that exists is harmoniously arranged, so too do the things that happen show a wonderful relationship.

Always remember Heraclitus's saying that the death of earth is to become water, the death of water is to become air, and the death of air is to become fire, and vice versa. Remember also that people forget where the path leads and that they quarrel with the reason that governs the universe, even though they interact with it constantly. They find everyday things surprising, but we should not act and speak as if we were asleep, even though in sleep we seem to act and speak. We should not simply accept what we are taught like children with their parents.

If a god told you that you would die tomorrow or the day after tomorrow, you wouldn't care much whether it was the third day or the next day, unless you were extremely fearful because the difference is so small. So think it's no big deal to die after however many years you can name rather than tomorrow.

Think constantly about how many doctors have died after worrying about their patients, how many astrologers have died after predicting the deaths of others, how many philosophers have died after debating endlessly about death or immortality, how many heroes have died after killing thousands, how many tyrants have died after using their power over life and death with cruelty, as if they were immortal. And think about how many cities are now completely gone, like Helice, Pompeii, Herculaneum, and countless others. Consider all the people you've known, one after the other: one man buries another, and then he is buried, and all this happens in a short time. The conclusion is that you should always see human life as brief and of little value. Yesterday, you were just a drop of semen; tomorrow, you'll be a mummy or ashes. So live according to nature, and when your time comes, leave life content, like an olive that falls when it is ripe, blessing the earth that bore it and thanking the tree on which it grew.

Be like the rocky headland against which the waves constantly break. It stands firm and calms the fury of the water around it.

You might think, "It's my bad luck that this happened to me." But you should say, "It's my good luck that although this happened to me, I can endure it without pain, without being crushed by the present or afraid of the future." Because something like this could happen to anyone, but not everyone could bear it without pain. So why consider the event more of a misfortune than your ability to endure it a good fortune? And would you call anything a misfortune for a person that isn't a deviation from human nature? And does something seem to you to be a deviation from human nature if it doesn't go against what human nature intends? Well, you know what the purpose of nature is. So will this thing that has happened stop you from being just, courageous, self-controlled, wise, careful in your decisions, truthful, honorable, and free? Or from having all the other qualities that, when combined, fulfill human nature? So, in any situation that might make you sad, remember this principle: "This is not a misfortune, but to bear it well is good fortune."

It's a simple but effective way to lessen your fear of death by thinking about those who clung to life for a long time. What did they gain compared to those who died young? In the end, they all lie in their graves—like Caedicianus, Fabius, Julianus, Lepidus, and all the others who attended many funerals and then had their own. The time we have to live is short, and we drag it out with such effort, in poor company, in weak bodies. So don't consider life a great thing. Look at the endless time behind you and the infinity ahead of you. In this vastness, what is the difference between someone who lives for three days and someone who lives for three generations?

Always take the shortest path, and the shortest path is the natural one. Do and say everything according to the soundest reason. For such a purpose frees a person from trouble, from conflict, and from all artifice and display.

Book 5

When you wake up in the morning and don't feel like getting up, remind yourself: "I'm getting up to do the work of a human being." So why am I unhappy if I'm about to do what I was made for, the purpose for which I was brought into the world? Or was I made just to stay in bed and keep warm? But staying in bed feels so nice. Were you made to enjoy comfort, or were you made for action and effort? Don't you see how little plants, birds, ants, spiders, and bees all work together to make the world what it is? And yet you're unwilling to do the work of a human being and hurry to do what's natural to you? But we need rest too. Yes, rest is necessary, but nature has set limits to this, just like with eating and drinking, and yet you often go beyond these limits, beyond what's enough; but in your actions, you stop short of what you could do. This means you don't really love yourself, because if you did, you would love your nature and its purpose. Other people who love their work push themselves to the point of neglecting washing and eating. But you value your own nature less than a craftsman values his craft, or a dancer values dancing, or a lover of money values his wealth, or a person who loves fame values his reputation. Such people, when they are passionate about something, will skip meals and sleep rather than stop perfecting what they care about. But do you see the acts that benefit society as less important and less deserving of your effort?

It's easy to push away or erase any troubling or inappropriate thoughts and immediately find calm.

Consider any word or action that aligns with nature to be appropriate for you; don't let criticism or the opinions of others make you doubt yourself. If something is good to do or say, don't consider it beneath you. Others have their own principles and follow their own paths; don't be distracted by them. Stay on your path, which is aligned with both your nature and the universal nature—they are one and the same.

I continue through life according to nature until I fall and rest, breathing my last breath into the air from which I draw it daily, and returning to the earth that gave my father his seed, my mother her blood, and my nurse her milk; the earth that has fed and watered me for so many years; the earth that bears my footsteps and endures all the ways I use and abuse it.

People may not admire you for your intellect. So be it. But there are many other qualities you can't say you lack by nature. So show those virtues that are entirely within your power—honesty, dignity, hard work, self-discipline, contentment with what you have, kindness, openness, simplicity, moderation, and magnanimity. Don't you see how many qualities you can display without needing any special talent? And yet you still choose to fall short. Or do you think your lack of natural talent forces you to complain, to be stingy, to flatter, to criticize your own body, to try to please others, to boast, or to let your mind be so restless? No, by the gods, it does not! You could have freed yourself from these things long ago. If you are slow to understand, work on it—don't ignore it or take pleasure in your dullness.

Some people, when they do a favor for someone else, expect to be thanked. Others don't expect thanks but still think of the other person as owing them something, and they remember what they've done. A third kind doesn't even think about what they've done, just like a vine that produces grapes and expects nothing more after it's borne its fruit. Just like a horse that runs, a dog that hunts, or a bee that makes honey, a person who does a good deed doesn't call for others to notice, but moves on to the next good deed, just as a vine moves on to bear grapes again in its season. So you should aim to be like those who are almost unaware of the good they do. But you might say, "Shouldn't I be aware of my actions? Isn't it part of being a social creature to know when I'm acting in a social way and to want others to recognize it too?" That's true, but you're misunderstanding my point. If you focus on understanding this, you won't fall into the trap I mentioned before. Even those who misunderstand what I'm saying do so because of a seemingly logical reason. But if you want to understand, don't worry that this will make you neglect your social duties.

The Athenians prayed:
"Rain, rain, O dear Zeus,
on the plowed fields

and plains of the Athenians."
We should pray in this simple and honest way, or not pray at all.

Just as people say that Asclepius prescribed horse-riding, or cold baths, or going barefoot to someone, we should think of nature as prescribing disease, injury, loss, or anything else of the kind. In the first case, "prescribed" means that it was ordered for the person's health. In the second, it means that what happens to each person is arranged as part of their destiny. We talk about things "fitting" just as masons say that stones fit together in walls or pyramids when they join in a certain way. In the whole of the universe, there is one harmony, and just as all bodies combine to make one harmonious whole, so all causes combine to make one harmonious destiny. Even those who don't know much can sense what I mean. They say, "It was fate that brought this on him." So if "brought," then also "prescribed." So let's accept these things as we accept Asclepius's prescriptions, even if some of them are harsh, because we trust they will lead to health.

You should take the same view of what happens to you as you do of your own health, and welcome everything that happens, even if it seems harsh, because it contributes to the health of the universe and the prosperity of Zeus. He wouldn't bring anything upon anyone unless it also benefited the Whole, just as no natural principle brings anything unsuitable to what it governs.

So there are two reasons you should be content with what happens to you. One, because it was meant for you and is related to you, like a thread of destiny spun for you from the very beginning. The other, because what happens to each individual contributes to the welfare, perfection, and even the very continuity of what governs the universe. For the integrity of the Whole is compromised if you cut off even the smallest part of its connection and continuity, whether of its parts or its causes. And you do cut something off when you fret about your lot; in a sense, this is an act of destruction.

Don't be disheartened or impatient if you don't succeed in doing everything according to the right principles. If you stumble, get back up, and be glad if most of your actions align with human nature. And love what you return to. Don't return to philosophy like a schoolboy returning to his teacher, but like a person with sore eyes returning to his sponge and ointment, or someone else returning to their bandage or compress. In this way, you'll show that following reason isn't a burden but a relief. Remember, philosophy requires only what your nature requires, but you wanted something unnatural. And what could be more pleasant than following your nature? This is how pleasure deceives us, but think whether there isn't something more pleasant in magnanimity, generosity, simplicity, consideration, or piety. And what could be more pleasant than wisdom itself, when you think of the security and peace it brings through understanding and knowledge?

Things are so wrapped up that several philosophers have thought them completely beyond understanding, and even the Stoics find them difficult. Every agreement we give to our perceptions is open to error. No one is infallible. So look at the objects of our experience—how short-lived they are, how poor in quality: even a criminal, a prostitute, or a thief could own them. Look also at the character of the people around you; it's hard to put up with even the best of them, let alone endure yourself. In all this darkness and filth, with everything constantly changing and passing away, what could possibly be worth valuing or pursuing? Instead, we should comfort ourselves with the thought of natural release, not being impatient for it, but holding on to two principles: one, that nothing will happen to me that isn't in line with the nature of the Whole, and two, that it's within my power not to act against my god and daemon, because no one can force me to do that.

What am I using my soul for right now? I must ask myself this on every occasion. I must examine myself and ask, "What kind of soul do I have right now?" Is it like that of a child, a young man, a woman, a tyrant, a domestic animal, or a wild beast?

We can understand what most people consider to be "good" by looking at their behavior. If someone truly valued qualities like wisdom, self-control, justice, and courage, they wouldn't be interested in anything that didn't align with those values. But if someone values what most people think is good, they'll readily agree with the comic writer who said that some people have so many goods they have no room to relieve themselves. This difference is obvious to most people. Otherwise, the saying wouldn't be offensive or rejected when applied to real goods, but we accept it when it's about wealth, luxury, and fame.

I'm made up of form and matter, and neither will disappear into nothingness, just as neither came into existence out of nothing. So every part of me will change and become some other part of the universe, and that part will change again into another part of the universe, and so on forever. The same process that brought me into existence also brought my parents into existence, and so on infinitely backward. Nothing prevents us from saying this, even if the universe follows definite cycles.

Reason and philosophy are powers that are sufficient for themselves and their own actions. They move from their own first principles to the end they aim for, which is why these actions are called "right" actions—they proceed along the right path.

You should ignore anything that isn't a part of your role as a human being. These things aren't required of you; they don't fulfill your nature or help you achieve your purpose. Therefore, they aren't good. Moreover, if any of these things were truly a part of you, it wouldn't be right for you to disdain them or resist them. We wouldn't praise someone for not needing them. If these things were truly good, then a person who deprives themselves of them or tolerates being deprived of them wouldn't be a good person. But in fact, the more a person deprives themselves of such things or tolerates their loss, the better they are.

Your mind will take on the character of your most frequent thoughts, for the soul is dyed by your thoughts. So dye your soul with a continuous series of thoughts like these: "Wherever a person can live, they can live well." But you must live in a palace. Well, then, you can live well in a palace. And again: "Each thing is made for a purpose, and it moves toward that purpose; its end lies in that toward which it moves; and where its end is, there also is its advantage and good." The good for a rational creature is community. It has been shown above that we are born for community. Is it not clear that the inferior exists for the sake of the superior? But things that have life are superior to those without life, and those with reason are superior to those without.

To seek what is impossible is madness, and it is impossible for bad people not to act according to their nature.

Nothing happens to any person that they are not naturally equipped to endure. The same things happen to others, and either because they don't realize it or because they show great spirit, they remain calm and unharmed. Isn't it strange that ignorance and arrogance can be stronger than wisdom?

Things themselves don't touch the soul at all; they have no entry to the soul and can't move it. The soul alone moves itself and makes whatever judgments it sees fit about the things presented to it.

In one respect, other people are the closest things to me because I must do good to them and tolerate them. But when some people obstruct my proper work, they become indifferent to me, no different than the sun, the wind, or a wild animal. These may impede some actions, but they don't impede my will or my disposition, which have the power to adapt and change. The mind converts and changes every hindrance to its activity into a help, so that what was an obstacle becomes a furtherance to the work.

Revere what is best in the universe: the power that uses all things and directs all things. Similarly, revere what is best in yourself: the power that uses everything else in you and governs your life.

What doesn't harm the community doesn't harm the citizen. Apply this rule in every situation where you think you've been harmed: if the community isn't harmed, neither am I. But if the community is harmed, you shouldn't be angry with the person who caused the harm—show them where they went wrong.

Think often of how quickly things pass by and disappear, both the things that are and the things that are produced. Existence is like a river in constant flow, with its actions always changing and its causes working in endless ways. Hardly anything stands still. And think of the vastness of the past and future, in which all things vanish. How foolish is it, then, to be puffed up with ambition, to struggle and worry over things, or to be upset about them as if they were permanent or could trouble you for long?

Think of the whole of existence, of which you are a tiny part; think of the whole of time, of which you have been assigned a brief and fleeting moment; think of destiny—what a small fraction of it are you?

Another person wrongs me. What's that to me? Let them deal with their own actions and disposition. I now have what the universal nature has given me, and I do what my own nature requires me to do.

Let the part of your soul that leads and governs stay undisturbed by the movements in the flesh, whether they are of pleasure or pain. Don't let it unite with them, but let it stay within its own bounds and limit those effects to their proper parts. But when these effects reach the mind through the natural connection that exists in a unified body, you shouldn't resist the sensation, for it is natural. But don't let the ruling part of yourself add the judgment that the sensation is either good or bad.

Live with the gods. And you live with the gods if you constantly show them that your soul is content with what is assigned to you and that it does everything your daemon wishes, which Zeus has given to every person as a guardian and guide—a part of himself. This is every person's understanding and reason.

Are you angry with someone whose armpits smell? Are you angry with someone whose breath is foul? What good will your anger do you? That's just the way his armpits or mouth are, and it's necessary that they produce such smells. But you might say, "He has reason, and if he tries, he can realize where he's offending." Good for you if he does! And you have reason too, so use your rational faculty to stir his rational faculty. Show him his mistake; correct him. If he listens, you'll cure him, and there's no need for anger.

You can live your life here on earth just as you intend to live when you've left it. But if people don't allow you to live as you wish, then leave life, but don't see it as a misfortune. "The house is smoky, so I'm leaving it." Why think this is such a big deal? But as long as nothing like that drives me out, I stay, I am free, and no one can stop me from doing what I choose to do. And I choose to do what is in line with the nature of a rational and social being.

The intelligence of the universe is social. It has made the lower things for the sake of the higher, and it has harmonized the higher with each other. You can see how it has arranged everything to fit together and work together, bringing the best things into unity.

How have you behaved so far toward the gods, your parents, siblings, wife, children, teachers, tutors, friends, relatives, and servants? Have you followed the principle of "do no harm" with all of them? Remind yourself of all you've been through and how much you've endured. Your life story is complete, your service is done. Think of how often you've seen beauty, disregarded pleasure and pain, rejected glory, and been kind to those who were unkind to you.

Why do unskilled and ignorant minds confuse those who have skill and knowledge? What kind of mind has true skill and knowledge? It's the mind that knows the beginning and the end and understands the reason that governs all existence, guiding the Whole through its appointed cycles for all eternity.

Soon, very soon, you'll be ashes or a skeleton, just a name or not even that. If you do have a name, it will be just a sound and an echo.

The things people value in life are empty, rotten, and trivial—like little dogs biting each other or children quarreling, laughing, and then crying. But fidelity, modesty, justice, and truth have fled up to Olympus from the wide-spread earth.

So what's left to keep you here if the objects of sense are constantly changing and never stable, if our senses are dull and easily misled, and if the soul itself is just an exhalation of blood? To have a good reputation in such a world is meaningless. Why not wait calmly for your end, whether it's extinction or transition to another state? And until that time comes, what's enough? Only to worship and praise the gods, to do good to others, to practice tolerance and self-restraint. And as for everything beyond the limits of your body and breath, remember that it's neither yours nor in your control.

You can always keep your life on the right path if you follow reason in your judgments and actions. Two things are common to the souls of all rational beings, both gods and humans: they are free from any external hindrance, and their good lies in a just disposition and just actions, with these being the limit of their desire.

If something isn't caused by my own wrongdoing, or if it isn't the result of any wrong done to me, and if it doesn't harm the community, then why should it trouble me? And what harm could it do to the community?

Don't let other people's grief carry you away indiscriminately. Help them as best you can and as the situation deserves, even if their grief is for the loss of something insignificant. But don't imagine their loss as any real harm—that's the wrong way to think. Instead, be like the old man in the play who reclaimed his foster child's favorite toy at the end, never forgetting that it was only a toy. So when you feel pity for others, remind yourself of what things are really worth. "Yes, but these things are important to them." Is that any reason for you to join in their foolishness?

"There was a time when everything seemed to go my way." But good fortune is what you make for yourself: and good fortune is having good inclinations, good impulses, and good actions.

Book 6

The universe is made up of a substance that can be shaped and directed, and the reason behind it has no intention to do harm. There is no malice in it, and nothing it creates is done wrongly or with ill intent. Everything that exists is made according to this reason.

If you are doing what you should be doing, it shouldn't matter whether you are cold or warm, sleepy or well-rested, praised or criticized, or even if you're close to death or busy with something else. Dying is just another part of life, and in this, as in everything else, it's enough to do your best.

Look inside yourself. Don't overlook the unique quality or value of anything.

Everything that exists changes quickly. Things either turn into vapor if all substance is one, or they disperse into smaller parts.

The reason that governs everything knows its own nature, what it creates, and the material it uses to create.

The best way to get back at someone who has wronged you is not to become like them.

Take joy and find peace in moving from one good action to another, keeping your thoughts on the divine.

The mind is what wakes itself up, shapes itself, and decides how it wants to see everything that happens to it.

Everything in the universe happens according to its nature. It couldn't happen according to anything else—whether something outside controls it or it controls something within it.

The universe is either a random mix of things, where everything is jumbled together and eventually falls apart, or it is a unified whole with order and purpose. If it's the first, why do I care about anything? Why do I worry about anything other than the fact that I'll return to the earth someday? And if it's the second, I should respect it, stay firm, and trust in the one who governs it all.

When something upsets you, quickly return to your calm state. Don't stay out of harmony longer than necessary. You'll master this more by constantly returning to it.

If you had a stepmother and a mother at the same time, you'd pay attention to your stepmother, but you'd always go back to your mother. The court and philosophy should be like that to you: the court is your stepmother, and philosophy is your mother. Return to philosophy often and rest in her. She will help you see the court's demands as bearable, and make you bearable in the court.

When we have meat before us and other types of food, we should recognize that what we are seeing is the dead body of a fish, or the dead body of a bird, or the dead body of a pig. Similarly, when we look at Falernian wine, we should remember that it is nothing more than a little grape juice, and when we see a purple robe, we should realize that it is just some sheep's wool dyed with the blood of a shellfish. These are the real impressions of what these things truly are, and when we see them in this way, we penetrate their real nature and understand them for what they truly are. In the same way, throughout our lives, we should act by revealing the true nature of things that seem most worthy of our approval, laying them bare, and examining their lack of value. We should strip away all the words that make them seem grander than they are. Outward appearances can be a powerful deceiver of reason, and when you are most convinced that you are dealing with things that are worth your effort, it is then that they deceive you the most. So, consider what Crates said about Xenocrates himself.

Most of the things that the masses admire are basic objects, those that are held together by cohesion or natural structure, such as stones, wood, fig trees, vines, or olives. But the things that are admired by people who are slightly more reasonable are connected to things that are held together by a living principle, like flocks or herds of animals. The things admired by people who are even more educated are those that are connected to a rational soul, but not a universal soul, only rational to the extent that it is skilled in some art, or expert in some other way, or simply rational to the extent that it possesses a number of slaves. But the person who values a rational soul, a soul that is universal and fit for social life, cares for nothing else except this. Above all things, they keep their soul in a state and activity that conforms to reason and social life, and they work together with others who share the same kind of values.

Some things are rushing into existence, while others are rushing out. Even as something is born, part of it is already dying. The world is constantly being renewed by motions and changes, just as time keeps flowing endlessly. In this river of life, where nothing stays still, what is really worth valuing among all the things that rush by? It's like falling in love with a sparrow that flies by, but it's already gone out of sight. Life is just like that—transient, like a breath you take in and let out.

Breathing and taking in impressions are not things to be valued, just like how plants transpire and animals breathe. Nor is it valuable to be driven by desires like a puppet on strings or to gather in groups. Even eating is just about getting rid of the waste later. So, what should be valued? Applause? No. Nor should we value the clapping of tongues, which is just empty praise from the crowd. If you've given up on trivial fame, what's left to value? To me, it's this: to act or refrain from acting according to your own nature, as skills and crafts teach. Every craft aims to make its product fit for its purpose, just as a gardener, a horse-trainer, or a dog-trainer does. The same goes for educating and teaching young people. That's where the real value lies, and if you hold onto this, you won't need anything else. Will you not stop valuing so many other things too? Otherwise, you'll never be free, never be self-sufficient, and never be without passion. You'll be envious, jealous, and suspicious of those who can take away what you value, and you'll plot against those who have what you want. If you desire any of these things, you'll be in a state of turmoil, and you'll often find yourself blaming the gods. But if you honor and respect your own mind, you'll be content with yourself, in harmony with society, and in agreement with the gods, praising all that they give and have arranged.

Everything around you—the earth, the sky, the elements—is constantly in motion. But the movement of virtue doesn't follow these; it's something more divine and moves forward along a path that's hard to understand.

People act in strange ways! They won't praise those who are alive at the same time and living alongside them, but they place great value on being praised by future generations, by people they have never seen and never will see. This is very much like being upset because those who lived before you didn't praise you.

If something is difficult for you to accomplish, don't think that it is impossible for any person. But if something is possible for a human and in line with their nature, then you should believe that you can achieve it as well.

In gymnastic exercises, suppose someone scratches you with their nails or hits your head and causes a wound. We don't show signs of anger, nor are we offended, nor do we suspect them afterward as being treacherous. Yet, we remain cautious around them, not as an enemy, nor with suspicion, but simply by quietly staying out of their way. Let your behavior be like this in all parts of life. Let us overlook many things in people who are like opponents in the gymnasium. It is within our power, as I said, to avoid them without suspicion or hatred.

If anyone can convince me and show me that I am not thinking or acting correctly, I will gladly change, for I seek the truth, by which no one was ever harmed. But the person who stays in their error and ignorance is the one who is injured.

I do my duty; other things do not trouble me because they are either things without life, or things without reason, or things that have lost their way and do not know the right path.

As for animals that have no reason, and generally for all things and objects, since you have reason and they do not, make use of them with a generous and liberal spirit. But towards human beings, who do have reason, behave with a social spirit. And on all occasions, call on the gods, and do not trouble yourself about how long you shall do this; for even three hours spent this way are sufficient.

Alexander the Macedonian and his groom were brought to the same state by death; they were either received into the same primary elements of the universe, or they were equally dispersed among the atoms.

Consider how many things happen at the same moment within each of us—things that concern the body and things that concern the soul. So do not be surprised if many more things, or rather all things that exist in the one whole, which we call the Cosmos, exist at the same time.

If someone should ask you how the name Antoninus is written, would you loudly and impatiently shout out each letter? What if they become angry—will you become angry too? Wouldn't you rather calmly spell out each letter in order? In the same way, in this life, remember that every duty is made up of certain parts. It is your duty to observe these parts, and without being disturbed or showing anger towards those who are angry with you, continue on your way and complete what is set before you.

How cruel it is not to allow people to strive after the things that seem suitable to their nature and beneficial! Yet in some way, you do not allow them to do this when you are vexed because they do wrong. For they are certainly moved towards things because they believe them to be suitable to their nature and beneficial to them. But if it is not so, then teach them, and show them without being angry.

Death is the end of impressions through the senses, the end of the pulling strings that move our desires, the end of the wandering thoughts, and the end of serving the flesh.

It is a shame for the soul to be the first to give up in this life when your body does not give up.

Take care that you do not become like a Caesar, that you are not stained with that dye; for such things happen. Keep yourself simple, good, pure, serious, free from affectation, a friend of justice, a worshipper of the gods, kind, affectionate, and diligent in all proper acts. Strive to remain the kind of person that philosophy intended to make you. Reverence the gods, and help people. Life is short. There is only one true fruit of this earthly life—a pious disposition and social acts. Do everything as a disciple of Antoninus. Remember his consistency in every act that was in line with reason, his even temper in all things, his piety, the calmness of his expression, his gentleness, his disregard for empty fame, and his efforts to understand things; and how he never let anything pass without first carefully examining it and clearly understanding it; and how he bore with those who blamed him unjustly without blaming them in return; how he did nothing in a hurry; how he ignored slander; how exact he was in examining manners and actions; how he did not reproach people, nor was he timid, suspicious, or a sophist; and how little he was satisfied with—such as his lodging, bed, clothes, food, and servants; and how hardworking and patient he was; and how, because of his frugal diet, he could last until evening without needing to relieve himself except at the usual hour; and his steadiness and consistency in his friendships; and how he tolerated free speech from those who opposed his opinions; and the pleasure he took when someone showed him a better way; and how religious he was without being superstitious. Imitate all of this so that you may have as clear a conscience when your last hour comes as he had.

Return to your sober senses and call yourself back. When you have awakened from sleep and realized that it was only dreams that troubled you, now in your waking hours look at the things around you as you did at those dreams.

I am made of a small body and a soul. Now to this small body, all things are indifferent because it cannot perceive differences. But to the mind, those things are indifferent only if they are not the works of its own activity. Whatever things are the works of its own activity, all these are within its power. However, of these, only those which are done with reference to the present matter; for as to the future and past activities of the mind, even these are indifferent at the present moment.

Neither the labor that the hand does nor that of the foot is against nature, as long as the foot does the foot's work and the hand does the hand's. So then, neither is a person's labor against nature, as long as they do the things of a person. But if the labor is not against their nature, neither is it harmful to them.

How many pleasures have been enjoyed by robbers, parricides, and tyrants.

Do you not see how craftsmen adapt themselves, up to a certain point, to those who are not skilled in their craft—yet they hold firmly to the reason and principles of their art, and do not allow themselves to depart from it? Is it not strange if the architect and the physician show more respect for the reason and principles of their own arts than a person does for their own reason, which is shared with the gods?

Asia and Europe are small corners of the universe; all the sea is just a drop in the universe; Athos is just a small clod of earth in the universe; all of the present time is just a point in eternity. All things are small, changeable, and perishable. All things come from there, from that universal ruling power, either directly or as part of a sequence. Accordingly, the lion's gaping jaws, that which is poisonous, and every harmful thing, like thorns or mud, are byproducts of the grand and beautiful. Do not then imagine that they are different from what you venerate, but form a just opinion of the source of all.

He who has seen the present has seen all—both everything that has taken place from all eternity and everything that will happen for time without end. For all things are of one kind and one form.

Frequently consider the connection of all things in the universe and their relation to one another. For in a way, all things are intertwined with one another, and all are friendly to one another. One thing comes in order after another, and this is by virtue of the active movement and mutual cooperation and the unity of the substance.

Adapt yourself to the things with which your lot has been cast, and love the people among whom you have received your portion, but do it sincerely.

Every instrument, tool, or vessel is good if it does what it was made to do, even though the one who made it is not there. But in the things held together by nature, there is within them, and there remains in them, the power that made them; therefore, it is more fitting to revere this power, and to think that if you live and act according to its will, everything in you is in harmony with intelligence. And thus also in the universe, the things that belong to it are in harmony with intelligence.

Whatever things are not within your power that you suppose to be good or evil, it must necessarily follow that if such a bad thing befalls you, or if you lose such a good thing, you will blame the gods and hate people—those who are the cause of the misfortune or the loss, or those who are suspected of being likely to be the cause. Indeed, we do much injustice because we make a difference between these things, because we do not regard these things as indifferent. But if we judge only those things which are within our power as good or bad, there remains no reason to either find fault with God or to stand in a hostile attitude towards people.

We are all working together towards one end, some with knowledge and intention, and others without knowing what they do; as with people who are asleep, as Heraclitus, I think, said that they too are laborers and cooperators in the things that take place in the universe. But people cooperate in different ways: even those who find fault with what happens and those who try to oppose it and hinder it also cooperate; for the universe had a need for such people too. So it remains for you to understand what kind of worker you place yourself among; for he who rules all things will certainly make good use of you, and he will place you among some part of the cooperators and those whose labor contributes to one end. But do not be such a part as the mean and ridiculous verse in the play, which Chrysippus speaks of.

Does the sun try to do the work of the rain, or Aesculapius the work of the earth, which bears fruit? And how is it with each of the stars? They are different, yet they all work together towards the same end.

If the gods have determined about me and the things that must happen to me, they have determined well, for it is not easy even to imagine a god without forethought. As for doing me harm, why should they have any desire for that? What advantage would result to them from this or to the whole, which is the special object of their providence? But if they have not determined about me individually, they have certainly determined about the whole, and the things that happen as part of this arrangement should be accepted with pleasure, and I should be content with them. But if they decide about nothing—which is wicked to believe—then we should neither sacrifice nor pray nor swear by them or do anything else as if the gods were present and living with us. But if the gods don't decide about anything that concerns us, I can still decide for myself, and I can seek what is useful, and what is useful to everyone is what aligns with their nature. My nature is rational and social, and my city and country, as far as I am Antoninus, is Rome, but as far as I am a human, it is the world. So, the things that are useful to these cities are also useful to me.

Whatever happens to each person is for the good of the whole. That should be enough. But if you look closer, you will also see that whatever benefits one person also benefits others. However, let the word "benefit" be understood here in its common sense, referring to things that are neither good nor bad.

Just as you find the continuous sight of the same things in the amphitheater and similar places tiresome and boring, so it is with life as a whole. Everything above and below is the same and comes from the same source. How much longer will this continue?

Think often about how many different types of people, with different professions and from different nations, have died, and let your thoughts go down to even Philistion, Phoebus, and Origanion. Now think about other types of people. We too must eventually move to that place where there are so many great orators, noble philosophers like Heraclitus, Pythagoras, and Socrates, so many heroes of old, and so many generals and kings who came after them. Add Eudoxus, Hipparchus, Archimedes, and other men of great intellect, vision, and dedication, as well as rogues, bigots, and even satirists like Menippus who mocked this short and fleeting human life. Think about how all of them have long been in the dust. What harm has come to them? And what about those whose names are completely forgotten? There is only one thing of value in this life: to live in truth and justice and be tolerant of those who are neither true nor just.

Whenever you want to cheer yourself up, think about the good qualities of the people around you—for example, one person's energy, another's decency, a third's generosity, and another's talent. Nothing cheers you up more than seeing virtues in the character of those you live with, especially when they are abundant. So keep these examples in your mind.

You don't resent your weight, do you—that you weigh only a certain amount and not three hundred pounds? So don't resent that your life span is only so many years and not more. Just as you are content with the amount of matter given to you, so be content with the amount of time you have.

Try to persuade people, but act even if they don't agree when the principles of justice demand it. But if someone uses force to stop you, accept it peacefully, and use the obstacle as an opportunity to practice another virtue. And remember that you started on this path with a condition—you didn't aim for the impossible. So, what were you aiming for? A certain effort, which you have accomplished if the things you were driven to do are not completed.

A person who loves fame thinks another person's actions are his own good; a person who loves pleasure thinks his own sensations are his good, but a person with understanding considers his own actions as his good.

It's within our power to have no opinion about something and not be disturbed in our soul because things themselves have no natural power to form our judgments.

Get used to listening carefully to what others say and try as much as possible to understand what is in the speaker's mind.

What isn't good for the hive isn't good for the bee either.

If sailors spoke badly of their captain or patients of their doctor, would they listen to anyone else? If not, how could the captain ensure the safety of the passengers or the doctor the health of those in his care?

How many people who were born around the same time as me are already gone?

Appearances: to someone with jaundice, honey tastes bitter; to someone bitten by a mad dog, water is terrifying; to little children, a ball is a wonderful thing. So why am I angry? Do you think a false opinion has less power than the bile in someone with jaundice or the poison in someone bitten by a mad dog?

No one will stop you from living according to the reason of your own nature. Nothing will happen to you that goes against the reason of universal nature.

Think about the kind of people others want to please, the things they aim for, and the actions they take. How quickly time will cover everything—and how much it has already covered.

Book 7

What is badness? It is what you have often seen. Remember this when anything happens: it is what you have seen before. Everywhere you look, you will find the same things, as in ancient histories, medieval times, and in our day; cities and houses are filled with them now. There is nothing new: all things are both familiar and short-lived.

How can our principles die unless the thoughts corresponding to them are extinguished? But you have the power to keep these thoughts alive. I can hold the opinion about anything that I should hold. If I can, why am I disturbed? External things have no relation to my mind. Let this be your state, and you will stand tall. You have the power to reclaim your life. Look at things as you once did, for this is how to reclaim your life.

The idle business of show, stage plays, flocks of sheep, herds, spear exercises, bones cast to little dogs, bits of bread in fishponds, laboring ants, scurrying mice, and puppets on strings—all alike. Your duty is to show good humor amid such things, not pride; to understand that every man is worth as much as the things he busies himself with.

In conversation, focus on what is said; in every movement, observe what is happening. In conversation, see what end it refers to; in movement, carefully watch what is signified.

Is my understanding sufficient for this or not? If it is, I use it as an instrument given by universal nature. If not, I either step aside for someone more capable unless there's a reason I shouldn't, or I do my best, aided by someone who, with my guidance, can do what is fit and useful for the general good. Whatever I do, alone or with another, should be directed to what is useful and suited to society.

Many celebrated by fame are forgotten; many who celebrated others' fame are long dead.

Do not be ashamed to be helped; it is your duty to do your part like a soldier in a town assault. What if you are lame and cannot climb the battlements alone, but can with help?

Let not future things disturb you, for you will face them, if necessary, with the same reason you use for present things.

All things are interconnected, and the bond is sacred; hardly anything is unconnected with any other thing. Things are coordinated and form the same universe (order). There is one universe of all things, one God who pervades all, one substance, one law, one common reason in all intelligent animals, and one truth; if there is one perfection for all animals of the same stock and reason.

Everything material soon disappears into the whole's substance; everything formal (causal) is taken back into universal reason; and the memory of everything is soon overwhelmed in time.

To the rational animal, the same act is natural and reasonable.

Stand tall, or be made tall.

Just as members in one body are united, rational beings, though separate, are constituted for one cooperation. This is more apparent if you often say to yourself that you are a member of rational beings. But if you say you are a part, you do not yet love people from your heart; beneficence does not delight you for its own sake; you do it as propriety, not as good for yourself.

Let external things fall as they may on parts that feel them. Those parts may complain if they choose. But I am not harmed unless I think it is evil, and I have the power not to think so.

Whatever anyone does or says, I must be good, as gold, emerald, or purple says, "Whatever anyone does or says, I must keep my color."

The ruling faculty does not disturb itself; it does not frighten or cause pain to itself. If someone else can frighten or pain it, let them. The faculty itself will not turn into such ways by its own opinion. Let the body take care not to suffer, and let it speak if it suffers. But the soul, subject to fear and pain, has the power of opinion about these things, and it will suffer nothing, for it will not deviate into such a judgment. The leading principle wants nothing unless it creates a want for itself; it is free from disturbance and unimpeded if it does not disturb and impede itself.

Eudaemonia (happiness) is a good daemon, or a good thing. What are you doing here, imagination? Go away, I beg you by the gods, as you came, for I do not want you. But you have come as you always do. I am not angry with you: only go away.

Is anyone afraid of change? Why, what happens without change? What is more pleasing or suitable to universal nature? Can you take a bath unless the wood changes? Can you be nourished unless the food changes? Can anything useful be accomplished without change? Do you not see that you, too, must change, just like everything in the universe?

Through the universal substance, as through a torrent, all bodies are carried, united with and cooperating with the whole, like body parts with one another. How many Chrysippus, Socrates, and Epictetus has time swallowed? Let this thought occur to you with reference to everyone and everything.

One thing only troubles me: lest I do something against human nature, or in a way it does not allow, or at the wrong time.

Near is forgetfulness of all things; near is forgetfulness of you by all.

It is unique to man to love even wrongdoers. This happens when you remember they are kin, do wrong through ignorance and unintentionally, and both will soon die. Above all, the wrongdoer has not harmed you, for he has not worsened your ruling faculty.

Universal nature, like wax, molds a horse, then a tree, then a man, then something else, each for a short time. It is no hardship for the vessel to be broken, just as there was none in its making.

A scowling look is unnatural; when often assumed, it extinguishes comeliness. From this, conclude it is contrary to reason. If even the perception of doing wrong departs, why live longer?

Nature, which governs the whole, will soon change all things you see and make new things from them, to keep the world new.

When someone wrongs you, consider with what opinion of good or evil they did it. When you see this, you will pity them, not wonder or be angry. For you either think the same thing is good or another similar thing. Your duty is to pardon them. If you do not think such things are good or evil, you will more readily be kind to the errant.

Think not of what you lack but of what you have. Select the best of what you have and reflect on how eagerly you would have sought it if you lacked it. However, do not overvalue them so as to be disturbed if you lose them.

Retire into yourself. The rational ruling principle is content when it does what is just, securing tranquility.

Wipe out imagination. Stop the pulling of strings. Confine yourself to the present. Understand well what happens to you or others. Divide and distribute every object into the causal (formal) and material. Think of your last hour. Let the wrong done by someone stay where it was done.

Focus on what is said. Let your understanding enter into the things being done and those doing them.

Adorn yourself with simplicity, modesty, and indifference to things between virtue and vice. Love mankind. Follow God. The poet says Law rules all. It is enough to remember Law rules all.

About death: Whether it is dispersion, resolution into atoms, or annihilation, it is either extinction or change.

About pain: Intolerable pain carries us off; long-lasting pain is tolerable. The mind maintains tranquility by retreating into itself, and the ruling faculty is not worsened. Let harmed parts, if they can, express their opinion.

About fame: Observe the minds of those seeking fame, what they are, what they avoid, and what they pursue. As piles of sand hide former sands, life's events soon cover past ones.

From Plato: Can a man with an elevated mind and view of all time and substance think human life is great? It is not possible. Such a man thinks death is not evil. Certainly not.

From Antisthenes: It is royal to do good and be abused. It is base for the countenance to obey and compose itself as the mind commands, but the mind not to be self-regulated and composed.

Do not vex yourself over things, for they care not about it.

To the immortal gods and us, give joy.

Life must be reaped like ripe corn: One is born, another dies.

If gods do not care for me and my children, there is a reason.

For the good and the just are with me.

No joining in others' wailing, no violent emotion.

From Plato: A sufficient answer is: You say wrong if you think a good man should consider the hazard of life or death, rather than whether he does just or unjust works of a good or bad man.

For men of Athens, truly: wherever a man places himself, thinking it best, or is placed by a commander, he should stay and abide hazard, considering nothing, death or anything else, above deserting his post.

Reflect if the noble and good differ from saving and being saved. A real man should dismiss such thoughts. A man must entrust these matters to the deity, believing women say no man can escape destiny. The next inquiry is how best to live the time given.

Look at the courses of stars as if traveling with them; consider the elements changing into one another; such thoughts purge the filth of earthly life.

Plato says: He who talks about men should view earthly things from above, in assemblies, armies, agriculture, marriages, treaties, births, deaths, courts, deserted places, barbarians, feasts, lamentations, markets, a mix of all things and orderly combination of contraries.

Consider the past's political changes. Foresee future things; they will be similar, not deviating from the present order: contemplating life for forty years is like contemplating ten thousand. What more will you see?

That which has grown from earth returns to earth;

That which springs from heavenly seed returns to heavenly realms.

This is dissolution of atoms' involution or dispersion of unsentient elements.

With food, drinks, and cunning magic arts,

Turning the channel to escape death,

The breeze heaven sent

We must endure and toil without complaint.

Another may cast his opponent better; but he is not more social, modest, or better disciplined to meet what happens, nor more considerate of neighbors' faults.

Where work can be done conformably to gods' and men's reason, fear nothing: where activity proceeds according to our constitution, no harm is suspected.

Everywhere and always, you can piously accept your condition, behave justly to those around you, and focus on present thoughts, examining them well.

Do not look around for others' principles; look to what nature leads you, the universal nature through events and your own nature through your actions. Every being should act according to its constitution; all else is for rational beings, like inferior things for superior ones, but rational for one another.

The primary principle in man's constitution is social. The second is not yielding to the body's persuasions, as rational and intelligent motion circumscribes itself, never overpowered by senses or appetites, both animal; intelligent motion claims superiority, not allowing itself to be overpowered. With good reason, for it is formed to use all. The third thing in rational constitution is freedom from error and deception. Let the ruling principle hold these things and go straight on, with what is its own.

Consider yourself dead and have completed life up to now; live according to nature the remainder allowed.

Love only what happens to you and is spun with destiny's thread. What is more suitable?

In everything that happens, consider those who experienced the same, how they were vexed and treated them as strange. Where are they now? Nowhere. Why act the same? Why not leave these agitations, foreign to nature, to those causing and moved by them? Why not focus on the right use of things happening to you? Use them well; they will be material for you. Only attend to yourself and resolve to be good in every act.

Look within. Within is the fountain of good, ever bubbling if you dig.

The body should be compact, showing no irregularity in motion or attitude. The mind's intelligence and propriety should show in the face and the whole body without affectation.

Life's art is more like wrestling than dancing: stand ready and firm for sudden, unexpected onsets.

Observe those whose approval you want and their principles. You will not blame involuntary offenders or want their approval if you know their opinions and appetites' sources.

Every soul is involuntarily deprived of truth; it is deprived of justice, temperance, benevolence, and everything of the kind. Bear this in mind, and you will be gentler towards all.

In every pain, remember it is not dishonorable nor worsens the governing intelligence; it does not harm intelligence rationally or socially. Epicurus said most pains are neither intolerable nor everlasting if you remember they have limits and add nothing in imagination: remember many disagreeable things are like pain, such as drowsiness, heat, lack of appetite. When discontented with these, say you yield to pain.

Do not feel toward the inhuman as they feel toward men.

How do we know if Telauges wasn't a better person than Socrates? It's not enough that Socrates died in a more honorable way, argued better with the sophists, endured a cold night more strongly, or that when he was told to arrest Leon of Salamis, he thought it was more honorable to refuse, or that he walked confidently in the streets—though we might doubt if this last part is true. Instead, we should ask what kind of soul Socrates had. Was he able to be satisfied with being fair to people and respectful to the gods? Did he avoid being upset by people's wrongdoings, or becoming a slave to anyone's ignorance? Did he accept everything that happened to him as part of life without thinking it was too much to bear? Did he keep his mind from being affected by the troubles of the body?

Nature hasn't mixed your mind with your body in a way that stops you from controlling yourself and mastering what is truly yours. It's entirely possible to be a great person without anyone noticing. Always remember this: very little is needed to live a happy life. And even if you've given up on becoming a great thinker or scientist, don't lose hope of being free, modest, social, and obedient to God. You have the power to live free from pressure with a peaceful mind, even if the whole world shouts at you, and even if wild animals tear apart this body that surrounds you. What stops the mind, in all this, from staying calm, judging everything around it fairly, and using what it has wisely? So that the mind can say to what it sees: "This is what you really are, even if people think you're something else." And the mind can say to what it uses: "You're exactly what I was looking for." For me, whatever happens is always an opportunity for virtue, whether it's rational or social, and in short, for the practice of the art that belongs to humans or gods.

Everything that happens is connected to either God or humans and is neither new nor hard to deal with. It's familiar and useful material to work with. The perfection of moral character is to live each day as if it were your last, without getting overly excited, sluggish, or pretending to be someone you're not. The gods, who never die, aren't upset that they have to put up with humans for so long, even though many of them are bad. In fact, they still care for them in every way. But you, who will die so soon, are you tired of putting up with the bad, even though you're one of them yourself?

It's ridiculous for a person not to escape their own badness, which is possible, but to try and escape other people's badness, which is impossible. Whatever the rational and social part of us finds to be neither intelligent nor social, it rightly judges to be below itself. When you've done something good and someone else has benefited from it, why do you still look for something else, like fools do? Whether it's to gain a reputation for doing good or to get something in return? No one gets tired of receiving what's useful. But it's useful to act according to nature. So don't get tired of receiving what's useful by doing good for others.

The nature of everything decided to create the universe. Now, either everything that happens is a result of that, or the main things that the universe's ruling power moves towards are governed by no rational principle. If you remember this, it will help you stay calm in many situations.

Book 8

This thought can help you stop caring about empty fame: you no longer have the chance to live your whole life, or even just your adult life, as a philosopher. It's clear to many, including yourself, that you are far from being a philosopher. Your life has become disordered, making it hard to gain the reputation of a philosopher, and your way of living goes against it too. If you truly understand this, stop worrying about how you appear to others. Instead, be happy if you can live the rest of your life the way your nature wants. Focus on what your nature desires and let nothing else distract you. You've already wandered through many paths without finding happiness anywhere—not in logical arguments, not in wealth, not in fame, not in pleasure, not in anything. So where can happiness be found? It's found in doing what human nature requires. And how do you do this? By having principles that guide your feelings and actions. What principles? Those that relate to what is good and bad: understanding that nothing is good unless it makes you just, self-controlled, brave, and free; and nothing is bad unless it does the opposite.

Before every action, ask yourself: "How does this affect me? Will I regret it?" In a short time, I will be dead, and all will be gone. What more do I need if what I am doing now is the work of an intelligent, social being who follows the same laws as God?

Alexander, Julius Caesar, and Pompey—how do they compare to Diogenes, Heraclitus, and Socrates? The latter understood things, their causes, and their essence, and their guiding principles were in harmony with their pursuits. But as for the others, how many things did they have to worry about, and how many things were they slaves to?

Remember that people will keep doing the same things, even if you burst with frustration.

The most important thing is not to be disturbed, for everything happens according to the nature of the universe, and soon you will be nobody and nowhere, just like Hadrian and Augustus. Then, focus steadily on your task, look at it, and remember that your duty is to be a good person and to do what human nature demands. Do this without straying, and speak as you think is most just, but do so kindly, modestly, and sincerely.

The nature of the universe constantly works to change things, to move them from one place to another. Everything is changing, but there's no need to fear anything new. Everything is familiar; what happens is neither new nor hard to deal with but is a usual part of the whole.

Every living thing is satisfied when it follows its nature. A rational being follows its nature when it agrees with truth, directs its actions towards social good, limits its desires to what is within its power, and accepts everything that happens as part of the universal order. This universal nature includes every individual nature, just as a leaf is part of the plant's nature. However, the nature of a leaf is part of a plant that cannot perceive or reason and can be stopped in its growth, while human nature is part of a larger nature that is not impeded and is intelligent and just, giving everything its fair share of time, substance, cause, action, and experience. But don't expect everything to be exactly equal in all respects; instead, look at the whole picture and how one thing compares to the sum of another.

You may not have time to study, but you do have time to control your arrogance. You have time to rise above pleasure and pain, to let go of the love of fame, and not to be upset by foolish or ungrateful people, but to care for them instead.

Don't let anyone hear you complaining about your life or the life in the court.

Regret is a form of self-blame for missing out on something useful. But if something is truly good, it must be useful, and a truly good person should pursue it. No good person would ever regret not indulging in a sensual pleasure, so pleasure is neither good nor useful.

Ask yourself, "What is this thing, really? What is it made of? What is its purpose in the world? How long will it last?"

When you wake up and feel reluctant to get out of bed, remember that it is in your nature, as a human being, to perform social duties. Sleeping is something you share with animals, but acting according to your nature is something that belongs uniquely to you and is more fitting and pleasant.

Constantly examine your impressions—every single one if possible—look at its cause, identify the feeling it brings, and analyze it logically.

Whenever you meet someone, immediately ask yourself: "What opinions does this person hold about what is good and bad?" If he believes certain things about pleasure, pain, fame, dishonor, life, and death, it won't be surprising if he acts in a certain way, and you'll understand that he's compelled to do so.

It's as silly to be surprised at a fig tree producing figs as it is to be surprised when the world produces things that are natural to it. Similarly, it would be foolish for a doctor to be surprised by a patient having a fever or a sailor by an unfavorable wind.

Remember that changing your mind and following someone who corrects your mistake is just as much a part of your freedom as sticking to your original opinion. This change comes from your own choice, your own judgment, and your own understanding.

If something is within your control, why aren't you doing it? But if it's under someone else's control, why do you blame atoms or gods? Both are senseless. You should blame no one. If you can, fix the cause; if you can't, at least fix the effect. But if even that's not possible, what good does it do to complain? Everything should have a purpose.

What dies does not leave the universe. If it remains here, it changes here and dissolves into its basic parts, which are elements of the universe and of yourself. These elements also change, and they don't complain about it.

Everything has a purpose—like a horse or a vine. Why are you surprised? Even the sun would say, "I exist for a purpose," and the other gods would say the same. So what is your purpose—to enjoy pleasure? See if that makes sense.

Nature's purpose includes everything, from the beginning to the end. Just like someone tossing a ball, how is it good for the ball to go up and bad for it to come down or even to hit the ground? The same could be said of a bubble when it forms and when it bursts. Or a candle, when it is lit and when it goes out.

Turn it (the body) inside out and see what kind of thing it is, what it becomes when it grows old, and when it is sick. Both the praiser and the praised, the rememberer and the remembered, are short-lived, and all this happens in a tiny corner of the world. Not even here do people agree, not even with themselves. And the whole earth is just a point in space.

Focus on the matter at hand, whether it's an opinion, an action, or a word. You deserve what you're going through because you choose to become good tomorrow instead of today.

Am I doing something? I do it with the good of humanity in mind. Is something happening to me? I accept it as coming from the gods and the source of all things, from which everything is connected.

Just like bathing seems—oil, sweat, dirt, filthy water, all things disgusting—so is every part of life and everything in it.

Lucilla saw Verus die, and then Lucilla died. Secunda saw Maximus die, and then Secunda died. Epitynchanus saw Diotimus die, and then Epitynchanus died. Antoninus saw Faustina die, and then Antoninus died. And so it goes for everyone. Celer saw Hadrian die, and then Celer died. Where are those sharp-witted men now, those prophets or proud individuals? Charax, Demetrius the Platonist, and Eudaemon—where are they? All of them were just temporary, and now they're dead. Some haven't been remembered at all, some became legends, and others have even disappeared from legends. So remember that this little body of yours will either be scattered, your breath will be extinguished, or you will be moved to another place.

A man finds satisfaction in doing the right work for a man. And the right work for a man is to be kind to others, to rise above the distractions of the senses, to judge things fairly, and to understand the nature of the universe and everything that happens in it.

There are three relationships: one to the body that surrounds you, the second to the divine source from which everything comes, and the third to the people you live with.

Pain is either an evil to the body—let the body say what it thinks of it—or to the soul. But the soul has the power to keep itself calm and not to think that pain is an evil. Every judgment, movement, desire, and aversion is within, and no evil can rise above it.

Erase your harmful thoughts by often reminding yourself: "Now it's in my power to keep this soul free from any badness, from any desire, from any disturbance at all. By looking at things as they are, I can use each one according to its value." Remember this power that nature has given you.

Speak plainly, whether in the senate or to any person, without being pretentious. Use straightforward language.

The court of Augustus—wife, daughter, descendants, ancestors, sister, Agrippa, relatives, friends; Areius, Maecenas, doctors, and priests—all are dead. Then think of others, not just one person's death but the end of a whole family, like the Pompeii. And consider the words written on the tombs: "The last of his race." Then think of all the effort those before them put in to leave behind an heir, and that eventually, one must be the last. Again, think about the end of an entire family.

You must organize your life action by action, and be content if each action achieves its purpose as well as it can. No one can prevent you from achieving this. "But there will be some external obstacle." No obstacle can stop you from acting justly, with self-control, and with reason. "But maybe some other action will be blocked." Accept the block gladly and make a wise change to meet the situation. Another opportunity for action will immediately take its place and fit into the plan for your life.

Receive wealth or prosperity without arrogance, and be ready to let it go.

If you've ever seen a hand, foot, or head cut off and lying apart from the body, that's what you do to yourself when you refuse to accept your lot or do something unsocial. Imagine you've cut yourself off from the natural whole—you were born to be part of it, but now you've separated yourself. But here's the amazing thing: it's within your power to reunite with the whole. God has allowed this to no other part, once it's been cut off, to come together again. But think of the kindness by which he has distinguished humans, giving them the ability not to be separated at all, or to return and reunite if they are.

Just as the nature of the whole has given every rational being all other powers, so we have received this power too. Just as the universal nature turns everything that stands in its way into a part of itself and uses it, so the rational animal can turn every obstacle into material for its own purpose and use it to achieve its goal.

Don't let the thought of your whole life overwhelm you, and don't dwell on all the troubles that may have happened in the past or may happen in the future. Just ask yourself, "What is there in this situation that I can't bear or handle?" You'll be ashamed to admit it. Then remember that it's neither the future nor the past that burdens you, but only the present. This present burden is very small if you isolate it and challenge your mind if it can't handle even this.

Does Panthea or Pergamus still sit by the tomb of Verus? Does Chabrias or Diotimus sit by the tomb of Hadrian? That would be ridiculous. Even if they did, would the dead be aware of it? And if they were aware, would they be pleased? And if they were pleased, would that make their mourners immortal? Was it not their fate also to grow old—old women and men like everyone else—and then to die? And with them dead, what would those they mourned do then? It's all just foul-smelling decay in a bag of bones.

If you have sharp sight, use it, but also add wise judgment.

In the structure of a rational being, I see no virtue that opposes justice, but I do see a virtue that opposes pleasure, and that is self-control.

If you take away your judgment about something that seems painful, you yourself remain unharmed by it. "Who is this self?" The reason. "But I'm not just reason." True, so let your reason not trouble itself. But if another part of you suffers, let it have its own judgment about itself.

An obstacle to sense perception is harmful to animal nature. An obstacle to desires is also harmful to animal nature. And something else is equally an obstacle and a harm to the nature of plants. So, anything that blocks the mind is harmful to intelligent nature. Apply this to yourself. Is pain or pleasure affecting you? That's for the senses to deal with. Have you met an obstacle in your efforts? If this effort was unconditional, then yes, the obstacle is harmful to your rational nature. But if you consider the usual course of things, you haven't yet been harmed or even impeded. Nothing can impede the proper functions of the mind. The mind can't be touched by fire, steel, tyranny, or slander in any way. When it's made perfect, it remains complete.

I shouldn't harm myself, as I've never intentionally harmed anyone else.

Different things bring different people joy, but my joy comes from keeping my mind clear, not turning away from anyone or anything that happens, but looking at and accepting everything with kind eyes and using each thing according to its value.

See that you make the most of this present moment. Those who chase after fame after death don't realize that the people of the next generation will be just like those they dislike now. Both groups will die. And what does it matter to you if those future people say this or that about you?

Take me and put me wherever you will; wherever I am, I'll keep my inner self calm and satisfied if it can act according to its nature. Is this situation any good reason for my soul to be unhappy and worse than it was? Expanded, shrinking, scared? And what would be a good reason for that?

Nothing can happen to any human being that isn't natural to humans, just as nothing happens to an ox that isn't natural to oxen, or to a vine that isn't natural to vines, or to a stone that isn't natural to a stone. So if everything happens as is usual and natural for it, why should you complain? The universal nature brings nothing that you can't handle.

If something outside you is causing distress, it's not the thing itself that's bothering you, but your judgment of it—and you can erase that judgment right now. But if it's something in your own attitude that's bothering you, who's stopping you from changing it? If you're upset because you're not doing something that seems right, why not do it instead of complaining? "But there's an obstacle in the way that I can't overcome." Then don't be upset, because the reason it's not being done isn't your fault. "But life isn't worth living if I can't do this." Then leave life as graciously as someone who has achieved their goal, and in peace with those who stood in your way.

Remember that your inner self is invincible when it withdraws into its own self-sufficiency, doing nothing that it doesn't choose to do, even if that choice is stubborn. How much stronger will it be when it acts according to reason and deliberation? That's why a mind free from passions is a fortress—people have no stronger place of retreat, and someone who takes refuge here is invincible. Anyone who hasn't realized this is ignorant, and anyone who knows it but doesn't take refuge is unlucky.

Say nothing more to yourself than what your first impressions report. Suppose you're told that someone speaks ill of you. That's all you've been told, nothing more. I see that my child is sick. I do see that, but I don't see that he's in danger. So always stick to your first impressions and don't add anything from your own thoughts. Then nothing more will happen to you. Or better yet, add something like a person who understands everything that happens in the world.

A cucumber is bitter—throw it away. There are thorns in the road—go around them. That's all you need to do. Don't ask, "Why are these things in the world?" because you'll be laughed at by someone who understands nature, just as a carpenter or shoemaker would laugh at you if you complained about seeing shavings or scraps in their workshop. And yet they have places to throw those scraps, while the universal nature has no external space. But her amazing skill is that even though she's confined herself, she changes everything within her that seems to decay, grow old, or become useless into something new, so she doesn't need any material from outside or a place to throw away what decays. She's content with her own space, her own material, and her own skill.

Don't be sluggish in your actions, unclear in your speech, or wandering in your thoughts. Don't let your mind become troubled or overjoyed. Allow some leisure in your life.

Suppose people kill you, cut you into pieces, or curse you. What can these things do to stop your mind from staying pure, wise, sober, and just? For example, if someone were to stand by a clear, sweet spring and curse it, the spring would still keep sending out good water to drink. If someone threw mud or filth into it, the spring would quickly disperse it, wash it away, and not be polluted at all. How can you make your mind like an everlasting spring and not just a well? By training yourself every hour to be free, kind, simple, and decent.

Someone who doesn't know what the world is doesn't know where he is. Someone who doesn't know the purpose of the world doesn't know who he is or what the world is. And if someone fails in any of these things, he couldn't even say what his own purpose is. What do you think of someone who seeks or avoids the praise of people who don't even know where they are or who they are?

Do you want to be praised by someone who curses himself three times an hour? Do you want to please someone who doesn't even please himself? Can someone who regrets almost everything he does be pleased with himself?

Don't just breathe the surrounding air—breathe in the thoughts of the mind that embraces all things. The power of the mind spreads everywhere and penetrates everything, just like the air for those who can breathe it.

Wickedness does no harm to the universe as a whole, and one person's wickedness doesn't harm another person. It only harms the one who commits it, and he can get rid of it as soon as he decides to.

My neighbor's will is as indifferent to me as his breath and his body. We're born to help each other, but the ruling mind of each of us is sovereign. Otherwise, my neighbor's wickedness would harm me, which God didn't intend, so that my misfortune wouldn't depend on another person.

The sun seems to pour its light everywhere, and it does spread out in all directions, but it doesn't run out. This spreading is an extension, and that's why its rays are called "extensions." You can see what a ray is if you look at sunlight entering a dark room through a narrow opening. It extends in a straight line and stops when it hits a solid object. The light stays there and doesn't slide or fall off. This is how the mind should spread and shine, not pouring out or colliding violently with obstacles, but staying fixed and illuminating whatever receives it. Anything that doesn't reflect the light will only deprive itself of it.

He who fears death fears either losing all sensation or gaining a different kind of sensation. But if you have no sensation, you won't feel any harm, and if you gain a different kind of sensation, you'll be a different kind of living being and won't stop living.

People exist to help each other. So either teach them or put up with them.

An arrow moves one way, and the mind moves another. But even when the mind is cautious or curious, it still moves directly towards its goal.

Enter into the mind of everyone you meet, and let them enter yours.

Book 9

When someone acts unjustly, they are acting against the will of the universe. The universe has created rational beings to help each other, not to harm one another. So, when someone goes against this, they are disrespecting the highest power. Similarly, lying is also disrespectful to this power because the universe is based on truth. Everything that exists is connected, and truth is the foundation of it all. A person who lies on purpose is guilty because they are being unjust by deceiving others. Even someone who lies without meaning to is still guilty because they are going against the nature of the universe. They disturb the order by opposing truth, using the abilities nature has given them incorrectly.

A person who chases after pleasure won't avoid doing wrong, and this is clearly against the will of the universe. Now, when it comes to things like pain and pleasure, or life and death, or honor and dishonor, the universe treats them all the same. It wouldn't have created these opposites unless it viewed them equally. So, those who want to live according to nature should also see them the same way. If someone doesn't, they are clearly going against nature. When I say the universe treats these things equally, I mean that they happen to everyone as a result of cause and effect. Everything that exists comes from a plan that the universe set in motion from the beginning, creating everything and allowing changes and cycles to happen.

It would be best for a person to leave this world without having ever lied, pretended, indulged in excess, or been proud. But if someone has experienced these things, the next best thing for that person is to become tired of them before he or she dies.If you choose to stay with such behaviors, has your experience not yet shown you that you should avoid them? The corruption of the mind is much worse than any disease of the body. The latter only affects animals, but the former destroys what makes us human.

Do not fear death, but be content with it, since it is also something that nature wants. Just like being young, growing old, maturing, getting teeth, a beard, and gray hair, having children, and giving birth, all the other natural events that happen throughout life, so is dying. This, then, is fitting for a thoughtful person—to be neither careless nor impatient nor scornful about death, but to wait for it as just another natural process. Just as you now wait for the time when your wife will give birth, so be ready for the time when your soul will leave this body.

But if you also need a more vulgar kind of comfort that can touch your heart, you will find it easier to accept death by thinking about the things you will leave behind, and the kind of people you won't have to deal with anymore. It's not right to be angry with others, but you should care for them and treat them kindly. Still, remember that when you die, you will be leaving behind people who don't share your values. If there is anything that could make us want to stay alive, it's the chance to live with people who think like us. But now, you see how difficult it is to live with people who don't agree with you, so you might say, "Come quickly, death, before I too forget who I am."

When someone does something wrong, they are really hurting themselves. When someone acts unfairly, they are making themselves worse.

Sometimes, doing nothing can be just as wrong as doing something bad.

It is enough for you to have clear thoughts, act in a way that helps others, and accept whatever happens with a calm mind.

Erase your imaginations, stop your impulses, control your desires, and keep your mind in charge.

Animals that don't have reason share one life, but animals with reason share one intelligent mind. Just like how all things of the earth share one earth, and we all see by the same light and breathe the same air.

All things that share something in common naturally move towards others like them. Everything that is earthy goes back to the earth, everything watery flows together, and everything airy does the same, unless something separates them. Fire moves upward because it is drawn to other fire, and it is so ready to join with any fire that even dry things easily catch fire because they don't have much to stop them from burning.

In the same way, everything that shares the same intelligent nature moves towards others like itself, even more strongly than the elements. The higher something is, the more it wants to mix with things like it. That's why among animals without reason, we see bees forming hives, cattle forming herds, birds caring for their young, and a kind of love. Even in animals, there is a kind of soul that brings them together, stronger than what we see in plants or stones or trees. But in animals with reason, there are communities, friendships, families, and gatherings of people; even in wars, there are treaties and truces. But in things that are even higher, like the stars, there is a kind of unity even when they are far apart. So, as we go higher, we find more sympathy and connection, even in things that are separated. But look at what happens now: only intelligent creatures, like us, have forgotten this desire to be united. Only among us do we see no coming together. Even though we try to avoid it, we are still drawn together, because our nature is too strong. If you look closely, you'll see what I mean. It's easier to find something earthy that doesn't return to the earth than to find a person who is completely separated from others.

Both people, gods, and the universe produce results in their own time. Even though we usually talk about this when we discuss vines and similar things, it doesn't matter. Reason also produces results for everyone and itself, and it creates other things that are like reason itself.

If you can, teach those who do wrong; if you can't, remember that you have the ability to be kind. The gods are also kind to such people, and they even help them achieve things like health, wealth, and reputation. You can do the same. So, who is stopping you?

Work, but not like someone who is miserable or looking for pity or admiration. Focus on just one thing: doing what you need to do or holding yourself back, as reason requires.

Today I escaped all my troubles, or rather, I got rid of them, because they were not outside of me, but inside, in my own thoughts.

Everything is the same: familiar in experience, short-lived in time, and worthless in substance. Everything now is just like it was in the time of those who have died.

Things stand outside of us, by themselves, without knowing anything or judging themselves. What judges them, then? Our minds.

Good or bad for a rational being comes not from feeling but from action, just as our virtue or vice comes not from what we feel, but from what we do.

A stone thrown into the air isn't harmed by falling down, and it isn't helped by being thrown up.

Look into the minds of those you fear and see what kind of people they are. You'll realize that there is no reason to be afraid of their judgment, and you'll see how poorly they judge themselves.

Everything is changing: and you yourself are constantly changing and, in a way, being destroyed. The whole universe is, too.

You should leave another person's wrong act where it is.

The end of an action, the stopping of a movement or thought, is like a death, but it's not something to fear. Think about the different stages of your life: your childhood, your youth, your adulthood, your old age. In each of these, every change was like a death. Is there anything to fear in that? Now think about your life with your grandfather, then with your mother, then with your father. Just as you find many differences and changes and endings, ask yourself, is there anything to fear? In the same way, the end and change of your whole life is nothing to be afraid of.

Quickly examine your own mind, the mind of the universe, and the mind of your neighbor: your own mind, so you can make it just; the universe's mind, so you can remember what you are a part of; and your neighbor's mind, so you can know whether they are acting out of ignorance or understanding, and remember that their mind is like yours.

As you are a part of a social system, let every act of yours be a part of social life. Any act that doesn't contribute to a social goal tears apart your life and makes it incomplete, like when someone in a meeting stands apart from the group.

Children's arguments and games, and poor souls carrying around dead bodies—such is everything. What we see in depictions of the underworld seems clearer.

Look closely at the form of an object, separate it from its material part, and then think about how long it is naturally made to last.

You have gone through so many troubles by not being satisfied with your mind when it does what it was naturally meant to do. But that's enough of this.

When someone blames or hates you, or says something hurtful about you, look into their soul, see what kind of person they are.

You'll realize that there's no reason to be troubled by their opinions of you. But still, be kind to them because, by nature, they are your friends. And the gods help them in many ways, through dreams, signs, and other means, to achieve the things they care about.

The cycles of the universe are always the same, up and down, from age to age. Either the universal mind moves everything for a reason, and if so, be content with the result, or it started everything in motion once, and everything else follows naturally. Or everything is made up of atoms. In any case, if there is a god, all is well, and if it's just chance, don't let yourself be controlled by it. Soon, the earth will cover us all, and then the earth will change, and the things that come from change will keep changing forever. When a person thinks about the changes that come one after another, like waves, and how quickly they happen, they will lose respect for everything that is temporary.

The universal cause is like a winter flood: it carries everything along with it. But how worthless are those people who are busy with political matters, thinking they are being philosophers! They are just wasting their time. So, what should you do? Do what nature requires right now. If you can, act, and don't worry about whether anyone notices. Don't wait for some perfect situation like Plato's Republic. Be content if even the smallest thing goes well, and consider that to be no small achievement. Because who can change people's opinions? And without a change in opinions, what is left but the slavery of people who pretend to obey but are really suffering? Now, tell me about Alexander, Philippus, and Demetrius of Phalerum. They can judge for themselves whether they understood what nature required and trained themselves accordingly. But if they acted like tragic heroes, no one has forced me to imitate them. Philosophy is simple and modest. Don't lead me to arrogance and pride.

Look down from above on the countless groups of people and their countless activities, all the different journeys in storms and calm weather, the differences among those who are born, live together, and die. And think about the life of people who lived long ago, the life of those who will live after you, and the life being lived now in other parts of the world. How many people don't even know your name, how many will soon forget it, and how many who might praise you now will soon criticize you. Realize that neither a lasting name, nor reputation, nor anything else is really important.

Accept calmly whatever comes from an external cause, and act justly in everything that comes from your own actions. In other words, let your thoughts and actions be fulfilled in social conduct, as that is an expression of your own nature.

You can remove many unnecessary troubles that only exist in your own opinion. And by doing so, you will make a lot of room for yourself by understanding the whole universe, contemplating the eternity of time, and noticing how quickly each thing changes—how short the time is from birth to death, and the limitless time before birth and after death.

All that you see will soon disappear, and those who witness this disappearance will soon disappear too. Whether you die in extreme old age or before your time, it will all be the same.

What are the leading thoughts of these people? What are they focused on, and what do they care about? Train yourself to look at their minds, without any disguise. When they think their criticism will hurt you or their praise will help you, what a silly thought that is!

Loss is nothing more than change. The universal nature loves change, and everything that comes from nature happens for a reason. Similar things have happened forever, and will continue to happen forever. So why would you say that everything has always been bad and always will be, and that the gods have never had the power to fix these things, leaving the world condemned to constant misery?

The decay of everything that is the foundation of everything: water, dust, bones, filth. Or, marble rocks, the hard parts of the earth; and gold and silver, just sediments; and clothes, only bits of hair; and purple dye, just blood; and everything else is the same. And what we call the soul is also just something that changes from one thing to another.

Enough of this miserable life, complaining and acting like a fool. Why are you upset? What is new here? What is bothering you? Is it the way something looks? Look at it. Or is it the material? Look at that. But besides these, there is nothing else. Now, finally, become simpler and better in your thoughts toward the gods. It's the same whether we examine these things for a hundred years or three.

If someone has done wrong, the harm is theirs. But maybe they haven't done wrong.

Either everything comes from one intelligent source and works together like one body, and the part shouldn't complain about what is done for the good of the whole, or there are only atoms, and nothing else but a mix and scattering. So, why are you upset? Say to your mind, "Are you dead, are you corrupted, are you pretending, are you just going along with the crowd?"

Either the gods have power or they don't. If they have no power, why do you pray to them? But if they do have power, why not pray for them to give you the strength not to fear the things you fear, or to stop desiring the things you desire, or to not be upset by anything, instead of praying for those things to not happen or to happen? Because if they can help people, they can help with these things too. But maybe you'll say that the gods have left these things in your control. Well then, isn't it better to use what is in your power like a free person than to desire in a weak and helpless way what isn't in your control? And who told you that the gods don't help us with the things that are in our power? Start praying for these things, and you'll see. One person prays, "How can I get to be with that woman?" You pray, "How can I stop wanting to be with her?" Another prays, "How can I get rid of that person?" You pray, "How can I stop wanting to get rid of them?" Another says, "How can I keep my little child safe?" You say, "How can I learn not to be afraid of losing them?" In short, turn your prayers this way, and see what happens.

Epicurus says, "In my sickness, I didn't talk about the pains of my poor body, and I didn't go on about it to those who visited me. Instead, I kept discussing the main points of philosophy, focusing especially on how the mind, even when affected by what happens to the body, can still stay calm and keep its own good. I didn't give the doctors a chance to act like they were doing something great, but my life went on fine and happy." Do the same as he did, whether you are sick or in any other situation. Never abandon philosophy, no matter what happens, and don't engage in silly talk with people who don't know any better. Focus only on what you are doing right now and the tool you are using to do it.

When you are offended by someone's bad behavior, immediately ask yourself, "Is it possible for the world to not have people like this?" It's not possible. So don't ask for the impossible. This person is just one of the many bad people who must exist in the world. Think the same way when you deal with dishonest people, unfaithful people, or anyone who does wrong in any way. When you remind yourself that it's impossible for the world to be without people like this, you'll find yourself being kinder to each person individually. It's also helpful to remember what virtue nature has given you to deal with each wrong action. Nature gave us gentleness to deal with unkind people, and other qualities to deal with other kinds of wrongs. In every case, you can teach the person who has gone astray because every person who does wrong is missing the mark and has gone off course. Also, how have you been harmed? You'll find that none of the people you're angry with has done anything that could make your mind worse; the only thing that can harm you is in your own mind. And what harm is there, or what is so strange, if someone who hasn't been taught does the things an untaught person would do? Think about whether you should blame yourself instead, because you didn't expect this person to make that mistake. Your reason should have helped you see that it was likely they would make this mistake, and yet you are surprised that they did. But most of all, when you blame someone for being untrustworthy or ungrateful, look at yourself. The fault is clearly yours if you trusted that a person with that character would keep their promise, or if you did something kind without doing it completely and without expecting anything in return. What more do you want when you've done someone a favor? Isn't it enough that you've done something that fits your nature? Why do you seek to be paid back for it? It's like if the eye demanded something in return for seeing, or the feet for walking. Just as these parts of the body are made for a certain purpose, and by doing what they were made to do, they get what they need; in the same way, when a person does something kind or helpful for others, they have done what they were made for, and they get what they need from it.

Book 10

My soul, will you ever be good, simple, and clear, without any confusion, brighter than the body that surrounds you? Will you ever enjoy being kind and content? Will you ever be full and satisfied, without wanting anything, not desiring anything, either living or non-living, just for the sake of pleasure? Will you ever stop wishing for more time to enjoy things, or a better place, or a nicer climate, or the company of people who agree with you? Instead, will you be happy with your present condition, pleased with everything around you, and convinced that you have everything you need, that it all comes from the gods, that everything is good for you, and will continue to be good, no matter what the gods decide to give you? Will you finally become someone who can live peacefully with gods and men, without finding fault with them or being judged by them?

Observe what your nature requires as long as you are just a living being: then do it and accept it, as long as your nature as a living being is not harmed by it. Next, observe what your nature requires as a rational being. Follow all these things, as long as your rational nature is not harmed by them. And remember, a rational being is also a social being. Use these rules, and don't worry about anything else.

Everything that happens either happens in a way that you are naturally able to bear it, or it happens in a way that you are not naturally able to bear it. If it happens in a way that you are naturally able to bear it, don't complain, but bear it as you were made to do. But if it happens in a way that you are not naturally able to bear, don't complain, because it will end after it has affected you. Remember that you are made to bear everything, as long as you believe it is either in your interest or your duty to do so.

If someone is mistaken, kindly teach them and show them their error. But if you can't do that, blame yourself, or perhaps don't even blame yourself.

Whatever happens to you was prepared for you from all time; and the causes have been working since forever, creating your being and everything that happens to it.

Whether the universe is made of atoms or is a natural system, the first thing to understand is that you are part of the whole that is governed by nature; second, that you are closely related to other parts that are like you. With this in mind, since you are a part, you will not be upset by anything that happens to you, because nothing that benefits the whole can harm the part. And the whole contains nothing that is not good for it. All living things have this in common, but the universe also has this additional feature: no external cause can force it to create anything harmful to itself. Remembering that you are part of such a whole will make you content with everything that happens. And since you are closely related to other parts like you, you will act in a social manner, focusing on what is good for everyone and avoiding the opposite. If you live this way, life will go smoothly, just as the life of a citizen who acts in ways that benefit others and accepts what the state gives them is happy.

The parts of the whole—all the things that naturally exist in the universe—must perish; but understand this as a change. If this change is naturally both harmful and necessary for the parts, the whole could not stay in good condition if its parts are always changing and are made to perish in various ways. Did nature design itself to harm its own parts and make them fall into harm by necessity, or did it just not notice? Both ideas seem impossible. But even if someone drops the idea of nature as a force and just says things happen as they do, it's still ridiculous to be surprised or upset that things naturally change, especially when everything dissolves back into its basic elements. Things either break down into the elements they are made of, or they change from solid to earth and from air to air, returning to the universe's reason, whether it is consumed by fire or renewed through eternal cycles. And don't think that the solid and airy parts belong to you from birth. They only recently came from the food you ate and the air you breathed. What changes is what you've added, not what your mother gave you. Even if what your mother gave you is deeply connected to this added part that changes, this doesn't change what's been said.

When you've taken on names like good, modest, truthful, rational, calm, and noble, make sure you don't lose them. And if you do lose them, return to them quickly. Remember that being rational means paying close attention to everything and not being careless; that calmness is accepting what nature gives you willingly; and that nobility is raising your mind above the pleasures or pains of the body, above fame, death, and all such things. If you can keep these names without needing others to call you by them, you will become a different person and start a new life. Continuing to live as you have been, while being torn apart and corrupted, is the sign of a foolish person who is too attached to life, like those gladiators who, though covered in wounds and blood from wild animals, still beg to live another day, only to face the same claws and bites again. So, hold onto these few names, and if you can stay true to them, do so as if you were living in the islands of the blessed. But if you find yourself falling away from them and losing control, retreat to a quiet place where you can regain them, or leave life altogether—not in anger, but simply, freely, and with dignity, having at least achieved this one good thing in your life: leaving it in this way. To help you remember these names, it will be very useful to remember the gods and that they do not want flattery, but want all rational beings to become like them. And remember that what makes a fig tree a fig tree is doing the work of a fig tree, what makes a dog a dog is doing the work of a dog, what makes a bee a bee is doing the work of a bee, and what makes a man a man is doing the work of a man.

Every day, farce, war, surprise, dullness, and slavery will wipe out those principles of yours if you don't constantly study nature. It's your duty to think and act in a way that perfects your ability to deal with circumstances while also exercising your understanding, maintaining confidence in what you know without showing off, but also without hiding it. Because when will you finally enjoy simplicity, dignity, and the knowledge of each thing—what it really is, its place in the world, how long it lasts, what it's made of, who owns it, and who can give or take it away?

A spider feels proud when it catches a fly, and a man feels proud when he catches a hare, a fish in a net, a wild boar, a bear, or captures Sarmatians. But if you look closely at their motivations, aren't they all just robbers?

Adopt the habit of seeing how all things change into one another, and constantly practice this part of philosophy. Nothing helps you develop a great mind more than this. A person trained this way has detached themselves from the body and, knowing that they will soon leave this world and everything in it, focuses entirely on being just in their actions and accepting whatever happens as part of nature. They don't worry about what others say, think, or do against them, but are content with two things: acting justly in the present moment and accepting what is assigned to them now. They set aside all distractions and desires, wanting nothing more than to follow the straight path of law, and by following this path, they follow God.

What need is there for fear when you can always ask yourself what should be done? And if you see the way clearly, follow it contentedly, without hesitation. But if you don't see clearly, stop and ask the best advisers. If other things block you, proceed with caution, but always do what seems just. Justice is the best goal, and if you fail, let it be because you aimed for justice. A person who follows reason in everything is both calm and active, cheerful and collected.

As soon as you wake up, ask yourself: "Will it matter to me if someone else does what is just and right?" It won't matter. You haven't forgotten, I hope, that those who act arrogantly when praising or blaming others are the same as they are when they eat and sleep, and you haven't forgotten what they do, what they avoid, what they pursue, how they steal, and how they rob—not with their hands and feet, but with their most valuable part, the part that can produce trust, modesty, truth, law, and happiness.

To nature, who gives and takes back all things, the educated and humble person says, "Give what you want; take back what you want." And they say this not with pride, but with obedience and satisfaction.

The little time you have left to live is short. Live as if you were on a mountain. It doesn't matter whether you live there or here, as long as you live everywhere in the world as part of a community. Let people see and know a real person who lives according to nature. If they can't handle it, let them end your life. That's better than living as they do.

No more talk about what a good person should be. Just be one!

Always keep in mind the whole of time and existence, and consider that each thing, in terms of substance, is like a grain of a fig, and in terms of time, like the turn of a drill.

Look at everything around you and realize that it is already breaking down, changing, and decaying, or that everything is made to die.

Think about what people are when they are eating, sleeping, having sex, going to the bathroom, and so on. Then think about what they are like when they have power over others—arrogant, quick to anger, and harsh in their punishment. And yet, just a little while ago, they were slaves to all those needs, and soon they will be slaves again.

What nature brings to each thing is good for it. And it is good for it at the time when nature brings it.

"Earth loves the rain, and the sky loves to give it." The whole world loves to create the future. I say to the world, "I share your love." Isn't that what it means when we say, "This loves to happen"?

Either you live on here, getting used to it; or you leave by your own decision; or you die, having done your duty. There's no other choice. So be cheerful.

Always keep in mind that "the grass is not greener" anywhere else, and that everything is the same here as it is on top of a mountain, by the sea, or anywhere else you choose to be. You'll find Plato's words fitting: "living within the walls of a city as if in a fold on a mountain."

What is my mind to me right now? What am I turning it into? What am I using it for? Is it lacking understanding? Has it become disconnected from social life? Has it become so mixed with the body that it just follows along with it?

A slave who runs away from their master is a fugitive. Law is our master, so breaking the law makes you a fugitive. In the same way, feeling pain, anger, or fear means you are rejecting something that has happened, is happening, or will happen—something that has been determined by the one who governs all things, who is law and assigns to everyone what is right. So, feeling fear, pain, or anger makes you a fugitive.

A man deposits his seed in a womb and leaves. Then another force takes over and makes a child. What an amazing result from such a simple beginning! Then the child takes in food, and another force creates sensation, movement, life, strength, and all sorts of other things. Look closely at these mysterious processes and see the power at work, just as we see gravity pulling things down or up—not with our eyes, but just as clearly.

Constantly remember that all the things happening now have happened before and will happen again in the future. Keep in mind the full stories from history or your own experience, like the court of Hadrian, the court of Antoninus, the court of Philip, Alexander, or Croesus. All the same as now, just with different actors.

Picture everyone who complains about anything as being like a pig that's being sacrificed, kicking and squealing. And think of the person who silently resents things as being like this pig too. Consider how we are all bound together and how only rational creatures can choose to willingly accept what happens; everything else must submit.

For everything you do, ask yourself if losing it through death makes death something to fear.

When you're offended by someone's wrongdoing, immediately think about how you might be doing something similar—like valuing money, pleasure, or reputation too much, and so on. This will help you quickly forget your anger, especially if you also remember that the person may be acting out of compulsion—what else could they do? Or, if you can, remove the cause of their compulsion.

When you see Satyrion, Eutyches, or Hymen, think of Socrates' circle; when you see Eutychion or Silvanus, think of Euphrates; when you see Tropaeophorus, think of Alciphron; when you see Severus, think of Crito or Xenophon; and when you look at yourself, think of one of the Caesars. In each case, think of someone similar from the past. Then, let this thought strike you: Where are those people now? Nowhere, or wherever. In this way, you will always see human life as nothing but smoke and dust, especially if you remind yourself that what has changed once will never exist again for the rest of time. So why stress? Why not be content with moving through this short life in an orderly way? What situation or role are you trying to avoid? What is all of this other than an exercise for your reason, which has carefully studied and understood life? Stay until you have taken in everything, just as a strong stomach digests all food, or a bright fire turns everything you throw into it into flame and light.

Don't let anyone truthfully say that you are not sincere or good; make sure that anyone who thinks this is lying. This is entirely within your power—who can stop you from being sincere and good? Just decide that you will not live any longer if you can't have these qualities. And reason will abandon anyone who won't have them.

In any situation, what can be done or said that is most reasonable? Whatever that is, it's within your power to do or say it—don't pretend there are obstacles. You will never stop complaining until you find the same joy in responding appropriately to each situation as a hedonist finds in their indulgences. Because you should consider it enjoyable to do what fits your nature, and you can do that anywhere.

A roller doesn't have the power to roll wherever it wants, nor do water or fire, or anything else controlled by nature or an irrational soul—many things can block them. But mind and reason have the power to move through everything that opposes them, by their nature and choice. Keep in mind this ability of reason to move through everything, like fire rising, a stone falling, or a roller going down a slope, and don't look for anything more. Any remaining obstacles either affect only the body, which is dead, or, without the judgment and consent of your own reason, they cannot hurt or harm you in any way; if they could, then the person affected would immediately become worse. But in the case of all other things that have a certain constitution, whatever harm happens to them makes them worse; however, a person becomes better and more praiseworthy by making good use of whatever happens to them. Finally, remember that nothing harms a citizen of nature unless it harms the city, and nothing harms the city unless it harms the law. None of the things we call misfortunes harms the law. So, what doesn't harm the law doesn't harm the city or the citizen either.

For someone who truly understands the principles of life, even the shortest and simplest reminder is enough to remove all pain and fear—for example:

"The wind blows last year's leaves to the ground ... and in the same way, the generations of men come and go."

Your children are like leaves, and so are those who praise you or curse you, or secretly blame or mock you. And those who will carry on your reputation in the future are like leaves too. All these things are like "leaves that grow in spring," as the poet says; then the wind blows them down, and the forest produces more leaves in their place. Everything is short-lived—that's their common fate—but you chase after things as if they would last forever. Soon, you will close your eyes, and soon someone else will mourn the person who buries you.

A healthy eye should see all there is to see and not say, "I only want to see green things"; that's a sign of disease. A healthy ear and nose should be ready to perceive all sounds and smells. A healthy stomach should be ready to accept all food, just as a mill grinds whatever it is made to grind. And in the same way, a healthy mind should be ready for all situations. A mind that says, "My children must live" or "Everyone must praise everything I do" is like an eye that only wants to see green or teeth that only want to chew soft things.

No one is so fortunate that there aren't people who will be pleased when they die. Even if they were a good and wise person, someone might still think, "At last, we can breathe freely, now that we're rid of this teacher. He was never harsh to any of us, but I could feel his silent judgment of us all." That's what they might say about a good person. But in your case, how many more reasons are there for people to want to get rid of you? Think about this when you're dying, and you'll leave more peacefully, thinking, "I'm leaving a life where even those I've worked, prayed, and cared for want me gone, hoping to get some small benefit from it." So why should anyone cling to a longer life here? But don't leave with less kindness towards them because of this. Instead, keep true to your own character—friendly, kind, generous— and leave life as easily as a soul leaving the body in a peaceful death. Nature connected you to them and made them your companions, but now she's releasing you. My release is like parting from family, but I do not resist or need to be forced. This, too, is part of following nature.

As much as you can, get into the habit of asking yourself, whenever someone else does something, "What is their purpose?" But start with yourself: examine yourself first.

Remember that what controls your actions is the part of you that's hidden inside: that's where the power to act comes from, that's the principle of life, and that's what you could call the real you. So, don't give as much thought to the body or the tools attached to it. These are just instruments like an axe, differing only in being attached to the body. There's no more use in these parts without the mind that moves and controls them than in a shuttle without the weaver, a pen without the writer, or a whip without the coachman.

Book 11

The rational mind has certain abilities: it can understand itself, shape itself, and make itself into whatever it chooses to be. It benefits from the results of its own actions—unlike plants and animals, whose fruits are used by others. The rational mind achieves its purpose no matter when life ends. It's not like a play or a dance where the whole performance is ruined if interrupted. Instead, at any moment, the rational mind is complete and fulfilled, and it can confidently say, "I have what is mine." It also explores the entire universe and the empty space around it, thinking about its shape. It stretches its understanding into infinite time, embracing the idea that everything renews in cycles. It understands that those who come after us won't see anything new, just as those before us didn't see anything different. Since things are so similar, a person who is 40 years old, if they understand anything, has in a way seen everything—both past and future.

Another quality of the rational mind is its love for others, its honesty, and its integrity. It values nothing more than itself, just like the law, which values justice above all. Therefore, true wisdom is no different from justice.

You'll think less of music, dancing, or wrestling if you break down a song into its separate notes and ask yourself about each one: "Is this something that controls me?" You'll be too embarrassed to admit that it does. Do the same with dance, analyzing each movement and pose, and with wrestling, too. For everything, except for virtue and virtuous actions, break it down into its parts, and you'll come to value it less. Apply this rule to your whole life as well.

What a noble soul it is, ready to leave the body at any moment, prepared for whatever happens next—whether that's disappearing, scattering, or continuing to exist. But this readiness should come from a thoughtful decision, not out of stubbornness like the Christians, but with dignity and in a way that others can respect, without being overly dramatic.

Have I done something good for others? Then I've also benefited. Keep this thought always in your mind, and never stop doing good.

What is your job? To be a good person. And how do you do this well, except by understanding the nature of the universe and the proper way for humans to live?

Tragedies were first performed to remind us of what can happen in life, showing that these events are natural. If you are moved by a play, you should not be upset by the larger stage of life because things must happen the way they do. Even those who cry out "Oh, Cithaeron!" in pain must bear it.

There are some wise sayings in tragedies, like,

"If my children and I are no longer cared for by the gods, this too has a reason,"

and,

"We should not get angry at mere things,"

and,

"Just as ripe corn is harvested, so are lives."

And there are many others like this.

After tragedies came the old comedies, which had value in their straightforward and honest humor, warning us against arrogance. Diogenes used this type of humor for the same purpose. Then came middle comedy and new comedy, which became more about imitation than teaching. Although these later works had some useful sayings, it's important to ask what the overall goal of this type of art was.

It's clear that there is no better way of life for practicing philosophy than the one you are currently living.

If a branch is cut from a tree, it is separated from the whole tree. In the same way, when a person separates from another person, they are cut off from the entire community. The branch is cut by someone else, but a person separates themselves by rejecting or hating their neighbor, not realizing they are cutting themselves off from society. But Zeus, who created human society, gave us the ability to reconnect with our neighbors and become part of the whole again. However, frequent separation makes it harder to reunite and return to the original state. In short, a branch that grows with the tree from the beginning is different from one that is cut off and then reattached, no matter what gardeners might say.

Share in their substance, but not in their beliefs.

Just as those who try to stop you from following reason won't succeed in diverting you from doing the right thing, don't let them push you away from your goodwill toward them. Keep an even balance, maintaining steady judgment and action while also being gentle with those who try to hinder you or who are against you. Being angry with them is just as much a weakness as abandoning your course out of fear. Both are failures to fulfill your duty—whether by running away in fear or by turning against your natural friends and fellow humans.

No nature is lower than art because art imitates nature. If this is true, then the most perfect and comprehensive nature could never be surpassed by any artistic invention. All arts create lower things for the sake of higher ones, and this is also how universal nature works. Justice originates from this, and all other virtues come from justice because justice cannot be maintained if we focus on indifferent things or are easily misled or changeable.

The things outside of you that you chase or avoid don't force themselves on you, but you go after them. If you keep your judgment of them calm, they will remain still, and you won't be seen as either chasing after or avoiding them.

The soul is like a sphere that keeps its shape if it does not stretch out toward anything or contract inward, flare up, or sink down. It should stay constant in its light, seeing the truth of all things and the truth within itself.

If someone looks down on me, that is their concern. But I will make sure that I don't say or do anything that deserves contempt. If someone hates me, that is their concern. But I will be kind and good to everyone, and I will be ready to show that person their mistake, not with criticism or showing off my tolerance, but with genuine goodwill, like the famous Phocion (if he wasn't being sarcastic). This should be the quality of our inner thoughts, which are open to the gods' eyes: they should see a person not complaining or feeling sorry for themselves. And what harm can come to you if you are acting in line with your own nature and accepting what suits the purpose of the universe as a human being at your post, working for the common good?

People may despise each other and flatter each other at the same time. They may want to surpass each other and yet bow down to each other.

How fake it is for someone to say, "I prefer to be honest with you!"—What are you talking about? There's no need to announce it. Your actions will show it soon enough. It should be obvious in your voice and the look in your eyes, just as a lover can read everything in their beloved's eyes. In short, a good and honest person should be like someone with a strong smell—anyone nearby will notice it, whether they want to or not. But pretending to be simple is like being a crooked stick. Nothing is more disgraceful than fake friendship. Avoid it most of all. The good, honest, and kind person shows these qualities clearly in their eyes, unmistakably.

Living well is within the power of the soul if it is indifferent to things that don't matter. It will be indifferent if it looks at each of these things separately and together, remembering that none of them forces an opinion about itself on us or comes to us on its own. These things remain still, and we create judgments about them, writing them into our minds. But we don't have to write them, and if any judgments slip into our minds, we can erase them. Remember, our attention to these things is brief, then life ends. So what trouble is there in doing this? If these things are natural, embrace them, and they will be easy; but if they are against nature, look for what fits your nature and go after that, even without recognition. Everyone is allowed to seek their own good.

Think about where each thing comes from, what it consists of, what it changes into, and what it will become when it changes. It will not be harmed.

If someone offends you, first consider: What is my relationship to others? We are made for each other. In another sense, I was made to lead them, like a ram leading its flock or a bull leading its herd. But start from the beginning: If everything is not just atoms, then nature governs everything. If this is true, then lower things exist for the sake of higher ones, and the higher ones for each other.

Next, consider what kind of people they are in private, and under what pressures they act as they do. Regarding their actions, consider how proud they are of their deeds.

Third, if what they do is right, you should not be upset; but if it's wrong, they are acting out of ignorance and not on purpose. Just as no soul likes to be robbed of truth, no soul wants to treat others worse than they deserve. People are upset when accused of being unjust, ungrateful, or selfish—wronging their neighbors.

Fourth, you also have many faults, and you are no different from them. Even if you avoid some wrongs, you still have the tendency to commit them, though you may abstain because of fear, concern about your reputation, or some other low motive.

Fifth, you may not even understand whether they are wrong, as many actions are done with regard to circumstances. A person must know a lot to judge another's actions correctly.

Sixth, when you are angry or upset, remember that human life is brief, and soon we will all be dead.

Seventh, it is not their actions that upset us, because these lie in their own minds, but our judgments of them. Remove these judgments, decide to dismiss your belief that an act is harmful, and your anger will disappear. How do you remove these judgments? By reflecting that no wrongful act of another harms you unless you also do many wrongs, becoming a thief and worse.

Eighth, more pain comes from our anger and frustration about these acts than from the acts themselves.

Ninth, a kind disposition is unbeatable if it is sincere, not fake or forced. What can the most aggressive person do to you if you remain kind? If, when they try to hurt you, you gently correct them and show them what they're doing wrong, saying, "Not so, my friend; we were meant for something better. You can't hurt me, but you are hurting yourself." Show them kindly how things are, without being ironic or critical. Your advice should be friendly, without bitterness or a desire to impress, whether alone or in the presence of others.

Remember these nine rules as gifts from the Muses, and start to be a good person while you are still alive. Avoid flattering others and being angry in your interactions, as both are harmful to society. When you feel anger rising, remind yourself that there is nothing strong about being angry; calmness and gentleness are more human and, therefore, more manly. Those who are gentle have strength, resilience, and courage, unlike those who are angry and upset. The more a person controls their emotions, the closer they are to real power. Anger and pain show weakness, as both have been wounded and have surrendered.

Finally, remember this tenth lesson from the leader of the Muses: It is madness to expect bad people not to do wrong, as this is impossible. But it is cruel to allow them to act this way toward others while demanding they do no wrong to you.

There are four main errors of the rational mind you should watch out for and remove when you notice them, saying to yourself: "This thought is unnecessary," "This thought harms social unity," "This is not an honest thought," and "This is a failure of the higher, rational part to the lower, bodily part, giving in to physical pleasures."

The air and fire elements in you naturally tend to rise, but they obey the order of the whole and stay within the body. The earth and water elements naturally tend to sink, but they are also raised up and stay in place. So even the elements obey the universe, staying in their assigned places until the universe signals their release.

So isn't it strange that only your intelligent part rebels and complains about its place? And yet nothing is forced on it—only what fits its own nature. But still, it refuses to comply and goes in the opposite direction. Any movement toward injustice, excess, anger, pain, or fear is a rejection of nature. When the rational mind feels resentment about anything, it is deserting its proper role. It was created not only for justice toward others but also for reverence and service to the gods, which is another form of fellowship, perhaps even more important than justice.

A person who does not have one consistent goal in life cannot remain the same throughout their life. We need to decide what that goal should be. People have different ideas about what is good, but only one thing is universally recognized as good, and that is the well-being of the community. Therefore, we should aim to benefit others, and a person who directs all their efforts toward this goal will be consistent in all their actions, remaining the same throughout their life.

Think of the country mouse and the town mouse and how the town mouse was frightened and anxious.

Socrates called the common beliefs of many people "bogeymen," things to scare children.

At public events, the Spartans set up shaded seats for visitors but sat wherever they could find a spot.

Socrates once declined an invitation to visit Perdiccas of Macedon, saying, "I don't want to die the worst death," meaning accepting a favor and then not being able to return it.

The writings of Epicurus tell us to constantly think of those who followed the path of virtue before us.

The Pythagoreans advised looking at the sky at dawn to remind ourselves of the constancy of the stars, their unchanging duty, order, purity, and openness. No star is covered by a veil.

Think of Socrates, who wore just a skin when Xanthippe took his cloak, and how he spoke to his friends who were embarrassed when they saw him dressed like that.

In writing and reading, you must learn before you can teach. This is even truer in life.

You were born a slave: you have no voice.

And my heart laughed within.

And virtue they curse, speaking harsh words.

It is foolish to look for figs in winter, just as it is to hope for a child when it is no longer possible.

When you kiss your child, Epictetus said, you should remind yourself, "Tomorrow, they may die." But some people think these are bad words. Epictetus replied, "Nothing is bad if it reflects nature's process. Otherwise, it would be bad to talk about corn being harvested."

The unripe grape, ripe bunch, and dried grape all change, not into nothing, but into something else that is not yet.

No one can take away our free will. Epictetus also said, "We must develop a skill in agreeing with things, and in all our actions, we should ensure they are appropriate to the situation, have a social purpose, and match the value of the goal. We must avoid personal motivation and not reject anything outside our control."

The dispute, Epictetus said, is not about a small matter, but about whether we are sane or mad.

Socrates used to ask, "What do you want? The souls of rational or irrational people?" "Rational souls." "What kind of rational souls? Healthy or unhealthy?" "Healthy." "Then why don't you seek them?" "Because we already have them." "Then why are you fighting and quarreling?"

Book 12

Everything you want to achieve through a long and difficult path, you can have right now if you allow it. This means if you stop worrying about the past, trust that the future will take care of itself, and focus on doing the right thing in the present. Be satisfied with what life has given you because nature chose it for you, and you were made for it. Always be truthful and fair, saying what is right and doing what matches the worth of every person. Don't let someone else's bad actions, opinions, or words, or even the feelings in your body, stop you. Let your mind take care of that. If, when you are close to death, you focus only on your mind and the spirit within you, and if you fear not that life will end, but that you might not have lived it according to nature, then you will be a person worthy of the universe that made you. You will no longer feel like a stranger in the world, surprised by what happens as if it were unexpected or dependent on this or that.

God sees our minds without the covering of the body and all its impurities. His connection is only between His intelligence and the intelligence He gave us. If you learn to do the same, you will free yourself from many distractions. It is unlikely that someone who ignores the body would waste time worrying about clothes, houses, reputation, or other superficial things.

You are made up of three things: a little body, a little breath, and intelligence. The first two are yours to care for, but the third—your intelligence—is truly yours. If you separate your mind from what others do or say, from what you have done or said, from worries about the future, from what your body experiences or what the breath (life) within you feels, and from all the chaos around you, then your mind will be free to act justly, accept what happens, and speak the truth. If you can do this, you will be able to live the rest of your life peacefully and in harmony with the spirit inside you.

I often wonder why people love themselves more than anyone else but value other people's opinions more than their own. If a god or a wise teacher told you to only think and plan things you would openly share as soon as you think of them, you wouldn't be able to do it for even one day. This shows that we respect what others think of us more than what we think of ourselves.

How could the gods, who arranged everything so well for us, overlook one thing—that good people, who have the most connection with the divine through their actions, would completely cease to exist when they die? But if this is true, trust that if it should have been different, the gods would have made it so. If it were fair, it would be possible; if it were natural, nature would have made it so. Since it isn't different, be sure it should not be different—for in questioning this, you are arguing with the divine. And we should not argue with the gods unless we believe they are just and good—if so, they would not let anything in the universe be neglected unfairly or without reason.

Even if you don't think you can achieve something, practice it anyway. Just like how your left hand might be weaker, but with practice, it can hold the reins stronger than your right.

Think about what kind of person you should be when death comes for you. Consider how short life is, how vast the past and future are, and how weak all material things are.

Look at things without their coverings; think about the reasons behind actions; consider what pain, pleasure, death, and fame really are, and how no one can truly harm you unless you let them.

In applying your beliefs, be like a boxer, not a gladiator. The gladiator can drop his sword and be killed, but the boxer always has his hands ready to defend himself.

See things as they truly are by breaking them down into their basic parts—material, cause, and purpose.

Remember that humans have the power to do what is right and accept what happens according to nature. We should not blame the gods, for they do no wrong, nor blame humans, as they only do wrong without meaning to. So, we should blame no one.

How silly it is to be surprised by anything that happens in life.

There is either an unchangeable destiny, kind Providence, or complete chaos without a plan. If it is destiny, why fight it? If Providence, make yourself worthy of divine help. If chaos, be happy that you have a mind to guide you. Even if chaos takes your body, breath, and everything else, it cannot take away your mind.

A lamp's light keeps shining until it goes out; will the truth, justice, and self-control within you stop before you die?

When you think someone has done wrong, ask yourself, "How do I know this is really wrong?" And even if it is, how do I know they haven't already punished themselves for it? Wanting a bad person not to do wrong is like wanting a fig tree not to produce figs, babies not to cry, or horses not to neigh—these things must happen. What should you do if someone has a bad character? If you get angry, work on fixing that in yourself.

If it's not right, don't do it; if it's not true, don't say it.

Whenever something makes an impression on you, break it down into its basic parts—what causes it, what it's made of, what its purpose is, and how long it will last.

Understand that inside you is something stronger and more divine than the emotions that make you act like a puppet on strings. Ask yourself, "What's in my mind right now? Fear, suspicion, desire, or something else?"

First, do nothing without purpose. Second, make sure everything you do is for the common good.

Remember that soon you will be nobody and nowhere, and the same is true for everything and everyone you see now. Everything is made to change, die, and transform so that new things can come into being.

Remember that everything is just how you think about it, and you have control over your thoughts. So, whenever you want, you can change your thoughts, and like a sailor who has safely sailed past a dangerous cape, you'll find calm waters and a peaceful bay.

When any activity ends at the right time, it doesn't suffer because it has ended. And the person who did this activity doesn't suffer either just because it stopped. In the same way, when all the activities that make up a person's life come to an end at the right time, it doesn't suffer because of that. The person who finishes their life at the right time hasn't been treated unfairly either. Nature decides the right time and end, sometimes because of old age, and always because of the universal nature, which keeps the whole world fresh and young by constantly changing its parts.

Everything that helps the whole universe is always good and happens at the right time. So, the end of life for every person isn't bad because it's not shameful. It isn't something we can control, and it doesn't harm the common good. In fact, it's good because it happens at the right time and helps the universe. When we follow this natural process, we're moving in the same direction as the divine will.

There are three important principles to remember: First, in everything you do, act thoughtfully and justly, just as justice itself would. Second, when things happen to you from outside, understand that they happen either by chance or by divine guidance, and don't blame chance or accuse divine providence. Third, think about what each living being is, from the moment it's conceived to when it first receives a soul, and from that moment until it gives the soul back. Think about what each being is made of and what it will become after it dies. If you were suddenly lifted high above the earth and could look down at all human activities, you'd see how small and short-lived they are. You'd realize that every time you looked down, you'd see the same things—things that aren't worth being proud of.

If you get rid of your judgment, you save yourself. Who is stopping you from letting go of it?

When you worry about something, you've forgotten that everything happens according to the universal nature. You've forgotten that someone else's wrong act doesn't harm you. You've also forgotten that everything that happens has always happened this way and will continue to happen everywhere. Lastly, you've forgotten how closely connected you are to the whole human race—not just by blood, but by shared intelligence. You've forgotten that each person's intelligence is divine, that nothing truly belongs to you, not even your child, your body, or your soul, because they all come from the divine. You've forgotten that everything is just opinion and that every person only lives in the present moment, losing only that moment.

Think often about those who have complained a lot or who have been famous, unfortunate, or successful in any way. Then ask yourself, where are they now? They're nothing but smoke and ashes, just a story or maybe not even a story anymore. Remember people like Fabius Catellinus in the countryside, Lucius Lupus in his gardens, Stertinius at Briae, Tiberius at Capri, and Velius Rufus. Think about how they chased after things with pride, but how worthless those things are now. It's much wiser to use the opportunities you have to be just, self-controlled, and obedient to the gods, and to do this simply and without pride. The worst kind of pride is the kind that's proud of not being proud.

To those who ask, "Where have you seen the gods, or how do you know they exist and worship them?" I would answer first that the gods can be seen with our eyes. Secondly, even though I haven't seen my own soul, I still honor it. In the same way, from all the experiences I've had of the gods' power, I'm sure they exist, and I respect them.

The safety of life lies in examining everything completely—what it is, what it's made of, and why it exists. With all your heart, do what is right and tell the truth. What else is there but to enjoy life by doing good things one after another, without leaving any gaps between them?

There is one light from the sun, even though it is blocked by walls, mountains, and many other things. There is one common substance, even though it is spread out among many different bodies with their own qualities. There is one soul, even though it is shared among many different living beings. There is one intelligent soul, even though it seems divided among many individuals. All these parts—like air and matter—don't have feelings and don't naturally connect with each other. But even these parts are held together by an intelligent force that pulls them towards each other. The mind, in a special way, reaches out to others like itself and connects with them, so the sense of fellowship isn't broken.

What do you want—to keep living? Do you want to keep feeling, moving, growing, and then stop growing, speaking, and thinking? Which of these things seems worth desiring to you? If you can easily set aside all these things, focus on what remains—following reason and God. But if you value these other things and worry about losing them because of death, you're going against reason and God.

How small a part of endless and unknowable time is given to each of us, and how quickly it disappears into eternity! How small a part of all the matter in the universe! How small is the tiny piece of earth you crawl on! When you think about all this, don't think anything is important except acting according to your nature and accepting whatever happens according to universal nature.

How does your ruling mind use itself? Everything depends on this. Everything else, whether you can control it or not, is just lifeless ashes and smoke.

A powerful reminder to think little of death is that even those who think pleasure is good and pain is bad have not feared death.

For someone whose only good is what happens at the right time, who is equally satisfied with more or fewer opportunities to act according to reason, and who doesn't care whether they view the world for a long or short time, death has no fear.

Mortal human, you have been a citizen in this great world; what difference does it make if it's for five years or fifty? For what follows the laws is fair for everyone. So where is the difficulty, if it's not a tyrant or an unjust judge sending you away from the world, but nature itself, which brought you into it? It's like a director who hired an actor dismissing him from the stage. "But I haven't finished my five acts, only three," you might say. You're right, but in life, three acts can be the whole play. What makes a complete drama is decided by the one who caused its beginning and now its end; you are not the cause of either. So leave satisfied, for the god who releases you is also satisfied.

Thank You for Reading

Dear Reader,

We hope this timeless classic has sparked your imagination and enriched your literary journey. Now that you've turned the final page, we want to share a vision for the future of reading—one where every classic you've ever wanted to explore is at your fingertips, in a format that best suits your life.

We'd like to invite you to gain immediate, unlimited digital & audiobook access to hundreds of the most treasured literary classics ever written—along with the option to secure deluxe paperback, hardcover & box set editions at printing cost. Together, we can spark a new global literary renaissance alongside our small, independent publishing house called "The Library of Alexandria."

Thousands of years ago, the Library of Alexandria stood as a beacon of knowledge—until it was lost to history. We aim to reignite that spirit of preservation and discovery right now, in the modern age—only this time, it's accessible to all, in every language and every format.

Picture a world where every timeless classic, novel, poem, or philosophical treatise is not only available to read but also updated for today's readers—modernized, translated into any language or dialect, and ready to enjoy in any format you choose, whether that is in an eBook, audiobook, paperback, or deluxe hardcover & box set version a printing cost.

By joining our movement to rebuild the modern Library of Alexandria, you become part of an unprecedented mission to offer:

- **Unlimited Audiobook & eBook Access to the Greatest Classics of All Time**

  Instantly explore thousands of legendary works, from Plato and Shakespeare to Jane Austen and Leo Tolstoy. All are instantly ready to read or listen to, giving you a complete literary universe at your fingertips.

- **Paperback & Deluxe Editions at Printing Costs:**

  Purchase any title in a paperback, deluxe hardbound, or deluxe boxset edition at printing costs, shipped right to your doorstep. Curate your personal library of Alexandria with editions worthy of display—crafted to last, designed to captivate, and delivered straight to your door.

- **Modern translations for Contemporary Readers in all languages and dialects**

  Discover a vast selection of classics reimagined in clear, current language—no more struggling with outdated phrases or obscure references. Next to the original versions, we aim to offer translations in as many languages and dialects as possible.

  As we continue our translation efforts and add new languages, readers everywhere can connect with these works as if they were written today. By bridging linguistic divides, you're contributing to ensuring that these timeless stories become more meaningful, accessible, and inspiring for people across the globe.

- **Your Personal Library of Alexandria:**

  Over the months and years, you'll curate a unique physical archive of classics—each volume a testament to your taste, curiosity, and love of knowledge. It's not just about owning books—it's about curating a cultural legacy you'll cherish and pass down for generations to come.

- **Join a Global Literary Renaissance:**

  Your support fuels an ongoing mission: allowing us to reinvest in offering deluxe print editions (including special boxsets) at their true cost, broaden the range of available formats and translations, and extend the reach of these works to new audiences worldwide. By joining today, you're not just preserving a legacy of masterpieces; you set in motion a powerful wave of literary accessibility.

We are more than a publisher—we're a movement, and we can't do it alone. Your support lets us scale our mission, preserving and reimagining history's greatest works for tomorrow's readers.

Become a Torchbearer of knowledge.

Thank you for picking up this book and allowing us into your literary journey. As you turn the pages, know that you're part of something larger: a global effort to keep these stories alive, share their wisdom across borders and generations, and spark a true cultural revival for the modern era.

If this resonates with you—please consider taking the next step by visiting:

www.libraryofalexandria.com

With gratitude and a shared love of knowledge,

The Modern Library of Alexandria Team

Visit:

www.libraryofalexandria.com

Or scan the code below:

www.ingramcontent.com/pod-product-compliance
Lightning Source LLC
Chambersburg PA
CBHW011402010726
47495CB00009B/2741

* 9 7 8 1 8 0 6 2 9 7 2 0 7 *